CW01467598

To contact the writer by mail write to Andreas Solomos, 1172 Danforth Avenue, Toronto, Canada M4J 1M3; by telephone call: (1) 416 465-9955; by email: solomos@allstream.net

Note for Librarians: A cataloguing record for this book is available from Library and Archives Canada at www.collectionscanada.ca/amicus/index-e.html
ISBN 1-4120-5094-4

Printed in Victoria, BC, Canada. Printed on paper with minimum 30% recycled fibre. Trafford's print shop runs on "green energy" from solar, wind and other environmentally-friendly power sources.

TRAFFORD
PUBLISHING

Offices in Canada, USA, Ireland and UK
This book was published *on-demand* in cooperation with Trafford Publishing. On-demand publishing is a unique process and service of making a book available for retail sale to the public taking advantage of on-demand manufacturing and Internet marketing. On-demand publishing includes promotions, retail sales, manufacturing, order fulfilment, accounting and collecting royalties on behalf of the author.

Book sales for North America and international:
Trafford Publishing, 6E–2333 Government St.,
Victoria, BC v8t 4p4 CANADA
phone 250 383 6864 (toll-free 1 888 232 4444)
fax 250 383 6804; email to orders@trafford.com
Book sales in Europe:
Trafford Publishing (uk) Ltd., Enterprise House, Wistaston Road Business Centre,
Wistaston Road, Crewe, Cheshire cw2 7rp UNITED KINGDOM
phone 01270 251 396 (local rate 0845 230 9601)
facsimile 01270 254 983; orders.uk@trafford.com
Order online at:
trafford.com/04-2902

10 9 8 7 6 5 4

In memory of my parents, Ionannis and Maria

1

VILLA MUSTAFA. PAFOS, CYPRUS. November 11, 2001.

I will *never* be free of the Mustafas, Marianna feared.

"Jason is waiting in the living room," the elderly maid mumbled as she drew the curtains.

A cluster of sunrays pierced the wide bay windows and temporarily blinded Marianna. For the past seven months, she'd been happy to awake to the same dutiful maid who walked into her bedroom with a cup of Greek coffee. But this morning she felt an urge to chastise her for doing just that. "I wish you wouldn't ...."

"Are you okay madam?"

"I'm fine. You may go now."

"Yes, madam."

Marianna remained in bed, staring at the ceiling, thoughts swirling in her head. Jason arrived in the town of Pafos unexpectedly the day before. He'd called her from the Mustafa Beach Hotel to announce his return, and she pretended to be delighted. In reality, this piece of news troubled her. Apart from some brief visits, Jason had lived in Canada for the past fourteen years, so she hoped this would be another of his short stays.

"I'm back for good," he'd said.

Marianna's concern about his return, however, was not as great as her desire to be free to raise her three children the way she wanted; free to spend her money as she saw fit; free to enjoy music and dance; free to travel. And free to continue to see Maximus.

Jason's arrival again sparked memories of her husband, Richard Mustafa, Jason's older brother, who had gone missing seven months ago this very day. His disappearance was still a mystery.

She wanted to forget about Richard, but his spirit was far from gone; everything reminded her of him. Every now and then, she feared he would come back. His pictures on the walls of Villa Mustafa were like ghosts. Her father-in-law, Faris Mustafa, had made sure of that by pointing his finger at them any time he and Marianna had an argument.

Until recently, Faris had kept reminding her of his son almost daily (constantly uttering his name, treating her visitors with suspicion, eavesdropping on her telephone conversations, giving her unsolicited advice, and scolding her any time she went out). She wasn't permitted to wear anything else but black. How tyrannical! she huffed. She suffered less humiliation now that Faris's illness confined him to a wheelchair.

She got out of bed, dressed, and swallowed two Tylenol tablets with a glass of water, hoping that her headache would fade away. She was worried that Jason might bombard her with questions about his brother's disappearance; the idea of having to sit down and answer his questions made her feel like a suspect about to be interrogated by the authorities. As she brushed her hair quickly, she decided to be pleasant but also make him understand that she would not tolerate any attempts on his part to rule her life. Marianna vowed to keep her distance from Jason and walked downstairs to greet him.

2

Jason saw Marianna emerge from the rotunda. She stood under the arch for a moment, apparently having forgotten something. She wore a black, long-sleeved, maxi dress, and high-heel black shoes. Her long hair was sandy, untamed, like she'd been running in the sun for hours. Marianna's light-brown eyes offered an illusion of innocence. Her curvy lips had a slight, peculiar twist. She had a classical Greek nose. *She must have lost some weight,* Jason mused, as he noted her slim tall figure and the black dress which made her look younger than her thirty-one years. Her hair covered much of her forehead and part of her left eye, as if she were hiding something. Jason stood up with his arms extended.

Marianna raised her eyebrows. "I can't believe it!" she said. She gave him a smile and they embraced.

Jason noticed how she avoided meeting his eyes. "Are you happy to see me?"

"Are you certain you want to stay here, for good?"

"I must know what happened to Richard."

"Why?"

"He's my brother. We were very close, once. You know that."

"That was a long time ago, and you've kept your distance all this time."

"Despite our differences, deep down I've always cared for him."

"You waited seven months after your brother's disappearance to show up?"

"That's how long it took for me to find a replacement."

"That's no excuse."

Jason maintained his composure. He recalled swimming in the Mediterranean Sea with Richard. The games they used to play, the fun they shared. His throat tightened, and he swallowed hard. "I miss him incredibly."

"We all miss him," Marianna said defensively.

Jason ignored the sharp edge in her voice. "How are the children coping?" he asked.

"They keep asking me, 'When is Daddy coming home?' I'm so upset." She placed her hands on her face and seemed to be on the verge of tears.

3

When she'd calmed down, he asked, "Would I be able to see them?"

"They're sleeping."

Jason wondered if she'd even told the children he was back in Cyprus. "May I see them later?"

"Oh, maybe. I'm hosting a dinner party. Will you join us at seven?"

"I'll be glad to."

She paused. "Your father doesn't live here anymore. After he got sick, Richard moved him to Villa Oasis."

"I know."

"Why does he want to meet you in this house, then?"

"You should ask him."

She looked at her watch and said, "I must get going. I have a busy schedule ahead of me."

"Is there anything I can do to help?"

"No."

Jason hesitated. "I want some time and space to think things over, after the long trip, before I meet with my father again. Is the library—?"

"I don't want to upset the children. If they see you there, they may think you're their father."

She hurried upstairs before he could ask her any questions about Richard.

He left the living room and walked over to the open patio. He stood there holding onto the balustrade, waiting for Faris, still thinking of his older brother.

Richard had always been good to him. Many times, as teenagers, they had pulled off hilarious look-alike incidents. One time Jason wanted a day off school to take a girl he liked to the mountains for a day of skiing and fun. Richard sat in Jason's class, and no one ever noticed.

And why had they drifted apart? Well, Richard decided to work for their father. And Jason despised Faris and how his capitalist concerns had always taken priority over his family life.

Jason's eyes brushed the broad horizon to the southwest where, a few kilometers away, the sky merged with the sea in two shades of blue. He let himself wander in the vacuum for a few brief moments. No thoughts, no feelings—just drifting in the expanse of the massive blue canvas. He saw sailboats, the coastline, quaint towns, seaside resorts, the lighthouse, and the harbour with its impressive castle, a vestige of Venetian glory. To his right, on the rolling hills, he recognized the luxury villas and their graceful arches, red-tiled roofs and landscaped gardens.

To his left, the traditional Cypriot village of Peta, with its one thousand residents, provided a striking contrast. It was quiet. Occasionally, he heard cocks crow and dogs bark.

Closer to his vantage point, he took in the stretch of the Mustafa estate. A five-foot high white-stone wall with smooth curves and uneven elevations resembling a miniature Chinese wall bordered the 45-acre olive grove.

Jason could see the rustic log-and-stone cabin with its small man-made pond, both of which were constructed amidst the olive grove to provide the setting for special outdoor occasions, such as picnics.

Villa Mustafa, its lawn and servant quarters, and the small Villa Oasis, were surrounded by another – a bit taller – wall. Graceful white gates led from the public road to the estate. He noticed a group of workers who appeared to be harvesting the olives. The front lawn was dotted with the palm trees Jason's father had imported from northern Africa. The garden was amply landscaped with fig, apricot, orange, lemon, pomegranate, and carob trees, and many grape vines that were beginning to lose their leaves.

He heard a rolling noise. When he turned his head, he saw Faris in a wheelchair and the nurse pushing him toward Villa Mustafa.

3

Marianna was having a shower. Richard would have been celebrating his thirty-fourth birthday ten days ago, she reflected. The two brothers, born one year apart, resembled each other, and she recalled many occasions when people could not tell them apart. The only physical difference between them that she knew of was that Richard had a two-inch tattoo below his right shoulder – an Old English R typeface.

The last time she had seen them together was two years ago when they had been attending the funeral of their American-born mother, Rachel Mustafa, who died in Pafos at age fifty-seven from cirrhosis of the liver. Her death had thrown Richard into a spell of depression.

Rachel was a rich blonde from the United States. She had grace and a sweet voice. When she was sober she showed remarkable devotion to her family. Rachel had been a devout Roman Catholic, but in this predominantly Greek Orthodox community, it was difficult at that time to find a Roman Catholic priest. Following Richard's instructions, the funeral service was held at the Greek Orthodox chapel of the Holy Monastery of The Saint Mary Magdalene, with Abbot Maximus officiating.

Richard, clean-shaven, was fitted with a black BOSS suit, black silk shirt and black silk tie. Jason, his face rough with a beard, wore dark grey trousers, a black V-neck sweater and a black cotton shirt, unbuttoned at the top. The two brothers with their long curvy light brown hair, large hazel eyes, big chests, prominent chins, and similar facial features were two modern, six-foot-tall, mourning Apollos. Richard stood by his mother's coffin and held his father's hand. Jason, pale from the long Canadian winters, was six feet away—alone. In happier times, Marianna had seen their broad smiles and heard their deep voices, but this time their lips were closed tight.

Their Arab father, a Saudi national in his early sixties, had brown eyes. He wore a black gabardine suit. His pale handsome face frowned. Marianna believed that his show of grief was a facade for an angst beyond the usual sorrow of a man who mourned the loss of a wife. His slow talk and measured gestures portrayed a well-balanced man, but in Marianna's eyes he was quite the opposite.

Among the family friends who attended the solemn funeral service was Alex Manning, an American. A few months before Rachel's death, he had set up an offshore company in Cyprus.

Marianna observed Abbot Maximus; her heart secretly trembled with familiar lustful yearnings. His owlish eyes were implanted deep in his face, eyebrows black and shaggy. His long black hair was carefully folded and covered by his *calimmafchio*, a traditional Orthodox hat. He was six-foot-one, taller than the average Cypriot male height, and wearing a *rason*, a black gabardine monk's robe, with a low collar embroidered with golden silk threads. The robe gave an aura of mysticism about him, and although it covered much of his body, Marianna could not help admiring his square shoulders. With his robe and long black beard, Maximus could fit the perfect picture of a monk in any Greek Orthodox monastery, but to Marianna he was more than that.

After the funeral, she tried to arouse Richard into lovemaking, but she felt the apathy of his frigid body. She now remembered how she'd felt sick and shivery, not by loss of her mother-in-law, but by Richard's apparent coldness.

Between the two brothers, she'd always known that the winds of fortune favoured Richard, who enjoyed a close relationship with his father. The locals in Pafos recognized the successful young Mustafa architect a block away.

Richard used his wealth and influence to benefit the local community. He set up the first humane society in the area; he convinced local politicians to construct a central, modernized sewage system that was appropriate for the sprawling cosmopolitan town of Pafos, often described as the Riviera of Cyprus. He persuaded Faris to donate five million dollars toward that project. Richard revitalized the local department of antiquities and was engaged in efforts to maintain the town's rich cultural heritage—the ancient Greek mosaics, monuments, and theatres, Byzantine churches, Venetian castles and ruins that spoke a silent story about the long and rich history of the sunny place.

He also organized and paid for excavation projects to unearth and maintain the buried ancient treasures that lay along the Pafos shores; he brought teams of professors and students of archeology from as far away as the United States to participate in these excavations.

Marianna remembered how Richard enjoyed discussing the history of Cyprus, especially the history of Pafos, where many had left their mark, including Greeks, Romans, Byzantines, the Crusaders' Richard the Lionheart, the Venetians, the Ottomans, and the British.

The United Nations included many archaeological sites in the area as part of its official list of cultural and natural treasures. After all, it was from the sea beneath the cliffs of Pafos that Aphrodite – an icon with whom Marianna strongly identified – had emerged. In antiquity, Aphrodite, the goddess of love and beauty, played a central role in the religious life of the island, and Pafos was the centre of her cult and home to her shrine.

4

Jason encountered his father: a beaten, slim, frail-faced man. The sight of Faris's wrinkled skin alarmed him. He embraced his father in silence.

"I feel energetic today," Faris said.

"I'm happy to hear that, father."

The elderly housemaid arrived with a tray full of grapes and a cup of tea for Faris. "Would you like something to drink?" she asked Jason.

"A glass of water and an aspirin will be fine," he answered. He felt embarrassed about feeling sorry for Faris. He looked away, pointing at the vast olive field. "I see people over there."

"I hired them. They're collecting the olives," Faris responded. "We have the darkest and thickest olive oil in the whole world. It's a good medicine."

The words were coming out in rapid succession, as if Faris was making a presentation. He was too spirited for a sick man, Jason thought.

"To find these people, Dr. Plato had to take me to the village at least seven times."

"You should be resting more often now."

"If I do, no one will do anything around here. Marianna is too busy with other things."

"Perhaps you expect too much from her—"

"We have to watch our steps!" Faris said impatiently. "Someone is out to destroy us! Be mindful of the intentions of the people around us."

"I came back to find out what happened to Richard."

Faris shook his head. "Don't get involved. I don't want you to get hurt."

"I'll take care of myself."

"I'm thirsty," Faris mumbled. His cup was empty.

Jason hurried to the kitchen. There he saw a woman who seemed familiar, but he did not pay much attention to her. "Where is the maid?" he asked the woman who was busy sorting the utensils.

The woman responded like a disciplined soldier, "Can I help you?" she asked.

"I'm looking for the maid."

"She finished her shift, sir. I'm her replacement."

"Get us some water, please." He felt uncomfortable and turned around. His nagging curiosity needed to be satisfied. He turned his head. "Do I know you?"

She didn't respond. She walked out and over to Faris, bent forward, held Faris's hand and placed a glass of water firmly in his grip.

Jason followed her closely and could see the round, firm upper edges of her breasts, separated by smooth cleavage that disappeared into her thin white blouse.

She's so elegant. She can't be more than thirty-two. She appears too ... sophisticated for this type of work. He observed her from head to toe. She was medium built, about five-feet-nine, a slender woman. She wore a black, loose-fitting, knee-length skirt. He could smell her subtle body scent. Dark shoulder-length hair was twisted and tied at the back of her neck with a bright red silk handkerchief. Her face was long and thin, eyes wide and bright black.

As he was watching her, a sudden brisk wind raised her skirt upward, revealing curvy buttocks and long, slender fair legs.

She moved her left hand below her lower back, pulling her skirt down. She glanced at Jason, but he pretended not to have noticed and lazily looked the other way.

Faris begged her to massage his stiff shoulders, and she did so.

When she left, Faris waved at Jason to come closer. "I'm dying."

"No, you're not!"

"Please, listen."

Jason sat down.

5

After breakfast, Marianna went to the library to read, but she had been unable to concentrate. Jason's arrival reminded her of the day Richard disappeared, on a drizzly April night ...

April 11, 2001 – It was getting late. Close to midnight, Richard called Marianna to say he would be working late at the office because he was putting the final touches on a construction project. Their three children (twins George and Andrew, age six; and Claira, age four) were asleep when he'd telephoned. Shortly after they'd spoken, Marianna took a sleeping pill and went to bed.

The morning came swiftly, and with her eyes closed, Marianna turned to her left to kiss Richard's cheek, but he was not there. "Richard?" There was no response. "It's six o'clock," Marianna uttered.

Outside, a fog hung like a dense blanket over the villa. Clad in a silk nightgown, she grabbed the woolen housecoat she had bought in London, and threw it on her shoulders. She hurried out of the master suite, walked through the rotunda and entered the library.

He wasn't there. Marianna glanced into the living room, family room and dining room, even peeked into the galleria. Then she walked faster, looking for him in the kitchen, breakfast room and finally the covered patio. He was nowhere in the house. *Had he gone to meet his father in Villa Oasis, next door?*

She followed the private patio between Villa Mustafa and Villa Oasis and knocked on the door, hoping to find him with his father, but she found only the nurse who was crying. "What's the matter?" Marianna asked.

The nurse, wiping her tears, pointed at the road.

"What's going on?" Marianna demanded.

The nurse could not say a word.

Marianna hesitated and then walked over to the gates. The morning carried cool, light sea winds, blowing from the south, dampening her eyes when she heard a voice.

"*Kalimera* Marianna."

The voice wishing her good morning came from outside the gates and when she reached them, she saw Dr. Plato. "Hello sir," she responded.

Dr. Plato was an 80-year-old physician from the nearby Peta village. He was six-feet-five, lean, and quite agile for his age. He sported a twisted mustache, and frequently wore British tweed suits, a custom Marianna thought too pompous for a village doctor. His hair was receding, and his face was square and solemn, like a Byzantine icon. In Marianna's circle of friends, he was an iconoclast and a man prone to hallucinations.

A group of men, Faris amongst them, were gathered outside the gates, agitated.

At the entrance, Richard's Alfa Romeo, with both doors open and the engine running, was facing the gates of the compound.

She approached Faris who looked defeated. "Where's Richard?" she huffed, almost out of breath. "What are these people doing here?"

"Apparently," Faris sighed, "my son has been abducted."

"No!" In her shocked and scared state, it struck Marianna as strange that she was not completely devastated by this news.

"I won't rest until they find him," Faris said. "They haven't got a single lead yet."

"Someone must have some idea what happened!" said Marianna.

Faris pointed to a group of six men in civilian clothes. "The Special Investigation Branch is discussing possible motives."

A man took Marianna gently by the hand and had a private word with her. She didn't suspect anybody, and she was too distressed to answer his other questions.

"Let's go," the inspector said to his men. The smoke left behind by the cars plastered Faris, Dr. Plato and Marianna, leaving her nauseated and trembling.

6

"Unfortunately, things didn't turn out as I'd planned," Faris said to Jason. "I fear, if you dig into Richard's disappearance, someone may try to harm you."

"The police have no clues?"

"That night, there were several shoe prints found in the mud. What else, I don't know." He took Jason by the hand. "You stay in the background. The people I hired will do the investigating."

Jason wondered if Faris knew more than he was willing to say. "Do you expect me to simply lie here in the sun?"

"I want you to assume the family business."

The warm breeze chilled him for a second before he responded, "I'm not interested in the family business. You have Nadir Makin, the General Manager. He's doing a good job, I understand."

"But who will step into my shoes?"

"I told you why I came back."

"No, Jason. You can't handle this."

It's hard for him to crack his old perceptions of me, he thought. "Perhaps I'll surprise you."

"I've already asked Helena to examine the bank books. They may give us some clues about Richard's disappearance."

"Helena? I don't understand."

"The woman you just saw … she is not whom she appears to be. She has the talent, intelligence and training to do the job."

"You must be kidding!"

"She's not an ordinary accountant. She's specially trained in forensic accounting."

Jason suddenly realized that Helena (the maid impersonator) was the girl he'd been infatuated with fourteen years ago—when he was nineteen. She's even more alluring now, he thought. "Isn't she the daughter of one of our former maids?"

"She is."

"Yes, I remember her mom, years ago. Angela! What's her daughter doing here?"

"I hired Helena shortly after Richard's disappearance. She'll take on her real duties when and if necessary. Until then, treat her as a maid. She knows I'm briefing you today about her involvement."

Jason was thunderstruck. He tried to say something, and again Faris took him by the hand.

"Don't say a word."

"Nothing stays secret for too long in this part of the world," Jason responded.

"She's lived away from Pafos for a long time."

"What about Marianna? Don't you think she should know?"

"She's a nervous one. I can't expect her to handle any pressure. Besides, she and Katerina are close, despite their silly skirmishes. Who knows about those two!" Then Faris whispered, "Remember they're Persinaras's daughters!"

Jason took a deep breath. "I'm going for a walk," he said.

"Wait, not just yet. I want you to move out of that hotel."

"But that's your hotel … I mean yours and Persinaras's."

"It's not safe there."

At two-hundred-and-ten dollars a night, the hotel room was tight on Jason's pocketbook, but he felt it was worth the expense. He was a man used to taking risks. "People should know where to find me."

"Did our staff recognize you?"

"At first, they mistook me for Richard. After I handed them my passport and they saw my name, they realized who I really was. The hotel manager sent me flowers and a 'welcome home' card."

"Mmm," Faris said, "I don't like it. I'll find you another hotel."

"It's not necessary, thank you."

"Do you need any money?"

Jason had calculated ahead of time that he had enough savings for his hotel charges, food and transportation to last him for three months. "No."

"I don't want you to start asking people around Pafos questions about Richard. You don't know them very well, and some may see you as a threat."

"Please don't tell me what to do," Jason insisted. "I make my own decisions, father."

"We must be patient in our search for answers."

Jason shook his head. "It's been seven months since Richard disappeared. Your patience has achieved precious little."

"You've lived in Canada for so long, I wonder if you've kept any of our traditions."

14

"Dad, exactly what do you want from me?"

"In a few days, after you settle down, I want you to start working for Mustafa Holdings."

"You're dreaming."

"I will make sure you receive a handsome salary."

"The answer is no!"

"Jason," Faris said calmly, "what would it take to make you see my point?"

"Your unconditional support for my efforts in finding out what happened to Richard."

"No problem, son," his father replied. "You need money—"

"Money has always been front and centre in your mind!"

Money, indeed! Throughout most of Jason's childhood and adolescence, Faris had been away from home. He'd learned through others about his father's business acumen. And, back then, Faris had never discussed with him details of his financial wizardry. Meanwhile, Richard had become more of a father figure to Jason than Faris could ever be. Richard was both father and friend. Remembering and missing his brother terribly, Jason bit his lower lip.

"Jason, I wish you could see things differently."

"Dad, why can't *you* see things differently?"

Faris paused before muttering, "Too late for me."

Just like old times, Jason felt uncomfortable challenging his father. He needed to focus on the problem at hand. "Every hour is valuable," he said. "I want to examine Richard's personal items, such as his passport, driver's license, identification card, diary, and as many other items as you can find."

"Helena is looking into that already," Faris said.

He thought of Helena and felt some relief, for he could turn to her for help if she wasn't as unyielding as Faris.

As Jason was about to go for a walk, Helena announced that there was someone at the gates. "He refuses to tell us who he is," she said. "His chauffer says his passenger is an Arab friend. They're asking permission to drive into the compound. Shall we open the gates?"

"Let them in," said Faris.

7

As the black Mercedes with its tinted windows slowly entered the compound, Jason wondered about the mysterious visitor. He knew that his father had huge real estate holdings in Saudi Arabia, Kuwait, Dubai and Bahrain. Faris had assisted the Kuwaiti delegation with the drafting and negotiating of a double tax treaty between Cyprus and Kuwait. The Saudi, Kuwaiti and other Arab ambassadors to Cyprus were frequent visitors, but, for security reasons, they always called before their visits.

His father's sympathies for the Palestinian cause were well-known throughout the Middle East. Faris had also participated in the committee which was put together at the Arab Summit in Fez, Morocco, in 1982, to consider Saudi Arabia's eight-point plan that envisaged a peaceful solution for a Palestinian homeland and an end to the Arab-Israeli conflict. The plan became the basis for the "Fez Declaration."

Many people described Faris as one of the most astute merchants and land developers in the Arab world. He had even earned the respect of American diplomats for his proven loyalty to U.S. national interests. An Arab diplomat to Canada once told Jason that Faris Mustafa could see value in anything, even plain hard rock. Faris was even quoted as telling an Arab king that the sand could one day be more valuable than the oil underneath it. That comment sparked the construction of brand new roads and airports, land distribution, and the development of huge irrigation projects and farming enterprises.

Lush, fertile fields replaced the kingdom's deserts, and produced most of the vegetables and fruits of the area (which relieved its heavy dependence on expensive imports). And at the same time the projects fulfilled the religious beliefs of the Muslim worshippers in accordance with the spiritual values of Islam. The desert country became a large-scale exporter of wheat, dairy products, fruits and vegetables, to the point that the kingdom could boast one of the world's largest integrated dairy farms. The people were happy, and the king was grateful. At least this is what Jason was told.

The big car turned into the limestone-interlocking brick forecourt and slowed down, opposite the north-side door of Villa Oasis. The chauffeur parked it between Richard's Alfa Romeo and Marianna's silver BMW SUV.

Tinted windows lowered, revealing a middle-aged man with curly hair, dark brown face and a long white beard.

"Do you recognize him?" asked Jason.

"It's Kamal, a friend from Saudi Arabia. He and I spoke on the phone recently. Three things you must remember. First, if you hear anything you don't already know, don't look surprised. Second, talk as if you are in charge here. Third, listen to what he's not saying."

Jason was lost for words.

The driver got out first. He was wearing a black wool suit, black turtleneck sweater, dark sunglasses and a black sailor's hat. He opened the door for the passenger, who was thin and more than six feet tall. This man wore a white collarless cotton shirt, buttoned all the way to the neckline, a long beige cotton coat, and dark baggy brown pants.

Jason stared at the strange man who walked slowly toward the door of Villa Oasis.

"You don't have to agree with everything he says," Faris added. "Don't be hostile either."

"Now let's go meet him outside the door. I don't want him to wait long. No maids are to be present."

While Kamal waited by the door of Villa Oasis, Jason steered the wheelchair with his father sitting comfortably in it toward the access ramp. When they reached him, Kamal opened his arms, bowed and embraced Faris, kissing him on both sides of his bony cheeks. Kamal then looked up at Jason.

Faris rattled off fast introductions, and Jason tried to smile.

Kamal extended his right hand, and Jason felt discomfort as the man's strong hand squeezed his own.

Faris struggled to pull the key from his coat pocket, while holding on to the left arm of his wheelchair. Realizing his father's difficulties, Jason reached to help, but by the time he bent to assist, Faris had the key in his trembling hand. Jason took it, opened the door and wheeled his father inside.

Kamal followed, shutting the door behind him. Jason looked out the window and saw Kamal's driver standing, gazing at Richard's car.

The morning sunlight shone into the cozy octagonal breakfast nook of Villa Oasis. For a moment, there was complete silence. Jason heard the clock ticking on the wall.

Kamal asked, "Has the tension across the Middle East affected your business much?"

Faris said, "Many tourists have cancelled their visits, and some of our new villa buyers revoked their construction contracts with us. Our hotel is sixty percent empty."

Kamal sighed, "I'm afraid things are only going to get worse for you."

What a pessimistic statement, Jason thought. "We're not any different from others whose businesses have suffered due to terrorism," Jason said confidently.

Kamal hesitated. "The Americans are putting pressure on the Saudis to freeze the assets of Mustafa Holdings everywhere. We notified your father recently. The Americans demand that we act soon. I was sent here for a reason."

"Oh?" Jason awaited further information.

"Someone has alleged that your father, or someone close to him, might be involved in funding a terrorist cell whose main aim is to destroy American embassies around the world and to assassinate American tourists."

"That's ridiculous!" Jason shouted. "You can't use allegations to wreck people's lives."

"Admittedly, we don't have hard proof. But because of possible consequences, we must take every allegation seriously and act upon it."

"We're not that kind of people!" Jason said.

Kamal shrugged.

Jason noticed that his father was unperturbed. *Why does he want me to be in charge?* There was dead silence inside the villa. Outside, the chirping of sparrows filled the autumn air. Jason felt nauseated— perhaps trapped.

8

Kamal broke the silence. "The good news is that the Saudis are reluctant to freeze Faris's assets, but they must audit your books."

Jason was flabbergasted. "That's against international law, you know!"

Kamal laughed. "International law? Such idealistic impositions! If you resist, we will act swiftly to freeze your assets as we deem fit."

"And we'll fight you 'til the bitter end!" Jason blurted out.

"But we are not prepared to freeze your assets—not at this stage."

"Not at this stage?" Jason said, confused.

"Your father's offshore bank, Mustafa Bank (Cyprus) International, must also be included in the audit. Eleven years ago, when one of our banks provided the Central Bank of Cyprus with the appropriate letter of comfort, we took a big risk. Your father's bank is supposed to operate as an OBU, and we shall make sure it does just that."

Jason understood that OBU meant 'Offshore Banking Unit.' He also knew the policy of the local licensing authorities was that only reputable international banking enterprises (and their subsidiaries that had good banking supervision) were eligible to operate in Cyprus as OBUs. "We had the appropriate clearances before the bank was established."

"We know your father's bank has financed legitimate construction projects in Dubai, but our agents suspect that this particular bank is using the Hawala system to fund a terrorist cell."

"We have nothing to do with Hawala," Faris protested. "We based our offshore financial services in Cyprus because Islamic countries prohibit the payment of interest, and we use Dubai because it has a free zone with no limitations on the movement of goods or currency. We record everything—"

"There are many legitimate Hawala dealers who have no terrorist connections," Jason interjected. "But can we avoid all this?"

Kamal became defensive. "Our policy has been to give the impression that we are working in partnership with the Americans, and

19

you can't do that and be tolerant of those who use their wealth and power to assist the terrorists at the same time."

"So what will happen?"

"If the United States and England together cannot defeat terrorism with their military might, then we must have another tool at our disposal: confiscation and control of all financial sources that the terrorists feed on. If they are starved and left struggling to maintain their networks, we can beat them."

Jason was furious. "Audit our books? You've no business sneaking into our operations. Outsiders aren't allowed to examine books without a court order. And who's to say you won't abuse your powers and engage in a fishing expedition to tax us or accuse us of tax evasion? You could use information pulled from us to help out our competitors. Once others find out we're being audited for alleged terrorist connections, we could face economic ruin—even though we're totally innocent! Besides, the Persinaras family has control over the Persinaras-Mustafa Group, and all our shareholders have to consent to such an audit. It's part of our agreement with Persinaras."

"We don't need their permission to audit their books. You'll get the books for us."

Finally, Faris broke in. "The Persinaras-Mustafa Group used to operate out of our building, but recently they laid off some employees and moved all their records to the hotel. We don't control the Group."

"Then maybe it's about time you took control of your affairs," Kamal said.

"Katerina gives us copies of the financial statements every year. The Group has been earning good annual profits," Faris said. "We don't have any cause to dig deeper than that."

"We've heard that business is slow and you're losing money."

Jason was growing weary. "I think you know my brother Richard is married to one of Persinaras's daughters?"

"We know Marianna is not involved with the day to day operations of the Persinaras-Mustafa Group."

Jason was silent.

Kamal turned to Faris. "We don't believe Marianna will turn against you, if this is your worry."

If something went terribly wrong, Jason could see the possibility of the two families colliding in a bitter dispute. He wondered if Faris could do anything to stop this mess. Jason knew Faris hadn't become rich by being a squeezed lemon. Furthermore, he wasn't completely convinced that allowing the Saudi accountants to go over the books with a fine-tooth comb was in any way acceptable. He turned to Kamal. "You said your people aren't out to get us."

Kamal frowned. "If, after the audit, our accountants determine that you are not involved in funding the terrorist cell, we'll walk away with pleasure."

"We need guarantees that the purpose of the audit will be strictly limited."

"Look, we want you to continue to operate your legitimate businesses. If you fail, our bank stands to lose the thirty-five-million dollar loan to your father."

A certain Arab bank has a stake in all this? No wonder Kamal was so unyielding. He looked at his father, who nodded. "I understand," Jason mumbled, trying to conceal his shock.

"I hope you do understand," Faris said, looking at Jason. "I was not at liberty to divulge this loan to anyone, unless absolutely necessary. But now it appears the time has come for you to know."

"That's correct," Kamal said. "The loan documents are with our lawyers. The agreements bind your father's estate and the estate's beneficiaries. Your father's will was given to me for safekeeping, and I'm the first to notify Makin who's named as the executor of the estate."

Jason looked at his father in disbelief. He was about to say something, but swallowed instead.

"The forensic group will be coming from Riyadh in a few days," Kamal said. "They'll be staying at your hotel. A young representative is coming to Pafos before their arrival to prepare their stay. His code name is Aziz. We want complete anonymity."

"We understand," Faris replied. "Is Mr. Manning aware of all this?"

"Yes," Kamal responded. "Alex is fully informed. He's prepared to allay any American fears about you, but he cannot prevent them from investigating your dealings."

Alex Manning and Faris were friends. Jason wondered, though, if their friendship wasn't merely the product of expediency. "What role do I play in all this?" he asked.

"I want you to represent Mustafa Holdings in these meetings. And I expect you to give our people everything they ask for."

This fellow quite enjoyed being imposing, Jason concluded. "You want me to be the link between Mustafa Holdings and the Saudis?"

"Yes."

Jason saw immediately how challenging the task would be. He hid his anxiety, resisted the temptation to get up and leave. He looked with sadness at Faris. "My father's health is poor."

"Can I count on you, then, to cooperate with our men?"

Jason's desire to find out how Richard had disappeared was suddenly uppermost in his mind. If his brother was involved in any shady deal, the audit would help him discover it, and he could follow the trace after that. "Yes, of course," Jason replied cautiously.

Kamal stood up. "Here," he said.

Jason saw a narrow strip of paper with numbers on it held out in front of him.

"That's a telephone number in Riyadh, just in case you need to reach me. My assistant will find me."

Jason took the paper and put it in his pocket.

"I must get going," Kamal said. "I have to be on time for the flight back to Riyadh. I envy you, gentlemen. The temperature here is a comfortable 26°. In Riyadh today it is 35°."

Nevertheless, Jason's blood was boiling.

9

After Kamal left, Jason looked at his father. Sweat dripped from the old man's forehead, and his breathing was heavy. "You're exhausted," Jason said gently. He picked up the phone and dialed the number of Villa Mustafa. Helena answered, and he asked her to send the nurse over to Villa Oasis.

He stayed with his father until she arrived. "I'm going for a walk," he said to Faris. "I'll be back soon. Keep the gates open for me, please."

He left to stroll through the garden. The wild bulbs his mother had lovingly planted at the edges of the driveway had begun to grow and flower again. He exited the gates, walked a couple of hundred metres into the country terrain and sat on a rock surrounded by anthills. Watching ants moving in and out of their nests, memories of his boyhood resurfaced. When he was ten he enjoyed sitting on the ground, looking at the ants milling around on the earth, like mini-caravans travelling in little deserts. Breathing in the scent of wild thyme and fresh earth invigorated his spirit, although he still worried about the health of his father and the whereabouts of his brother.

Suddenly, a familiar male voice turned his head. He saw Dr. Plato, walking a black sheep dog.

"Jason!" Dr. Plato trumpeted raising his arms.

Jason was shaken with pleasant surprise. Dr. Plato was an old and trusted friend of the Mustafa family, and his presence soothed Jason's soul.

They embraced.

"You're in good form," Jason said with a wide smile.

"This is Azor," Dr. Plato introduced his dog. "Come, meet Jason."

Azor turned his head sideways to size up Jason, and wagged his tail.

"He's very friendly," Dr. Plato said.

"I like him," Jason said.

Dr. Plato said, "I was with your father early this morning. When I entered his bedroom, I saw him looking out the window, steadily and patiently waiting for you. He was so happy when you got out of the taxi.

I examined him quickly and left to get Azor." A momentary silence fell. "How are you?"

Jason saw no reason to pretend. "I've been away so long, I feel like a stranger."

"Your father needs you."

Jason found Dr. Plato's statement quite extraordinary. He and his father had crossed swords on many occasions, and he knew him well by now. Faris had no need for anybody unless he had something to gain. "How is my father's health?"

"Not well, I'm afraid."

Jason had learned shortly after his mother's death that Faris contracted leukemia and was receiving chemotherapy and radiotherapy. After Richard disappeared, Faris's situation worsened, and a nurse was assigned to look after him at Villa Oasis. Jason thought it was absurd that the guesthouse, which lacked the splendor of Villa Mustafa, would become his father's home. "What does 'not well' mean, specifically?"

"All the doctors agree that the treatments are not helping him."

"What can I do?"

"Stay as close to him as you can. Tomorrow I'll take him to the hospital for his regular chemotherapy. Why don't you come along?"

He remembered the days his father enjoyed perfect health. It must be painful, Jason thought. "I'd like that. What time?"

"Ten o'clock."

Jason knew where the new Pafos Hospital was. "I'll be there."

Dr. Plato focused his eyes on Villa Mustafa. "Ever since your brother's disappearance, things have certainly changed around here."

"Well, all things considered, isn't that only natural?"

"No. Marianna is a different person." He lowered his voice. "She goes out a lot … you know."

Jason had no personal reason to doubt Dr. Platos's words, but he knew others thought of him as a man whose mind conjured up imaginative goings-on. He recalled one particular story that had become the gossip of the villagers. In the early 1950s, the British occupying forces (on a tip from Dr. Plato) stepped up their hunt for a serial rapist who was ravaging the area. Dr. Plato told them that he'd witnessed the rapist drag a young woman into the bushes, raping her at gunpoint.

Based on that information they arrested and charged a man who, despite Dr. Plato's testimony, was acquitted. The defence lawyers had branded Dr. Plato a man whose story was nothing but a figment of his imagination. The truth never came out because the alleged victim, perhaps fearing for her safety, refused to testify.

"Have you seen Marianna recently?" Jason asked Dr. Plato.

"Very briefly, last week, when I came to visit your father. It seems … she was trying to avoid me."

They stood there quietly for a minute, and then Dr. Plato said, "I must go home and feed my dog. Azor has been my sole companion since December, when my wife passed away."

"I was told of that. I'm so sorry for your loss, Doctor."

Dr. Plato embraced Jason and said, "Will you come visit me? I have something important to tell you. In case you've forgotten, my house is next to the church in the village square. It has a red-tiled roof and a front veranda."

Jason could see the Peta village nestled in the lower hills, barely a kilometre away. "Sure I will," Jason said jovially.

"Let me write down my phone number for you," Dr. Plato said. He took out his pen and searched for a piece of paper but couldn't find one.

After taking it from the top pocket of his shirt, Jason opened his little notebook and flipped to a blank page. "Write it here," he said.

Dr. Plato took the note pad, wrote down the number, and returned it to Jason. "See you later."

10

While Dr. Plato and his dog headed back toward the village, Jason's mind travelled seven months back.

He'd heard of his brother's disappearance while dining at a Toronto restaurant with some colleagues from the University of Toronto, in celebration of his tenure. At the tender age of thirty-three, he was a full-time professor of Political Science and International Affairs. While his colleagues were laughing and drinking around the table, Jason could not find the appetite to finish his meal. Just before his father called from Cyprus, he'd had a nagging premonition of some sort, but he could not nail down the source of his irritation. Then his cell phone rang.

"I don't know how to begin," Faris said.

"You sound alarmed," Jason said.

"Richard has gone missing."

They spoke for at least an hour.

Jason's head swirled in disbelief, shock and anger. Immediately he wanted to forget about his tenure, sell everything in Canada, and move to Pafos to investigate. But returning to Pafos was not an easy task. Jason had been living in Toronto for fourteen years, and although he had occasionally travelled to Pafos to attend important family functions, his visits there were brief, mainly because he loathed and despised his father. Faris was the successful businessman, the man who could do no wrong, the man who demanded and received respect, loyalty and blind obedience. And Jason was too free-spirited for such a serf-like existence.

Early on in life, Jason had rebelled. When he became of legal age, he left home in search of his own identity. In retaliation, Faris gave up on Jason and nurtured and supported his son Richard, whom he treated as his only rightful heir. Jason lost hope of ever reconciling his differences with his father. He refused to keep in touch with anyone in his family—though he missed and longed for the affection of his mother. His detachment from his father amplified when his mother died.

Jason did return to attend his mother's funeral. During that visit, he'd intended to stay in Pafos for ten days, but his departure was delayed for two weeks because he lost his passport, driver's license, birth certificate and other personal documents. He suspected that someone stole them from his hotel room. Disgruntled and disappointed, he notified the hotel management and local authorities. However, no one ever found his items of identification. Eventually he received a temporary travel document from the Canadian Embassy, allowing him to return to Canada. He was able to replace the missing documents later in Toronto.

The day after he'd learned of Richard's disappearance, Jason walked aimlessly along the boardwalk on the shores of Lake Ontario. His eyes searched over the surface of the lake while a mixture of smog and stale weeds agitated his nostrils. He felt in perfect physical and mental health. He thought of the small, frugal apartment which he rented a few blocks from campus. Jason could afford a larger home, but he enjoyed living in more compact places. His work demanded too much of him; so much that, apart from some brief sexual flings, he had no time for a lasting and meaningful relationship with any woman. He felt out of balance, and he ached for love and companionship. The cool wind touched his forehead.

Jason remembered his high school years, when he had a platonic romantic affair with the daughter of the Mustafa housemaid. Helena Andreou was a year younger than he, and they often met secretly, wandering bare-foot, stealing kisses across the isolated beaches of Pafos. He recalled the day he left Pafos for Toronto, looking into her dark eyes, whispering the poetic words of Lord Byron:

When we two parted
In silence and tears,
Half broken-hearted
To sever for years,
Pale grew thy cheek and cold,
Colder thy kiss;
Truly that hour foretold
Sorrow to this.

The soothing wind on the Toronto boardwalk turned into a storm, and as Jason made his way up the narrow stairs to his apartment, his soaked-through clothes were dripping water all over the floor. Once he got inside, he threw off all his clothes and sat by the side of his bed, leaned back on the mattress and closed his eyes.

Jason kept a box of things that he'd brought with him from Cyprus – the rope from his favourite kite, some sea shells, and some drawings he he'd done as a child. In the same box he kept the twenty-six letters Richard had written to him. Jason wrote back only once, and he had kept a copy.

He reached under the bed, his arm still damp from the rain, and pulled out the tattered cardboard box. Jason picked up the letters, the paper soft from being handled so many times, and words caught his eye as he shuffled through them looking for the one he wanted, scanning Richard's handwriting. 'I went to the beach today' ... 'You know that ice cream you like?' ... 'They introduced me to another woman just last night' ... 'Architecture is okay, but I work far too much' ... 'I wish you hadn't gone' ... 'I miss you Jason; we all do.'

And then he found it. The words were still as clear as when they had been written.

'Dear Richard, there is nothing to excuse my lack of response. But there is also nothing to excuse how father has treated me. I'm sorry that it has to be this way, but I can't have him in my life, and with you, comes him. I hope you understand why I cannot be there for you.'

Water from Jason's hair fell onto the paper, leaving marks and soaking through the typewritten letters, smudging the black ink. It was streaming down his face now, as his head bent forward towards his knees. He caught his breath when he tasted the salt on his lips.

11

Jason wondered if Richard's body might be buried in the terrain surrounding the compound. The only way to find out was to walk around the land and look for signs. But surely the police had their dogs sniffing around soon after his brother disappeared. And he could still be alive.

He gazed back at Villa Mustafa. The place was too grand for his taste. He had never liked big homes anyway. His eyes shifted to Villa Oasis, as Kamal's suspicions reverberated in his mind. *Is my father involved in something clandestine or illegal? What happens if the Saudis prove the unthinkable?*

He remembered having talks with his mother. One day he asked her how she and Faris met. He learned that Rachel had been working on architectural designs for the construction firm owned by Faris's father in Riyadh. Faris was twenty-eight and Rachel was twenty-four. "We fell in love the moment we met," Rachel boasted. They married in Riyadh a year later, but not before Faris had promised her two things: that they would live in the Mediterranean, and that he would not try to convert her to Islam.

Rachel told Jason that her American parents, Joseph and Jessica O'Neill, were foreign correspondents for a New York newspaper. In 1950, they'd been sent to cover the situation in the Middle East. Although the United Nations intended to create a separate Palestinian state, the Arab war with Israel led to the Jordanian occupation of Palestine's West Bank. Abdullah, the Emir of Jordan, annexed the West Bank and renamed his enlarged state the Hashemite Kingdom of Jordan. Rachel was only eight at the time. Her parents used Cyprus as home base, but they often travelled back and forth to Jordan.

They sent Rachel to an English school in Amman, but they also wanted her to learn Arabic. Within two years Rachel became fluent in the Arabic language. When her parents returned to the United States in 1960, Rachel was ready for University. She chose Architecture because the ancient Greek buildings enchanted her. When she graduated in 1965, she felt drawn to Cyprus, and wanted to live there. But because she needed an income to support her, she decided to work in Riyadh for a few years.

She was planning to earn enough money to buy a villa in Cyprus and eventually move there.

Rachel often spoke fondly to Jason about her experiences in Cyprus. Before Jason's birth, Rachel and Faris had visited there seven times. When Jason was born, his parents moved their young family to the town of Kyrenia, on the northern part of the island. They purchased a villa and hired a Greek Cypriot maid named Angela.

Each summer, from 1968 to 1974, the Mustafas stayed in Kyrenia, but after the 1974 Turkish occupation of northern Cyprus, Angela and her child, Helena, became refugees and fled to Pafos. Then Faris sold the villa to a Turkish army officer, and the Mustafa family never returned to Kyrenia. Instead, they started visiting the town of Pafos on the southern part of the island, and in 1978 they moved permanently from Riyadh to Pafos, where Angela returned to work for the Mustafa household.

While the family was living in Riyadh, there were some unpleasant memories Jason wished he'd forgotten. Rachel started drinking heavily when Jason was nine. Others became aware of her alcohol use and raised quite a fuss. Faris and Rachel were under great pressure to leave Riyadh or face persecution for violating the tenets of Islam.

Faris's construction business was facing huge challenges, too, and needed to expand its operations. Jason had later learned that during this time, Cyprus had enacted attractive offshore tax legislation, which prompted thousands of foreign companies to take advantage of very low taxes (4.2%) and offshore secrecy laws.

Since his parents already knew Cyprus, they didn't have much of a problem when they settled there for good. They made many friends, including John Persinaras and his wife. Faris and Rachel maintained their friendship with the Persinaras family throughout the years, but Faris had kept his business matters to himself, until one day Persinaras offered to be one of Faris's business partners.

In 1985, Faris and Persinaras formed the Persinaras-Mustafa Group, the consortium that oversaw the ownership, management and operation of the hotel and the villa development projects on the hills. But Faris held onto other investments in Saudi Arabia, Jordan, Kuwait, Dubai and Bahrain. He also set up offshore banking operations in Cyprus to facilitate the banking needs of his Arab friends.

When his family moved to Pafos, Jason was ten. He remembered the first time his parents took him and his brother to see the area that later became the Mustafa estate. Rachel fell in love with the land the moment she set foot on it. "I love it, I love it," she sang, and her song danced in all directions. It was an idyllic environment: strolling hills to the north-east, a valley to the south-west, the sea expanse to the south, the Peta village upland, and in-between, hundreds of olive, carob, orange, lemon and almond trees. A few hundred feet to the east, green strips of cultivated grape vine orchards complemented the landscape. Multi-coloured wild flowers sprang everywhere.

Jason remembered that it had been so quiet he heard the hum of bees. Further to the west, he saw flocks of sheep and goats grazing freely on the land. At an elevation of 1,200 feet, he viewed Pafos and the whole surrounding area. At sunset, it was the perfect spot to sit and do nothing. There was a fragrance in the air so intense that Rachel turned to Faris and said: "Honey, this place rejuvenates my spirit." She looked forward to leaving her bitter memories of the Tuxedo Park Estate dispute behind her.

Jason had never been to Tuxedo Park. Rachel had described it as 'an architectural masterpiece', designed and built by Jason's great-grandfather in 1928. It was situated on twenty-four acres of private, tranquil, heavily wooded and landscaped grounds in the exclusive, private community of Tuxedo Park, just fifty minutes from Manhattan. It was set amidst 2,300 acres of mountains with three lakes. "After your great-aunt Elizabeth inherited it, she sold it to a shipping tycoon. I was so upset that I began a lawsuit to block the deal, but in the end I couldn't stop it from being sold."

When Villa Mustafa was being built, Rachel was scrupulous with details; she loved all kinds of wood. She hired some of the best craftsmen in the area to prepare hand-carved gilded moldings, staircases and mantelpieces. The place had lots of room. Jason wanted a smaller house, but his opinion didn't matter. "We need the space, my boy!" Rachel told him cheerfully. And her enthusiasm made young Jason giggle.

She used to love playing the piano. Schumann's *Dreaming* was her favourite piece.

The years had passed. Now he missed his mother's kind and sensitive nature.

Jason also remembered the days he and Richard had spent together as teenagers, and his heart sank, as reality dropped its heavy anchor on his nostalgia.

12

Back in the present, Jason began to walk to the Mustafa compound. Faris's caustic comments about Katerina reminded him of something that happened during a celebration to which he'd been invited almost five years ago.

January 31, 1997 – Dignitaries and local celebrities joined the festivities. The Persinaras and Mustafa families, their friends, employees, local politicians, clergy and hundreds of clients and guests gathered at the Mustafa Beach Hotel (the consortium's Crown jewel) to commemorate the twelfth anniversary of the consortium, The Persinaras-Mustafa Group. John Persinaras controlled Persinaras Estates Ltd., while Faris Mustafa controlled Mustafa Holdings.

At the appropriate moment Faris took the podium and said, "The land development business in Pafos is a lifetime aspiration. We do not build homes; we build dreams. We offer our select clients the opportunity to enjoy a lifestyle comparable to the best French, Spanish, Italian, Mexican, Caribbean and Greek resorts. Million-dollar ocean and hill views, spectacular beaches and many of Cyprus's finest hotels are only part of the long list of features that continue to make this fabled stretch of Pafos coast a world-class address. And if history repeats itself, those who buy into this opportunity (while prices are held back due to the political impasse) have most to gain when Cyprus becomes a full member of the European Union."

At the same gathering, Persinaras's eldest daughter, Katerina, then thirty and already a lawyer, suddenly announced that the Persinaras-Mustafa Group had reached an agreement with a land development company from Sudan to expand the construction of luxury villas in Pafos. The announcement, as Katerina had later tried to tell Faris, was kept secret until the last moment in order to achieve a competitive advantage. But Faris felt left out and betrayed. Jason was equally concerned, but Richard and Marianna intervened to pacify their families. The proposal was put to a vote during a subsequent meeting, and although the Persinaras family (with its 51% holdings in the consortium) prevailed, Mustafa Holdings (with its 49% interest in the Persinaras-Mustafa Group) remained resolute.

As he entered the gates, Jason felt that he needed to know for certain that his father was not aiding and abetting a terrorist group. He walked toward Villa Oasis, determined to confront Faris.

13

Marianna was sitting in the private patio of her bedroom, drinking tea, and watching a black Mercedes leaving the compound. Grains of cold sweat rolled down her spine and burst on the edges of her buttocks. Jason had barely set foot on the Mustafa estate and now he was welcoming visitors, she thought with disapproval.

When they'd met in the living room, she'd noticed how fit he was in his dark, neatly-pressed grey trousers. His black turtleneck sweater was thick and loose, making him appear comfortable and self-confident, but she could also sense that he had gone through personal anguish. His voice, deeper than it once was, yet soft and steady, portrayed inner strength, and his big hazel eyes were full of child-like curiosity. She wondered if he had a woman in his life, but she was pleasantly distracted by the scent of grilled calamari, baked bread, and roasted pine nuts, all of which filled the villa and reached her nostrils.

She decided to walk to the kitchen and inspect dinner preparations for the party she was hosting that evening. Her guests were to include: her sister, Katerina and her husband; her father, John Persinaras; her mother, Alexia Persinaras; the mayor of Pafos, and his wife; the Pafos police chief; the general manager of the Persinaras Estates and his wife; the General Manager of Mustafa Holdings and his wife; two female architects, and their husbands; the Bishop of Pafos; and of course her brother-in-law, Jason. But most important to Marianna was Abbot Maximus.

She'd barely finished giving her instructions to the chef and his helpers, when Helena walked into the kitchen.

"Is Jason still there?" Marianna asked, pointing toward Villa Oasis.

"I don't know, madam."

"Have you seen Katerina?"

"A few minutes ago, her car left with the children inside."

Marianna knew that her children enjoyed Katerina's company. Katerina was Claira's godmother, and Marianna remembered their argument when the topic of choosing the child's name came up.

Marianna wanted to call her 'Anna', but Katerina's choice, 'Claira', prevailed. Katerina had an air of authority about her.

"She took them to church again?" Marianna voiced in amusement.

Helena said, "The children are rather fond of her!"

The maid's comment reminded Marianna of Katerina's loss when the latter was only nineteen. It was a sad chapter in Katerina's life, a grief of which few people were aware. "Yes, well she loves the children very much," Marianna said and paused. "If Katerina had her own, I'm sure she would spoil them just as much."

"She certainly loves Claira."

"I know," responded Marianna with a dismissive wave of her hand. "I don't mind. Claira is five, and she needs all the love she can get."

"Yes, children can never have too much."

"I don't mind her spoiling Claira. But the twins were so disciplined when Richard was around, and look at them now. They're so insecure."

Their conversation was interrupted when the gate telephone entry system rang. Helena answered. It was Monk Modestos, one of the twenty-one monks of the nearby Holy Monastery of The Saint Mary Magdalene. Marianna gave permission for his entry into the compound, and Helena pressed the numeric access code.

Half a minute later Marianna welcomed him at the north-end porch. They walked across the rotunda through the galleria hall and into the kitchen. Marianna knew Modestos well. He was twenty-two, an effeminate man whose short, stocky stature contrasted sharply with that of his master, Abbot Maximus.

Modestos was carrying a huge and heavy bamboo basket full of halloumi cheese, three jars of mountain honey and five loaves of monastery bread. "Abbot Maximus is pleased that you've invited him to dinner tonight and is sending you his heartfelt regards with these presents," said the monk.

Marianna was unable to hide her excitement. "How thoughtful! Please thank him on my behalf and tell him that I will be most honoured by his presence in my home tonight. Dinner starts at seven."

The monk nodded, and left.

Marianna took a loaf of bread from the basket, placed it on a platter and walked over to the master bedroom, through the sitting area and outside onto the private patio. She sat on one of the cushioned cast-iron chairs and sighed. There, alone, she touched and smelled the bread as if it were a rare flower she hadn't seen or smelled before. She got carried away – touching, feeling and smelling the loaf. The source of her stimulation was not the bread but the image of Maximus.

The fresh, cool November air, blowing from the sea, caressed her face. How invigorating, she thought. It would be perfect if he were here now! With a magnificent sea view, this was the right place to relax, dream and contemplate. She craved to be in his arms once again, and these feelings prompted her to think even more about him. The private patio offered a sanctuary for her secret thoughts. She could come here and sit and stare at the blue sea, the rolling hills and the blue sky. At night, she would put the children to bed and come out here to relax, looking at the stars, the moon and its reflection on the sea, a reflection that resembled rivers of flowing golden lava; changing, expanding or contracting, matching her moods and agitating her sensual desires.

Abbot Maximus made Marianna feel attractive, important and wanted. She could hardly wait until he came tonight!

She'd tried to keep her affair with Abbot Maximus top secret, but in this region of sixty-two thousand inhabitants, she learned that only the bats in their caves kept secrets. It was impossible. Innuendos and gossip flew everywhere, but she couldn't care less. Her sister Katerina was the only person who knew all the details of Marianna's intimate moments with Maximus. She'd told her about everything between them. She could trust her sister, but no one else.

Maximus was the man who could touch her on the right spot, at the right time and fill her with ecstasy. Even the thought of him caused her body to moisten with longing. She remembered their first erotic encounter more than nine years ago. It had been a hot summer evening …

14

At Katerina's wedding, music bellowed below a star-filled night sky. People danced and drank wine generously. Family, relatives, friends and guests gathered at the five-star Mustafa Beach Hotel, which belonged to the consortium, to celebrate the marriage of Persinaras's eldest daughter to George Lagos, an Athenian. Marianna was single and carefree. Maximus had just been ordained an abbot, and at forty-two, he was old enough to be her father, but she found this stimulating. He was sitting with some other local notables, near the head table when they began a casual conversation.

"Men and women are growing farther and farther apart," he said. "Someone even came up with the crazy notion that the two genders come from different planets. We should stop stressing what makes us separate from one another. We're different, okay, but those things that make us similar are greater than our differences."

Marianna absorbed every word he said. The conversation moved on to the topic of love and religion. Maximus drew a line between non-sexual love (selfless and spiritual) and erotic worship. He called the first Agape the second Erotas. "The Ancient Greeks defined and refined these terms."

Marianna took over from there. "Agape and Erotas," she said, "are supposed to be two totally different forms of love, but they have a common thread, and this joining is the strong bond and attachment that one person feels for another. Erotas and Agape can co-exist. I can desire you sexually, but I can also feel a sense of Agape, pure selfless and giving love for you."

"Erotas," he responded, "is a form of love based on sexual gratification, designed to procreate humankind. It doesn't always turn out that way; it can become hedonistic."

Marianna was curious. "What do you think of hedonism, exactly?"

"Hmm," he said. "The Cyrenaics, or egoistic hedonists, of Ancient Greece believed that immediate gratification of personal desires was the supreme climax of existence. Knowledge, they said, exists in the fleeting sensations of the moment. So it's useless to formulate a system of moral values when urges for plain and present pleasures is weighed against any pain they may cause in the future. Now, the Epicureans (or rational hedonists) argued that true pleasure is reached only through reason. They extolled virtues of self-control and prudence. I'm somewhere between these two theories. Sexual gratification is part of our makeup, our destiny, and our relationship with God. But hedonism can be so powerful it often creates conflict between us."

As the band's music blasted the air with bouzouki tunes, and people danced in circles, Marianna and Maximus kept talking, disregarding their surroundings. Maximus listened more than he talked, a sharp contrast to the self-centred, bragging, immature young men of Marianna's age. She observed how he had the cunning ability to change topics (and facial expressions) in an instant—from austere and pious, to jovial and casual. Marianna's boredom completely disappeared.

It was close to two o'clock in the morning, and the guests began to leave the hall. Marianna had excused herself, kissed her sister and brother-in-law, said goodbye to her parents and friends, and left.

As she was starting her car in the hotel parking lot, Marianna saw him, through the rear-view mirror, walking toward his four-wheel drive utility car. As soon as she drove off, past the exit, she saw his car following hers closely. She hadn't planned it, but suddenly she craved to be cradled in his arms. Speeding past the tourist area, she followed a rural road and stopped about six metres from an isolated beach.

Marianna turned the lights off and waited. She rolled down the car window. The fresh smell of the sea hit her nose. Oxygen was flowing around her. She could hear the gentle force of the waves hitting the sand in constant, never-ending strokes, causing the sea to moan.

Maximus's car appeared from the dark, and he parked it parallel to Marianna's coupé. She got out and walked over to the passenger side of his car. The door was already open. Without a word, she threw herself in his arms. She felt his warm, wet lips on the back of her neck, kissing and sucking her, while his fingers were already inside her black silk underwear.

His hard, thick fingers lingered on the edge of her lips, pressing them together, then setting them apart. He moved his middle finger into her slowly, numbly, agitating her clitoris and stimulating the vaginal walls. Marianna uttered disjointed words, gasped and whispered in quivers.

Overtaken by feverish lust, they found themselves outside the car. The moon was clear. Their eyes met and their gazes burned under the night's bright sky. As she tugged off his robe, his hot hand crawled

38

between her legs and pulled off her panties. Maximus removed her dress and bra and began to devour her breasts. She unzipped his pants. He spun her around in his arms, and she felt his embrace, like that of a wild animal anxious to mate. His skin was tanned, the hair of his chest soft and bushy. And he had a musky odour: part salty sweat, part sweet wine.

When he laid her upon the warm sand, she knew she was at the mercy of his desires. She spread her legs and arms apart, embedding her body on the sand, stroking it, becoming part of it. He caressed the outer lips of her vagina with one hand and sank the fingers of his other hand into her round buttocks. He squeezed them, and she squealed from the force of his grasp. He then pushed his long, strong tongue deep inside her, slipping it in and out, and it felt as if he was fucking her. Marianna moaned and trembled. "Let me taste you, too," she begged.

She crawled on the sand and faced the large, round head of his penis. With delightful lust, she stroked it repeatedly with both hands. She salivated as she opened her mouth and sucked him deeply inside her throat. She sensed that Maximus enjoyed it, and kept licking and sucking until she began to nag with spasms of desire. "Maximus, fuck me hard!" she pleaded.

As he penetrated her, the full moon was about to set into the depths of the sea. Maximus was taking her slowly, teasing her with pauses at each end of his thrust. She felt his stiff erection flowing into her, and she wanted the pleasure to last forever. But the ecstasy came bright and strong, and her orgasm was long and deep, agitating her senses – elevating her consciousness.

For the next six weekends, they were to meet secretly like this. Then some fishermen saw them, and gossip reached John Persinaras's ear. Her father confronted her, and she denied the affair, playing it down as platonic. Nevertheless her parents had their men follow her steps very closely, and they forbade her from seeing Maximus for a long time.

15

Many memories stuck in Marianna's mind. Many men had wanted to marry her. Her parents and relatives had introduced her to some suitable candidates, but when she dated them, she never felt as aroused and excited as when she was with Maximus. He knew how to touch her, grab her and seduce her with tantalizing hedonism, making her cry with ecstasy. She reacted to her parents' strict control by becoming obnoxious to the men who dated her, playing with their feelings, putting them down, teasing them and ignoring them altogether.

She'd felt so restricted by her parents that she began dreaming of leaving Pafos and moving to Athens. Marianna hoped that Maximus would follow her, and they could start a new life in Greece—she as an interior designer, he as professor of Byzantine Studies and Monasticism. After all, she had lived in Athens from 1988 to 1992, as a student of Interior Design at Athens Polytechnic. But she'd abandoned such thoughts after Maximus called them "precarious."

Marianna had tried to cope with her sense of loss (not having Maximus in her life). She persuaded her parents to help her set up three adjacent galleries near the Pafos harbour. She found three nineteenth century Cypriot homes, which she renovated, connected together with wide Venetian arches and aptly named them: "Marianna's Galleries."

She was fond of Cyprus history under British rule, which began in 1878 when the British arrived on the island to find it in a state of wretchedness from years of Ottoman occupation. Victorian Cyprus (1878-1901) had organized government but no democracy, since the British were interested only in using the island as a colonized base for their Middle East interests.

Marianna had collected thousands of artifacts, from ceramics to clocks, prints to paintings, silverware to sculpture, textiles and tapestries, precious jewels, dress and household items, down to handcrafted locks and hinges. She had purchased most of these items at auctions, exhibits and other private collections. Then she restored and sold them at a premium to British tourists and others. To enhance the reputation of her galleries, she also hosted exhibits and works of contemporary Cypriot artists.

There was another moment that stayed with her. It had been seven years ago, one day in June, three months after she'd married Richard. It was a Sunday.

June 5, 1994 – While her sister Katerina and she were in Marianna's Galleries hosting an art exhibit, Marianna saw Maximus with a group of British guests, chatting with the artist and gazing at the paintings. The name of the artist's exhibit was *"stochasmos,"* and each painting seduced patrons into contemplation. As Maximus's and Marianna's eyes met, she turned and stared at the hall leading to the two washrooms and a storage room.

A few seconds later, unnoticed by anyone, they sneaked into the ladies' washroom. Standing up, he unzipped his pants, and she saw him swollen and pink with lust. He grabbed her by the buttocks, pulled off her panties and lifted her up to his lower waist. While her legs spread apart, swallowing his body, he entered, holding her with his strong hands and striking gentle strokes against her.

16

Marianna wondered if her lack of concern about cheating on Richard had more to do with the resentment she bore over her parents controlling her, rather than with Richard's workaholic tendencies.

Her marriage to Richard was arranged by both their parents in an effort to solidify the two families' joint business ventures with a blood bond. Twenty-seven-year-old Richard had been cool to the idea at first, and he declined to go along with his parents' suggestion. His initial rejection infuriated her so much that she resolved to win his heart at all costs. Using all manner of overtures and pampering, she, at age twenty-four, finally won his affections. After a brief engagement, they married in 1994 at a Greek Orthodox Church with the special blessings of Richard's mother, Rachel.

She now realized that she'd never wanted to marry Richard, but had got used to his company and as time travelled she adopted a sense of duty to him and their three children. After Rachel's death, Marianna caught on that Richard was having an affair: *Chanel #5* wafted from his suits; lipstick traces were left on his handkerchiefs; and overnight stays in Nicosia (capital of Cyprus), which he claimed were for "business reasons."

But Marianna chose to ignore these signs because he was a good father to their children and a dedicated professional. Richard gave her a great deal of freedom, though he lacked the passion she had once known with Maximus. She made Richard content, she thought, only because he'd never experienced such pure and primitive sex. *Maybe I made him feel inferior to me, which would explain his affair – or affairs?*

After Richard's disappearance, she began seeing Maximus again. *I'm free now, and Maximus might not remain a monk all his life.* Marianna justified her behaviour simply by stating to herself that she was the product of her society.

Her friends spoke about the increasing permissiveness of Cypriot morals. She ignored such talk, keeping her opinions to herself. Societal views were as diverse as the Cypriot citizens themselves. Monasteries (with their business ventures, land development projects and other non-religious undertakings) were the primary targets of criticism. Some blamed the immorality on the hypocrisy of the church, and its hoarding of wealth. Others blamed the influx of Russians and offshore money for the increase in criminal activity and general lack of respect for the law. A sizeable group blamed the Cypriot politicians, branding them selfish and arrogant, practicing nepotism and unwilling to change. Some blamed everything and everybody. Marianna believed that the loose moral standards and the increase in criminal activity had more to do with the self-indulgence of the Cypriots themselves than with the influx of foreigners and foreign money.

From her elevated private patio, she enjoyed a tremendous view of the west end of the villa grounds. She saw the six-foot bronze statue of Aphrodite on a pedestal in the middle of the fountain. Facing the statue and raising their hands to the sky, ten small naked nymphs of the Mediterranean Sea (the Nereids), daughters of the sea god Nereus, surrounded the edges of the cyclical fountain.

She saw the statue in an Athens gallery while she and Richard were vacationing in Greece (six months following the death of Richard's mother), and she decided to purchase it. When the statue arrived back home in Pafos, she recalled the scorn of her parents. They believed the price tag ($38,000.00 US) was too high, and they tried to get her to mark up the price and sell it at her gallery.

However, for Marianna, the statue represented a relationship that was sensual and liberating, and she wanted to be close to it, to make it a part of her life. With Richard's blessings, she hired a professional landscape contractor to build a fountain and the statue was placed in the middle of it.

Why do I love it so much? she wondered, looking at the statue. Perhaps there are some similarities between Aphrodite and me, she mused. She was fond of Greek mythology: she knew, in Homeric legend, that Aphrodite was said to be the daughter of Zeus and Dione, one of Zeus's consorts, but in the *Theogony* of Hesiod she was described as having sprung from the foam of the sea of Pafos, and her name meant "foam-risen." According to Homer, Aphrodite was the wife of Hephaestus, the lame and ugly god of fire. Her lovers included Ares, the god of war, who in later mythology was represented as her husband. Aphrodite was the rival of Persephone, queen of the underworld, for the love of the beautiful Greek youth, Adonis. *Isn't it odd? I tend to admire older men.*

The legend about Aphrodite that Marianna found most enticing was the cause of the Trojan War: Eris, (the only goddess not invited to the wedding of King Peleus and the sea nymph Thetis) tossed resentfully into the banquet hall a golden apple on which were inscribed the words "for the fairest." When Zeus refused to judge between Hera, Athena, and Aphrodite, the three goddesses who claimed the apple, he asked Paris, prince of Troy, to make the award. Each goddess offered Paris a bribe: Hera promised him that he would be a powerful ruler; Athena whispered that he would achieve great military fame; and Aphrodite guaranteed that he would have the fairest woman in the world. Paris declared Aphrodite the fairest and chose as his prize Helen of Troy, the wife of the Greek king Menelaus. Paris abducted Helen, which led to the Trojan War. Marianna smiled. *It's amazing how goddesses influenced both men and gods.*

17

After Rachel's death, Marianna convinced Richard that they should rearrange the interior of the villa. "This is our home now," she remembered telling him. Marianna felt it was important to make the rooms appear more inviting. "We want our family, friends and guests to feel good about sitting down and staying awhile."

Marianna wanted the living room to be a mix of Arab and Greek themes, a daring technique that she knew only the most skillful interior decorator could put together. Richard had been collecting Arabian art: original oil paintings, water colours, antique maps of the Middle East, contemporary Arabic calligraphy antiques and artifacts such as wooden engravings, chests, Bedouin weavings, rugs and textiles. Marianna had rearranged these items and added some paintings and sculptures, replicas of semi-nude and other classical Greek themes, floral fabrics on the pillows and ottomans to soften the rooms. She always had fresh flowers and scented candles throughout the home.

Before Richard's disappearance, she'd been getting used to the idea of having a lasting marriage. She felt comfortable and thankful for the blessings in her life and she felt the need to contribute to local charities, with both her time and money. She remembered being interviewed by a Pafos TV hostess. The television station was organizing a marathon for children with disabilities, and Marianna was the main matron of the charitable institution promoting it.

"Having been born under the astrological sign of Cancer," she said to the interviewer, "I desire my social environment to blend harmoniously with my own personal world, my home and my children. I like to think that we are all connected and dependent on each other, and that no one should be left behind. I can change my home, but I can't change my society by myself. That's why I need the help of all Pafians to ensure the happiness of all our children."

When she was asked to describe how her children spent their time, Marianna's face glowed with excitement. "When we moved to the hills, rabbits were populating all around us. The children were having fun feeding and watching them. A friend of mine wrote a children's book about the rabbits of Villa Mustafa, and rabbits became a part of our home. The children's rooms are filled with art and pieces of furniture that mean something to them: small sculptures of animals and children, and every time I look at them I feel like a child again myself."

Marianna also transformed the swimming pool from its worn-out condition into a colourful and exotic painting of glass mosaics surrounding three-dimensional, hand-carved fish-motif tiles. She finished the bottom with a smooth background of sky-blue pebble-tech that blended into a mysterious moon and silent stars. The children's favourite part of the pool was the warm and relaxing spa, which had tile inlays, but (at this time of year) it was too cold to swim.

She wished it were summer. She could not wait for summer; it was her favourite season. Marianna and her friends would often sit by the covered patio for hours, watching the children play, while lizards would roam freely in the garden's grounds. And on the trees above, blond male canaries serenaded their female companions.

18

Marianna hadn't seen the children all morning, at least not since Katerina had taken them to church. She looked left, at Villa Oasis. The doors were shut. She saw Jason wandering alone on the hills nearby, and she was tempted to call him to join her for tea. But she changed her mind. She wondered what Jason and his father had been discussing with the stranger in Villa Oasis, and she was unnerved. It could have been another one of those business deals, she thought. Faris was very sick, she knew that, but she also knew that a certain Pafos doctor who had examined him believed that he might recover. He'd overcome a mild stroke before, she remembered and came back to take charge. She resented him for making all the major decisions. Even now, in his condition, he continued to pull the strings that directed the management of Mustafa Holdings.

Shortly before Richard's disappearance, Faris had promoted him Chief Architect, a position which Richard was pleased to accept. Still, his father oversaw all his activities. Richard had once told her that he doubted his father would ever groom him for the job of chief executive, because it seemed Faris had already handpicked Nadir Makin (General Manager of Mustafa Holdings) to be in charge of the day-to-day running of the company.

I hate this Arab connection, Marianna told herself. Although Richard was an Arab's son, she never saw him as an Arab. He was not a Muslim. She remembered with amusement the day before her wedding, when Richard was baptized a Christian. It happened at a secret religious ceremony presided over by Abbot Maximus. Richard's mother, Marianna's parents and sister, were among the few witnesses. Richard always worried what the fall-out might be should his father find out about his baptism.

Faris did not approve of the present lifestyle of his daughter-in-law, which he labelled "frivolous." Faris held title to the two villas and the surrounding olive grove, and she feared that he, or his beneficiary, could evict her anytime.

Richard had always liked the place with its graceful arches, five bedrooms, six baths, two half-baths, fabulous eat-in gourmet kitchen

47

complex, long galleria with its skyline, twenty foot in diameter rotunda, exercise room, game room, spacious library and four-car garage. The living room featured a seventeenth century Italian-carved marble mantle, nine-foot tall stained glass windows with panoramic views, and a nineteenth century Cypriot fireplace. The dining room had local terra-cotta floors and a beamed ceiling. Vaulted ceilings enhanced the breakfast room and a Greek Cypriot artist painted its walls with local countryside themes. The master suite with its two baths had separate dressing rooms for Marianna and Richard; it also had a private patio. The library, which was Richard's favourite place, was richly panelled in cherry wood. It had a fireplace and a wet bar. On the eastern wall of the library, a door led to a private area, which was Richard's conference room. In the basement, there was a temperature-controlled wine vault with a capacity for one hundred cases.

From her vantage point, Marianna saw the cabin nestled in the olive grove. Nearby, an arched wooden gazebo overlooked the blue Mediterranean, and farther to the southwest a small maid's quarters housed both the female nurse and the older housemaid.

Marianna felt incomplete without the two villas, the maid's quarters, the cabin and the olive grove.

She sunk her teeth into the monastery bread when the phone rang. "Hello," she answered, holding the loaf with her teeth marks embedded in it.

"I hear you're hosting a dinner party tonight," Faris said.

She cringed, preparing to be criticized again. "I thought with Jason's arrival, we should have a little celebration," she lied. "I meant to invite you, of course, but I got so busy with the preparations."

"Mr. Manning and his wife have arrived from Nicosia and will be staying at the hotel for a couple of nights."

"Really? I want them to join us for dinner."

"I'll invite them," Faris said. "Make sure they're looked after properly."

As always, Faris wanted to be the master; the man who was in control. "Well, I always enjoy their company .... You know that," she protested.

"No loud music or dancing," Faris continued. "The atmosphere should be formal and restrained."

He's not going to spoil my party, Marianna resolved. "I can't tell my guests how to enjoy themselves."

Faris said, "By the way, I'll invite Dr. Plato, too."

"Why?"

"Remember, this is my residence. I'm the father of the missing Richard Mustafa."

"How many times do you have to remind me?" she grumbled and hung up.

To take the children to the chapel of the Holy Monastery of The Saint Mary Magdalene, Katerina drove along a dirt road, which was a shortcut of seven minutes. On the way to the monastery, she remembered when she was nine years old.

December 18, 1975 – Katerina's parents, John and Alexia Persinaras, entertained their long-time friends, Faris and Rachel Mustafa, who were visiting from Riyadh. During that time, the Persinaras house was located near the Pafos Harbour. After lunch, Katerina's father drove the family and their two guests to the monastery to visit Abbot Alexandros.

Their car followed the scenic route along the southern coastline where ageless erosion had carved deep rifts that ran southward. The altitude grew gradually higher from south to north, ending with a large difference in height above sea level that marked the beginning of the Pafos Hills. From there, the secluded setting drew the eye hundreds of metres downward to the choppy sea, then farther up again the monastery emerged at 1,500 metres, like an arched theatre balcony overlooking the Mediterranean. To the north, the highlands merged with the Troodos Range, the highest mountains of Cyprus.

Katerina looked at the valley, which blended with the smooth hillsides, where villagers led poor agricultural lives. The landscape had been practically unaltered by humans whose humble houses blended harmoniously into the natural lines of the slopes. But the green meadows that made agriculture possible in this Mediterranean environment vanished whenever the olive slopes became too deep.

Venturing onto the narrow path towards the monastery, the car gradually reached a distant place and time. Katerina's imagination was stirred by the efforts of the monks to ensure their seclusion and consecration.

The landscape surrounding the monastery was untamed, with ravines, wooded peaks interspersed with steep gorges and views of an inexhaustible coastline. Streams of clear water ran under the deep shade of the carob trees. Amidst this wilderness were the high walls of the monastery with vegetable fields around them. Olive trees encircled the fields. Visible among the greenery and the impenetrable gorges—hovering in the most unexpected position—was the spectacle of a large cave carved out of the mountain by the first hermits who hundreds of years ago spent their days in isolation and meditation there.

It was a land where reality was intertwined with legend, and faith fused with mysticism.

A façade of ten huge arches guarded the entrance to the monastery. Layers of monks' quarters were built in a U shape, resembling a fortified Venetian castle, and Katerina was astonished to see fat, black-robed monks living in this luxurious place.

She said to her mother, "I don't see the prince!"

The architecture was palatial and spacious. Adjacent stylish units stood on verdant terraces, exhaling a charm of Venetian splendor, and although blending in a perfect balance with the environment, they were set apart from it with their style and comfort. Well-constructed double stonewalls had been roofed with red-tiles laid over wooden beams and boards hewn from the finest pine or cedar. Arch-covered corridors led to a large reception room at the midpoint of the 'U' formation. In the centre of the monastery, a Byzantine chapel stood firm and solemn.

They went straight to the chapel. It was past 3:00 p.m., and the Mass had already finished. Only a handful of worshipers were inside. While Katerina and Marianna were lighting candles, their father stood in the middle of the church, pointing at the frescos and explaining to the Mustafas the history behind them.

"These are locally produced paintings," he said. "They are a synthesis of regional iconography and Byzantine influence. The crowning focuses our attention on The Virgin by means of circular geometry that defines the Trinity, the heavenly world and earth."

They left the church and headed for the reception room. Abbot Alexandros was sitting on his throne, smiling, blessing and talking to his guests. Maximus, who was at that time an archimandrite, stood by his side.

The abbot was sick and frail. He said, "This monastery is one of the oldest in Pafos, created by a group of Byzantine monks more than a thousand years ago. It's a unique monastic place which, although part of Cyprus, is governed by its own local administration."

Katerina called the monastery "the prince's castle." The place occupied part of the hills of Pafos, an extension of the Troodos Range. "Due to its isolation, the monastery has remained one of the most unspoiled parts of Pafos," the abbot continued.

Katerina was too young to understand the politics of monastery life, but she gathered that Maximus was in charge of the monastery's affairs, the one who made all major decisions. Katerina's father was so impressed with the scenery and the panoramic view of the sea that he proposed to purchase 3,000 acres of agricultural land surrounding the monastery. Her father and Maximus excused themselves and proceeded to Maximus's private office. Katerina went along.

During their private discussions, a deal was struck between Maximus and Katerina's father. They spoke about rezoning and other terms she found boring at that time. But she listened, and she understood.

A few weeks later, John Persinaras began the first phase of villa developments in the area. Katerina, who accompanied her father to the area again and again, watched the bulldozers gutting the hills, uprooting trees, and carving roads. Paving machines, trucks carrying asphalt, and hundreds of workers followed the bulldozers.

The abbot died shortly before Katerina's wedding, and Maximus was ordained an abbot in order to succeed him.

20

Over a span of twenty-six years, Katerina saw how steadily the area surrounding the monastery had developed into one of the most prized villa developments on the island, transforming the monastery's tranquil past, and forever fixing its future. Every plot of land was zoned residential. The average villa was selling for 700,000 US dollars, and some villas were being snatched for as much as $2.2-million. She had done the calculations a thousand times. The profit margin was nearly 80%.

Now, as she stopped her car on the parking grounds by the eastern walls of the monastery, the ten arches guarding the entrance were not as magnificent as they had seemed to her so many years ago. Scores of cars were parked on the cobblestone square, and street vendors were peddling their dry nuts and fruits to the visitors. She opened her purse and flipped the pages of her small diary until she found Sunday, November 11, 2001. She wrote: *I came to see Maximus at the monastery.* She left the diary in the glove compartment. "Come on children; let's go!"

They went inside the crowded chapel. Katerina dropped some cash into the opening of a square wooden box by the entrance. Next, she took four candles from the dispenser beside the box, lit and placed them in the sand box among hundreds of other burning candles. She made the sign of the cross and kissed the icon of Saint Magdalene.

Her first prayer, as always, was for the safety of that special child, that healthy, bright-eyed, little girl, who was christened Claira (her only child), the baby girl she gave up for adoption sixteen years ago. Katerina had kept the child for three months, breastfeeding and caring for her as would any other loving mother. At the end of three months, her parents would not wait another day, and had people at the adoption centre bring the papers to sign.

They came to pick up the baby the next day. Two people at the adoption agency, a nurse, Marianna, her parents, and the man who had left her upon being told that he was to be a father, were the only people who knew about the child's existence. Her sadness, anger and sense of loss increased over time, but she kept her tears inside.

One by one she lifted Marianna's children and they too kissed the icon, while others behind them waited in line to do the same.

As Katerina held Claira's hand, the twins, Andrew and George, stood restless behind them, bored, whispering in each other's ears. "Aunt Katerina," said Andrew, "what are they saying?" He pointed at two groups of singing monks who were standing in front of the arched entrance to the apse on either side of the bema.

"Shhhhh!" George whispered, placing his index finger in front of Andrew's mouth.

Poor boys, Katerina thought. *It's all foreign to them. I wish I could explain all the Byzantine psalms, but I don't understand them myself; and the cacophonous monks, with their shrill voices, make things worse.*

Katerina surveyed the aisles. Most youngsters appeared disinterested, standing, as if planted there against their wishes by someone. Many were throwing empty stares at the walls. Others appeared to be praying, but Katerina saw evidence that their minds were elsewhere. Older girls and boys exchanged secret glances, and their mothers were meticulously examining other mothers' dresses, hair styles and make-up. Only the old ladies, their heads covered with black veils, were meditative.

Abbot Maximus walked in, wearing his ornamental robes, robes over robes, gold crosses and crown, and stopped in the middle of the apse, his hand raised in the air, begging God's forgiveness on behalf of his flock: *"Kyrie Eleison, Kyrie Eleison."*

The steady rhythm of the Byzantine psalms mesmerized her and took her mind to another world, her private world.

A few days before, she had spoken with K3, a Cypriot informant with alleged ties to the Cyprus Special Investigation Branch (SIB). The Americans had hired K3 at the beginning of Ronald Reagan's presidency to keep an eye on movements of the large contingent of diplomatic and military personnel in Cyprus of "The Evil Empire," as President Reagan had labelled the U.S.S.R. After the collapse of the Soviet Union, the Americans kept K3 on a contract-by-contract basis and gave him odd jobs as needs arose. After the September 11 attacks, the Americans asked him to penetrate the ranks of senior Arab diplomats in Cyprus and to look for ties to the money-laundering activities of the Muslim fundamentalists who were operating in the Middle East.

Before her power had grown within the consortium, Katerina was a legal practitioner, and K3 was one of her clients. She was fully aware of his gratitude for her successfully defending him on two counts of armed robbery. The charges were dismissed for lack of sufficient evidence. During their most recent meeting, K3 was unusually reticent. She remembered their conversation perfectly ...

21

"Why are you so quiet today?" Katerina said.

"I don't know if I should tell you this," said K3.

"I'm your lawyer, remember?"

"Yes, but this is not about me. It has to do with … possible terrorist links."

Katerina's curiosity was suddenly replaced by concern, which she concealed beneath her steady voice. "What is this terrorist business?" she asked, nonchalantly.

"You swear you'll keep it confidential?"

"It's always been that way between us."

"No, you must swear."

"Why?"

K3 explained, "Your relative, Faris, may be involved."

Katerina was somewhat relieved. "Is it something illegal?"

"Possibly, yes. Promise not to tell anyone."

"Do you trust me?"

"I always do," said K3.

"Then, don't ask me to make silly promises."

"I'm concerned about the secrecy of the plan."

She saw clouds of uncertainty. "Is there a *plan?*"

"I won't tell you unless you give me your assurances that you will treat this information as strictly confidential."

Katerina saw the futility of resisting K3's wishes. "I promise to tell no one."

"The Americans suspect Faris is affiliated with a terrorist group. They're putting pressure on the Saudis to do something about it. The Saudis are sending their team of forensic experts to audit Faris's books. But they won't stop there. They also want to get hold of the books of your father's company."

"Then they're wasting their time," she said casually.

"It sounds to me like it's a conspiracy to destroy your father."

Katerina laughed while the blood inside her veins stormed to her head in rapid thrusts.

K3 said, "The Mustafas may be behind it, but this is conjecture on my part. Apparently Faris has been forewarned, and he will cooperate fully."

"I don't understand these Saudis. They have no business to mingle in our affairs."

"They're very anxious."

She wondered if Manning and Cynthia knew anything about these developments. "I find this extraordinary," Katerina said.

"Why?"

"Faris is considered a good friend of the Americans."

K3 was silent.

"You don't believe the Americans are now turning against one of their staunchest supporters, do you?" Katerina asked.

"Everything is possible."

Katerina managed to keep her uneasiness below detectable levels. "When are they coming?"

"Soon."

Once K3 left Katerina's office, she picked up the phone and called Maximus. "I have something to discuss with you on Sunday after Mass."

They agreed to meet at his private office.

22

Immediately after the end of the liturgy, Abbot Maximus hurried to his private office, which was located on the second level of the monastery. The room was dark, but warm sunlight penetrated the arched windows striking the bookshelf, which was full of old, leather-bound books. He could hear people chatting and walking away from the monastery's grounds toward their cars.

Besides his bedroom, the office was his most private place. It was vitally important to him to have a space of his own, and he felt blessed that this place was an extension of whom he tried to be. It was cozy, warm, soft and had a reflective atmosphere. The craftsmanship that was put into creating his office (with its wood-carved walnut bookcase to the leather chairs, leather-top desk, Persian carpets, paintings of the heavenly angels and icons of Mary Magdalene and other saints) made him feel like an Archbishop every time he entered it.

On the mantelpiece, two gold communion cups flanked a huge candelabrum, and two huge stone lions of St. Mark (similar to the one that soared on the column in Venice's Piazzetta) stood on either side of his mahogany desk, as if ready to attack intruders. *I truly adore this place*, he smiled. It was the place where, since his ordination, he spent most of his Sundays napping on the leather sofa or relaxing and reading. But today, he was expecting a visitor.

As he anxiously awaited Katerina's arrival, his thoughts became more distasteful.

He could never let go of his humble beginnings, for he was always fearful of the insecurities of the past. Maximus recalled the days when as a sad little boy, before his tenth birthday, he was frantically searching for food in his home village. His little sister cried in the bitter cold of a January winter, her stomach aching with pain from days of malnutrition. He dug through the muddy earth with his bare hands, his numb feet immersed in the soil, anxiously groping for potatoes in their neighbours' land. His father shouted beside him: "Dig deeper! Dig deeper!"

He'd envied the neighbours' children for their good fortune: fertile land, fruit trees, animals, servants, abundance of food and good clothes. He had resented that God had blessed them with fine destiny and treated him so cruelly. This unhappiness had been the start of a long and tortuous barefoot walk through the rough, snake-infested hills one night, which had taken him from his village to the deep Pafos' interior and finally, to the monastery itself.

As a plain monk, he had very few possessions. But as he assumed more duties (and earned more privileges), he succumbed to temptations.

Maximus remembered the great deal of thinking and planning that went into structuring a transaction with Katerina's father so as to ensure his shield from outside scrutiny. Only a small portion of the money that Persinaras had agreed to pay for the purchase of the monastery lands went straight to the monastery. The balance of the price was part of a scheme designed to benefit him.

This plan was John Persinaras's payback for getting the land at a bargain price. The arrangements were paperless and the plan was flawless, except for certain bogus documents and the corporate Swiss bank account that Persinaras had set up in the name of Persinaras Estates. From this account, pay orders were funneled to others, year in and year out, justifying the transfers as *Commissions and Overhead Expenses for Overseas Operations*. The payments were transferred to Persinaras's contacts on the Island of Guernsey, and through an offshore bank there, his men re-channelled the payments to Maximus's sister who was living in London under an assumed British name, which was also on the payroll as an *'overseas estate agent'*.

To safeguard the continuation of payments to Maximus, he and Persinaras had signed four bogus documents: a Vendor Take Back Mortgage under seal, in the amount of $7.6-million, supposedly the balance due and owing to the monastery from the sale of land to Persinaras Estates; a Promissory note from John Persinaras (as debtor) to the monastery (as creditor) in the same amount for the same purpose; a Power of Attorney, authorizing Maximus to set up a Trust to hold the funds in the Swiss bank; and a Trust Deed, appointing the monastery as sole beneficiary of the funds in the trust account.

They'd agreed that Maximus would keep the original documents, but he should never use them as evidence of debt obligation to the monastery for the land transaction between the monastery and Persinaras Estates, unless Persinaras reneged on the secret deal. But the agreement called for the destruction of these documents as soon as Persinaras Estates finished paying the $7.6-million to Maximus's sister. Based on these documents, Maximus could at any time request the transfer of the account to any of his nominees.

To protect Persinaras, in case of Maximus's death, Maximus had agreed to issue bogus receipts, from the monastery to Persinaras Estates, each time a payment was made to Maximus's sister. Persinaras assured him that he would keep the receipts and copies of the bogus documents locked in his private safety deposit box. The receipts thus far totalled $2.6-million.

Maximus had a tacit understanding with Persinaras that Katerina will respect their agreement and continue the payments. But he knew that Katerina was conniving and controlling, and this awareness bothered him.

He looked for his favourite bittersweet chocolate and found one. As he crunched into it, Katerina appeared at the arched entrance of his office.

23

It was so dark in the room, he barely recognized her. As she entered his office, he could see the lines of her slim silhouette. She was wearing a tight fitting long dark blue dress, which almost sank in her flesh. With her long, amber hair, she was at once more photogenic and mature than he'd remembered.

Katerina's expression was solemn but pleasant. The sunlight sneaked through the window, illuminated her face, and created a colour not unlike the complexion of the moon. Her face was wider at the forehead and rounded at the chin, like a well-curved acorn. Dark green were her eyes, wide and oblique, resembling two large, sun-dried ripe olives, but the sunlight gave them a glittering spark that Maximus thought might even scare a lion. Her nose was well-curved and raised upward at the tip, overexposing her nostril cavities.

He could not finish the chocolate. "Where are the children?" he asked her.

"They're downstairs, playing hide-and-seek," Katerina said, and sat on a chair in front of the desk.

From the inside window, Maximus saw Andrew chasing George. Claira was hiding behind a column. "They grew up so fast!" he exclaimed.

"George and Andrew will be seven in March. Claira will be five in February."

He turned to face Katerina who was noticeably nervous. "What's wrong?"

Katerina said, "The Americans want the Saudis to investigate the Mustafa family. They're sending forensic accountants to do a thorough audit of their books, and such an audit will include our books. The Cyprus secret service is against the idea, since it will open a can of worms for everybody, including us."

Maximus understood where Katerina was leading him; he made a mental note to avoid getting involved. He waived his hand in a gesture that signified his doubts about the validity of the story.

Monk Modestos, Maximus's personal assistant, brought them coffee and biscuits, and after he left, Maximus shut and locked the door.

"The fact is," Katerina went on, "Faris Mustafa wants to keep his close ties with the Saudis, and is determined to get to the heart of the matter."

Maximus was unmoved, but he nodded.

"Do you know his son, Jason, is back?"

"Jason. Who cares about him?" Maximus said, smiling contemptuously.

"There are two Mustafas now."

"Those two will never get along," Maximus said.

"Faris will soon die, and Jason may take his place."

"He's a drifter. If he was interested, he would have been in charge of the Mustafa wealth long before now."

"But he has hereditary rights."

"We'll cross our bridges when we come to them."

"It will be too late by then."

"Well, buy him out. He'll likely be glad to sell you whatever he inherits."

"I despise uncertainty," Katerina said with a worried look on her face.

"Be patient."

"I can't. Something must be done." She sighed. "If the audit goes ahead, it won't be Faris who'll be exposed."

"You can handle it."

Katerina said, "In an ordinary audit we could give some plausible explanations and hide our offshore connections, but if this private audit goes ahead we won't be protected by Cyprus legislation. We'll have to provide names, amounts, justification for payment and produce supporting documentation. Think about it!"

What could possibly happen if the Mustafas and the Saudi men go ahead with their audit? Maximus wondered. He said, "I was told that if a Swiss bank violated its banking secrecy it might be subject to administrative sanctions imposed by the Federal Banking Commission, which might, in turn, withdraw a bank's license and order the bank's liquidation. So, I have nothing to fear."

"Swiss banking secrecy is in not absolute," Katerina said. "In criminal investigations, banking secrecy can be lifted by a court order. It's possible that your private and confidential arrangements with Persinaras Estates could become a public domain. If uncovered, you'll lose your own wealth. You'll be unfrocked of your religious duties, and you'll face prosecution for fraud and embezzlement of monastery and church property."

24

Katerina was telling Maximus that the arrangement was imperfect. He was naïve enough, he thought, to trust John Persinaras unreservedly. He feared his public humiliation and complete destruction, but the thing he feared most was poverty. It was things like these that made Maximus vicious. "I thought I had absolute protection!" he yelled, staring at Katerina.

"We shall think of the little ones," she said.

"The little ones?"

She got up. "Come," Katerina said. They walked closer to the window.

He watched the children playing.

"Look at George and Andrew. Do you see their features?" She paused to take a deep breath. "They have your hair, your eyes, your nose, even your personality!"

Maximus pulled back. His rage reddened his nose and enlarged his eyes. "Do you realize what you're doing to me?" he shouted, and his hands trembled with anger.

"Face reality, damn it!" screamed Katerina. "I don't want these two innocent souls to learn one day that their real father is in jail. I want them—"

"This is my private affair," Maximus interrupted. "You'd better not play with my sentiments."

"Whether you like it or not, you are responsible for the boys' security and happiness."

Maximus was flabbergasted, but he looked for a different way to handle this challenge. His face changed colours. "What is it you want from me?"

"I want us to destroy all the documents."

His face turned from pale yellow to bright red. "I can't destroy these papers without guarantees. I can't give up $5-million just like that."

"I can give you my word, nothing more."

She thinks she has power over me, but it's the other way around, Maximus thought. *As long as I have these contracts, she has no power over me, he reasoned.* I'll keep control of the documents, he resolved. *If I were to die* *now, for any reason, she knows the monks will find them and use them to either void the deal or force Persinaras Estates to pay up the $7.6-million to the monastery. If she gets hold of the papers now, she can get rid of me, he feared. As long as I have them, she can never destroy me.*

He remembered that fateful night many years ago when, under the watchful eye of his father, he had been stealing potatoes. He was digging for them with bare hands and the deeper he dug, the muddier he got. To change his fate, he rose and ran to the monastery, away from his cruel father. He grabbed his coat. "I'm getting out of here."

"You can't run away from our problem."

"Don't panic. They'll never discover the purpose of the account."

"Marianna loves you. You must know that. She wants the children to grow up around you."

"Marianna is happy where she is. The children … I'm not even sure they're mine. If I am their father, it's best for them to never learn the truth."

"One day they will, and it'll be too late for us to do anything."

Maximus saw Katerina trembling, and he sensed that there was something more wrong than what he knew about. His right hand touched her shoulder lightly. "Are you hiding anything?"

"I need your help," she said weakly. "I don't know what my husband would do if he learned that they're after our books."

Maximus's toughness melted. "If I can help, I will."

The room was suddenly quiet. Katerina sat down and put her hand on her face. "Oh, my God," she gasped. "It's getting late." She glanced at her watch. "The children must be starving. I'll be back on Tuesday at 2:30. You're coming tonight, aren't you?"

"Yes."

As soon as Katerina left, Maximus collapsed into the leather sofa and closed his eyes. The familiar ringing of the monastery's bell was calling the monks to gather at the dining room for Sunday lunch. He felt famished, but was too tired to move. He saved his appetite for dinner at Villa Mustafa.

25

In the living room, Jason watched as the nurse measured Faris's blood pressure and took his temperature. She then helped him take his medicine and when she finished, Jason asked her to leave them alone.

"Dad, do you have any friends who are terrorists?" Jason asked.

Before Faris gave an answer, the telephone rang. It was Dr. Plato. From Faris's response, Jason understood that Dr. Plato was briefing Faris on the events of the day. Dinner was mentioned, too, and Faris invited the doctor to attend Marianna's dinner party. Faris also hinted at "announcements" to be made at the dinner table. They said their goodbyes, and Faris turned to Jason who was sitting next to him. "Where were we?"

"Do you have any terrorist friends?"

"Before I forget," Faris said, "Alex and Cynthia arrived at the hotel from Nicosia a couple of hours ago. They want to see you again, and I've invited them to dinner."

"It's Marianna's dinner party," Jason objected.

"She doesn't mind. The Mannings were good friends of Richard and Marianna, mainly because of my good relations with Alex."

"I see." Jason was eager to know more about Faris's connections with Manning, but he lined up his thoughts. "I deserve an answer," he said.

"The only terrorists I ever fought against were some rebels in the Saudi dessert in 1953, when I was fifteen. It was after the death of King Abdul Aziz, and the country was mobilized, but things returned to normal soon afterwards."

"I'm talking about the terrorists Kamal spoke of today."

Faris furrowed his brow. "Do you think I'm so naïve as to believe that the way to change American policy toward Arabs and Muslims is to attack America?"

"When it comes to fanatics, reason takes a back seat," Jason said.

"Those who back a religious war forget that the Koran was formulated more than thirteen hundred years ago, when the world order was totally different."

"But the rapid expansion of Islam was achieved through conversion and military conquest," Jason ventured.

"Force and war did play a role in the spread of Islam. But that was then."

"Can force prevail again?"

"That's not my view," stated Faris.

"Do you support the Islamic fundamentalists?"

"Islamic fundamentalism includes a mix of ideas. It's too complex a topic to get into."

"You sound ambivalent, and I find it unsettling," Jason stated.

"It has to do with the origins of Islam."

"Do you sympathize with any terrorists?"

"Let's not kid ourselves."

"Do you support the Americans in their fight against terrorism?"

"I have no choice in the matter. They are in power now as the Arabs were in power 1300 years ago."

He's playing the issue pragmatically, Jason thought. "So what you're saying is the Americans today are like the Arabs were back then?"

"In a way ... yes."

"We can't blame the Americans for protecting their interests, then."

"I don't blame anyone."

"Do you believe that recent attacks on America are rational?" Jason asked.

"I thought you were an educated man—not an impatient child."

"Well, Dad, I don't understand you at all!"

"We're all upset." Faris raised his voice, "Arabs and Muslims are troubled, too!"

"I remember you once telling me that during the early days of Islam there was great tension and opposition to Islamic rule, but the Muslims prevailed. Do you think that someday the Muslims will rule the world, once again?"

"People no longer fight with hands and swords."

"Why do Muslims mix everything with religion?"

"We are not alone in mixing religion with everyday life. There is nothing wrong with that."

"It depends," said Jason.

"Muslims feel persecuted."

"I think you can start the process of cleansing and rejuvenation by cleaning your own backyard first."

"We refuse to surrender to non-believers."

"But Islamic law also states that all nations must surrender to Islamic rule, if not their faith."

"Islam is like most religions on this planet," insisted Faris.

Jason was not fully satisfied with the answers he was getting. "Do I have your promise that you're not linked to any terrorist cell?"

"Yes, absolutely."

"Do you think that Richard might have been involved?"

Jason watched Faris's face become angry. "How can you dare say such a thing? Richard would never do something like that!"

"Then, you have nothing to fear. I mean, you and I have nothing to fear; I don't know about Persinaras Estates."

"If Persinaras or his daughter Katerina is implicated, we will soon know," Faris said.

"How?"

"Before it catches its prey, the octopus must first extend its tentacles."

"This is what drives me mad!" Jason shouted. "You appear to know how the system works, but you have no clue about the cause of Richard's disappearance!"

"I'm just as frustrated. Let us now bestow trust in each other's abilities."

"I have the feeling you don't trust me with your secrets," Jason grumbled.

"You didn't inform me about your decision to become an agnostic until I found out through my own contacts."

"It's not true! I believe in God. I just don't classify my beliefs."

"It doesn't matter anyway."

Faris tried to brush aside the significance of Jason's response and Jason was skeptical of his father's professed understanding. Past accusations and counter-accusations still lingered in his memory, and it was difficult to write them off completely. The best option, he concluded, was to allow time to test his father's intentions.

26

It was getting late, and Jason needed to go back to the hotel for a short rest, a shower and a change of clothes for the dinner party. "I must be going. I'll see you tonight at Villa Mustafa." He telephoned for a taxi.

"I'm reluctant to attend," Faris said, "but I'll do it for you and Alex."

"Speaking of Manning," Jason began, "what is his role in Cyprus, exactly?"

"Alex is a smart businessman," Faris answered. "Our friendship goes back at least ten years. He would never sneak behind my back."

"But I thought he came to Cyprus in September 1999. I met with him when he attended mother's funeral."

"I was introduced to Alex long before that."

"Can you ask him to find out what the Saudis and the Americans are after?"

"I've already had a long chat with him. There's nothing he can tell me about American foreign policy that I don't already know. He's no longer a politician."

Manning arrived right after Kamal's visit. *Coincidental?* Jason doubted it. "I wonder what he's up to."

"I extrapolate; I never speculate," Faris responded. "Obviously Manning has a reason for being in Pafos. He and I discussed your future, and he wants some assurances from you."

Discussed my future? "Like what?"

"I told him you'll soon assume your responsibilities as the new Chief Executive Officer of Mustafa Holdings."

"I don't need this job. I'll find my own work. I committed myself to cooperate with the Saudis as your representative, but I've never agreed to assume control of the family business."

"You can cooperate all you want; however, if you can't put your signature on a document when the right time comes, your authority is meaningless. I already called Makin and ordered him to draw up the papers for your appointment as CEO. You'll have a comfortable salary and the formal authority to deal with the Saudi delegation."

Jason changed the subject. "Clearly you and Manning are involved in some kind of business together, correct?"

"Yes."

"Is he aware of the past rift between you and me?"

"He considers your rebelliousness a sign of asserting your individuality. In fact he finds it commendable that you were able to become a professor solely through your own efforts."

"Manning said that?"

"Yes," Faris affirmed. "Now, will you help me walk to the washroom?"

Jason held Faris by the arm as they walked. He opened the door and helped his father to sit on the toilet. He then closed the door and waited outside.

Jason remembered his first encounter with Manning and his wife Cynthia. It had occurred two years ago ...

27

November 1999. After Rachel's funeral service, friends and notables had gathered at Villa Mustafa. Jason and Alex Manning met in the living room and engaged in a cordial conversation. Manning was a thin gentleman with short blonde hair and a parrot nose. His thick spectacles were too large for his small face. Jason figured he was about forty or so.

Manning introduced Jason to Cynthia. She was just as thin as Manning, but taller. Jason guessed she was at least ten years younger than her husband. Her short bright hair mushroomed in all directions; she seemed the type of woman who would welcome new experiences. The lack of make-up and lipstick enhanced her high cheekbones and green eyes. She was wearing a lush three-piece silk set: solid cabernet-coloured pants; and autumn paisley-patterned blouse with a tank top. There was something mysterious about her.

During the memorial gathering, Jason couldn't help noticing that Cynthia and Richard were locked in a long discussion with each other.

Manning had practiced law in the U.S. for two years as a prosecutor of juvenile offenders. He joined the Foreign Service in 1985, and the Department of Defense sent him to Bahrain in 1990 as the Defense Attaché. That same year, he met Cynthia in Manama, the capital of Bahrain, and they married a year later. She worked in the Information Management unit of the Embassy. In 1993 he was appointed Deputy Chief of Mission and Chargé d'Affaires at the U.S Embassy in Paris, and by 1996 he'd become the Deputy Assistant of State for legislative Affairs. Finally, in September 1999, he quit his job, became a private citizen and went to Cyprus to operate an offshore corporation.

28

"I wouldn't mind meeting them again," Jason said as he helped walk Faris back to the living room.

"I can't join you. Alex wants to have lunch with you alone, tomorrow, at the hotel's Palace Restaurant."

This could be my chance to get the American to help in finding out what happened to Richard. The local authorities seem to be dragging their feet, Jason thought. After all, his mother had been an American citizen. "I think that'll be fine," Jason said. "I'll confirm it with Manning tonight."

"There's something about this couple you should know," Faris added.

Jason nodded.

"They're both very dedicated American citizens. For them, America is number one."

Jason hesitated. "How did you and Manning hit it off?"

"Before I forget let me first tell you about this malicious rumour, to which I refuse to give any credence."

"Why should I know?" Jason asked, very unsure of how to react.

"Because Manning's dignity and pride depend on it."

"You're so protective of him. I wish you had been as protective of me when I was growing up."

"I'm not protective of anybody," Faris complained. "There were times when I also had my suspicions, but I didn't think your brother was ever unfaithful to Marianna. Besides, Cynthia seems very devoted to Alex."

Richard was a handsome man. He attracted women—young and old—anywhere he went. "It is possible," Jason said.

"No!" Faris blasted. "Richard would never do anything to upset me."

Jason regretted his off-the-cuff remark. "Very well," he retreated, hands up in the air.

"Richard would not do such a despicable thing," Faris reiterated.

"Whatever you say." Jason was eager to appease Faris. "Tell me about your friendship with Manning."

"It's not easy to understand. You … the people of your generation … come to conclusions too fast, without the facts."

Jason, his face expressionless, listened.

"It was September 1990. Your mother and I were visiting a handful of my business associates, who were living in Manama. I was eager to know how this small state of some thirty-three low desert islands on the western side of the Persian Gulf—in a small area and with a population of 600,000—was able to develop a stable economy considering its modest petroleum reserves. The key, I learned, was services—such as banking and tourism."

Jason had never been to Bahrain. The state was ruled by the Sunni al-Khalifa family, who came from the Central Arabian Peninsula in 1783 and established themselves as Bahrain's rulers from then on.

By the late eighteenth century, the British had defeated the Dutch for supremacy in the Persian Gulf. Beginning in 1820, Britain imposed a series of Treaties on Bahrain and its neighbours. When petroleum was discovered in Bahrain in 1932, it was the first such discovery on the Arabian coast of the Persian Gulf. As a result, Britain exercised its influence there more strongly than in other protected states, and Britain's naval forces in the Persian Gulf established their port at Al Jufayr. But in 1968 the British government, short of revenue, announced that British forces would withdraw from positions west of Suez, Egypt, by the end of 1971.

"Bahrain became an independent state on August15, 1971," Jason said.

"After 1975," Faris continued, "the Lebanese Civil War began, and Bahrain took over much of Lebanon's financial services industry, including its offshore banking units."

"That was a good move on the part of the Emir," Jason interjected.

"It was these OBUs in Bahrain that attracted my most keen interest, for their model was good and sound. Your mother and I attended several commercial functions in Manama during that visit. We met Alex at one of those gatherings."

Jason nodded in silence.

"The United States had a large mission in Manama, for geopolitical reasons. The U.S. Navy's lease of Bahrain's facilities dates back to 1949. In 1987, Bahrain provided vital facilities to the U.S. naval forces escorting Kuwaiti vessels through the Persian Gulf to shield them from possible attacks by Iran, which accused them of carrying Iraqi oil.

By 1990 Bahrain began to shift its foreign policy and sought measures to strengthen its ties with the U.S government."

"I know all this," said Jason abruptly.

"And I know you. You're impatient. You were always like that." Faris continued, "There was, however, one internal problem that had existed in Bahrain for many years. The Islamic revolution of Iran, which brought a Shia government to power on the other shore of the gulf in 1979, heightened tensions between the Sunnis and Shias in Bahrain."

"That was inevitable," Jason added. "About seventy percent of all native Bahrainis belong to the Shia branch of Islam and the rest (such as the ruling al-Khalifa clan) are Sunnis."

"High unemployment among the Shia population was a cause of discontent. The Bahraini Defense Force was not even 10,000 strong at that time. Its tiny navy depended on the assistance of the U.S. Navy, whose Fifth Fleet uses Bahrain's harbour facilities even now."

Faris's voice sounded dry.

"Do you want anything to drink?" asked Jason.

"No."

"I need something to quench my thirst," Jason said.

"There's Coke in the fridge. Where is she?"

The nurse was busy in the laundry room. "I'll get it," Jason offered.

When Jason came back to the living room with a can of cola in his hand, Faris asked, "Are you hungry?"

"No. I don't have an appetite right now."

"Neither do I. I'll finish what I have to say, and I'll let you go because I'm getting tired."

"Do you prefer we continue this discussion another day?

"No. During our visit, there was political unrest among Bahrain's Shias, and the government responded by reinforcing its military. They turned to the U.S. government for help. The U.S. Administration, anxious to avoid mingling into the internal affairs of the state, was looking for ways to cool off both sides. When Alex learned of my extensive experience in Arab relationships, he came to me seeking my input. I gave him some advice, which he appreciated immensely."

"Did you ever ask for his help?"

"When I needed his help, he was there for me." Faris looked Jason straight in the eye. "Let me make something clear," he said, "Alex has never compromised his position and his duty to his country, and I never betrayed his confidence."

"That's good to know," Jason said.

The taxi was outside the gates.

"I have to go," Jason said.

"Here's a transmitter for the gate," Faris said handing him the keypad.

29

The gates were open when Jason reached Villa Mustafa at 7:45 p.m. Among the many cars, a limousine was parked in the driveway. Two men stood beside it, chatting.

Inside the house, Jason saw Marianna interacting with her guests, who were gathered in the living and family rooms. The perfumes of wild marjoram, oregano, basil and rosemary pervaded the air, mingling with the more pungent smell of olive oil. Food aromas blended with the soft tunes of Greek music in the background. It was Jason's favourite Greek song: *Never on Sunday*. He felt energized.

Marianna mingled in the middle of the living room, resplendent, wearing a loose and baggy checkered black and white suit with a long hemline skirt, a design reminiscent of the early 1920s. A flame-red silk scarf around her neck complemented her striking appearance. The Cyprus sun had bronzed her well. Jason remembered how solemn and distant she had been that morning, but this evening she seemed a totally different person. She cheerfully greeted her guests with meticulous attention, smiles, and a squeeze of their hands.

When she saw Jason, Marianna waived happily at him, and after he approached her she threw her arms around him.

There were whispers in the room. He overheard a woman say, "My goodness, I could swear he's Richard."

Jason was a bit surprised by Marianna's sudden demonstration of affection, although he knew her to be a great hostess. He decided to mix with some of the guests for a few moments, making a conscious decision to stay in the background. He sensed that behind all the beaming faces and cordial socializing there was a subtle – but nevertheless present – aura of angst, accentuated by Richard's pictures on the walls and Jason's presence in the living room. Yes, his appearance drew some sharp stares from Abbot Maximus, George Lagos and Katerina. Manning and his wife Cynthia recognized him instantly and said hello.

Manning gave him his card and asked, "Will you meet me for lunch tomorrow?"

"Where?"

"The Mustafa Beach Hotel."

"Is one o'clock okay with you?"

"That's perfect," Manning said.

"Unfortunately I won't be able to join you," Cynthia interjected.

"She has a charitable function to attend," Manning explained.

The three of them spoke for a couple of minutes and then dispersed to mingle with the others.

Jason saw some guests kissing the hands of Bishop Panaretos and Abbot Maximus, a practice he knew was prevalent – especially among the older generation – but not too appealing to him. When he approached them, he shook their hands firmly and assertively. The only person who seemed completely relaxed was Dr. Plato. Then the nurse pushed in Faris, in his wheelchair. Jason went over to stay with him for a few minutes. It was Marianna's party, and he didn't want the occasion of his arrival in Pafos to overshadow it. He could not wait to meet the children, and he planned to spend some time with them.

30

Surveying her guests, Marianna reassured herself that she had done the right thing inviting Jason to dinner. She had to demonstrate to him that she was in charge at Villa Mustafa and that she had the support of many friends, some of them more powerful than others. She felt comfortable seeing that the majority of the guests were people close to her. Abbot Maximus was unusually quiet, listening and nodding to whatever the Bishop was saying. She felt the desire to be closer to him, but the physical distance between them was not as forbidding as the puddle of people around her. Intentionally, she chose to talk with women rather than men, but her eyes wandered freely around the living and dining rooms, observing all her guests.

Jason now stood beside his father, and when Marianna noticed him again, she recalled his body scent when they embraced. He had Richard's looks, demeanor and posture, with his white cotton pants, blue denim, long-sleeved shirt, and dark blue cardigan. But he appeared lonely, and she relished his isolation. For a quick moment, she even felt sorry for him, as he resembled a lonely and frail shrub on a windswept, desolate, rocky beach. Poor Jason, she thought. His large nose extended smoothly into the air. Five uneven stressed-filled lines were cluttered on his forehead, resembling waves crossing each other in a choppy sea, finally caressing his curved eyebrows. She pictured him packing up and leaving Pafos for good.

A village man's loud song jarred Marianna out of her reverie. While attending to the rotisserie of barbeque lamb on the covered patio, the perspiring village man was holding onto and drinking from a bottle of ouzo. She prayed he would remain in that semi-intoxicated stage until the lamb was cooked. Meanwhile, the chef in the kitchen was feverishly preparing to serve the main courses, and two female waitresses were helping the guests with drinks. She was satisfied that the party was running smoothly.

Soon, the guests took their seats in the dining room and began nibbling on appetizers and dips. Katerina's husband, George Lagos, filled his plate with caviar and began devouring it with a tablespoon, splattering clusters of the delicate fish roe on the bright white, embroidered tablecloth. Marianna who was sitting on his left-hand side, unable to conceal her embarrassment, whispered in his ear, "Behave."

She turned to Maximus who was sitting on her other side. "Forgive me for being unable to come to church today," she said. "You must have been busy as well."

"Nothing extraordinary for this time of the year," Maximus said smiling. He finished chewing on a piece of halloumi and was about ready to wash it down with a glass of *White Lady*. He looked at Katerina who was sitting opposite him and said, "Did the children enjoy the sermon today?"

"They loved it," Katerina said steadily. "They always love going to church."

Persephone Koleas (the mayor's wife) said, "I wish I could say the same for our son. As soon as he turned eighteen, he stopped going to church."

Mayor Spiros Koleas glanced at Maximus. "Tell me, your Grace, is it normal for children of this age to avoid going to church?"

"Children need role models in their lives," Maximus said solemnly. "We have a collective responsibility to keep them closer to the church."

I wish he wasn't so didactic, Marianna thought of Maximus. She wanted to change the subject but didn't know how to do it without seeming annoyed. "Would you like some soup, father?" she asked her father-in-law who was sitting on Jason's left.

Faris sipped tea with the assistance of the nurse, and Marianna noticed that he seemed disinterested in the outside world. Frail, beaten, he managed to utter, "I'm fine, thank you."

Marianna was ready to ask the maids to serve the main course dishes, when Helena walked into the dining room with the children. The boys went straight to Faris, and Claira ran toward Katerina, who turned around to hug her.

George said, "Grandpa, please tell me a story. Can I stay with you?"

Andrew echoed his brother's request. "Yes, can we stay? I want to drink some wine."

"Me, too!" George said excitedly.

Everyone laughed.

Helena took the carafe of grape juice that lay on the demi-lune table by the wall and poured juice into two small glasses. "Here," she said, smiling, "this is the closest to wine I can find."

George took the glass of juice with both hands, had a sip, and then turned to his grandfather and said, "This wine comes from grandpa's cellar. I drink it all the time, right grandpa?"

Most guests burst into laughter. Faris nodded. Marianna noticed that Lagos was self-absorbed.

Andrew said, "This wine is different. Last time Uncle George gave me red wine, it made me so sleepy ..."

Everybody's eyes turned to George Lagos, and he was clearly embarrassed. "Oh, yes, yes," he said. "I gave him ... red grape juice ... strong grape juice. They must have left the alcohol inside for added flavour!"

A few guests laughed, but Marianna thought what Lagos had done to Andrew was outrageous. "George," she said, staring at Lagos, "next time you should try to keep the added flavour to yourself."

Claira whispered to Katerina, "I want you to sleep in my bed tonight."

"I'd love to," Katerina said, "but your Uncle George won't let me. He'll feel lonely if I don't sleep by his side."

"Uncle George won't notice," Claira announced loudly. "He snores too much ..."

Everyone laughed, except Lagos.

Marianna noticed how Helena graciously gathered the children, and despite their protestations, took them to the game room. She then saw Jason getting up and heading in the same direction.

31

Manning was sitting next to Steve Naharos, the Pafos police chief. Marianna was anxious to see Manning and Naharos having a good time. She asked the female waitress to attend to Manning who was drinking Jack Daniel's on the rocks, while Naharos said, "Young people are not as innocent as they used to be."

"Why is that?" Manning asked.

"During the last ten years we have been experiencing an increase in juvenile crime in Pafos, from petty theft to arson, from public mischief to serious drug offences," Naharos continued.

"I know youth crime," Manning said. "I used to prosecute young offenders in America. Your problems with the youth of Pafos are insignificant."

Marianna feared that Naharos, an egomaniac who hated to be contradicted, might explode.

"They're too unruly," Naharos objected.

"You know best about crimes in your territory," Manning said, apparently happy to reverse his prior comment.

Maximus, who'd overhead the conversation, said, "The root of evil is foreign-generated crime. The foreigners are changing our economic, social and political environment, and their actions are threatening traditional Cypriot relationships."

"Crimes have no colour," Cynthia said.

Mayor Koleas joined in the conversation. "I envy the way Marianna's children live in this village setting," he said. "I think the problem is urbanization."

Panaretos, the Bishop of Pafos, sat next to Koleas and added, "We should count our blessings. We live in good times."

"But we are breeding a society that is lazy, opportunistic and hedonistic," Dr. Plato intercepted.

Marianna sensed that Dr. Plato and Bishop Panaretos were heading toward one of those confrontations for which they were famous. She remembered one that had taken place when she was about six. It had been a noisy evening that resulted in a fierce physical scene. The incident flashed in front of Marianna's eyes as she twisted in her chair, searching for something to say, but not able to think of anything.

32

"I have an announcement to make," Faris said anxiously. Everybody's eyes turned to him. He continued, "I have decided to set up an educational foundation for the benefit of the poor, bright students of Pafos. Many of these exceptional students cannot afford to pursue university studies because their parents don't have the financial resources. I've named it the 'Richard Mustafa University Foundation' in honour of my son. I pledge to make an initial contribution of 50,000 Cyprus pounds, and will continue to contribute the same amount every year for ten years. But I pledge, right now, to contribute more if the church of Pafos and Abbot Maximus can match my contribution, pound for pound."

He hopes to live that long, Marianna reflected.

Everyone applauded, but neither Bishop Panaretos nor Abbot Maximus echoed Faris's challenge for equal contributions. Suddenly, there was dead silence which was broken by the whispers of the maids who were beginning to serve the main dishes, one by one, in a quick succession. A selection of steaming roasted chunks of lamb, kebabs, broiled calamari, fried red mullet, mousaka and cleftiko was put out.

Dr. Plato rose from his chair and said, "I propose a toast to my good friend Faris. May we all drink to his health and longevity."

Katerina stood up and said, "There is a man among us who deserves equal honour and recognition. This is a man who made Pafos the place of choice for homes in the sun; a man whose dedication has produced some of the best architectural creations that Pafos has to offer; a man who created employment and opportunities for thousands of workers and their families. This man is no other than my father, John Persinaras. Let us drink to his happiness!"

As the guests toasted their glasses, John Persinaras smiled and turned to Maximus, who was sitting to his right. "It's so touching," he said.

Marianna fixed her eyes on her father, while he surveyed the room; he looked at the drapes, the paintings on the wall, the high ceiling, and then lowered his eyes and fixed his gaze on Katerina.

He remained seated as he spoke. "When you reach my age, you'll understand why I'm not going to stand up," he said smiling. "But when I was a boy, I was always on my feet. So much so, that my father once remarked, 'Learn to be on your feet less, by using your mind more,' and I'll never forget that. In fact, I have used this motto all my life, and it has helped me stay away from menial jobs. I wanted to use the pen more than the shovel. My father wanted me to be a lawyer, but much to his disappointment, I became an architect. But I'm glad that Katerina is a lawyer, for I find many similarities between architects and lawyers. The lawyer's true calling is to fight for justice with grace and purpose; the architect's mission is to design homes and buildings with grace and purpose."

Persinaras then turned his eyes and looked at Marianna, sitting a few seats to his right. "Yes, grace and purpose are common themes that continue to guide our family, and I'm proud that my daughters are continuing this tradition with devotion and enthusiasm."

A group of dancers came out of nowhere, and Marianna shouted, "Surprise!" The bouzouki music reached its peak, and the dancers began to dance 'Zorba the Greek.' They danced and danced, as the guests watched and clapped. Other dances followed: Kalamatiano, Hassapiko, Tsifteteli, Karsilamas, Tsamiko, and Zeybekiko. Then, the group began to dance local Cypriot dances. Marianna's face was shining with pleasure at the success of the night. As they were ready to finish, the dancers went to the table and steered the guests to the floor. The only people who remained seated were John Persinaras, Faris, Dr. Plato, Abbot Maximus and Bishop Panaretos.

While the dancing guests returned to their seats, their faces perspiring form the physical demands of the Greek dances, Marianna and Katerina kept dancing. This time, Katerina asked the leader of the dancing band to show her the intricate steps of the dance Hasapiko.

The masculine man, in his early 30s, explained, "This was the dance of the Butcher's Guild of Constantinople during the Byzantine period, and was known as *Makellarikos*, from the 'pure' word for 'butcher'. The dance was popular in Constantinople, and some islands for centuries until the 1922 catastrophe when the Turks slaughtered thousands of Greeks. Afterwards, the dance has captivated the mainland Greeks. It has also become popular with Greek sailors who gave it a name of their own, *Naftiko*, and they danced it in ports."

"But I thought this dance was first introduced in the movie 'Zorba the Greek'" Marianna said.

"Not really, the man said. "Thanks to the movie "Zorba the Greek," it has become the best-known Greek dance in the world. There are countless variations, and no two groups of dancers do the same routine." He then explained to her that the dance is done with a hand-to-shoulder hold, and the dancers may improvise the order of the variations, communicating with taps on the shoulders of the adjacent dancer. "There are two parts to the dance," he said; "one slow, and one fast, especially for very fast songs. The slow and fast parts of the dance are sometimes done separately, sometimes together." He demonstrated. Everybody was watching with keen interest, except Maximus and Lagos. They were outside, on the open patio, smoking and chatting. Marianna saw them leaving the dining room and wondered why they looked so keen to leave the group during the moment she and Katerina were learning how to dance *Hasapiko*.

By the time the dance instructor finished his dancing steps, Cynthia was on her feet, holding hands with Katerina and Marianna. The American woman, anxious to participate, began to dance and drive the two to daring steps that caused broad smiles on the faces of many who were pleasantly surprised to see that she had some prior exposure to this dance. When they finished the steps, the instructor congratulated Cynthia and said, "What you just danced was a simplification of the slow *Hasapiko*, the *Syrtaki*. It was first done in France in the 1950s and spread back to Greece. In addition to simpler steps, the style is more casual compared to the deep concentration of the slow *Hasapiko*."

Cynthia was joyful. "The names don't matter to me. I just love to dance!"

"Bravo!" the instructor laughed.

"It's a fabulous party," mentioned Manning. "We're having great fun!"

"Yes," Cynthia echoed. "Too bad Jason looks so sad. I wish I could cheer him up."

At that moment, Marianna realized that Jason was making no effort to join the other guests. She saw him sitting in the game room. He had devoted most of his time to the children who, from time to time, kept peering at the party, running back and forth from the game room. But she also saw Helena talking to Jason when the children were not present, and Jason paid close attention to what she was saying. Marianna wondered what they were discussing. She glanced at her watch. It was nearly midnight. She asked Helena to take the children to their bedrooms.

"Let's go, children," Helena said.

"Would you join us for coffee and liquor," Marianna asked Jason.

"Perhaps later," Jason said. "First I must take my father home."

"The nurse can do that," she suggested as she picked up the phone.

"No, it's getting late and she's probably sleeping."

"She's supposed to stay up, waiting for my call," she said.

"I'll take him," he insisted.

At about 12:15, Marianna saw Jason pushing the wheelchair with Faris sitting in it, his head hanging on one side and his eyes closed.

Soon after Jason and Faris left, Marianna served her guests fruits, desserts, coffee, and liquor, but she couldn't wait for the moment to be with Maximus again, and she wished for the party to be over soon. Any time she approached him, she felt intoxicated by his body scent; any time their eyes met, her lips got hot and wet. She resolved to make love to him that same morning, so she went to the washroom and wrote on a piece of paper the words: 'Meet me at the log cabin in the olive grove at 2:35.' She put the note in her pocket and waited for the right moment to hand it to Maximus.

Close to 2:00, her guests finally began to exit. When she saw Maximus leaving, she ushered him to the door, embraced him, and slid the piece of paper in the top left pocket of his cassock.

33

After Jason took his father to Villa Oasis, he waited until he had fallen asleep and then called a taxi.

As he was sitting in the back seat of the cab taking him to the Mustafa Beach Hotel, Jason took solace in the fact that during the evening he had found the opportunity to speak to Helena, in the absence of the children, who were running back and forth from the dining room to the game room. During the conversation, he'd persuaded Helena to gather for him some of Richard's personal items. She agreed to meet him on Tuesday morning, which was her day off. They didn't wish to be seen together in public, so the meeting place was problematic for both of them, but she ultimately came up with a suggestion.

He tried to imagine how he and Helena would interact with each other during their first private meeting, after not having seen each other for fourteen years. Memories of the naive times they'd shared together resurfaced, but this time his body was craving sexual gratification, and he was overtaken by naked lust. She had offered to meet on Tuesday morning at the corner of Pallas and Odeion streets, in downtown Pafos. "Dress like a fisherman," she said. "And put on a pair of dark sunglasses."

Back at the hotel, he tried to sleep but, despite his exhaustion, he lay awake, staring at the ceiling, his mind wandering from topic to topic (faces, places and events passed through the screen of his thoughts, like a motion picture without a logical sequence). For a brief moment he fantasized about making love to Helena. He then tried to focus on the actions of the people who had come to Marianna's dinner party—their demeanors, words, facial expressions, body language—looking for clues.

The happiest moments of the evening were those that he'd shared with the children. The twins were calling him 'Uncle Jason', whereas Claira called him 'mister'. Andrew was playfully steering Jason into a fistfight, jumping all over him, challenging him and twisting Jason's fingers, while George was telling Andrew to 'stop it'.

Jason said to the boys, "Do you like kites?"

"I wanted to have one, but my mom wouldn't let me. She's afraid I may get struck by lightning."

86

"Well, we can fly them on a clear day. How's that?"

"Yes, Yes," both boys exclaimed simultaneously.

Claira offered to draw pictures for him. She sat on his lap, her head resting on his chest, like a trusting cat, and she began to draw trees, houses, birds, and people. She said, "This is me," pointing to a girl holding hands with a man and a woman.

"And who are these two people?" Jason asked.

"My mommy and daddy."

Jason embraced her tenderly, caressing her soft hair. He stiffened his lips and lowered his eyes. "You draw so well!"

"Where is my daddy?" Claira said. "You look just like him."

Jason drew a long, deep breath. "He's travelling."

"I want him to come back, soon!"

"Yes dear, he'll be back."

"Will you get him back for me?"

Jason felt Claira's heart pounding softly against his chest. "I promise you I'll look for him, and I'll not rest until I find him."

During dinner, he'd noticed Maximus habitually scratching his nose, and at times laughing uncontrollably.

Persephone, the Mayor's wife, frequently raised her fine eyebrows during her conversation with others, as if everything that was said was something new to her. A slim, blonde woman of medium height, she looked younger than her forty-five years.

Mayor Koleas, an obese gentleman with long curly white hair and a watermelon-shaped face, seemed comfortable as he spoke to Panaretos.

Katerina and Lagos never said a word to each other, as if they were complete strangers. Lagos, forty, was short but wiry. His pale face was dotted with dark brown acne scars. He was dressed in a pin striped, custom-made, *Giorgio Armani* suit and was wearing a gold Rolex watch. Although others were drinking, Lagos never had a single sip, but his glass, filled with wine, stood on the table. Jason sensed that Lagos was somehow uptight, because every few minutes his reddish eyes blinked rapidly.

The hunchbacked Bishop Panaretos, a pious-looking chap pushing eighty, smiled broadly to everybody, but when he spoke to Koleas, Panaretos' face became solemn.

Niki, one of Persinaras' female architects, kept getting up every twenty minutes to go to the bathroom, and she often passed by the game room. The other architect, Vickie, was fixed on her chair like a dull statue.

Niki's husband had obviously enjoyed himself; Vickie's spouse ate uncontrollably, even when throwing enigmatic glances at Makin.

At one point Jason saw John Persinaras getting up to approach Faris, touching him on the shoulders as they spoke. Jason figured Persinaras must be about sixty now. He was of medium physique, had short straight white hair and a thick grey mustache that extended well beyond the edges of his thin lips. His pink nose was flat, and his eyes were as dull as those of a shark.

Alexia Persinaras was tall and full-figured. She had a long, thin neck, and when she walked, Jason thought of a giraffe – he examined her narrow white face, harsh green eyes and short curly hair which was dyed dark brown. Alexia was on her feet most of the evening, telling the waiters what to do, handling dishes and sending back food items that she thought were poorly prepared. On more than one occasion, she demanded that Marianna put the children to bed.

Ken Stavro, the general manager of Persinaras Estates, was fifty, a short, slender Paphian, bearing a perpetual smirk as if he was born with it. First, he attempted to sing, but he stopped abruptly when no one seemed to enjoy his cacophonous voice; he then proceeded to tell jokes, but nobody laughed; later he got up and dragged Lagos to join him for a Zeipekkiko dance. Athena, Stavro's wife appeared totally disinterested in what the others were doing and saying. Jason sensed that the two of them were supporting actors in the Persinaras crew.

As she shouted, "Opa, Opa, Opa," Marianna increased the music volume. Lagos didn't miss the chance to show off his dancing skills. Makin, the thirty-eight-year-old general manager of Mustafa Holdings, got up with a cigar in his mouth and started to clap, clap, clap, clap, clap … in a fashion that Jason thought was an overt declaration of comradeship. Jason did not believe that Lagos and Makin could hit it off, but their demeanor toward each indicated otherwise. Makin's portly body was too large for his suit. His dark face had two vertical scars on his left cheek, giving him a ruthless appearance.

After he sat down, Makin never passed an offer to fill his glass, and Jason noticed how he was mixing his drinks, much to the dismay of Makin's wife, Aisha. *How unusual for a Muslim to drink so much in front of so many guests.* Jason noticed that Faris who was sitting to Makin's right seemed just as puzzled.

Naharos, the police chief, a tall mustached man in his mid-forties, was sitting between Manning and Dr. Plato, and Jason could see that Naharos's face was turned away from Dr. Plato for a good part of the evening. Naharos's solemn expression was overshadowed by a vicious glare in his eyes that made him more fearsome than he was pretending to be.

Alex Manning appeared to be enjoying every moment, but there was something enigmatic about his disposition, Jason reflected.

Cynthia was the star of the evening, Jason thought. He watched her dance, drink, talk and laugh, with a flair and passion that well suited her elegant figure. Quite frequently she would toss charming glances at him. Not knowing what to make of her boldness, Jason was simply mystified.

This succession of thoughts was rapid. He wondered if he was losing his mind. He tried to focus his thoughts on one topic, and suddenly he remembered Toronto in 1990. He was on a student's visa at that time, studying business management at Ryerson Polytechnic University. He found the Toronto residents conservative, but pleasant. One of his professors had branded Toronto "the most multicultural city in the world," and Jason enjoyed this characterization, for he had felt the need to be accepted by a society which espoused ethnic diversity. After all, he personified diversity in many ways: his father was an Arab Muslim, and his mother was a devout American Christian; he grew up in Saudi Arabia, and when he was ten years old, his family moved to Pafos (a Greek-dominated environment where many of his schoolmates were Greek Cypriots).

He knew that with its Charter of Rights and Freedoms, Canada was the only constitutionally multicultural country in the world, but this entrenchment of rights did not impress him a great deal, for despite these freedoms, most police officers in the streets of Toronto were white Anglo-Saxons and very few minorities, except Jews, held positions of power and influence. He felt that most immigrants – Indians, Pakistanis, Tamils, Sinhalese, Italians, Greeks, Chinese, Serbs, Croats, Ethiopians, Eritreas and Arabs – were treated as institutionalized modern slaves, doing all the menial, dirty and physically demanding jobs (cleaning offices and houses, attending parking lots, serving food, sweeping streets, driving taxis, and constructing roads and houses).

At first, he felt lonely and homesick. But as time went on, he learned to appreciate Toronto. With his fair characteristics and Western looks, he fit very well into mainstream Toronto society. But, deep within, he always saw himself as an outsider.

Now in Pafos, alone in his hotel bed, he felt the same way. He punched the pillow repeatedly. *I have to settle down. I need to share happiness and pain with a woman beside me.*

34

After Maximus left Villa Mustafa, he got into his Land Rover, turned on the ignition and while the car was warming up, he pulled out Marianna's note. *How can I possibly meet her there?* The log cabin was in the middle of the olive grove and walls surrounded the estate. Maximus wasn't sure what to expect once inside the grove, let alone inside the cabin. He wondered whether the reward was worth the risk. After driving to a deserted field, he parked his car under a carob tree, turned off the engine, got out and began to walk. He estimated the distance between his car and the cabin to be about five hundred meters. He was familiar with the surrounding area, but with the bright moon, he recognized individual trees and shrubs. He followed a hunter's track that led him outside the walls of the olive grove. He climbed up the trunk of an olive tree that was barely rubbing the outside wall, stepped on the top of the wall and then jumped inside the grove, landing hard on his feet. He cried out, holding his knees.

Maximus stood still, trying to catch his breath. He glanced at his watch. It was close to 2:35 a.m. The brisk night wind slapped his perspiring face, and he felt as if he were immersed in the bottom of a cool well after a hard day's work under the blazing sun.

He saw the cabin but no lights were on inside. He could hear the mating calls of a group of frogs nearby. As he walked steadily toward the cabin, he saw a hand waving at him from the window.

Marianna opened the door slowly to let him in. He touched her face, kissed her and exclaimed a sigh of relief. "I didn't know if I should come here," he said, breathing deeply.

"It's safe, don't worry."

"I just realized how high these walls are; I almost broke a leg landing on the ground."

"The walls around here are not as high as those walls famous lovers had to climb."

"I guess I won't be able to measure up to their accomplishments."

"You look flushed," Marianna said.

"It must be all that wine." Maximus slid his hands under her jacket to unbutton her blouse. He reached her bra, pulled it down, lifted up her jacket and began sucking her breasts.

She dropped her jacket, blouse and silk scarf. While lowering her head backward, she whispered, "You know how to arouse me."

He grabbed her by the waist to keep her from falling. "I can't see anything around here," he said. "Where's the bed?"

"One second," she said. She found some matches and lit a candle. She pointed to a queen-size bed at the edge of the inner wall of the room. "There it is."

Now Maximus saw Marianna's round, firm breasts with their erect nipples reflecting the candle's rays. He pulled off her skirt, leaving only her white panties on, and while he was kissing her upper back, he extended one hand between her legs, the fingers of his other hand playing inside her mouth. He felt her wetness on both of his hands. As he stroked his middle finger on the edges of her vagina, she began shivering. As he bit the edge of her earlobe, he whispered, "You're mine."

"Eternally," she whispered back.

He then took her firmly by the arms and kissed her lips. The subtle odor of her reached his nostrils; a delicate mixture of vaginal fluid, French fragrance, honey and Champaign swept over him.

"I want you," Marianna said.

Maximus gently placed her on the bed and bent down to her feet, where he began kissing her toes, one by one, while holding and caressing the arches of her feet. He then ran his tongue up her lower legs, blowing hot air softly, while kissing the area with his lightly salivated lips. His hands were rubbing her thighs in swirls, from the edge of her hips to her knees. He felt her hands on his crotch; the pressure of his penis inside his pants was pushing out. "Not yet," he said.

He threw short, sharp, brash strokes inside her thighs with his tongue, from her knees to the edges of her panties, occasionally lifting them with his fingers and kissing the surface of her thick pubic hair and the outer lips of her vagina.

Marianna grabbed his head and ran her fingers through his hair, stroking it, pulling it and rubbing it with her palms. "I like what you're doing to me," she said.

While his mouth was kissing and exhaling hot air on her panties (directly on top of her vagina), she tried to pull them off, but he gently took her hands and interlocked her fingers with his. His saliva was mixed with the wetness on the garment, soaking it lightly. His mouth lifted her panties and began kissing her skin at the spot between her vaginal opening and her anus, and he occasionally rubbed it with his nose and beard. He looked up and saw her mouth wide open and her eyes shut.

There was a faint smile on her face. Her chest was heaving. "Please, don't stop."

Maximus inserted his tongue between the outer and inner lips of her vagina opening, and he tenderly stroked her there from one end to the other—back and forth repeatedly, in slow movements. He felt spasms inside her vagina and was tempted to insert his tongue inside, but told himself to wait. With his mouth open wide, he sucked and pulled her pubis.

He then released her fingers and placed his on her lips, feeling her hot mouth devouring his fingers, and he almost reached his climax. He removed the wet fingers from her mouth and ran them down her side, under her arms, following the curves and paths of her body. Tracing his way down slowly, he wavered and made shapes in her sweat. His fingers trickled through the triangle of matted darkness that framed her and with the thumb of the same hand, he gently stroked the inside walls of her vagina.

"I like this!" Marianna panted.

He looked at her face again, and saw her tongue extended and twisted upward.

His mouth found her clitoris, erect and stiff. His tongue began circling around the base, but never touching it. He moved his mouth to her belly and kissed and sucked her navel. By now, his hands were caressing her breasts and rubbing her nipples.

Marianna pulled his head toward her face, and his mouth devoured hers. His body felt her hot body, quivering. "You want me inside you?" Maximus asked.

"Yes, please."

"I want every inch of you to be mine."

"Please, please do."

"I want to feel you from within and touch you deeper and deeper."

"Yes, Yes."

Maximus inserted his hands under her panties, grabbed them, and tore them apart. He rubbed one piece on her vagina and then used the same piece to rub his face. He could feel her excitement.

"Oh!" she said, admiringly. "That was naughty."

92

Marianna slipped her hands inside his pants and grabbed his penis. He could feel her delicate fingers rubbing and stroking it. The sensation dazed him.

Placing a pillow under her lower back, he elevated her buttocks for better penetration.

She directed his penis on the outer lips of her vagina and jerked him inside her. "Ah!"

He felt her flesh; she was warm and oily. He pulled back slowly.

She jerked him back in again.

Maximus pulled away again. "Oh, my God! Ah!" He pushed himself in slightly, lingered, and pulled back again, rubbing her pubic hair. He then inserted it slightly in again and kept stroking her there, slowly, for a few seconds. Then, he pulled back again. He reached his hands to her breasts, stroking and grasping uncontrollably. Then, in a curving stroke, he pushed himself a bit deeper into her this time, but he pulled back again and kept himself between the outer and inner lips.

"Stay inside me," she cried. "Please!"

He felt her soft vaginal lips opening up again, inviting him deeper and deeper inside her. He gently went back in, this time a bit deeper, half way in.

"Oh, I love it!" she yelled.

Her sweet smell made him mad and wild. He pushed deeper inside her, a full stroke, holding her locked in that position for a few seconds. He then rolled around, she on top of him, rooted far into her, and he felt her throb around him, while she kissed his chest. He could hear the sweet, splashing sounds of their bodies, a symphony of significance with the cries of the frogs outside.

Her breathing rate increased. Her movements intensified, and he fully harmonized hers with his, until he realized she was reaching the peak of her pleasure.

"Oh, Oh, I'm coming! My God, Maximus, I'm coming! Oh, oh, ah! Ooh. Ohhh! Ouuuuh! Ahh! Mmm."

She was moaning with pleasure, and he could feel a series of rhythmic contractions squeezing him tighter. He felt that ejaculation was about to happen, and he could not stop it. He clung to her harder and harder. "Me, too!" he cried. "Ahh!"

35

She stayed on top of him. "Did you enjoy it?" she asked.

"Yes, very much. You?"

"Oh, Maximus, you make me feel a complete woman."

He felt pleased. He knew she'd reached orgasm, but needed to hear her say it. "Did you come?"

"Oh, yes. It was strong and sweet. Couldn't you tell?"

"Sometimes women fake orgasms."

"Maximus, I've never faked an orgasm because I didn't even know what an orgasm was until I met you. You're the only one who's been able to exhilarate me."

Maximus felt gratified. They moved, and as he lay on his back, Marianna placed her head in the curve of his right arm, and he held her for a few minutes. He closed his eyes and almost dozed off, but he realized that dawn was behind the hills. He looked at his watch. It was close to 4:35 a.m. He had ten minutes to get dressed and leave the olive grove. "I must get going," he said.

"Please stay a bit longer," she said.

"I'll come see you again," he said. "Soon."

"Did you enjoy yourself at the party?"

"There is something that bothers me. Might as well get it off my chest."

"What is it?"

"I saw you embracing Jason and felt uncomfortable."

"Jealous, you mean."

"If you want to look at it that way, yes."

"But why?"

"The way you went about it."

"Don't be silly. Jason is my brother-in-law."

"He's not your brother. I thought it was a bit physical."

"Circumstances demanded it."

"Are you saying you feigned your affection?"

"I had no other choice."

Maximus furrowed his brow. "How do I know you're not doing the same to me?"

At this, Marianna became angry. "Because I don't sleep with Jason, damn it!"

"But you may sleep with him someday. The possibility worries me."

"No, it'll never happen. Jason is not my type. Besides, I love you," she insisted.

"How long will your love for me last?"

"Eternally."

"I'm only a monk. There're many things I won't be able to offer you."

"I have plenty of everything. All I need is your love."

"Ours is lust. How long can lust last before love lashes at it?"

"I know, I know. You're a philosopher. You once told me the difference between Agape and Erotas. For me, love and lust are the same."

Maximus tried to make her understand him. "You don't see beyond the now. We can't go on like this much longer before people start talking about us."

"People are talking about us already," Marianna answered in a carefree way. "I don't mind it. Why do you suddenly care?"

"I'm concerned about you."

"If you really care, you should leave the church and marry me."

"It's so simple for you."

"We can move away, anywhere."

"The problem is not the place. I can't leave the monastery, I'm committed for life."

"You won't be the first or last to leave the church."

Maximus knew she was right. But in his situation, he would not dare contemplate such a move; his sister in London depended on his continued financial support. If this steady stream of funds were to be cut off, she would lose everything, including her luxury apartment in London's West End.

The monastery gave him sanctuary; it fed and clothed him. The monks had bestowed on him their confidence in the management of the monastery property. He was head of a multimillion-dollar institution with land holdings and cash. Although his monastery allowance was small, he enjoyed the power and authority that came with his ordination as abbot.

If he left the monastery, he would be at Marianna's mercy. With her wealth, beauty and youth, she would be a constant challenge, and God knows if he could continue to maintain her affections. He was older, and the age difference between them was a big factor to consider. His sex drive was strong now, but he knew it would diminish with time, while Marianna's would remain the same, if not increase. *Sex is not enough*, he concluded.

His other concern was the two boys. If in fact he was their biological father, as Katerina claimed, he owed it to them to see that no one harmed them. Memories of his childhood years passed before him like a speeding bullet. He hated to imagine what would happen to them if they were ever left destitute, but he consoled himself with the knowledge that they were well cared for.

Still, he was not totally certain that he was their father. A simple blood test could determine this for certain. He'd have to get Marianna to agree, of course, but he didn't know how to mention it without alarming her. "My leaving the church is out of the question," Maximus finally stated.

Marianna began to cry. "You don't love me."

"I love you very much. Do you love me?"

"I'm madly in love with you. How many times do I have to say so?"

"If you truly love me, you should understand my situation."

"What situation? All you have to do is quit the church."

Maximus looked at his watch one more time. *If I stay here five more minutes, the daylight will find me, in the olive grove. I must get going.* "Your sister believes that the twins came from my sperm. Is it true?" He could not believe he managed to utter these words.

She paused and said, "I'm not sure."

Maximus felt that Marianna's answer was as painful for her, as was his desire for the truth. "We must submit blood tests for verification," he said.

"No!" she replied firmly. "I'm not putting my children through that ordeal."

"We'll discuss this again," he said. He kissed her, opened the cabin, and ran toward the walls of the olive grove. The darkness was disappearing fast, and narrow pinkish and golden strokes were slowly spreading on the eastern horizon. He climbed up the wall, jumped on the other side and began to run towards his Land Rover.

36

Jason spent a good part of Monday morning at the Pafos Hospital. Faris underwent his weekly chemotherapy cycle, with his son and Dr. Plato by his side. Jason watched how liquid drugs were injected into one of Faris's veins. The treatment was supposed to eliminate the cancer cells in his body, relieve symptoms and even prolong his life. But judging from the attending doctors' reactions, Jason knew that his father was nearing the end of his existence.

Jason left the hospital at noon and took a taxi to the Mustafa Beach Hotel. Entering his room, he found a note under the door which read, 'Hi, Jason. I'm sorry that I can't join you and Alex for lunch, but I hope to see you soon. Cynthia.'

He took a shower and changed clothes. His lunch appointment with Manning was scheduled for 1:00 p.m., and he rushed to be on time. He didn't feel hungry.

His elevator landed in the lobby of the hotel. He had a couple of minutes to look around. The place was spacious and rich with colour, arches and décor; the enchanting character of the huge mural on the wall—with its depictions of ancient Greek glory—brought the past to life; flower arrangements, tall palm trees and gently running water set the tone. The lobby was surrounded by a harmony of light and gold.

Jason walked into the Palace lounge and was astounded by the impressive pillars and statues. The place was packed. He saw Manning sitting in a private corner, and he waived at him. On his way to the table, he caught a glimpse of two men wearing dark blue suits who were sitting at the table next to Manning's. Jason recognized their faces—they were the same men who had been standing by the limousine on Sunday evening.

"I arrived early to get a good table," Manning said, extending a hand.

"You got us the best spot," Jason responded smiling, and he shook Manning's hand.

"Have you eaten here before?"

"No. It's a magnificent place."

"It belongs to your father," Manning said.

"Well ... only part of it."

Manning was conservatively dressed in a pin-striped blue suit. Perfectly barbered, he had a well-trimmed goatee, which accentuated his parrot nose.

Manning indicated a seat. "Please," he said, and they both sat down. There was a bottle of mineral water and a glass already on the table.

"When your brother was around, Cynthia and I used to come here often," Manning said.

"Richard was a great host," Jason said.

"So, how is your teaching post?" Manning asked.

"It was good while it lasted," Jason replied.

"Do you think you'll stay in Cyprus?"

"Yes. That's my intention."

Jason's response seemed to unnerve Manning. The waitress brought them the menus. "I won't stay long," Manning said. "I think I'll have a grilled chicken sandwich. What about you?"

"I'll have the Caesar salad."

"Your father tells me you're determined to find out what happened to Richard."

"My father wants me to step back."

"That's understandable. He's concerned about your safety."

"I know that my life might be in danger."

"Your father asked me to dissuade you from getting involved. I told him ... he should let you pursue the matter."

"Can you assist?"

"Yes, of course. My wife and I are available for anything you need."

"It would help if you'd approach the US Ambassador to Cyprus and ask him to exert some pressure on the Cyprus authorities to re-open the case."

"I'll see what I can do."

"Do you have any information you can share with me?"

"Unfortunately I don't, but if I stumble on anything I'll let you know."

"What are your thoughts about Richard's case?" Jason asked.

"I hate to speculate. Your brother was such a nice man. Cynthia and I find it difficult to believe that someone would want to cause him any harm."

"Do you suspect anyone?"

"If we had any clues I would gladly share them with you and your father. At this stage, we're in the dark—just as you are."

"Is there anything else I should know at this point?" Jason asked.

Manning scratched his parrot nose. "Well, not that it's any of your business, but someone had spread the word that my wife was having an affair with Richard."

"So I heard."

"This is another one of those legends that grow abundantly in this land. Cynthia is an extrovert. She makes friends fast. Some people misunderstand her intentions."

"I understand," Jason said.

"But let's suppose she had an infatuation with your brother. I'm perfectly capable of forgiving her."

Jason changed the subject. "The Saudis suspect my father has ties to a terrorist cell. They say the Americans are putting pressure on them to investigate my father's books."

"It's part of their duties," Manning said. "The US embassy and the Cyprus authorities are working together to combat terrorism. The Government of Cyprus has enacted anti-money laundering legislation. On terrorism financing, the government has adopted important treaties and is eager to act swiftly to freeze the assets of terrorists operating within its territory. My country is working toward a Mutual Legal Assistance Treaty which will strengthen co-operation between the U.S. and the Government of Cyprus."

"But, apparently, it's the Saudis who are anxious to get involved."

"Yes of course. Your father is a Saudi citizen."

"You've known my father all these years. My mother was an American citizen. As an American friend of ours, can you do something – for example speak to the US authorities – to prevent this unjustifiable interference?"

"In fact, we encourage this type of investigation."

"You encourage it?"

"My company does legitimate offshore business here, and I don't want to give the impression that we are not in accord with my country's national interests. The US embassy here handles issues that concern the welfare and protection of American citizens and their interests. The Americans want to combat all kinds of illegal activities."

"Are you suggesting that my father is working against these objectives?"

"I don't know. Something went wrong somewhere."

"I thought you were good friends. He tells me that he has never betrayed your confidence in him."

"That's what he says, which brings me to the topic of why I wanted us to meet today."

"I know. You want to extract some assurances from me."

"Your father is sick. He'll die soon. I did help him a lot, and he knows that."

"He's grateful."

"Well ... I want us to continue this close cooperation."

"In what way?"

"Soon, I understand, you'll take the helm of Mustafa Holdings and your father's other business interests. All I ask from you is to conduct your businesses in line with American national and international interests."

The waitress arrived with their lunch.

37

Manning waited for the waitress to leave the table. He grabbed the sandwich, sunk his teeth into it, and started to chew fast. "Your father has profited a great deal. We didn't interfere with his commercial activities, as long as US interests were not jeopardized. But lately we have suspected he's gone behind our backs."

Jason was thunderstruck. "Did you confront him with your suspicions?"

"I did. He denies any involvement with funding a terrorist cell."

"I've already told my father I'm not interested in assuming any role in his business," Jason said.

"You have no choice in the matter," Manning said. "You're the only person alive that stands to inherit your father's estate."

"I can refuse to accept any bequest from him."

"It's not that simple. You've already stepped onto the dance floor."

"How?"

"By assuming an investigative role into your brother's disappearance."

"What has that to do with my father's business dealings?"

"One is indispensable from the other," Manning said. He swallowed his last bite and got up.

"Wait," Jason said. "Tell me how?"

"I can't." Manning said. "I'm afraid I have to get going," he rushed. "I have to be in Nicosia before four."

The Caesar salad lay intact on the table. "I guess I'm leaving, too," Jason exhaled as he searched his pocket for money to pay for the meals.

38

The rays of the morning sun deflected on the smooth surface of Jason's dark sunglasses. With tourist-like indifference, he observed the hurried footsteps of storekeepers, as they got ready to open their shops for business. Cars and motorcycles were roaming around him in the busy downtown intersection. Newspaper vendors, their bicycles loaded with heavy bags, waved their papers and began broadcasting the news of the day, while street vendors filled up their kiosks with sandwiches and soft drinks.

Jason managed to cross the street and he stood in the corner of the intersection of Pallas and Odeion, waiting for Helena to show up. He turned around to face the showcase of a shoe store, pretending he was a shopper, only to see his figure on the mirror inside; he was wearing a black fisherman's hat, black sweater and black pants.

A taxi, with a female passenger in back, pulled up beside him. A dark blue silk scarf covered her hair, and huge sunglasses hid her eyes. He turned around and she gestured to him. He opened the rear passenger door and sat beside her. They exchanged glances, but kept quiet.

The taxi moved on, speeded up and turned into a narrow street that led to the southwest outskirts, a squalid neighbourhood where the old Turkish sector of the town, known to locals as "Mouttallos" was located. Old houses built of clay, typical of the Ottoman era, were clustered in a harried formation resembling a Gaza refugee camp.

The taxi slowed down and suddenly came to a stop in front of an old, square, small house. A wall enclosed the front yard, and a stonewashed arched gate faced the street.

"Get me the suitcase and leave us here," Helena told the driver.

The driver opened the trunk and pulled out a suitcase, which he placed on the sidewalk. She paid him, and the taxi left.

"Let me do the talking," she said to Jason.

A tall plump woman in her forties, her face painted with layers of makeup, was waiting for them in the yard. She let them in the house while a white poodle, running back and forth in the narrow corridor, was barking uncontrollably, and sometimes hiding under her long dress.

"Are you Roxana's friends?" the woman asked, as she lifted the poodle in her arms.

"Yes," Helena said, standing in front of the suitcase.

When the woman with the poodle proceeded to walk, her long dress was literally sweeping the dusty floor. "It's 150 pounds a month," she said, "including the furniture."

The rent is dirt cheap, Jason thought. The exchange rate was two US dollars for every Cypriot pound, and he knew that no place in Pafos could rent for less than that.

"How long do you want it for?"

"Six months," Helena said

Jason was puzzled. He walked around the floor with childlike curiosity. It had three rooms and a small bathroom. The room fronting the street was supposed to be the kitchen; it was equipped with a linoleum-top dinette table and two matching chairs. A needlepoint occasional chair and a coffee table were crowding the middle room. The room nearest the patio was furnished with a big brass bed and a wooden dresser. Jason opened the door that led to the patio and the backyard, which faced south.

The lawn was landscaped with orange and lemon trees that appeared neglected and forgotten. He had an unobstructed view to the seacoast, which he estimated to be about two kilometers from the house. He could see the Mustafa Beach Hotel. *It's a perfect house*, he contemplated. He calculated the driving distance between the hotel and the apartment to be less than five minutes.

Helena said to the woman, "We'll take it." She reached in her handbag, pulled out a stack of money and counted it. "Here is the whole rent for six months," she said thrusting 900 pounds in the woman's left hand. "I don't need a receipt."

Jason noticed that the woman was taken by surprise, and he turned his head to the floor.

"I ... forgot to ask for your names," she said.

"Oh," Helena said, "I'm Persephone and this is Moses," pointing at Jason.

Jason opened his mouth in bewilderment and stared at the wall, his back facing the two women.

"Where are you from?" the woman asked Helena.

"I come from Nicosia," Helena said. "I am a dancer. My friend is a fisherman from Haifa. We need a secret place to be together from time to time, you understand?"

The woman nodded.

VEILED ARCHES

Jason's eyes scanned his clothes. He touched his fisherman's hat. He felt mildly agitated and didn't know whether to smile or frown. Helena was obviously planning something. He also had the nagging feeling that these two women knew each other, but he wrote off his sentiment to sheer speculation.

"You won't see me, and you won't hear from me for six months," the woman said.

"I'm glad we can communicate so well," Helena said tenderly.

"Here are two keys and a piece of paper with my name, address and telephone number on it," the woman with the poodle said. She then left.

They sat on the two dusty chairs in the kitchen.

39

"How did you find out about this place?" Jason asked Helena. As he looked at her expressive, bright black, eyes, he had a jarring sense of déjà vu.

"A Romanian nightclub dancer used to live here," Helena said. "She and I were friends. She left Cyprus a few weeks ago."

Jason was amazed. "This place suits me so well," he said.

"I thought you would hate this place," she said laughing. "But don't get any funny ideas."

"But really, I like it!"

"I hope you don't like it too much," she said. "It's in the heart of the brothel quarters."

"Hmm, I like it regardless," Jason said, scratching his forehead with his index finger.

"After fourteen years in Canada, I thought you'd change your taste of things," Helena said.

"My taste of things," he said jovially, "has advanced from plain to bare."

"Bare necessities." She said with a grin. "That was your motto. I remember how you enjoyed mingling with the poor kids of the town. Everybody thought it was so odd!"

"You still remember?"

"You used to give me your roast beef sandwiches. You preferred my mother's pancakes. I remember when I was nine, I saw you one day flying your kite at the beach with Richard. Other kids your age were flying their kites, too, but yours was the one that soared in the sky, almost vertically, far above the other kites. You were full of pride, while the kids in the group were struggling to steady theirs.

"I asked you how you managed to fly your kite so high. You looked at me with your sad eyes and said, 'I make my kites with my own hands. I feel the weight of the cane on the tip of my hands for balance. It becomes part of me. My kite soars because it is very fragile, and when it soars, I soar with it. The bamboo strips that form the frame are so thin, they can break at any moment. The line is the finest I can find, and the tail is made up of real feathers.' And I said, 'You're not afraid you'll lose

105

it if the line breaks?' You answered, 'I'm prepared for it, I don't mind. I enjoy it when it breaks and disappears into the horizon.' Do you remember?" she asked tenderly.

"Yes, I used to enjoy the freedom of the sky. Too bad I didn't become a pilot. How's your mother, by the way?"

"After you left for Canada, she stopped working as a housekeeper in your parents' house. She took me to Greece for a better future. She often spoke about you with fondness."

Jason sensed that Helena was uncomfortable talking about her humble beginnings. He remembered Helena's mother working in the Mustafa household as a maid, washing dishes, scrubbing the floors and doing the laundry. He nodded thoughtfully. "Your mother spent more time with me than my own mother did. She's the one who taught me to speak Greek. How is she?"

"She died in a car crash."

"I'm terribly sorry to hear that," he said. "How long ago?"

"Almost six months now."

Jason took hold of his head with both hands and bent it down. "That's terrible."

"Do you still resent your father?" Helena switched topics rapidly.

"Resentment has kept us apart. We haven't been able to forgive each other, yet."

"You left so suddenly."

"I wish I'd kept in touch," he said reflectively.

"We were too young, anyway. We *both* wanted to run away from home."

"Tell me about your life. What's happened since then?"

"I'd rather not get into it, right now," she said. "Let's get down to business. You'll move all your valuables from the hotel and give them to me. I'll store them in a safety deposit box at a bank nearby. The box will be in both our names."

"Let me understand something," Jason said. "I thought you wanted us to meet so that you could tell me something important. Are you now telling me to move out of the hotel?"

"Jason, you must understand that Pafos is not the place it used to be fourteen years ago. The Russian Mafiosi are not the only bad guys around here. The place is infected with undesirables of all types."

"The criminals here are no more dangerous or cunning than those in North America."

"Ha! You're being naïve if you think you can apply your Canadian experience to this place."

Jason enjoyed a good debate, but this time he realized that Helena was simply trying to help. "Can you be more specific?"

"You'll tackle the problem only by learning to play the local game well."

"It's impossible to disregard what I already know," Jason said with a frown.

"You don't have to disregard anything. But first you must observe and learn the realities of this particular place. Then apply your knowledge based on these realities."

Only a fool could disagree with that statement, Jason mused. *This woman,* he reasoned, *is putting her life at grave risk and her career and reputation on the line.* "Why did you agree to assist my father in such a clandestine fashion?"

"It's not because of the money, if that's what you think. I was a senior accountant with an Athens accounting firm earning an excellent salary, without too much hassle."

"What is it then?"

"One day you'll know."

He nodded.

"Your father wants you to move out, but for now, you will keep your hotel room. Nobody should know about this house—not even your father. If people want to meet with you, the hotel will always be the meeting place, except for us. We meet here."

"I understand."

40

"And another thing," Helena continued. "You will not sleep at the hotel. You'll sleep here every night. I'll give you a cell phone and I will have a similar one. I will also arrange for a phone line to be installed in this place, and an answering machine. On my days off, we will meet to discuss the progress of our investigation."

"Whom shall we investigate first?" Jason queried.

"We should have a parallel investigation of all possible suspects in Richard's abduction. I'll do the paper trail and review all available records. You do the legwork. But we should also keep an open mind about other suspects we don't know of right now."

"How do we start?"

"Methodically," Helena said. "Think of it as a step-by-step process."

"What do you know so far about possible motives?"

"There are many. Your brother had many friends, but he also had enemies. Rumours are circulating that your brother had an affair with a married woman. He also locked horns with a local developer about water rights … there are a number of other players."

Jason sensed Helena's hesitation and said, "Please put all your cards on the table."

Helena gave a sigh and stated, "I think Maximus and Marianna are having an affair."

"Do you know this for a fact?"

"I haven't seen them in bed together, if that's what you mean. But on Sunday night, well into Monday morning, past two o'clock, Marianna left the children with me and went out alone. She said she was going for a walk to get some fresh air, but I suspect Maximus was waiting for her somewhere out there."

"I see. What do you know about Maximus?"

"Very little," Helena answered. She closed her eyes for a few seconds, as if she was trying to figure out something. "I don't know what he might do if he is cornered."

"I want to confront him … ask him some questions."

"I don't recommend a direct confrontation at this stage," she said. "He may be prompted into taking defensive measures."

41

Jason wanted to address Kamal's allegations. He wondered if Helena knew the purpose of Kamal's visit. "Did my father discuss with you the Saudis' concerns?"

"He told me all about it. I think you should fully co-operate with them."

"What makes you think I wouldn't?"

"Our training sometimes hinders our jobs. Your father is upset that you are reluctant to accept the position of CEO. He asked Makin to prepare the papers for your appointment, but he also informed him about your reservations. Apparently Makin is just as content to play the role of the CEO for now."

"What happens if the Saudis have a hidden agenda?"

"Why do you say that?"

"The real threat may not be the terrorists."

"In what way?"

"There may be other reasons, such as financial. They know my father is dying, so they may fear they'll lose their investment in his business."

"But if that's their concern," Helena said, "they have other means at their disposal. Your father told me that the loans are guaranteed with mortgages on the lands and buildings."

"Have you seen the mortgages?"

"No. But soon I will."

"I feel uncomfortable being in the dark about their financial dealings," Jason said with a puzzled frown.

"And what if the Saudis are behind Richard's abduction?" Helena said.

Jason realized that Helena had an open mind. He felt some satisfaction in knowing she was prepared to uncover every stone, to examine every option. "We need to map a plan," he said.

"First we need to define our strengths and weaknesses," she said, unzipping the suitcase.

"Yes," he said supportively. "Let's do that."

The suitcase lay open on the dusty floor. "These are the only items I found in the villa," she said.

It was full of bloated envelopes, plastic bags, documents and clothes belonging to his brother. Helena opened a large brown envelope. "Your brother is probably dead by now," she said quietly.

Jason's eyes fixed Helena with an astute stare. "How did you reach that conclusion?"

She heaved a heavy sigh. "It's the passage of time that worries me."

His stomach swirled as he watched Helena handling his brother's things. A subtle hint of stale scent reached his nostrils and he felt nauseated. Helena pulled from the large brown envelope a passport, a Rolex watch, a golden chain, a golden lighter, three Monte Cristo No. 4 cigars, two condoms, an appointment book, a leather-bound address book, and a business card organizer that was full. He could not bear the sight of his brother's personal things. "Please put them away," he said solemnly.

She placed the items back in the envelope. "Hold on to these," she said, handing the envelope to Jason. "They were in the library at Villa Mustafa. I think Marianna took these from Richard's office the day of his disappearance. There might be some useful information inside."

Jason placed the envelope in front of him on the kitchen table. "What happened to Richard's architectural blue prints, drawings and projects?"

"Makin probably has them locked in his office by the harbour."

"So far, Richard's body hasn't been found. Without the body, we can't say for sure what happened," Jason said.

Helena reached for another envelope. "If anyone wanted a ransom, they would have communicated their demands by now." There was a pause while she pondered. "We should start investigating the people that were closest to him. It looks to me like a premeditated murder," she said.

"You mean … because there were no signs of resistance?"

"Both car doors were wide open, and the engine was running," Helena said. "It seems your brother knew his abductor."

"I think there was more than one," Jason said. "Possibly one was with him in the car."

"Your brother's disappearance took place between midnight and 5:00 a.m."

"Many things can happen in five hours."

"We don't know if Richard was in his car, do we?" Helena said. "He might have been killed and disposed of kilometers away. Someone may have driven his car to the front of the gates to cause confusion."

"This scenario sounds too risky for the assailant," Jason said thoughtfully.

Helena opened the second envelope. It contained a handwritten note and several bundles of US dollars. "Here, your father wants you to have this," she said.

Jason shook his head firmly.

"Please read the note."

Jason took the note and unfolded it. It read: 'Dear son, this envelope contains fourteen thousand dollars. I want you to have it. This is the money I saved for your fourteen birthdays when you were away from home. Your father, Faris.'

"I told him, I don't need his charity," Jason said. "Return it to him." He tried to give back the note to Helena.

"I'm afraid I won't," she said.

"All I needed was his love," Jason said. "Now, after all these years, he gives me money."

"He's dying; you know that."

"I was at the hospital yesterday when he received his chemotherapy. It's a terrible experience for him. I could feel it. While I was holding his hand, he was trembling."

"If you don't accept this gift, you will never come to terms with your past."

He took off his hat and tossed it on the table. Cold sweat poured down his forehead, and he noticed the room's rising temperature. He felt hungry. When faced with a dilemma, he always felt hungry. It was a nervous effect he had learned to recognize. As though this wasn't enough, a mouse ran along the side of the baseboard, causing Jason's upper torso to jerk in reflex. His hunger was gone in an instant.

He got up and walked over to the window facing the street. The neighbourhood was small, and children were playing soccer at the edge of the street. He enjoyed hearing their voices and seeing them play. *I can't wait to watch the World Cup in June*, Jason dreamed as he watched the children shooting the ball.

Helena was standing beside him. He could smell her sweet scent.

42

Helena said to Jason, "When Turkey invaded Cyprus in July 1974, we became refugees, and my mother brought me to Pafos. We settled in a house two blocks from here. There were not too many children around in 1974. Their Turkish parents took them to the north of Cyprus when the two communities were divided. Some pockets of Turkish fighters stayed behind and there was fear in the streets. My mother wouldn't let me go out in the streets alone, even to buy ice cream.

"One day I sneaked out to buy ice cream from a tiny grocery shop whose owners were a Turkish Cypriot couple who had decided to stay. Their small house was a few hundred meters away from their store. They had many Greek Cypriot friends, and they probably felt protected. They were not in their shop. Their boy, my age, was behind the counter. I was short of money, and he felt sorry for me. He offered me the ice cream, but he refused to accept my meager change. I turned down his generosity.

"I ran back to my house, burst into the small bathroom, barred the door, and started to wail. I blamed my mother for our poverty. I didn't realize how fortunate I was until I learned that, on that same day, somebody had abducted and killed the boy's parents. It was an execution-style killing, they said. His parents were probably dead shortly before I saw his innocent face that day." Helena sighed. "But he didn't know it."

"That's very sad," Jason said. In spite of his genuine sorrow, his thigh almost touched her hip, and he was tempted to take her into his arms, kiss her and taste the ripe fruits of her body. He pressed his thigh against her hip to gauge her reaction and tried to put his arms around her, but she moved slightly away from him, signalling she was unreceptive to his advances. *This isn't the right moment,* he judged. "What happened to the boy?"

"The Red Crescent Society took custody of him."

His eyes turned to the floor. His lips were firm. He stood there, numbed by the nature of the atrocities.

Helena asked, "Do you know what had happened to their property?"

113

"Their property has no meaning considering their tragedy," said Jason, surprised by her question.

"Their shop is now in ruins. Their house remained empty for a long time until someone figured out how to make money out of it." She hesitated. "I don't know if I should tell you this," she wavered. "I'll tell you before our meeting is over."

Jason did not press for an immediate answer. "I resented my father for being so rich," he said.

"But you had it all," Helena said in a tight voice.

"Except for love, and I need love most of all!" Jason now felt like a boy who yearned for consoling. "My mother couldn't give me her love because she was drunk most of the time. And my father was distant and egocentric. I grew up thinking that poor children were more fortunate than me, because their parents showed them their love."

"Is that why you always identify with the poor?" Helena said.

Jason sensed sympathy in her words and felt vulnerable. "I am who I am," he said nonchalantly.

"Others in your shoes would ask and expect to receive," Helena spoke persistently.

"What do you mean?"

"Others are now enjoying your family's wealth. Marianna lives in a villa that she hasn't spent a penny for. She has maids, cars, money, privileges, and she treats all these as a matter of natural right. Does she have a higher right than us … I mean … than you?"

"She is the mother of my brother's children. And they deserve a good life."

"You deserve the same."

"If you mean, I deserve to enjoy the same wealth, I beg to differ," Jason said. "I deserve only the things that are rightfully mine. And right now, the only things on this planet that are rightfully mine are my own abilities."

"We should use our abilities to our advantage," Helena said.

"My brother utilized his talents to his advantage, and look what happened to him."

"Bad things happen to everyone, poor and rich. It is not wealth that destroys peoples' lives. Wealth is neutral. It is *how* people view and use wealth that determines their path."

"Wealth is one big temptation."

"Jason," Helena said firmly, "face your demons."

He had more tangible problems to tackle, so he kept quiet.

114

"Are you afraid that if you have wealth and influence, you'll become like your father?"

"Maybe I am," Jason whispered.

"You are not your father," Helena said. "You are yourself. You said it a few seconds ago."

"I tried to stay away from him."

"You can stay away from those who've hurt you, but you can't stay away from yourself."

"I face all my challenges."

"I know what you mean, but that's not good enough," Helena said softly. She suddenly pursed her lips. "Jason! Are you listening to me?"

"Richard wrote me letters after I left Cyprus. He kept sending them for a year, before giving up on me."

"He didn't give up on you, Jason. You know he didn't."

"I gave up on the place. Richard was there for me the whole time, and I hated him for it. I wished he'd been horrible to me, so that I could blame him for something. Looking at him was like looking at myself, except he turned out better—the way our father wanted. Richard was always there for me."

"If you're honest with yourself, you must face your internal challenges," Helena said sternly. "You can fight your external challenges all your life, but you may find the real answer inside yourself."

Jason was listening attentively. "Right now, what really matters is discovering what happened to my brother."

"You can't do it alone! To discover what's happened, you need the help and support of others, especially your father," Helena said. "Long ago you needed your father's love and didn't get it. You probably long for it now. Sometimes we don't realize that the reason we don't have something, is because we fear rejection. Your father offers you his love. Accept it. Accept his gift to you too."

"Love cannot be bought, it is there to be had for those who open their hearts." Jason said.

"Our need to love and be loved should not be incompatible with our comfort and prosperity."

Jason was contemplating Helena's words. "What I need and what I want are two different things."

"The dividing line between need and want is not always clear. You need balance."

"How do I achieve balance?"

"For starters, take the money your father has sent you and use it to pay for some of your expenses while you are working on your brother's case. It's not wrong," Helena said.

"You keep the money," Jason said. "You've already paid for the rent."

"I used your father's money for the rent," she said. "I have a budget too, you know!"

"You can use it for other expenses."

"Honestly, I have a feeling that you're afraid of money," Helena said.

"I'm not afraid of money," Jason said in protest. "I'm afraid of *his* money."

"Okay," Helena said facetiously. "I'll tell you what. I'll keep it, but with one condition."

"And what's that?"

"I'll give it back to you when you deserve it."

"Jason started to laugh. Her laughter mixed with his, and the tension between them began to wane.

43

"What do you know about Katerina?" Jason asked Helena.

"I learned a few things about her from third accounts," Helena said casually. "But before I tell you about those, I'm going to get us some take-out for lunch."

She left the house, and in practically no time she was back with two large pitas full of souvlaki. "I think better on a full stomach," she said, as she handed a pita to Jason.

He took the pita with appreciation. The aroma of parsley and char-broiled lamb was too strong to resist. He sunk his teeth into the warm pita. "Really," he said, "I never met your father, and you've never said anything to me about him."

"I'd prefer not to discuss that now," Helena said.

Jason detected Helena's discomfort. "I understand."

Helena said, "Katerina and Lagos met in Athens in 1989, when Katerina was a law student at the University of Athens. Lagos, a fraud artist and university dropout, seduced Katerina with his smooth talk. But Katerina let herself be seduced because she knew that Lagos's uncle was the head of the University's examining board. At Katerina's urging, Lagos stole his uncle's key to the office where the final tests that she had to write in the next few days where kept, broke in and copied the exams.

"Katerina passed the exams with flying colours and graduated with distinction. No one knew of the fraud until many years later when Lagos, intoxicated, sputtered it out – along with many other things – in vivid detail to his drinking buddies in a Pafos tavern. The man loves to talk. Discretion is not one of his attributes. But lately, he is reserved and rather serious, as if he underwent a complete transformation.

"Lagos and Katerina dated for a few years, and when Katerina returned to Cyprus, Lagos followed in pursuit. Fearing the displeasure of her parents who wanted her to marry a local wealthy surgeon, Katerina kept the relationship secret for some time. She enjoys controlling everything around her, even her parents. She led them to believe that she was fond of the local surgeon, but she was dating two other men at the same time, in addition to Lagos who was happy to be in Cyprus, living in a furnished apartment at Katerina's expense. But when Katerina learned that the surgeon was dating his Romanian nurse, Katerina used the occasion to convince her parents that the surgeon was a womanizer, unsuitable to her family's traditions.

"She then introduced Lagos to them as an archeologist who was on leave from the University of Athens, overseeing the mosaic excavations near the Pafos harbour. Lagos with his sweet tongue and charming ways convinced Katerina's parents that he was indeed a well-rounded man of culture. Her parents not only endorsed the union, they put pressure on Katerina to marry Lagos, fearing that such an opportunity would never arise again. To agree to the marriage, Katerina extracted from her parents the following: the promise to appoint her to the position of the Chief Executive when Persinaras was about to retire; cash; a luxury, fully-furnished villa in the Pafos hills; two luxury cars; and a position for Lagos in Persinaras Estates to compensate him for supposedly having to give up his promising university career.

"The fish did bite! Katerina's scheme worked very well. Katerina and Lagos finally married in Pafos in 1992. It was a lavish wedding. The wedding party was celebrated with thousands of distinguished guests, dignitaries, politicians and clergy. She has a reputation in the legal community as a woman who always gets her way."

Jason absorbed every word, now realizing the formidable nature of Katerina's character. "She's more scheming than I thought," he responded. Equally worrisome was the portrait Helena painted of Lagos. He saw the couple as interdependent. His eyes told him to rub them; his ears told him to listen; his body told him to lie down for a rest.

"People are often deceptive," Helena said.

That comment prompted Jason to wonder, *How do I know she's not one of them? How can I trust her fully? Many people are not what they seem.* He went by his gut feeling. "I can count on you," he said.

"I'm grateful for that," she said, then took out a piece of paper and wrote the name 'Crow' on it. "An anonymous caller telephoned your father on April 12, the day of Richard's disappearance, to say that a man named Crow the Butcher may have witnessed something. The police were notified but the tip didn't turn up anything. Someone suggested that Crow sells meat in the nearby Farmers' Market."

Jason took the piece of paper and put it in his pocket. "It sounds like a nick-name to me."

"I must get going," Helena said. "I have to be in Nicosia in a couple of hours. In the meantime, I will arrange for someone to clean this place."

"Before you go, finish the story about the Turkish couple," Jason said.

"I knew you wouldn't forget," Helena said thoughtfully. *"This* is the house that belonged to that Turkish family."

Helena's latest information caused a shiver down Jason's spine. "Who owns it now?"

"The money I gave to the woman with the poodle will eventually reach the hands of the rightful owner," she said.

"You mean the son is back?"

"Yes." She gave him one of the keys and left.

44

On Tuesday morning Katerina secluded herself in her office at the Mustafa Beach Hotel. She refused to accept any visitors, asked her secretary to screen all incoming telephone calls, and cancelled all her appointments. She needed time to think. She hoped to have a plan in place by the time she met Maximus at the monastery that evening.

A large frame on her desk contained her favourite photo: sitting in the front row, her father and mother were holding hands; their grand-children, Andrew, George and Claira were sitting on the carpeted floor, by their feet; Katerina and Marianna were standing at the back. All radiated huge smiles. Everytime she looked at this picture, she thought of her own child.

They did not allow me to take photographs of my child, Katerina remembered. *There are no photographs, no mementoes.* When she got pregnant at nineteen, her parents were furious with her and insisted that she give up the baby for adoption. The man who had fathered her child abandoned her, and her parents were horrified of what people would say about their family.

From the moment the baby was ripped from her arms, she became a different person. Katerina cried for weeks and refused to speak to her parents. Marianna was the only one whom she would allow to enter her room, and only then for company, because she wouldn't talk at all. She didn't speak to her parents for a year after that. Although she became strong and indifferent, there were times when she felt responsible for the loss. And this resulted in feelings of shame and guilt – emotions which she kept to herself.

She took the picture frame, kissed it and brought it close to her chest. *I will never allow anybody to take anything away from me again. These are the only people that matter to me now. I'm responsible for their well-being, their happiness, their future. I'll do anything for them. I'm the head of the family.*

She sat on the soft leather armchair, but as she pondered about the latest turn of events, she felt uncomfortable. Even the calm sea, a few meters away (her only visible connection to the outside world), could not soothe her soul.

She got up and began to pace back and forth, eyes darting, playing with her hair, fidgety but trapped, ready to pounce if the door were opened. She remembered how forcefully she'd stepped in to save her father from the brink of financial ruin a few years ago. She gave herself credit for the expansion of the Persinaras-Mustafa Group during the last five years, but also realized that this expansion would have been impossible without the influx of money from *Long Nile Development Corporation*. As she recalled the events that precipitated her family's involvement with the *Corporation*, a wave of resentment splashed against her.

Any time she thought of them, she felt powerless. The irony, she noted, was that the *Long Nile* people, with all their invisibility, exerted as much pressure upon her as any other regular board of directors would on the management of an ordinary public company. This pressure was too enormous to ignore and too embarrassing to admit. When the *Long Nile* people first appeared on the scene a few years ago, she saw them as carriers of hope and promoters of prosperity.

Her husband, George Lagos, had found them and introduced them to her father. It all began when her father had a heart attack and was facing bankruptcy due to his extravagant lifestyle and reckless business ventures. He was in desperate need of cash to keep his ventures afloat. Lagos got in touch with the *Long Nile* people and arranged for a meeting. She wanted to meet them too, so she went along.

They met at the Nicosia Hilton. Her father sought financial assistance in the form of a loan, and they were anxious to assist. But they demanded cumbersome and heavy repayment terms. As part of their willingness to loan her father the money, they insisted that one of their associate companies, *Sudan Star Construction Inc.*, a land development company, be awarded several lucrative contracts to build more luxury villas for the Persinaras-Mustafa Group of companies in Pafos.

Her father had been reluctant to do business with *Long Nile* under such circumstances, but things turned for the worst when the local banks called upon their loans and refused to consider any re-financing arrangements. Then, at Lagos's insistence, Katerina persuaded her father to consummate the deal with *Long Nile*.

She now wondered if she had any other choice. She shook her head in bewilderment. In return for the sixteen million dollar loan to John Persinaras, *Long Nile* demanded that the amount be recorded in the loan documents as twenty million dollars and be subject to 10% interest per year; Katerina protested that the four million dollars surcharge was excessive, but Lagos had insisted. "Are you crazy?" he said. "Don't spoil the deal." They justified the four million dollars as the risk part of the business, and they said 'the higher the risk, the higher the reward.' Interest payments, which amounted to two million dollars per year, had to be paid on the anniversary of the loan for four years, and the balance of the loan together with interest had to be paid on the fifth anniversary.

She flipped her diary and circled January 31, 2002. She calculated the number of days left for the loan to become due and payable. *Oh, my God, the loan is due in 79 days.*

Long Nile had demanded and received a guarantee, signed by John Persinaras and Katerina jointly, pledging to *Long Nile* all their personal assets. John Persinaras and Katerina also signed a general security agreement, assigning to *Long Nile* all assets, proceeds, revenues and profits of Persinaras Estates Ltd, the holding company that controlled the Persinaras-Mustafa Group of companies. John Persinaras and Katerina also agreed to hire *Sudan Star Construction Inc.* to construct several villas in the area.

As the villa development business was promising and lucrative, Katerina had every confidence that she would meet the yearly interest payments and eventually be able to pay off the loan when it came due. But now business was slow, and the cash flow was not enough to meet the $22-million payment to *Long Nile*. She had tried to refinance the loan and get an extension. She had spoken to the local representative of *Long Nile* about this possibility three months ago, and he had said: "absolutely out of the question." She could not turn to the banks, either, because of Persinaras's bad credit history.

Today Katerina felt uncomfortable as she remembered how Faris was annoyed by her decision to award some villa construction contracts to *Sudan Star Construction Inc.* She hated to think about Faris's reaction if he discovered the loan deal with *Long Nile*.

As soon as the loan deal was consummated, the *Long Nile* people disappeared. Katerina remembered how relieved her father had felt at the time. After the banks were paid off, at least $6-million was left for future expansion.

Now, gazing at the calm sea, she remembered the four happy years that followed, but her face stiffened when she recalled the unpleasant surprise she had experienced in the spring of 2001 when a local representative from *Long Nile* suddenly appeared and demanded that all loan payments be re-directed to a bank account in Northern Afghanistan. She had already begun to suspect that *Long Nile* might have ties to a radical group. When the representative threatened to kill her if she disobeyed his order, she obeyed the directive. *What will they do to us now if I miss the payment?*

She figured there must be a way to get out of the tentacles of *Long Nile*. She couldn't turn to Lagos for help, for she doubted his judgment and didn't trust him anymore. He could never keep a secret, especially when he was drunk. He'd embarrassed her so many times, by revealing confidential information to others. Ever since he'd bragged to his drinking friends about his break-in of the professor's office in Athens to steal the exam papers for her, she couldn't trust his discretion.

He promised her that he'd stopped drinking, but she knew he still did so behind her back. Lately, he was spending most of his time away from his office, playing golf or backgammon with Makin, or poker with the guys. On occasion he would say to her that he was visiting a job site, but when she looked for him, he wasn't there. Instead, he was in his powerboat with a group of people, fishing and drinking.

He's good for nothing. I wish I had a child, but not with him. He can't father any children, anyway. His goddamn sperm is rotten. I shouldn't have brought him to Pafos. I lied to my parents about his background, and now the boomerang has landed. She wondered where he found all the money to spend on his lifestyle with the $3,000 a month salary he was paid by Persinaras Estates Limited, but she realized she was paying for most of the household expenses, and he had no major debts (all big-ticket items, such as cars and the boat, were paid for). Their villa was also mortgage free.

The local *Long Nile* representative reminded her of the due date of the loan a few days ago and asked her to meet with him at her office on Wednesday to discuss it. Tomorrow is Wednesday, she reminded herself. She grabbed her Montblanc *Andrew Carnegie* piece and brought it close to her eyes. It was elegantly carved with an 18-carat gold nib and decorated with a sensuously winged feminine figure in sterling silver. She had never met the man who'd sent it to her for her thirty-fourth birthday, but the *Long Nile* representative had told her it came from the boss.

She squeezed the pen hard, raised it above her head and pointed the gold nib at the wall. She hesitated and, as she tightened her mouth, she struck the pen on the wall, puncturing the velvet wallpaper and destroying the golden nib. *I want Long Nile out of my life!* In her desperation to cling to something, she thought of Maximus and Marianna. She felt she could exert as much influence and control over them as *Long Nile* was exerting on her, and she felt somehow relieved.

Katerina thought of the vast Mustafa wealth, and she suddenly realized that if she could get her fingers on Faris's money, she could use all of it to pay off the *Long Nile* people and get them out of her sight once and for all. She could not bring herself to the prospect that Jason could soon gain control of the Mustafa wealth, which included Villa Mustafa and the surrounding land, to the exclusion of her sister, the children and her parents.

But with Jason out of the way, the only lawful heir would be Marianna and the children. She knew that with his ill health, Faris's days were few. Time was running out in both directions, and she had to act now and act fast.

45

When Helena left the Turkish house, Jason opened the suitcase. When he saw Richard's clothes, he felt a sharp pain in his chest. He took out two shirts, brought them closer to his face and imagined how handsome Richard would look wearing them. Hot tears rolled down his cheeks, heavy and cloudy, dropping on the still air of the quiet room and making shallow holes in the dusty floor by his shoes. He could not bear holding them. He sat at the kitchen table and tried to think straight. If Helena was correct and Richard was dead by now, he'd have to face it. He tried.

Rumours circulated that Marianna was having an affair with Maximus, and Helena alluded to parallel rumours about Richard having had an affair with a married woman. But there were no indications that Richard and Marianna were involved in a domestic dispute. However, he did not completely write off an argument-motivated murder.

He dismissed the possibility of Richard being murdered during a robbery.

He learned from his criminology course, during his graduate studies, that there is more to a crime scene than just physical evidence. He remembered Helena's forewarning not to blindly apply his knowledge to the Pafos environment, but nevertheless, he saw no reason to totally disregard what he had learned.

Based on the information he had gathered so far, Jason believed that whoever murdered Richard was an organized individual. Since there was no body, no cause of death could be determined. Jason reached the conclusion that if Richard was murdered, then his murder had been planned ahead of time. He was convinced that Richard's abductor was capable of moving and hiding the body, volunteering information or even returning to the scene.

The possibility of a terrorist abduction did not elude Jason. Kamal's visit was perhaps not as coincidental as it appeared to be. But why would a group of terrorists abduct and/or assassinate Richard? As far as Jason was aware, there was no political connection in Richard's life that would have prompted retaliation, besides Faris's own sympathies toward the Palestinians. Terrorists would have sought to generate a political show of force and mass publicity, both of which were lacking in his brother's case (unless Richard was a terrorist and didn't toe the line, or he had stumbled upon classified information).

Circumstantial evidence was pointing in all directions, but Jason had very little physical evidence. Helena's counsel to proceed methodically resonated in his ears, together with the naked realization that he had to devote a sizable part of his energy to gathering information. In most homicides, the victim knew the killer, so he had to focus his attention on Richard's immediate circle of friends, family and business associates. He knew that it was more difficult to get information from these people than from documents. Therefore he needed to examine many documents, and he had to devise a way to get them.

Jason looked at the suitcase and the bloated envelopes, which sat on the kitchen table.

He wanted to examine them first, but it was mid-afternoon; he was hungry, and needed some fresh air. He pulled out the piece of paper from his pocket with Crow's name on it. This is a perfect opportunity to look for Crow, he thought. He locked the Turkish House and set out to visit the Farmers' Market.

46

Shortly before 3:00 p.m on Tuesday, Katerina called K3 in Nicosia. "Any news from the Saudis?" she asked.

"Well, my contact in Pafos informed me that a person by the name of Aziz is supposed to be a guest at your hotel this Sunday. His associates from Saudi Arabia will join him a few days later."

"What time is his scheduled arrival at Larnaca Airport?"

"Five p.m."

"That's November 18, right?"

"Yes."

"Do you know who is picking him up from the airport?"

"Nadir Makin," K3 said.

"They're not sending Jason?"

"I guess not."

"Do you know why?"

"My source told me that yesterday Faris appointed Jason as the Chief Executive Officer of Mustafa Holdings, but apparently Jason is reluctant to assume that role."

This was both good and bad news to Katerina; doubly good in the sense that Jason and Faris were not getting along, and Jason was going to stay away from the day-to-day operations of Mustafa Holdings. But it was bad because Jason had an independent mind, and his distance from Mustafa Holdings would render him immune to any wrongdoing. "And who's going to make the major decisions?"

"Makin, I guess. But from what I understand, Faris wants Jason to take an active role in the investigations."

"You're an angel. I owe you one."

"I can never repay you for all you've done for me. Take care."

Katerina hung up. She had to take care, all right. She looked at her watch. It was time to leave for the monastery.

47

As Katerina drove to meet Maximus, she went over her plan one more time. Her objective was to convince Maximus to kill Jason.

At 3:30 p.m. she made her way from the monastery's parking lot, up the steep stairs, through the double-door arched entrance, up the second level corridor and into Maximus's private office.

As soon as she entered his office, she saw Maximus handing out some documents to Monk Modestos, his personal assistant. Modestos excused himself and as he left the office, Maximus shut and locked the door. They sat on the leather sofa.

Katerina began, "There are some rather disturbing developments. I had a telephone conversation with my contact in Nicosia. Apparently Faris has appointed Jason as CEO. Faris suspects certain irregularities with our books. I'm also concerned that when Jason learns of your love affair with Marianna, he'll want to know if it is true. He may ask to meet you face to face one of these days."

Maximus said, "But he has no right to mingle in Marianna's private life. He cannot expect Marianna to lock herself in the bedroom and cry all day. Getting involved at this late stage, his only motivation must be to prevent Marianna from receiving her rightful inheritance. You see, the most he hopes to accomplish is to accuse Marianna of Richard's death. The least he can do is cause embarrassment for Marianna, soil her reputation and create a layer of suspicion around her."

Katerina replied, "When I was nine years old he stayed in our home during one of his parents' visits. He was a quiet boy with sad eyes. He used to take my dog for long walks and stay out for hours, while I was dead scared that a car would run over my poodle. My parents ended up giving him my dog, because any time Jason left our house without him, the dog would howl uncontrollably. I haven't forgiven my parents for what they did. Richard's marriage to my sister didn't bring me any closer to Jason."

Maximus said, "I see. He's accustomed to finding ways to snatch other people's things. This type of personality can be ruthless, merciless and dangerous. I can't see what he hopes to gain by meeting me. I'll simply deny my affair with Marianna."

Katerina wanted to sandwich Maximus. "Whether you admit or deny your affair with Marianna will make no difference to Jason. He may use your admission to implicate you in Richard's disappearance. And he may disprove your denial and reach the conclusion that you had a hand in Richard's disappearance."

"Surely he must already suspect that I may be responsible."

Katerina was aware of Maximus's tendency to switch things around to suit his objectives. However, it was extraordinary, she thought, to hear Maximus say that he could be a possible suspect. Since Richard's disappearance, the only person she'd suspected was her husband Lagos. But she was not so naïve as to tell to Lagos that she considered him a suspect. With Maximus, she had the power to plant the seed in his mind that not only was he a possible suspect, but that Jason was determined to prove him as the only suspect. "The suggestion that you and Marianna conspired to kill Richard is a cause for concern."

"If there had been any suggestion that Marianna and I had something to do with Richard, the police would have brought such evidence to light by now."

"What if Jason has evidence that Richard has been murdered by you, or Marianna? You and my sister would be facing sure disaster. Seven months have passed, and Jason has brought Richard's ghost in the vicinity, ready to re-appear."

Maximus exclaimed, "Why did Jason have to come back? I had hoped I'd seen the last of him! He's the son of a Muslim. I'll consider his visit to our monastery as disruptive, an affront to our Christian values."

Katerina said, "One problem: his mother was a devout Christian and a benefactor of your monastery."

"He takes it for granted that he'll be welcomed by me. Still, that hardly entitles him to sneak into my private life."

"I fear Richard's disappearance will linger on and keep open the whole question of Marianna's participation, either alone or with you. We should try to find a way to put an end to this controversy. Perhaps you should stop seeing my sister."

"I can't stop Marianna from seeing me."

Katerina added, "There is another problem in regards to Jason's return. Villa Mustafa and the surrounding land belong to Faris. When he dies, I can see a legal battle unfolding between Marianna and Jason for the ownership of the property. He may prevail. And if he gets all that property, he will begin to exert tremendous influence on our people. He may then try to marginalize us."

"You overestimate him."

"It's easy for you to say that. I can just see Marianna and the kids packing their belongings and moving out of the villa. Marianna has spent a great deal of her time and money to fix that place. She tied her happiness to Villa Mustafa. Now Jason could pull the carpet out from under my sister's feet and humiliate her immensely."

"The other day, you asked me for my help. Today, I thought you had some startling revelations. All I have heard so far are your fears about what Jason might do."

Katerina searched for the sting. "You're ridiculous," she said. "Jason is coming after you with a vengeance. As long as he's alive, you'll never fuck my sister, again!"

"We can meet in Athens, Rome, or elsewhere."

"Your simultaneous absences will be two dry logs in his fireplace."

"Why don't you do something about it? You have just as much to lose, perhaps more," Maximus said.

"You forget we're relatives. My family's business is partnered with his father's business which, when Faris dies, will become Jason's business. So far, Jason has not threatened my family's business, and there is no indication that he will do that. On the contrary, he may prove to be a much better partner than his father ever was."

"Are you saying that Jason will not pose a threat to your aspirations?"

"What aspirations? I have no aspirations," said Katerina.

"Why are you so anxious to pin me up against him then?"

"You don't get it? I can learn to live with him, but you can't. One of you has to overcome the other. It's like two strong winds that meet mid air from opposite directions."

"If he's capable of destroying me, he's just as capable of destroying you."

Katerina felt that there was no way that she could demonstrate to Maximus the force of her argument. She now realized how formidable Maximus was when it came to playing mind games. She had to find a more practical, a more persuasive way, to hit the right nerve. "He may be planning to marry Marianna."

"Is that what you want her to do?"

"Personally, no. But you know Marianna. She swirls around like a sunflower. She may marry Jason if he starts to be influential around the place. And I won't blame her."

48

They were alone in the dark, cold room. The bell rang, calling the monks to evening liturgy at the monastery's chapel. Maximus scratched his nose, and Katerina sensed that he was thinking over something. She kept staring at him.

Maximus's eyes lowered. "What would it take for us to work together on this?"

At last he's losing his detachment, Katerina thought. "Do you have anything in mind?"

"What do you have in mind?"

"Time is running out."

"Your father owes me a lot of money. Now whether he or Persinaras Estates pays me, the money is still the same."

"How much do you still want to let off this?"

"You paid $2.6-million. You owe me another $5-million."

"You gave my father a sour deal. If it were up to me, I wouldn't have paid more than $1,000 an acre. Remember, we developed the land."

"Without this land, you would be scraping floors!" Maximus shouted.

You dirty, lousy scoundrel. "We don't have that kind of money. Business is slow, and the two main unions are getting bigger wages."

"Oh, come on! Each plot is selling for over $220,000. The villas on it go for $1.1-million a crack."

"Don't exaggerate."

"I've read your colourful brochures."

"But you haven't seen our balance sheet."

"Your creative accountants take care of that."

"We're losing money now."

"Maybe someone is robbing you blind."

Katerina's eyes brightened. "If we go under, you won't get a single penny."

"The monastery can get most of the land back."

"That's what you think. To get the land, you would have to have mortgages registered on the land, and the monastery hasn't done that, thanks to you!"

131

"Thanks to your crooked father!"

"I can't believe what's happening between us," Katerina said softly, as she paused. "I thought you wanted us to work together, and all I hear is money. If you do what I say, the money will follow. I mean lots of money, more than $5-million."

She could see Maximus in obvious bewilderment.

"It's very simple," Katerina stated. "You take care of Jason. I'll take care of this guy Aziz."

"Who's Aziz?"

"He's a Saudi, who's arriving on Sunday. The others will be coming in a few days."

"So, what's the plan?

Katerina didn't wish to look like she was taking the first step. If Maximus came up with the idea first, she schemed, it would make it easier for him to carry out the plan. "You know the handling of things. How should we coordinate our efforts?"

"Who goes first?"

"The one who will generate the greatest distraction."

"Jason?"

"Definitely not."

"Why?"

"We want Jason to be the primary suspect in Aziz's death. All eyes will turn on him. Then, when you kill Jason, the primary suspects will be the Saudis," said Katerina.

"Simply put, we pin one against the other."

"It is how the plan is carried out that worries me. We must work out the details carefully."

"I have a suggestion," Maximus said. "You handle the details for Aziz, I'll handle the details for Jason, and I'll move once I hear news of Aziz's death. Then, I'll do what I have to do."

Katerina had her doubts. "What guarantees do I have that you'll carry out this plan?"

"I'll give you the documents. You'll hold on to them until I kill Jason. If I fail, you keep them, and I'll lose my $5-million dollars. If I do kill him, you return the documents to me and pay me an additional $5-million ... cash."

"'That makes sense," Katerina said. "I must get going. I'll call you tomorrow night to tell you where to meet. Bring the documents with you."

49

It took Jason less than five minutes by foot to reach the centre of the Mouttallos quarter. In the Ismet Inonou Piazza, tourists wandered the corridors and kiosks of the bazaar, looking at the vast variety of artifacts, local embroidery and souvenirs, as peddlers called them to come in and make an offer. Despite the warm weather, the locals were wearing heavy clothing, in sharp contrast to the tourists who, with their shorts and skirts, were enjoying the break from the northern climates of their countries. Jason believed most of the tourists were British.

He entered the roofed Farmers' Market expecting to see sun-dried faces selling produce on makeshift counters. Instead, the place was crowded with shoppers among the organized fruit and vegetable booths, meat and fish cubicles, delicatessens and liquor kiosks. Sausages, cheeses, vegetables, fruit, bread, smoked and fresh meat, smoked fish, dried goods, herbs and flowers produced scents that blended with the body odours around him. This unparalleled sensation crawled and nestled around his most basic needs. He enjoyed seeing the variety of products on display and listening to the haggling of the local vendors.

At the east-end entrance, he saw a little boy about three years old running alone on the cobbled street while a van was backing up in the boy's direction. The boy was almost under the left wheel of the van when Jason shouted, "Stop!" He dived and pushed the boy out of harm's way.

Jason was happy he saved the boy's life, even as his forehead bled from hitting the rear end of the van.

The boy's screams got the attention of bystanders who gathered around to see what happened.

"Oh, my god, my boy!" a woman cried in a Greek Cypriot dialect. She pushed her way through the onlookers and lifted the shaken boy in her arms. Slim and neat, she was trying with one hand to fix her light brown hair that was blown in all directions from her frantic movements.

She looked no more than thirty. Her high cheekbones had a natural rose tint, and her large light brown eyes sparkled in the sun. She wore light pink lipstick. Her slightly open lips suggested a caring passion mixed with tones of sensual desires. Jason sensed that she could be both a good mother and an affectionate companion.

A few seconds later, her husband, a masculine mustached man in a white apron, came to shake Jason's hand. "Are you alright?" he asked, his face overflowing with appreciation.

"I'm fine, thank you," Jason responded in Greek, touching his bloodied forehead.

"Come," the man said. "My wife is a nurse."

They walked over to a small restaurant. The man's wife handed the crying boy to her husband and attended to Jason's injuries. She applied an antibiotic ointment and covered the wound with a bandage.

"What is your name," Jason asked her, somewhat uncomfortable as he secretly cherished her touches.

"Penelope," she said tenderly.

Jason thanked her for the treatment, and proceeded to leave, but her husband approached him and said, "I don't know how I can show you my appreciation for saving my boy's life. Thank you, thank you, a million times."

"Your words of gratitude are more than enough."

"Please sit down for a few moments," the mustached man said. "You must be hungry."

Jason watched the broiling steaming lamb on sticks, and his hunger was amplified. He ordered a large portion wrapped in a warmed pita and ate it hastily. He had no time for a leisurely meal. He pulled out his money to pay for the meal, but the mustached man waived his hand. "No, no. It's on the house."

"Thank you." Jason decided to reward him with a well-deserved compliment. "You make excellent kebab, the best I've ever had!"

A broad smile stretched the man's wide jaw. "Thank you, friend," he said twisting his huge mustache with his fingers.

"Tell me, please," he asked the man, "where can I find Crow the Butcher?"

The mustached man scratched his head. "How much meat do you need?"

"I must see *him*."

"I wouldn't buy meat from the Crow's hands," the man said contemptuously.

"What's his real name, do you know?"

"Dimitrios … I think."

"Oh, well, where's his booth?"

"If I were you, I would stay away from that swindler. He may feed you donkey's meat, if not something worse."

"I'm not interested in buying his meat. I just wish to meet him."

"It's none of my business, but I don't understand why a fine gentleman like you wants to meet a disreputable man like him."

"I thought he worked in this market."

The mustached man laughed. "Crow works everywhere. He used to have a booth in this bazaar, but the meat inspectors cancelled his license a few months ago. I learned he is now a pimp— he continues to sell meat on the black market."

"Would you happen to know where he lives, then?"

"He owns a brothel on Parthenon Avenue, not too far from here. I don't remember the number. If you ask for Crow's brothel, the people in that neighbourhood will direct you."

Jason fought back a chuckle. *Parthenon. The famous Greek temple dedicated to virgins had a namesake street in the heart of the bordello district.* Jason nodded and looked at his watch. "I must get going. Thank you for the information."

"If there's anything you need, anything at all, I'll be glad to assist," the mustached man said. He handed Jason a piece of paper. "My name is Nicholas. This is my home phone number. And below is my number here at the restaurant. Call me anytime, even if it's late at night."

"My name's Jason."

"It's a nice name," Nicholas said. "Are you American?"

"Half-Arab, half-American."

"The mid-east met with the mid-west, eh!"

They both laughed. It was getting dark and the shoppers began to leave. Jason left the market and walked straight to the Ismet Inonou Piazza, looking for Parthenon Avenue. He passed a deserted Turkish mosque with a minaret and entered Mechmet Pasa Street, a narrow one-way lane with two-level houses on either side. The female prostitutes standing at the entrances outnumbered the men walking on the sidewalks, and most men appeared to be blue-collar types. There were no nightclubs or discos—the neighbourhood wasn't conducive to romantic engagements.

50

As Jason ventured farther east and entered Parthenon Avenue, a completely different atmosphere unfolded before his tired eyes. He saw expensive European cars parked on the street and young men entering and exiting the brothels like hornets in and out of nests. A group of men were gathered inside a fancy-looking betting store, while on the sidewalk young prostitutes wearing mini-skirts and high-heel shoes shook their hips and made inviting gestures. He saw more brothels as he penetrated deeper into the edge of the street. He asked for Crow's brothel, and a man in his early twenties agreed to take him there.

It was a large pillared dwelling that resembled an ancient Greek sanctuary. A brass sign on the door read: *'The House of Adonis and Aphrodite.'* Jason wondered whether Dimitrios, the Crow, was inside.

After he went in, Jason observed in the atrium at least a dozen attractive women dressed in long white transparent gowns sitting on replicas of ancient Greek couches; waiting, nodding, smiling. Paintings and sculptures of semi-nude men and women, imitations of classical Greek art, adorned the walls. The polished marble floor gleamed. In each corner, a large vase full of fresh flowers blended with the light blue colour of the walls, and French perfume floated in the air.

A spectacled madam was sitting, prim and proper, behind a desk. She flipped and examined the pages of a large black notebook. Her dedicated manner reminded Jason of the business side of the operation. Behind her desk a huge painting depicted ten hetaerae dressed in fawn skins, surrounding, touching and feeding Dionysus, the god of wine. Female slaves were carrying trays of fruit, food and drinks. The god was holding a drinking horn and wearing a crown made of vine branches.

This masterful painting spoke silently about the man who owned the place, Jason mused. *Dionysus was good and gentle to those who honoured him, but he wreaked madness and destruction upon those who spurned him or the orgiastic rituals of his cult.* The repeated depiction of the nude human bodies reflected the hedonistic atmosphere of the parlour. It was a hall full of the most enduring Grecian themes. Jason speculated that only a professional decorator could have effected such an organized arrangement.

Two anxious young men walked in after him. They rushed to two of the best-looking prostitutes and took them by their hands, apparently anxious to take them to the rooms. However, the overbearing voice of the madam brought them to a dead halt.

"Over here first," she waived.

They obliged, paid their dues, and proceeded to their assigned rooms.

"What can I do for you, love?" she asked Jason, staring at him.

"Ah, yes," he uttered with his hands in his pockets, feeling his paper money. "Is Dimitrios in?"

"What do you want with him?"

Jason offered her twenty pounds. "May I speak to him?"

She took his money, shoved it in her breast and said, "No. You speak to me, love!"

He examined the painting behind her. The artist's signature at the right bottom of the painting read: 'D.Lucas/2001.' It occurred to him that he had seen an identical signature somewhere recently. "You've got a nice place," he said.

"This is not a museum," she said sternly. "Come back when you feel horny."

"I may do that sooner than later." He turned his head to the left and saw a shut door with a sign on it that read 'OFFICE.' "Is Dimitrios in there?" he asked.

"He doesn't wish to be disturbed."

He strolled out, turned left and spotted the window of the brothel office. He tried to peep at Crow's face inside, but the window's lower edge was one foot above his head. Embarrassed, Jason looked around to see if anyone was watching. He decided to head back to the brothel.

This time, he hurried in and rushed to the office door. He twisted the handle and opened it slowly. He saw a man, with a small round head and long curly hair sitting on a chair behind a huge square desk, smoking a cigar. In front of the desk, Jason noted the backs of three other men. Cigar smoke filled the room. A Doberman, standing ready beside its master, barked.

"Out! Out!" shouted the man behind the desk.

"I'm sorry to disturb you," Jason said. "I must speak to you." He felt a strong hand from behind pull him by the collar of his jacket. When he turned his head, he saw the madam's blazing eyes.

"I told you, he doesn't wish to be disturbed!" she yelled. "Now get the hell out of here!" Her arms were now locked around his neck, and he had trouble breathing.

"What the fuck is happening?" the man with the long curly hair asked.

"He insists on seeing you without telling me why," she said.

"Let go of him," the man ordered, and the madam obeyed.

Jason could breathe normally again. "All I asked was to have a brief word with Dimitrios," Jason exhaled.

The man appeared amused. "Dimitrios, eh! Every bastard in town calls me Crow. Come to the point. Fast!"

Jason felt lightheaded. "Do you know anything about my brother, Richard Mustafa? He's missing."

The three men who looked like thugs stood up, and at the sight of their faces Jason knew he was definitely in danger.

"I told the fucking police I know nothing. Why won't they leave me alone?" Crow screamed, pounding his fist on the desk.

Jason saw at least six prostitutes rushing to the farthest corner of the hall, standing there in silence. The Doberman barked at him uncontrollably and thick saliva was dripping from his jaw. He was thankful that the thug who was holding the leash was strong.

"Did you ever meet my brother?"

"Not face to face," Crow said.

"Have you ever done any business with him?"

"Never."

"Do you know anything about my brother's disappearance?"

"I know nothing."

"Can you tell me where you were on the morning of April 12, 2001?"

"It's none of your fucking business."

"Do you know Richard's wife?"

"Everyone in this fucking town knows Marianna."

"I mean, do you know her on a personal level?"

"You mean have I ever fucked her?"

"No, no, I mean—"

"Are you the fucking Revenue Department? What kind of stupid questions are these?"

"I'm sorry to upset you, Mr. Dimitrios," Jason uttered quietly. He hoped that his sudden show of courtesy might soothe Crow's temper.

"You're damn right you're upsetting me, and for nothing. Now that you're finished with your brainless snooping, we have nothing to discuss. Beat it!"

Jason feared if he persisted he would be eaten alive or found on the muddy grounds of some deserted field. "Thank you for letting me speak to you," he said and walked out of the brothel.

At least he did not leave empty handed. The signature, 'D.Lucas/2001,' on the lower right corner of the huge painting that hung in the hall of the brothel was still vivid in his mind. He had seen that same signature on three of the paintings that hung in the living room of Villa Mustafa.

51

When he returned to the Turkish house Jason found the floor spotless. A fresh lemon scent permeated the house. Clean sheets and blankets had been spread on the bed and a vase with twenty-four red roses stood in the centre of the kitchen table, which was covered with a white-cottoned embroidered cloth. Dishes, cutlery and other kitchen essentials were meticulously stored in the drawers and shelves. A cellular phone on top of the fridge was plugged into a charger. He opened the fridge and smiled when he saw a six-pack of his favourite beer, Carlsberg, waiting to wet his dry mouth. Cold cuts wrapped up in wax paper, bottled water, and sliced bread were also among the items.

For a brief moment he thought he was starting a holiday, then opened a bottle of Carlsberg and walked over to the bedroom. Jason sat on the bed, his head resting on the headboard, and he gulped the whole beer. He closed his eyes and fantasized about making love to Helena. Several minutes ticked on by.

He opened his eyes, feeling refreshed, but his hand felt the roughness of his face. Jason wanted to shave and change clothes but realized that all his belongings were at the hotel. He locked the Turkish House, and flagged down the first available taxi.

A dreadful suspicion had dawned on Jason. After arriving at the Mustafa Beach Hotel, he'd been unable to think about anything but Crow's unwillingness to answer all his questions. Although Jason couldn't specify further, he sensed Crow hid things and he was determined to get to the root of the matter. First, he resolved to locate D. Lucas, the artist.

He thought of all the questions he was going to ask Lucas. He couldn't tell whether the artist was a man or a woman. How large the artist's portfolio was? How many of Lucas's paintings were sold? Who was the main exhibitor of Lucas' art? Who had purchased the huge painting that hung in the Parthenon brothel?

Jason had to give the artist a false impression (that he was interested in purchasing a large chunk of the artist's work). He realized why the decoration of the Parthenon brothel seemed familiar. It was the same careful arrangement of Grecian themes and semi-naked bodies that existed in the living room of Villa Mustafa, a taste which (unless strangely coincidental), would reveal Marianna's connection to the walls of the brothel—and possibly shed some light on Richard's disappearance.

He had to discuss the details of the Dionysus painting with the artist, and tell him that he saw it at the brothel. He had to avoid causing any unnecessary suspicion. Jason knew that artists get excited talking about their work. *Artists are mercifully naïve*, he decided. *This D. Lucas fellow will tell me anything.* The purpose was not to raise the artist's ego; it was to discover the thread that might unravel the mystery of Richard's disappearance. Like the mythical Daedalos, Jason also had to pass a linen thread through all the shell's whorls.

There were of course many simple explanations to be considered. The painting could have been sold by D. Lucas to Marianna's Galleries, and she might have then sold it to the brothel as an ordinary commercial transaction.

He was merely speculating. Thinking of all the possibilities made his mind spin like a fan. Had Crow been to Marianna's Galleries, or had Marianna gone to Crow? She must have had a reason for approaching Crow, who was a pimp. Jason concluded that he'd been too direct with Crow. He made the mistake of revealing the purpose of his visit instead of pretending to be a customer. *I'm foolish*, he berated himself, *to assume Crow would ever cooperate, especially if he was involved in Richard's abduction.*

Jason pondered the possibility that someone else may have purchased the painting from Marianna's Galleries and re-sold it to Crow. Yet, even if this was true, Jason was still anxious to know the identity of the first purchaser who had dealt with the artist, D. Lucas, and the donor or seller who had ultimately sold it to Crow.

These thoughts whirled through his mind while he shaved, bathed and dressed. Mulling over things as he ate dinner alone at one of the hotel's restaurants, he found that he couldn't finish his meal.

52

Back in the Turkish House that evening, Jason recalled Faris's comments when he'd urged him not to get involved in the search for Richard's abductors. Nevertheless, it was not until the end of the evening, when he went to bed, that it occurred to him that his life was in real danger.

That he could be killed frightened Jason to the point that he got up to check the door and the windows one more time. *What if Crow sends his thugs to kill me?* He hoped that no one had followed him when he left the brothel. If Crow was involved in Richard's abduction, Jason wondered who hired him to do the job.

He got up and went straight to his brother's personal belongings. He picked up Richard's diary and flipped to April 11, 2001, the eve of his disappearance. Several notes, which Jason recognized as Richard's handwriting, were spread all over the page, and it was difficult to read them. April 11th was a Wednesday. Times began at 8:00 a.m. and ended at 8:00 p.m. A scribble at the 9:00 a.m. line read: 'Inspect progress of Delphi Villa Project.' Another note near the 1:00 p.m. line read: 'lunch with M.' Did 'M' mean Marianna, Maximus, Manning or Makin?

Another reminder at the 5:00 p.m. line read: 'Meeting with Makin and client to discuss Delphi Villa.'

A shorter note after the 6:00 p.m. line read: 'Call Mari.' Jason knew that Richard always referred to his wife as 'Mari'. He carefully placed the diary under his bed mattress.

Jason knew that Richard used to smoke cigarettes. Cigars? Never. Yet, among his items, he found three Monte Cristo cigars.

Next, while examining the business card organizer, Jason discovered at least fifty business cards inside. Many of the names on the cards he did not recognize, but he figured they belonged to Richard's suppliers, clients, friends and acquaintances. He found among them Makin's card with the title 'General Manager, Mustafa Holdings Inc.' He looked to see if he could find a card belonging to the artist, D. Lucas, but he could not. He carefully flipped the pages of the leather bound address book. There was no reference to any D. Lucas.

Who was the client that Richard was supposed to meet on April 11th to discuss the Delphi Villa Project? Jason wondered. Where did the meeting take place? Who else was present at that meeting?

He needed to find out about the Delphi Villa Project, but how? Jason learned that, after Richard's death, Makin had the entire collection of blueprints removed from Richard's office and locked in his own. He remembered Helena telling him that Faris had informed Makin that Jason was not interested in assuming the CEO duties at Mustafa Holdings. Any direct questions to Makin about the Delphi Villa Project would have alerted him, and he didn't know how Makin would react.

Jason decided to make up a story, but he must be careful not to appear too obvious. Or, he could get the key to Makin's office and enter at night when no one was around. Except that he'd have to evade security. He decided to risk a break-in to Makin's office.

He picked up the cellular phone and dialed the Cyprus Telecommunications Authority (CYTA), seeking directory assistance for a D. Lucas listing.

"There are five listings under this name," the operator said "Which address, please?"

"I don't have the address," Jason responded. "Could you give me all of them?"

"No sir, I'm sorry," the operator said.

53

On Wednesday morning, at eight fifteen, Jason visited the Farmers' Market and bought a bottle of *Five Kings*—the best quality Cyprus brandy he could find. He then went over to the restaurant where he had initially met Nicholas, the mustached man, and looked for him. "He comes here two days a week," a young waiter told him.

"I brought him something," Jason said.

"I don't know if he's awake yet."

Jason left the bottle with the waiter. "Please give it to him," he said.

"I know who you are," the lad said. "You saved his boy's life. I think he'll be happy to see you. Let me call him." He picked up the telephone, dialed a number, and spoke something in Greek. The dialect was so unusual that Jason couldn't fully understand what he was saying. The waiter then turned to Jason and handed him the telephone. "The boss wants to speak to you," the waiter said.

Jason put the phone to his ear. "This is Jason," he said. "I'm in the area … just thought I'd drop by to say hello."

"My regular job is a security man," Nicholas said. "I finished my shift at three this morning."

"I'm sorry to wake you up."

"Not at all. I'll be there in twenty minutes."

When Nicholas arrived at the restaurant, Jason befriended him with the bottle of *Five Kings* and spoke to him in Greek, thanking him for providing Crow's address the day before. Nicholas invited him to sit down.

During their conversation—partly in English, partly in Greek—Nicholas thanked him once again for saving his boy's life and asked him if he met Crow.

To avoid revealing the purpose of his visit to the Parthenon brothel, Jason lied, "I had a good time."

"I knew you would like it," Nicholas said. "Everybody loves that place."

He enjoyed the man's simplicity. "Have you ever been there?" Jason asked, grinning mischievously.

"Are you kidding? My wife would kill me!" He waved the palm of his hand across his neck.

"I want you alive. I wouldn't know where else to go for a good kebab."

Nicholas smiled broadly and rushed to open the bottle of brandy. "Let's celebrate this new friendship," he announced. He took two glasses, filled them with brandy and shoved one in front of Jason's mouth. "Cheers!"

Before Jason found the courage to say anything, the mustached man had already gulped the full liquor and was licking his lips. "Yes ... cheers," Jason hesitated. In a spirit of camaraderie, he chugged his shot. His throat felt the caustic strength of the sure-fire brandy, burning and nearly causing him to choke.

Nicholas cut a large chunk of luntza, a smoked and marinated, sun-dried pork tenderloin. "Eat this," he pressed.

Jason, with tears in his eyes but still anxious to please his new-found friend, devoured the whole thing. What a way to start the morning! he agonized.

"You speak Greek so well?" Nicholas said.

"I learned it from our housemaid. She was Greek."

"Good. Very good! Where is your house?"

Jason had promised to Helena to keep the Turkish House address a top secret. "I'm staying at a hotel in Kato Pafos."

Nicholas said, "I'm usually here on Tuesdays and Sundays. The other days I run a small security company. That's my regular business, really. I have fifteen men working for me." He filled his chest with air. "I've bought some modern surveillance gadgets recently," he boasted. "I'm an ex-police officer."

"You're a hard-working man," Jason said in admiration.

"Not really. This," he said pointing at the grill "is my hobby. Let's have some *mezedes*."

Jason had a love-hate relationship with *mezedes*; they were a rich collection of appetizers and savories. Any time he ate them, his stomach had no room for the main dish. "Thank you for the offer, but I'll reserve my appetite for some other day. May I use your telephone book?"

"I'll get you one." Nicholas rushed to the kitchen and returned a few seconds later with a huge telephone book. By then, Jason realized that Nicholas truly meant his words when he spoke about "new friendship."

"Thank you." Jason took the book with a grin of appreciation and flipped the pages, looking for 'D. Lucas'. Sure enough, he found five listings. He wrote them all down, thanked Nicholas and left the restaurant looking for a quiet spot to make his calls.

He called the first number on the list. The female voice on the other end said, "No artist lives here."

A cheerless, deep male voice answered his second call.

"Mr. Lucas, please," Jason said.

"This is he."

"Are you D. Lucas the artist?"

"No, I'm his father."

"When do you expect him in?" Jason asked naturally.

"You haven't heard? We buried him six days ago."

"I'm so sorry," Jason said softly. "Was it an accident?"

"No, my son…well, everybody knows … he had AIDS."

"That's horrible," Jason responded sadly. His sorrow was twofold: a good artist was lost to AIDS, and a possible leak source was now gone.

"He was my one and only child."

Jason could hear the man's sobs. He hesitated for several seconds, and then asked, "I don't mean to sound heartless, but can you please tell me who is now handling the sales of his paintings?"

"Some woman bought them all," he said. "I think she has a gallery by the harbour; that rich lady whose Arab husband disappeared a few months ago. Marianna Mustafa."

Jason thanked him and pressed the end button of his cellular phone. It was almost 9:50 a.m. He looked for a taxi that would take him to the hotel.

54

When Jason arrived at the Mustafa Beach Hotel, the lobby was crowded with tourists while travel agents explained their services and signed up clients for excursions. Jason approached one of the three receptionists who was wearing a blue miniskirt and a red sweater and asked her to check his messages.

"Are you Mr. Jason?" she asked. From the tone of her voice, Jason understood she knew who he was.

"Yes."

"You have six messages." She handed him six folded envelopes.

Jason sat in the main dining area, ordered a light brunch and proceeded to read his messages. The first note read: "Dr. Plato called. Please call him back."

The second message was from the nurse at Villa Oasis: "Your father is not feeling well. He's asking for you."

The third note read: "A woman called. She did not give her name. She will call back." Jason figured it could not be Helena because she had his cellular number. He dialed her cellular number but there was no answer. She must be working at this hour, he thought.

The fourth message was written in different handwriting: "Mr. Steve Naharos, the police chief, wants you to be at the Pafos police station today, at eleven o'clock sharp." It was almost 10:30 a.m. Jason wondered what it was about.

The fifth message was typewritten: "Jason I must see you. Please drop by my office soon. Katerina."

The last telephone message had a fax sheet attached to it, which stated: "Dear Mr. Jason Mustafa. Aziz will be arriving at Larnaca Airport on Sunday night at five o'clock. Cyprus Airways, Flight 269, direct from Riyadh. Please be at the airport on time." The fax was signed by Kamal Kamal.

55

Jason instructed the taxi driver to enter the gates of the Pafos Police Station. It was a few minutes before eleven o'clock, and the station was a throng of police cruisers. As he walked towards the main entrance, he noticed a black police car (with license plates marked: 'POLICE CHIEF') parked in the driveway.

The station was an old compound structure that was built by the British during the colonial administration of Cyprus. Jason knew that besides its austere offices, the station contained a prison that was once used for the detention, interrogation and torture of EOKA suspects—those liberation fighters whom the British had suitably referred to as 'terrorists'. Sharp pieces of broken glass bottles were embedded on the pointed top end of the high walls that surrounded the station.

He gave his name at the front desk and asked to see the police chief. He was startled when the sergeant in charge escorted him to a windowless room which had all the signs of an interrogation chamber. Chairs were scattered around. A microphone on the square wooden table was connected with cables, and Jason noticed the large mirror on the wall. A huge electric light fixture hung from the ceiling, directly above the table.

Jason had to answer a number of personal questions, such as place and date of birth, occupation, permanent residence, religious affiliation and marital status, while the sergeant made notes. He was also asked if he'd been convicted of a criminal offence and for how long he planned to stay in Pafos. The sergeant treated him as if he were a suspected trouble-maker and never mentioned the police chief during the interview.

About fifteen minutes later, the door opened and in walked Steve Naharos. "You are here. Good," the chief said. He stared at Jason, who tried to get up in protest. Naharos tipped his shoulders with a baton and motioned him to remain seated. "So you are turning this town upside down," he said with a frown.

"What have I done?"

"You went to a brothel yesterday and caused quite a scene." Naharos's left eyelash was blinking rapidly and uncontrollably, and his hands were trembling.

"I asked Crow if he knew anything about my brother's disappearance," Jason responded.

Naharos grabbed a chair and sat opposite. "Who gave you permission to play private investigator?"

"I didn't accuse anyone of a crime. I have the right to ask questions."

"Not the way you went about it," Naharos shouted. "You trespassed on their property and violated their privacy by bursting into their office uninvited. Do you know what we call this offence?"

"The courts will decide whether I have committed an offence, not you!" Jason shot back.

"Break and enter, that's what you've done."

"If you plan to charge me, do it now."

Naharos's facial muscles suddenly relaxed. "I'm assigned with the responsibility of policing this place. I assume, from your actions, you believe we've done an inadequate investigation regarding your brother's disappearance."

Jason noticed that Naharos' self-esteem was as low as the light fixture that hung in front of him. "What I think at this stage shouldn't matter to you."

"For your information, we interviewed Crow and his men. We've already determined that they're above suspicion."

Jason wondered if Naharos was being less than truthful. After watching Naharos interact with Marianna at Villa Mustafa on Sunday, with all the display of a trusted friend, Jason figured that Naharos couldn't possibly remain an impartial law enforcer. "Why did you allow Marianna to drive Richard's Alfa Romeo to the compound the morning of Richard's disappearance, without first examining the car for fingerprints and other possible physical evidence?"

"I'm not at liberty to disclose police procedures."

Jason felt frustrated. "You simply left the scene unprotected."

Naharos was silent.

"I'm disappointed," Jason murmured. "Do you even have a theory as to what happened to my brother?"

"He was killed by persons unknown," Naharos said calmly, but Jason sensed that Naharos was boiling inside.

"Why are you so sure he's dead?"

"Look," Naharos said firmly. "Cyprus is a small island. No one has ever been found alive after this much time has passed."

Jason said painfully, "I just can't believe you closed the file."

"Tell me why we should keep it open!" Naharos shouted.

"Those who killed him should be found, arrested and prosecuted."

"Right. That's easy for you to say. We have many unsolved cases. They're part of our reality. Our resources are very limited."

"Then why are you offended by my attempts to find some clues?"

"We're concerned that you may cause a big stir in this small community and embarrass innocent people, including your own family. Your indiscriminate intrusions into people's private affairs are also very dangerous."

Jason restrained his anger. "Have you ever considered Marianna as one of the suspects?"

A tired-looking Naharos smiled. "Everybody was a suspect, including your own father."

"You could have asked for a search warrant to search Villa Mustafa," Jason said calmly.

"It couldn't be done!" Naharos shouted again. "The scene of the crime was outside the compounds!"

"You could have found important evidence."

"It would be unconstitutional to search the villa on mere speculation."

"Did you search my brother's office?"

"No!"

"Why not?"

Naharos looked fixedly at Jason's eyes. "The bloody place was empty!"

Jason shook his head. "That's because you didn't move fast enough; that's why I'll go on with my own investigation."

Naharos pulled out a piece of paper and shoved it in Jason's face. "If you don't sign this, I will arrest you and charge you with break and enter," Naharos said. "It's your written assurance that you'll immediately stop acting as a private investigator."

"This is a violation of my legal rights!" Jason protested. "I refuse to sign it!"

"Very well, then." Naharos stormed out of the interrogation room, slamming the door behind him. The powerful light shone on Jason and he began to perspire. He couldn't see anything, but he could hear footsteps and occasional voices.

The door opened again, and Jason's stomach began to tighten. A tall and burly male police officer held Jason's hands behind his back and handcuffed his wrists.

"You can't do this to me," Jason stated nervously.

56

They met at her office shortly before noon. Katerina recognized him instantly. He was short and fat. The perpetual sour look on his face made her nervous. She had never known his name and dared not ask for it. His grey beard was meticulously trimmed, but it did little to take away his solemn appearance. He uttered his message slowly and harshly: "The boss expects repayment of the entire loan on time." His words were demanding, not pleading.

Katerina's heartbeat sped up. She had to cough up exactly twenty-two million dollars. The loan was due on January 31st.

How could she tell him that she couldn't acquire the money by January 31? This same man had previously threatened to kill her if she disobeyed his directive.

Instead of explaining her inability to repay the loan in timely fashion, she decided to transfer her worries to him. "Do you know the Saudis are sending a group of forensic accountants to investigate Mustafa Holdings and Persinaras Estates Ltd?" she asked casually.

"That's news to me."

"They suspect the Mustafas are funding a radical group. The Americans are putting pressure on the Saudis to locate and destroy them."

He was fidgety. "You are not going to co-operate, I hope."

"How can I co-operate? It's like digging my own grave."

"We want complete secrecy. We count on you, Katerina," he said pointing his finger at her.

"I have a plan that will frustrate their efforts."

"I hope you'll share it with me. We must know."

Katerina hoped to cause him sufficient apprehension, to the point that he would be amenable to any of her suggestions. "Before I reveal this plan, I want us to consider the possible consequences. If the Saudis discover the channeling of money to the *Taliban* ... 'clergy,' the authorities will prosecute us all. They may freeze or confiscate our assets. If your identity is revealed, you'll be arrested and imprisoned. The loss of twenty-two million dollars would be the least of your worries."

Grains of sweat rolled from his forehead.

"The Americans are determined to find you," Katerina continued.

"When are the Saudis expected to arrive?"

"Soon, very soon!"

"What's the plan, then?"

"They're sending a man named Aziz to Pafos this Sunday. He's supposed to make the preparations for the group's arrival. If you kill Aziz when he arrives at the Larnaca Airport, his execution will frustrate the Saudis. Our best-case scenario is for the Saudis to cancel their plans. The worst outcome is to delay the arrival of their accountants; by the time they turn up, I will pay your people the total amount. We'll then destroy the books."

The representative didn't seem convinced. "We're playing with several unknowns here," he said. "Many things can go wrong."

"Do you have a better plan?" she asked raising her hands.

"I guess not," he said.

"Now," she said firmly, "Can I count on you to kill Aziz?"

"What time on Sunday is he due to arrive?" he asked.

"Five o'clock in the afternoon."

"How will I know who he is?"

"Nadir Makin will be at the airport to pick him up. You know Nadir, don't you?"

"Anyone else?"

"Possibly Jason."

"I heard he's in town. Is he behaving?"

Katerina pretended she had no concerns about Jason. *Maximus was going to kill him anyway*. Her plan now was to convince Jason to pursue Marianna in order to ignite Maximus's ire to the fullest. Eventually, she hoped, the authorities would catch Maximus, prosecute him for Jason's murder and imprison him. As for *Long Nile*, once they were paid off, she thought, they would depart for good. At the end, she would be left alone in control of the Persinaras and Mustafa assets.

She'd talked to Marianna shortly before the representative arrived at her office. "They've arrested Jason" Marianna had said, but Katerina wasn't too happy. She wanted him out of custody, so she could carry out her plan. This is a perfect opportunity, she thought, to earn Jason's eternal gratitude and draw him to trust her.

"We have nothing to fear about him. He's not even interested in running his father's businesses," Katerina said.

"That's encouraging."

Katerina wanted to return to the topic of Aziz's assassination. She had to take it as given that the representative would do the job. "I cannot describe Aziz to you."

He frowned. "I'll use the process of elimination." He lit a cigarette and drew a puff. "Leave it to me," he exhaled.

Katerina got up. "I hate to rush you. I have to attend a meeting with my architects."

She was lying; she wanted to get to the police station.

The representative remained seated. "How's George?" he asked.

"He's very busy. We rarely go out."

He raised his eyebrows and stiffened his mouth. "Can I ask you a personal question?"

"Depends."

"You have been to the monastery recently. Are you having an affair with Maximus?"

Katerina was furious but kept smiling. She understood the subtle hint that she was being followed and that her moves were being monitored. This asshole, she thought, refuses to disclose his name; yet he has the audacity to ask personal questions! "We're friends, that's all."

He scratched his nose. "You're too young and too pretty to be a friend to a real man," he said scornfully.

She kept her cool. "I'm loyal to George."

"That's commendable."

Katerina was beginning to feel uncomfortable. She had to sit again to avoid offending him.

As soon as she sat down, he got up. "I'm leaving," he said. "Can you call a taxi?"

She could understand why he didn't drive to the hotel—a man as secretive as he wouldn't be so naïve as to own a car. She walked him to the lobby and told one of the receptionists to order a taxi. She left him standing outside.

She immediately went back inside, picked up one of the courtesy phones and dialed the security guards at the building's entrance. "I want one of you," she said, "to follow the man who is standing outside waiting for a taxi. Follow the taxi. When he gets out, follow him by foot. If he gets into another car, follow the car. Make a report of his activities for the rest of the day. Be back at the hotel by nine thirty tonight. I'll see you then."

57

Twelve other men shared the cell with Jason at the police station. From their comments and arguments, he presumed the majority were gamblers, drug dealers and wife beaters. They tried to approach him, but he avoided them all. He had to wait his turn to use the telephone. When his turn came up, a police officer asked, "Are you Jason Mustafa?"

"Yes."

"A woman is waiting for you in the office a few doors down the corridor. Follow me."

As he followed the officer, Jason's confidence got a boost. He felt sure it was Helena, and he wondered how she found out of his arrest. He saw the back of a woman. When she turned around to face him, he froze.

"Jason," Katerina said. "What's happened to you is terrible. I'm here to get you out."

Jason began doubting his perceptive abilities. He'd kept his distance from her, and he'd sensed she'd kept her distance from him. Now here she was standing in front of him, like a merciful saint offering her assistance. Maybe I was wrong about her, he wondered.

"Naharos informed Marianna about your arrest, and she called me. She couldn't come down because she had to take Claira to piano lessons."

"I was about to call my father," he said.

"You shouldn't do that," she hissed. "His health is rapidly declining."

"I had no one else to turn to." He couldn't believe he sounded so helpless.

"Jason what are you saying?" Katerina said in a mellow tone. She stroked his face with both hands.

Her sympathetic eyes caused him to shiver. He wished he were thousands of miles away, in a totally unknown place, a stranger amongst strangers. He wouldn't have to bear the brunt of such humiliation. "I'm fine," he murmured, trying to back off.

"The papers are ready," the officer said. He handed Jason a legal size paper that was headed: 'UNDERTAKING.' He read it from top to bottom. As a condition of his interim release, he had to undertake not to communicate with Crow and to stay at least one-hundred meters from the brothel at Parthenon Avenue. He estimated the Turkish House and the Farmers' Market were more than two hundred meters away from the brothel, and felt relieved. The document set out the date on which he must appear in court to face the charge of 'Break and Enter.' Jason signed it and handed it over to the officer.

"Consider yourself a lucky man," the officer said. "If it weren't for Mrs. Lagos, you would have remained in custody until your trial."

Jason glanced at Katerina and heaved a sigh of appreciation.

"By the way," the officer said, "your first court appearance is Friday, December 14." He handed a copy of the undertaking to Jason. "Make sure you're there on that day."

"Yes, officer," Jason mumbled.

Katerina put her right arm under Jason's left arm and held his left hand with her left hand. "Let's go," she said smiling broadly. "Would you buy me an ice cream?"

Jason smiled back. They crossed the street and walked over to a kiosk, where he bought her a cone-shaped wafer full of vanilla ice cream. As she was licking it, he wondered if her display of affection was genuine. "I'm grateful to you," he said. He suddenly remembered the message she had left for him at the hotel. "You were looking for me? Now that you've found me," he said smiling, "what can I do for you?"

"I see you living alone and my heart hurts," she said. "I know how much love Marianna can give to someone like you. You must make the first move, Jason. Marianna is still in mourning. She's a woman. You will have to show her that you can be a good lover and a good husband."

Jason felt as though somebody had hit him on the head with a heavy iron bar. He cleared his throat for a couple of seconds. Instead of saying 'no', he played her little game for whatever it was worth. Jason wanted to know where this was going. "I think you may be right," he said, feigning a relaxed manner. "First, you must make sure that Naharos knows that I may marry Marianna."

"I can take care of that," she said.

"Good," Jason said. "I have to go to Villa Oasis and see my father."

58

At quarter to two, Wednesday afternoon, on his way to Villa Oasis, Jason stopped by Peta Village Square and looked for Dr. Plato's house. He remembered Dr. Plato telling him that the house was next to the church. He recognized it just as Dr. Plato described: a Mediterranean-style bungalow with ceramic roof and front porch.

Dr. Plato led Jason to the living room. Books and newspapers were strewn all over the place, and classical music played softly from the portable stereo. The sheepdog shook his tail and turned his head sideways.

"Please sit down," Dr. Plato said with a worried look on his face.

Jason was reminded of his father. "Is he alright?"

"I'm afraid not. He's not responding to his treatments."

"Are there any alternative methods?"

"His leukemia has progressed to the stage at which no one and nothing can save him."

Jason felt guilty for spending most of his time away from Villa Oasis. He got up. "I must go," he said.

"Wait a minute," Dr. Plato begged. "I have something to tell you. I have agonized over this since Sunday. I can no longer keep it to myself."

Jason sat down.

Dr. Plato said, "Your brother is not the biological father of the twins, George and Andrew."

"How can you say that?"

"When the twins were six months old, Richard approached me in confidence. He expressed to me his nagging suspicion of Marianna cheating on him. He observed that the twins had none of his characteristics. I tried to alleviate his concerns by telling him that sometimes children do not resemble their parents, that they can inherit characteristics seven generations back. I hated to upset him, but his heart was already in turmoil. Rumours were circulating that Marianna had been flirting with Maximus before she married Richard and he suspected that she'd continued to see Maximus after their wedding."

Jason was anxious to know more. "Then?"

"At that time, I reduced down my medical practice to two days a week and was assisting an obstetrician at a private clinic. Richard had brought Marianna and the twins to the clinic for a routine general checkup. I took blood samples, and on Richard's instructions I performed DNA tests. I found that the twins shared one band with Marianna, but no bands were shared between them and Richard."

Jason was fully familiar with DNA paternity testing, but he was surprised that a clinic in Pafos had the facilities to carry out such procedures. "How accredited is the laboratory that did the tests?"

"You won't believe this, but the level of expertise in that clinic is comparable to Western European and American standards."

Jason knew that a DNA paternity test was the most accurate form of paternity testing. If the DNA patterns between the child and the alleged father do not match on two or more DNA probes, then the alleged father cannot possibly be the biological father of a child. "Did you inform Richard and Marianna of your findings?"

"No one knew about the results of the tests except Richard."

Jason imagined how painful it must have been for Richard, all those years, knowing that the twins came from the sperm of another man. Richard took no steps to divorce Marianna and Jason had no knowledge of any marital difficulties between them. "How did Richard react when he learned that he was not the twins' father?"

"The way every normal person would. He was devastated and refused to believe it. He asked me to repeat the tests, but I declined, fearing that if I got caught I would be sent to prison for a good number of years. Richard came to see me a few days later. His face was full of anger. He was mad at everybody, especially at himself. I was concerned for his mental health. Afraid he might kill himself, I prescribed tranquilizers and sent him home. He visited me again two days later. He was depressed and threatened to kill himself if I didn't do another test."

"He was not prepared to face reality, I suppose," Jason said.

"Yes, that's exactly it," Dr. Plato said. "He blamed himself for asking me to do the tests in the first place. Despite her indiscretions, he continued to love Marianna dearly."

"How do you think Richard was able to cope afterwards?"

"He wasn't! He kept pressing me for a second set of DNA tests. Basically he was fooling himself. Frankly, I felt sorry for him to the point that one day I promised to do a second analysis, but I never carried it out. Instead, I destroyed all the records and told him the next day that the results of the first test were wrong. I lied to him that the second set of tests showed that of the forty-six chromosomes of the children's nucleated cells, half of them came from Marianna and half of them came from him. He was so relieved he began to sob. I hated myself."

"I see," Jason said, his eyes fixed on the floor. "I guess we won't know if he fathered Claira."

"After that experience?"

Dr. Plato had proved his loyalty and dedication to the Mustafa family many times over, more with deeds than words, Jason thought. Yet, without the actual proof, it was difficult to accept the doctor's words unreservedly. "Why tell me about this now?"

"Someone in the Mustafa family must know the truth."

59

Faris lay on the bed, his eyes closed. Jason had never seen him so weak. I never got to know him, he reflected with a sigh.

"He's been asking for you since yesterday," the nurse said. "Jason is here," she whispered in Faris's ear.

Faris opened his eyes. "Is that you, Jason?" he murmured.

Jason touched Faris's hand and felt its coldness. "I'm sorry I couldn't come yesterday," he said. Then he lied, "I was out of town."

"Where's Helena? Call Helena," Faris pleaded in a rumbling voice.

"She's at Villa Mustafa. I'll call her right now," the nurse said, and she picked up the phone.

Jason didn't think it was a good idea to discuss Helena's clandestine activities at such a critical time (especially with the nurse in the room), but he wanted to reassure Faris that things were progressing well. "Helena is doing a fine job," he said. He left it at that.

"I loved your mother dearly," Faris said. His voice was a broken, hard mumble.

Jason felt Faris's hand trembling. "Please relax," Jason said. "This is not the time to discuss the past."

"The past and the present always end up merging," Faris said. "Today is the day."

"Yes."

Tears were falling from the corner of Faris's eyes and his face was as pale as a ripe lemon. "I broke the rules of matrimony."

Jason had never seen Faris cry, not even when Rachel died. Now watching him in such an emotional state, Jason was lost for words. However, his confusion did not come as a surprise, for Jason already knew that Faris had engaged in casual sexual affairs with several women. "That's in the past," Jason said.

"One woman, a special woman to me, bore me a daughter."

Jason was stunned.

"Angela," Faris whispered.

"Angela? You mean, Helena's mother?"

Faris closed his eyes, and Jason thought that Faris had stopped breathing. "Yes," Faris said with closed eyes. "Angela and I ... were lovers for a long time ... until she moved away." His dry lips moved slower. "She stayed a single mother all her life ... because of her love for me."

Jason was speechless. He was angry, embarrassed, pleased; all these sentiments were teeming in his heart at the same time. For a brief moment he wished Faris hadn't told him about his affair because his mind was filled with romantic feelings for Helena. He was mad at his father for taking advantage of Angela, a housemaid who was as vulnerable as any person of lower social status. He was sad that Helena grew up without a father in her life. He was embarrassed over harbouring sexual fantasies about Helena as early as yesterday. He was pleased to learn that Helena was his closest living blood relative in the whole world, apart from Faris. "Does Helena know this?"

"Yes," Faris whispered. "Her mother and I told her six months ago."

Now he understood why Helena had kept a physical and emotional distance from him at the Turkish House. "Why did you keep this a secret from me?"

"The secrets we keep ... become part of ... our individuality."

Jason stood in deep contemplation. He heard hurried steps behind him, and after turning his head he saw Helena.

She walked steadily toward the other side of the bed. She faced Faris and placed her palms on his face.

"I told him," Faris said. "I did as you said."

Tears dripped down Helena's face. Now Jason knew why she had accepted the dangerous mission which Faris had assigned her.

Jason wanted to embrace her, but she was his half sister. This scene was too surreal for him. The air in the room seemed thin to him.

"I love you dad," Helena gasped.

"Jason, please look after your sister," Faris gasped.

Helena lifted her eyes and glanced at Jason. "Forgive me," she said softly. Tears kept rolling down her cheeks. "I learned about this when my mother died." She looked at Faris. "I'm glad you told me. You have no idea how relieved I am." Her words were hushed by a loud sob that pierced Jason's emotional defense and reached into the inner, most sensitive spot of his heart.

Faris raised his hands in the air, signalling to Jason and Helena to come closer. On an impulse, Jason's hands clasped Faris's hand, as if he didn't want him to go. Helena's bent down to hold him.

Jason could almost feel Faris's fight with death. He placed his father's hand slowly by his side and touched his face. It felt cold.

Faris's eyes turned to Helena. "Take good care of … Richard's children," he said.

"I've appointed you … their guardian and trustee … in my will."

Jason saw Helena's surprised expression. "My appointment will upset Marianna," she said.

"I can't trust Marianna … with thirty-five million dollars," Faris said.

How ironic, Jason thought; that the twins will benefit from a man who would have disinherited them had he known Richard was not their biological father. Jason was torn in two: his sense of family honour; and his love for those two pleasant and playful boys. He wondered what a sensible person would do or say at a crucial moment such as this. Both logic and sentiment ran to his aid simultaneously.

What if Dr. Plato was wrong in his DNA analysis? The DNA results were destroyed anyway. Even if Dr. Plato was correct, what could be gained by stigmatizing two innocent boys? God knows how many children grew up that way. There was one very important reason for keeping their illegitimate status buried forever: the twins would grow up to be two Mustafas. These two boys would perpetuate the memory of Richard's name.

Faris stared at Jason. "I left you Villa Mustafa and the surrounding land, including the olive grove." I know you will take good care of this property. Make sure you continue to harvest the olive oil every year. Harvesting the crops of earth is not a hobby; it is a duty of the highest order."

Jason was not expecting Faris's generosity. "But father!" he exclaimed.

Faris interrupted. "There's no time for discussion. I have few words remaining in my life. I've left one half of the shares of Mustafa Holdings to you. The other half is Helena's."

"Marianna? What about Marianna?"

"I left nothing for her."

Jason remembered Kamal's comments about the thirty-five million dollar loan from he Saudis. That was the exact sum of money Faris was leaving in trust for the children. He was tempted to say: *I remember Kamal saying that certain loan documents were deposited with the Saudi lawyers. Is it true that these agreements bind your estate and the estate's beneficiaries?* He had no idea of the exact magnitude of the estate, but he estimated it to be well in excess of two hundred million dollars. If the estate had more than sufficient assets to protect these loans, the Saudis, he anticipated, would have no choice but to respect the specific bequeath for the children's benefit. Yet, he wanted to hear from Faris's own mouth how much his estate was worth.

"Father, forgive me for asking, but how much money do you have?"

"Money? I don't have just money. I own real estate holdings ... here and overseas, and ... I've got ... banking interests."

"That's what I mean. What does everything add up to?"

"I never kept ... close track. But ... I think ... the total net worth ... is ... about two hundred million dollars."

"Kamal claimed that your will was deposited with him and that Makin is the named executor," Jason said. "Is it true?"

"That's the old will," Faris whispered. "Dr. Plato has ... my new will."

Jason never expected to receive anything from his father's estate. When he was a boy, he had felt undeserving of Faris's love. He grew up thinking that way. The love he longed to receive never arrived. He would trade in Villa Mustafa and his share of Mustafa Holdings for an ounce of paternal love. He never heard the sweet words, "I love you, son." How sweet, how wonderful, the phrase would sound if Faris uttered it now.

"Thank you, father." But that was as far as Jason could stretch his words. He felt a force of resistance inside him, pulling him back from opening up his true feelings. The force was so mighty, it was preventing him from forgiving his father and letting go of his bitterness toward him. He longed for love, but now he realized that he was not prepared to receive it. This struggle between father and son was apparently meant to continue even after Faris's death.

His father's bequest of Villa Mustafa to him was a curse! He imagined Marianna's anger, resentment, contempt. *Why pin me against her? Am I to handle his unfinished business? Does he want to punish me one more time?* Worst of all, Jason now felt he had no choice but to deal with all the outstanding issues regarding Mustafa Holdings. Whether he liked it or not, he had to step into Faris's shoes. What he hated most had been thrust upon him: wealth and responsibility. *How can I love him?* Jason wondered.

Faris took a deep breath as if gasping for air. "I'm afraid ..." he murmured and stopped. His gaze was dim. "I'm afraid ... your brother .... Stop looking ... for him."

"I want a moment alone with Jason," Faris murmured. Helena and the nurse left the room.

60

Jason had never felt so close to his father. As he embraced Faris, he felt exactly the same way as when he was a little boy.

Faris struggled to make some room for Jason and signalled for Jason to lie down beside him.

As he lay down beside his father, with his arms around Faris's head, Jason sensed a tremendous force flowing from his father and entering his own body. His father's head was like that of a little helpless boy, who needed all the love a father could give. There he was, Jason, feeling like a father holding onto a helpless child (a child Jason knew was about to die). A sudden indisputable truth tripped his mind at that moment: You cannot feel love unless you are ready to give love. Caught in the reverse role, Jason clung to Faris and managed to cry out: "I love you."

Faris did not respond. A few minutes later, Faris opened his eyes, which were barely three inches from Jason's eyes. "I'm ready to go," he whispered. "I want a proper Muslim funeral."

"Oh, dad," Jason cried, "I don't want you to die."

"Your mother … and Helena's mother … are waiting … for me."

The three words Jason was waiting to hear did not come out.

"Yes," Jason's voice broke, "but I need you, too. We have unfinished things to do, Dad. Games to play, stories to tell, laughter to share, adventures to embark upon, roads to travel together … we haven't done any of these things!"

Faris, barely audible and ever so slowly, said: "We all have … one chance. I hope you'll … accomplish many things with … your own children … when you're a father … God willing."

Jason watched Faris's chest rising and sinking with irregular rhythms. "You're my father!" he cried, trying to salvage whatever precious something might be left. "I need to know that you love me!"

Faris whispered something unintelligible.

Sunrays darted in through the window, wanting to grab a glimpse of a dying man before darkness. Jason looked out the window and realized that the sun was about to set. The room seemed brilliant, as if illuminated by millions of crystals hanging from a giant chandelier. He heard Faris's breathing get heavier, seemingly sinking into a deep haze, and suddenly it stopped.

Jason wondered what it was like to enter the gates of Death. He could feel the stiff body lying there beside him, like a severed tree trunk. The sunrays weren't coming in so brilliantly as before. The room grew darker by the second.

61

Marianna had news. She lifted the phone and dialed Katerina's cellular number, while the nurse left the villa. Katerina answered and Marianna said promptly, "Faris is gone."

"Where?" Katerina asked.

"To hell, I hope."

"He died?"

"Yep."

"Well? You should be happy."

"I'm worried." Marianna hesitated. "Many of Richard's personal items are missing from the library."

"Did you call the police?"

"Not yet. Do you think I should?"

"What good would it do?" Katerina said. "If Faris took them, Jason would have them by now."

"Yes, he probably has. Could you search his hotel room?"

"I don't think Jason is stupid enough to have Richard's things lying around the hotel room."

Marianna gulped down a whole glass of white wine. She had drunk two glasses before she called Katerina, and she was feeling tipsy. "I might as well tell you the really bad news."

"For us or for them?"

"For me."

"If it's bad for you, then it's bad for me."

"The nurse came to see me a few minutes ago. She wasn't sure if she should tell me this. She overheard Faris talking on his death bed to Jason and Helena."

"What did she hear him say?"

"You won't believe this. Helena is the product of his adulterous relationship with one of his maids, a woman named Angela."

"Helena? His daughter?"

"It gets worse."

"Don't do this to me."

"Faris left me nothing! Yes, nothing! He willed to Jason the villa estate and half of the company. The other half of Mustafa Holdings goes

166

to Helena. The nurse heard him say that he set up a thirty-five million dollar trust fund for the children. And guess who will administer the fund?"

"Jason."

"Wrong! Helena."

"Where is the will?"

"Apparently, Dr. Plato has it."

"What?"

"That's right."

"Call Naharos right away!" Katerina cried.

"To do what?"

"Have him arrest Helena for impersonation. She posed as a servant to deceive you."

"I didn't hire her."

"We'll work out the technicalities later."

"This is crazy! Tomorrow I'll be thrown out of this place!"

"Don't worry."

But Marianna was even more anxious. "Please help me."

"Call Naharos, now," Katerina repeated. "And don't tell Maximus that Faris is dead."

"Why not?"

"I'll tell you later," Katerina said.

Other times when she needed her, Katerina was quick to run to her rescue, Marianna remembered. This time, she sensed Katerina's reluctance to intervene. "Fine," she said tensely and hung up.

62

As soon as she finished talking with Marianna, Katerina called her husband. "Have you heard?

"What?"

"Faris died."

"All right," George said. "I'll be home at ten-thirty. We'll discuss it then."

"Why so late?"

"I'm entertaining a British couple who are keen on purchasing a villa from us."

Katerina needed the extra time anyway. She called her parents and told them about Faris's death. She then called K3 and left a message on his voice mail, telling him the same thing. She tried to call Maximus, but his line was busy. I must see him tonight, she decided.

She did some paper work, but her mind was elsewhere and would not concentrate. She waited until nine-thirty and then she wondered if the security guard she had asked to follow the *Long Nile* representative was back from his mission. She called the security office, and sure enough he answered the phone. "I can't speak to you right now," he said, and she sensed that others were listening.

She bristled. "Come to my office right away," she ordered.

It didn't take more than two minutes for the guard to knock on the door of her office.

"Come in and close the door," she said, sitting behind her desk.

"I was afraid to speak to you on the phone," he hesitated. "You may be surprised by the information I gathered."

"Tell me," she uttered impatiently.

The guard sat down. "He had lunch with two other men at St. George restaurant, near Coral Bay beach."

"Who were the other two?"

"Your husband and Nadir Makin."

"My husband?" she gulped and looked around. "And Makin?"

"Yes," the man said softly.

"What time?"

"Shortly before two."

"Did you listen to their conversation?"

"I kept a safe distance to avoid detection. All I could see were their gestures, but I could hear a lot of laughing."

"Who did the driving?"

"Your husband."

"Where did they meet before he drove them there?"

"The man who left the hotel got out of the taxi at the Pafos Harbour. He walked about two hundred feet toward the castle. Your husband's car was parked behind Marianna's Galleries. The man who left the hotel went straight to the car."

"What did they do after lunch?"

"They drove from the restaurant at four-thirty. I followed them. They dropped him off near the Pafos Farmers' Market. I followed him. He entered a brothel on Parthenon Avenue. I waited. At eight-fifteen, he exited the brothel and got into a taxi, which was carrying another passenger in the back. I followed the taxi until it reached the outskirts of Pafos, and then I realized it was heading out of town. They took the main Pafos-Nicosia highway. At that stage, I saw no point in following them and it was getting dark."

"Thank you," Katerina said sternly. "You can go now." She then hesitated. "Stay home tomorrow and relax. You've earned a day off with full pay."

The security man smiled in gratitude, nodded and left. She remembered Maximus, and she started to scratch her legs, pondering her next move. The nails ripped her pantyhose and reached her flesh. *Would he refuse to hand over the documents if he knew that Faris was dead?* She resolved to get hold of the documents that night. She knew he didn't keep a phone in his luxury 'cell'. She called his office line, and he answered.

"We must meet tonight," she said. "Remember to bring the documents."

"It's getting late," he said. "I have to get up early."

"It's very important."

"I'll bring them to your office tomorrow," he said.

"No!" she insisted. "Tonight."

"I can't meet you here at this hour. The monks will start talking."

She remembered the derelict depot at the bottom of the valley. After the rezoning of the land, most of the carob trees were cut to make room for the construction of villas. "I'll wait for you by the carob storehouse. Be there at midnight."

"It's too far away," he said.

"That's the only secluded place in the area."

"As you wish," he said and hung up.

Her husband was supposed to be home in about thirty minutes, she thought. Two minutes later she was in her car heading for her villa.

63

Sadness overwhelmed Jason. The heavy fog that surrounded the compound depressed the hills and the olive grove, as the evening gloom drew closer.

Having promised himself to honour his father's wishes for a Muslim funeral, he must have the body buried within twenty-four hours. The difficulty was that Jason did not think it right for him to take charge of the funeral service which, according to Faris's religion, had to be performed by an Imam, a Muslim religious leader.

The body had to be cleansed by bathing and dressing it in a shroud, and then it had to be prayed for. The rite had to be brief and followed by an interment in an Islamic cemetery. Faris's burial had to be performed as quickly as possible in order to free his soul from his body, which lay rigid before Jason's eyes.

For Faris Mustafa, The Day of Reckoning had arrived and he had to account for his actions. Jason dared not to speculate about the rewards of heaven, or the punishment of hell, that may await his father.

He had no idea how to find an Imam, but he thought of one Muslim who might agree to cleanse Faris's body. He looked at the clock on the wall; it was 9:30. Jason left Faris's bedroom and walked into the kitchen where Helena was going over the list of guests for their father's funeral and calling them, one by one. He picked up the telephone and dialed Makin's residence. His wife, Aisha, answered.

"I have some rather sad news to tell you about my father," Jason said.

"What's the matter?" Aisha queried.

"He passed away two hours ago," Jason announced solemnly.

"Oh, no!" she exclaimed. "I thought he was fine when I saw him on Sunday. It can't be true."

"I can't believe it either," he exhaled. "Is your husband home?"

"No. He's gone to Nicosia for your father's business."

"Do you know when he's coming back?"

"He said he'll return Sunday night, after he picks up someone at Larnaca Airport. But if he learns your father has passed away, I'm sure he will come back sooner. I'll call him."

171

Jason wondered what time Makin had left town. He lied to Aisha, "I called him at the office at seven-thirty-five to tell him about my father's death but he wasn't in."

"That can't be," she said. "He called me from there a few minutes past eight."

If Aisha was telling the truth, then Jason figured Makin left town after Faris's death. Sunset was at 7:28 to be exact, and Faris died shortly before that. "Do you know who the visitor might be?"

"I'm sorry, I don't."

"By the way," Jason said, "I look forward to your presence at the funeral service tomorrow at three in the afternoon. It will take place at the mosque in the Ismet Inonou Piazza."

"I know where it is," Aisha said. "I will tell my husband."

After he hung up, Jason recalled Kamal's fax message. Aziz was due to arrive at Larnaca Airport at five o'clock Sunday night, and Kamal wanted Jason to "be at the airport on time." Jason wondered if Makin informed Faris of his plan to go to the airport to welcome Aziz.

It appeared, at first glance at least, that Makin did not think Jason would be going to the airport. Jason had declined to assume his duties as CEO of Mustafa Holdings, but he had every intention of cooperating with the Saudis. He had given his explicit promise to Kamal to do just that when they met at Villa Oasis on Sunday in Faris's presence. His absence from the airport would signal to the Saudis that he was opposing their plans, and he had no such intentions.

Jason turned to Helena. "I don't know an Imam. We also need to find someone, a Muslim, who will cleanse the body."

Helena gladly offered to assist. "Leave it to me," she said, casually lifting the telephone, apparently eager to demonstrate her connections. In a few minutes, she located and arranged for an Imam. Then, she called another number.

64

Helena's tone—while she spoke on the telephone—was so affectionate that Jason wondered if she knew the person beyond the bounds of mere acquaintance. This thought came and passed quickly through his mind and was replaced with the more pressing matters of the moment.

After she hung up, Helena turned to Jason and said, "Ismail can be here to look after father's body in three hours, perhaps earlier."

Jason said, "Makin is out of town. It seems he plans to pick up Aziz at the airport on Sunday."

"But tonight is Wednesday. Why would Makin leave three days early?" Helena said.

"Do you think he's aware of father's death?"

"I'm not sure. The nurse notified Dr. Plato and Marianna. I don't know who else."

"What are you suggesting?" Jason asked.

"Father told me that 110,000 dollars was missing from the company's vault the day of Richard's disappearance."

"Why tell me now?"

"He didn't want you to know about it until the time came."

"There was a plan, I suppose."

"The only people who had keys to the vault were father and Richard."

"Maybe Richard took the money."

"Or worse. Someone might have forced him to remove it at gun point."

"Or worse yet. His killers took the key and then removed the money."

"Yes, it's possible."

"Did Makin know about the money in the vault?" Jason asked.

"That's what bothers me. I don't really know. It's his movements that cause me some concern. When Richard disappeared, he removed Richard's architectural plans and put them in his office. Now, he's gone to Nicosia."

"I need the keys to Makin's office," said Jason.

Helena queried, "What are you looking for exactly?"

"In his diary, Richard had written a note. He planned a meeting at five in the afternoon with Makin and a client to finalize the Delphi Villa specifications."

"They have security there, usually a man at night."

Jason intentionally avoided addressing Helena's security concerns. "Do you know how much money is now in the vault?"

"Father withdrew $90,000 and gave it to me. I put it in the bank to use it for anticipated expenses." Helena paused. "He gave me a Power of Attorney, authorizing me to get the rest of the money, if I so decide. He left $50,000 in the vault deliberately. There are five hundred bills, one hundred dollars each. He photocopied them all. Do you want to see the photocopies?"

"Yes, please."

Helena walked to the bedroom and came back with a legal size brown envelope. She opened it and pulled out the sheets with the bills printed on them.

"How do we know that in fact he had $50,000 dollars in the vault?"

"I saw it this morning."

"Really?"

"Father had the vault checked every morning by the security attendants in my presence. They and I reported to him following each inspection. I sign in and out."

"Are you the only one with signing authority?"

"Yes."

"So if money goes missing, you'd be the main suspect."

"Yes, except that I can't gain entry to the executive offices on the fifth floor without first checking in at the security counter on the main floor. I think the offices are wired with surveillance cameras."

If Richard had been abducted and killed by robbers, Jason thought, they would have taken all the money. "Give me an idea of the layout on the fifth floor."

"Makin's office is sandwiched between father's and Richard's corner offices. Father's office is on the west side. There is a fire exit on the east side, by Richard's office."

"Who else has the key to father's office?"

"Makin," Helena answered.

"How do you know?"

"Father told me."

"Who occupies the other floors?"

"Secretaries, drawing booths, accounting, marketing and sales."

"Do you have the key to Makin's office?"

"I have all the keys now."

"I have an idea," Jason said.

Helena listened attentively.

"Call security over there. Tell them that Faris died tonight and that we're going to his office to get some cash from the vault to cover funeral expenses. When we arrive, you keep the security men busy, and I'll search Makin's office."

Helena raised her eyebrows. "You forgot about the cameras."

"To hell with the cameras! Father appointed me the CEO of Mustafa Holdings. Remember? I'm in charge now!" he barked.

Jason saw Helena taken aback. "Why the change of attitude?" she asked.

"You shouldn't be that surprised. Yesterday you told me to face my demons. I'm doing just that. It's up to me to choose how to deal with my experiences with Faris. He's now gone, unrepentant it seems, and I have to move on."

Helena, who was even more startled than before, gave him a questioning look.

"A CEO may visit his offices at any time," Jason said calmly. "Besides, if Makin has nothing to hide, he won't mind my intrusion."

"Why do you need me to be there, then?" Helena asked.

"To open the vault and count the money."

"The Power of Attorney I had is no longer valid now that father is dead."

He remembered Faris telling them that Helena was one of his executors. "I need your presence as a witness in case the vault is now empty. Besides, I doubt if the security men will question the validity of the Power of Attorney."

He dialed Dr. Plato's telephone number.

Dr. Plato answered with a soft, "Yes?"

"This is Jason. How are you, doctor?"

"I am trying to cope. Please accept my most heartfelt condolences."

"Thank you. The funeral service is at three tomorrow afternoon, at the mosque, near the Pafos Farmers' Market."

"I'll be there," Dr. Plato said with a broken voice. "We shall all meet afterwards at Villa Mustafa to read your father's will, which I have."

"Do you mind telling me who the executors of my father's estate are?"

"The three of us; you, Helena and I."

"Can I put you on hold for a second?"

Jason spoke to Helena. "We can use the authority of the will to gain entry at the offices."

"I've got reservations, but so be it," Helena said. "Who'll look after the body?"

"I need your presence at the Villa Oasis tonight," Jason said to Dr. Plato. "I must step out for a couple of hours."

"I'll be right over."

Jason remembered the separate gate telephone entry system for Villa Oasis "Ring me from the gates when you arrive?"

"It won't be necessary. I have the gate entry code and a set of keys to the villas."

"Sure." He paused. "Could you please bring the will to me?" Jason asked.

"I'm sorry," Dr. Plato responded. "The will must remain here until it is read after the funeral. I'll have to abide strictly by your father's instructions."

"As you wish."

When Jason hung up, Helena took the phone from him. "I have something important to do and a few more names to call," she said. "I'll be ready in ten minutes."

"Are you going to call the building security?" Jason asked her.

"No. I'd prefer it if we show up impromptu."

65

Jason and Helena got into Helena's Toyota Starlet 1.5 diesel and drove toward the Pafos Harbour, heading for the offices of Mustafa Holdings Inc., which were located less than two hundred meters from the harbour's restaurant strip. On their way, he briefed her on the events that followed after she had left the Turkish House on Tuesday.

They parked in the seaside tourist zone behind the *Theoskepasti Church*. It took them less than ten minutes to reach the building, a stuccoed five-storey structure competing for prominence with the Venetian Castle towering above the coastline across the luminous waters of the harbour.

Helena rang the bell, and a man of about forty, overweight in a green uniform opened the glass door. The sweater he was wearing read: 'MH Security'.

"Hello Helena," he said. "What brings you here at this hour?"

"Are you the only man on duty?" Helena asked.

"Yes."

"Mr. Faris Mustafa passed away three hours ago. This is his son Jason," she said gesturing at Jason.

"Hello sir," the man said, shaking Jason's hand. "My condolences."

"Thank you," Jason said, lips stiff, staring at the ground.

"We're here to get some cash from the vault," Helena said. "We need it for the funeral."

"I'm sorry," the security man said. "I have firm instructions to prohibit entry to anyone, including you and Jason."

Jason responded, "I'm the CEO of this company now. You've probably heard of my appointment."

"What's a CEO?" he asked.

"He's the boss," Helena interjected. "Everyone in the company was supposed to be notified."

"I'm sorry," the guard said apologetically, as if he did something wrong. "Mr. Makin has given me my instructions."

"Mr. Makin takes his instructions from me," Jason said calmly.

"That's not what he told me."

177

"I'm telling you now," Jason insisted.

"No, sir," the security man countered.

Jason tried to get in, but the security man blocked his entry. "I would hate to use my gun," he warned.

Helena intervened. "Please, Jason," she pleaded. "Let's go." She took him by the arm, and he didn't resist her. They walked across the street and stood there for a few seconds.

"Obviously, Makin has moved ahead of us," Jason said fuming. He suddenly thought of Nicholas. "I know of a friend who may be able to help us," he said.

He flipped through his small notebook, borrowed Helena's cell phone and called Nicholas's home number. A female voice answered the call. Jason asked, "Is Nicholas in?"

"No," she said.

"Are you his wife," Jason asked.

"Yes, and who are you?"

"Jason. You treated my wound. Do you remember me?"

"Yes, of course!" she said brightly. "How are you?"

"Fine, thanks."

"Nicholas is on a site tonight, but I can get hold of him. Give me your number and I'll get him to call you."

Jason gave her Helena's cellular number, and a couple of minutes later the phone rang.

"My friend, how are you?" Nicholas asked enthusiastically.

"Listen," Jason said hurriedly. "I need your help."

"Anything for you."

"I want you to find me five able men who can be employed as security officers right away."

"Where shall I send them?"

"Do you know where the Mustafa building is located?"

"The one by the harbour?"

"Yes. I'm outside the building. I want them to come here with a van and a good locksmith."

"Nothing illegal, I hope," Nicholas said.

"The building belongs to my father, who died a few hours ago. I have the authority to hire new personnel and change the locks."

"I'll bring my men down in ten minutes," Nicholas said. "Stay put."

Nicholas and his men arrived promptly. They parked their blue van on the street and got out. Jason and Helena greeted them, and Jason briefed Nicholas on the situation.

"I think I've seen you before," Helena said to Nicholas. "Aren't you the man who has that restaurant by the Farmers' Market?"

"That's my hobby," Nicholas smiled. Suddenly his face turned stern. "Stay here until we secure the building," he said.

Then he walked across the street to the front entrance of the Mustafa building with his men and rang the bell. When the security man opened the door, Nicholas had a chat with him, and Jason saw the security man nodding. Next he saw Nicholas smiling and heard laughter. Nicholas waived at Jason and Helena, signalling them to approach the entrance.

Jason was taken by surprise. *There was going to be no resistance, no trouble.*

"He's my second cousin," Nicholas explained, pointing to the security man. "We play poker every Sunday."

"I see," said a smiling Jason.

"He'll go home now," Nicholas said. He showed Jason a piece of paper with numbers and capital letters scribbled on it. "Write them down," he said. "This is the security code to access the building and this is the password that is registered with the alarm company. You can use them for now until we change the code number and notify the alarm company of the new password."

The security man handed the keys to Nicholas and left.

"From now on he works for me at the restaurant," Nicholas said smiling broadly.

Jason was astounded. "I hope he's not going to be in trouble for co-operating with us," Jason said to Nicholas in private.

"He had no choice really," Nicholas said. "I told him if he didn't do as I said, I would turn him in for working as a security guard without a proper license. He has a long criminal record. I know this for a fact because I've saved his ass many times."

Nicholas's men changed the locks and stood by the entrance as Nicholas, Jason and Helena proceeded inside the building. Nicholas then gave instructions to one of his security men to disable the internal surveillance system.

66

The place was quiet. They got into an elevator that took them to the fifth floor and passed through a large reception area. Helena opened Faris's corner office. It was carpeted and spacious. Flashing neon lights from the taverns to the west of the building penetrated the large windows and reflected on the white walls. Jason noticed how quiet the office was despite the heavy traffic on the street below. The density and movement of the traffic down there at this hour wasn't unusual for this tourist area, but the pedestrian walkway edging the semicircular harbour was almost empty.

Nicholas sat on one of the leather chairs and lit a cigarette.

"I'd prefer that you come close when I open the vault," Helena said to him. "You've got to verify the count and initial the ledger."

"Sure," Nicholas said and stood by the vault.

Jason watched as Helena turned the handles. He heard a breaking noise and saw the vault wide open.

Helena stood still. "It's empty," she said.

Jason took a fleeting look. The shelves were bare. He faced Nicholas. "Please make some notes." He then turned to Helena. "How much did you say was in there?" Without waiting for an answer, he read the ledger for himself: "$50,000."

With Nicholas busily writing notes, Jason unlocked Makin's office and went inside. Helena followed.

It was smaller than Faris's office, but packed with more furnishings and the walls were painted in brighter colours. A stereo on the credenza was at low volume, and Jason heard Arabic tunes. On one of the four walls, there were mounted layers of drawers six feet high, wide enough to fit architectural plans placed flat down. Each drawer was labelled with a different letter of the alphabet.

"Look for anything that might belong to Richard and put it in the corner," he said to Helena. "Start with the desk."

She pointed at a humidor that lay on the credenza. "Any cigars in there?" she asked.

Jason knew why she asked this question. He remembered the cigars he'd seen among Richard's items at the Turkish House. He opened

180

the box and saw at least fifteen Monte Cristo cigars, No. 4. He wondered whether Richard's cigars came from the same box. He took the humidor with the cigars inside and placed it in the corner. "We'll take this," he said.

Helena struggled with the credenza. "I can't open it," she said. "It's locked."

Taking from his knapsack a small crow bar, Jason inserted its forked end into the crack and pulled hard. It took a few seconds, but finally the door snapped open.

Inside the cabinet, were three cheque books with three different bank accounts. Two of the accounts belonged to local banks. The third account was with a Panamanian bank. He put them next to the humidor. Next, he found a stack of envelopes. He began to open them, one by one. Some of them contained love letters addressed to Richard from 'Mythic Blue.' In a separate bundle, a large envelope contained a birthday card. It read: "To my dearest and closest friend, I wish the happiest of birthdays and prosperity beyond your wildest imagination. From: George Lagos." There was no mention of the intended recipient.

Jason guessed it would take him at least two hours to look through all the envelopes. He collected and placed them all in the corner among the other items he planned to take with him to the Turkish House.

He saw a photo album and opened it. In it were photographs of Makin and his wife with friends. A photograph caught Jason's attention. It showed Makin, Aisha, Lagos and Katerina dining at a place that looked like a village tavern. The back of the photo read "September 2001."

Jason's eyes widened. "Come here," he said to Helena. In his hands he had a photograph.

"They seem to be having a good time," she said.

"This man," he said pointing his finger, "is Crow the Butcher."

Makin, Crow and another unidentified man were being hugged and kissed by three women. "The background has the same art that I saw hanging on the walls of the brothel," he said.

"Why do you think Faris didn't voice any of his concerns about Makin to us?" Helena asked.

"That's a good question, and I hate to speculate." As soon as he said that, he stopped and touched his head. It occurred to him that all the records of Mustafa Bank (Cyprus) International were in Nicosia. He's up to something sinister, he thought. "The bank records, the records!" Jason shouted. "We want those records preserved."

"I've already thought about it," Helena said. "As soon as Faris died, I arranged with my people in Nicosia to get an ex-parte court order, sealing the bank, freezing its financial assets and changing the locks of the bank building. I also hired security guards for the entrances, and two of my men are now looking for Makin with instructions to follow him and record his movements and actions."

Jason was lost for words.

"The court order is temporary and it expires in seven days," Helena continued, "unless it's renewed."

"But how could you get a court order so fast without much evidence?" Jason uttered in disbelief.

"Very simple," Helena said. "Faris is the only director of the holding company that holds the shares of Mustafa Bank (Cyprus) International. The holding company is set up in Cyprus as an offshore entity. According to the law, the minimum number of directors that an offshore company should have is one, and there's no maximum. With Faris dead, there is no acting director. An Affidavit explains to the court that without the appointment of replacement directors, the interests of the bank stakeholders are in jeopardy."

She's brilliant, Jason admired. "How many directors does the bank have?" he asked.

"Faris said that there were only three: Richard, Makin and himself," Helena responded. "According to the bank's by-laws, for loans over $100,000 at least two directors must sign for approval."

"We must get the bank books," Jason said.

"I already have those, and I'm in the process of reviewing them."

"Can you do that despite the court order?"

"Why not? The court had ordered a freeze of the bank's *financial* assets. Prior to his death, Faris (suspecting some irregularities) gave me power of attorney. This authorized me to gain possession of the bank's books and other records for audit. On Tuesday evening, after I left the Turkish House, I went to Nicosia with Ismail and two other men in a van, removed the most important records and books and brought them to my apartment in Pafos."

"Nobody noticed?" Jason asked curiously.

"Faris took care of that. He fired the security firm hours before we arrived there. We then disconnected the alarm system."

"Have you found anything important?"

"I'm working on it."

Jason put the album and the three chequebooks in his knapsack. He then remembered to look for the Delphi project. His eyes didn't take long to locate the letter D on the shelves. He opened the drawer and began to examine the architectural plans inside. After eleven plans, he found the project Delphi.

The front cover set out general information, such as the company's logo, building code requirements, soil conditions, civil engineering instructions, building permit directions, and framing notes. Jason counted sixteen sheets. Sheet number two showed an artist's impression of the front elevation and beside it the first floor plan was revealed. It featured an extravagant porch and wide window arches, an elegant upper balcony and a red tiled roof. Jason could not help admiring Richard's creativity. The design had a striking Mediterranean look. The plan detailed the formal living areas flanking the foyer, which was adorned with entry columns and arched window treatments. The central family room offered a fireplace. Sheet three offered a spectacular view of the rear elevation, featuring patio and pool.

Jason flipped the sheets in a hurry, looking for the name of the owner, but couldn't find one. Most of the information was technical, showing the basement plan, the first floor plan, the second floor plan, internal elevations, floor framing, external elevations, and the electrical plan. What attracted his attention most was the basement plan. It had a huge space, divided into compartments that extended underground far beyond the main floor plan. Jason wondered why. He rolled the plans and placed them on the floor.

Three seconds later, one of Nicholas's guards appeared at the door. "The police are on their way," he said. "What should we do?"

67

On her way home, Katerina stopped by a 24-hour supermarket and bought two bottles of expensive champagne. She planned to get Lagos drunk and she had good reason: Faris's passing. Her plan was to extract from her husband all the information she could get about his involvement with Makin and the *Long Nile* representative. Close to midnight, she was going to come up with a pretext (that she needed a prescription from the pharmacy) so she could drive to the carob storehouse, the place where she and Maximus had agreed to meet.

While driving through all the shortcuts, she received Marianna's call.

"A few minutes ago," Marianna said, "I saw Dr. Plato arrive at Villa Oasis. I went to him as he was walking toward the villa and asked him if Faris had left his will with him."

Katerina was surprised by Marianna's boldness. "What did he say?" Katerina asked.

"That he had Faris's will in his house and asked me to wait until tomorrow. Then he hurried over to Villa Oasis. When he came in the door, Jason and Helena left together."

With Dr. Plato away from his house, now was the perfect time to grab Faris's will, Katerina reflected. "Have you called Naharos yet?"

"I'll call him right now."

"Don't tell Maximus," Katerina said.

"Okay," Marianna said, and Katerina pressed the end button of her cellular phone.

She then stopped her car to think. She had to change her plans. She debated whether to call K3 or go straight home to speak to Lagos about Faris' will. Destroying a person's will carried a maximum punishment of ten years in prison, she thought, but someone had to do it before Dr. Plato had the opportunity to turn it over to Jason and Helena.

K3 was in Nicosia, a two-hour drive away, and she needed someone to act fast. She didn't trust Lagos with her family's secrets, but Faris's will was a different matter. Besides, Lagos was good at breaking in, and he knew exactly where to find Dr. Plato's house. With the Will destroyed and Jason dead, Faris's estate would fall into the hands of

Marianna's children, the closest next of kin to Faris. She thought of Helena as a possible contestant and claimant, but she was pleased when she remembered Marianna's words that Helena's mother was also dead. She knew that DNA paternity testing could be performed without the mother, but she knew of no case where a DNA test could be done with the putative father dead.

68

Marianna was on the phone again. "I want Helena arrested and charged," she said to Naharos.

"Helena? Is that the maid?"

"Well, she was hired as a maid—"

"What did she do?"

"Faris died a few hours ago. The nurse told me that while lying on his deathbed, Faris confessed that Helena was his daughter."

"That's interesting."

"She also stands to inherit a big chunk of his estate."

"How do you know?"

"The nurse told me."

"But I still need a reason to arrest her."

"She looked so natural, I know. Many of Richard's items are missing from the library. I think she took them."

"Has anyone seen her stealing?"

"No."

"I can't charge someone on mere suspicions. She might be innocent."

"She and Jason left Villa Oasis a few minutes ago."

"I wonder what those two are up to."

"Me, too."

"Get ready. I'll pick you up in twenty minutes."

It was a cool night, and Marianna dressed appropriately. She then called the maid's quarter. The elderly maid answered. "I'll be going out for a few hours," Marianna said. "Could you stay in the house while I'm gone. The children are in bed."

"I'll be over in five minutes," the maid said.

Naharos arrived on time.

"My officers were able to locate Helena's car and are now looking for her in the tourist district of the harbour," Naharos said to Marianna as soon as she closed the passenger door of his unmarked cruiser.

"If she knows she's being followed by the police, she may destroy or hide Richard's things," Marianna uttered.

"Leave the police work to us, please," Naharos said politely.

"She shouldn't get away."

They were cruising along the Tombs of the Kings Avenue, the main road between Coral Bay and Pafos, heading for the harbour when Naharos received a radio call. "Someone spotted them near the Mustafa building," a woman's voice said.

Naharos turned to Marianna. "Do you have the telephone number of the offices over there?"

"Yes. I also know the number of the security desk."

"He handed her a phone. "Please call them for me."

"This is Marianna," she said. "Are you the security?"

"Yes, why?"

"It's the security man," she said to Naharos.

"Ask him if he's alone in the building," Naharos said.

"Are you alone?"

"No."

"He said no," Marianna said.

"Who else is in the building?" she asked.

"It's none of your concern."

"He won't tell me," she said to Naharos.

Naharos grabbed the phone. "This is the chief of police," Naharos shouted. "I order you to lock the doors and prohibit anyone from leaving the building until I arrive."

Naharos pressed hard on the accelarator. He passed the Tombs of the Kings, reached the intersection of Apostle Paul Street and The Tombs of the Kings Avenue, turned right and drove about five hundred meters. He found a spot near the Mustafa building and parked. He radioed the police for reinforcements and turned to Marianna. "Stay in the car. If she's there, I'll bring her to you for an off-the-cuff chat."

Marianna was pulling her hair. "Is there any way you can find out what they're doing in there?"

"Relax," Naharos responded. "I don't even know if they're in the building. It won't take long."

69

George Lagos was lying on the chesterfield with his shorts on, watching the results of the day's horse races on television. "Get up," Katerina said.

Lagos seemed too comfortable to move. "You sound annoyed," he said, eyes still fixed on the screen.

"Faris is dead. He left a will, and Dr. Plato has it. Marianna is left out of his estate. The worst news is that Helena turned out to be his daughter, and he's left her a sizable portion of his assets."

"You're not serious."

She threw her purse at him. "Get up, damn it!"

Lagos stood up with lighting speed. "What do we do?"

"Get dressed. We must get hold of that will!"

"I don't even know where it is."

"You're not listening. I said Dr. Plato has it. Go over to his house now and grab it!"

"How?"

"You know how."

"Do you expect me to walk across the village square?"

"You simply break in from the rear of the house and get it. You're good at this type of work. Remember?"

"It's not that easy. I don't want to fight with an old man."

"He's not in the house right now."

"He may have stored it away. How do I know where to look? Are you crazy?"

"Dr. Plato is a messy gerontologist. He has a reputation for that. Papers are strewn all over his place. The man is a lousy organizer."

"That's even worse," he murmured. "What if I don't find it?"

"We can think of something else, if and when that time comes."

"I'll need to wear a mask and gloves, and someone will have to give me a ride to the outskirts of the village." He paused. "Wait, I think I have everything I need. Give me half an hour to get ready."

"Good. I'll drop you off, and I'll pick you up from the same spot at twelve thirty."

"Do you think it will take that long?"

"You might need the extra time to search around."

"Right."

He disappeared into the basement and came back thirty minutes later, fully attired for the job. Katerina noticed a bulge in his waist. "What are you carrying?" she asked.

He lifted his black sweater and stood there like a cowboy. "Just in case," he said.

"You're not going to use that I hope!"

"Only to scare intruders."

"No, no, put that away."

"Either I take it with me, or you do the job yourself."

Katerina dropped Lagos off at the edge of an agricultural road, half a kilometer from the outskirts of Peta Village. She then drove slowly through a muddy trail, went down a small valley, reached the Olive Storehouse and waited. It was eleven thirty-five, and the area was serene. It was not as dark as she thought, for the moon came from behind the hills and she could see the long shadows of trees shaking in the wind. She was tempted to get out and stretch her legs, but she hesitated when she noticed a crawling creature disappear into the thick underbrush. She feared the place might be infested with the killer Blunt-nosed Viper, and her body filled with shivers.

70

Jason lifted his knapsack by the straps and hung it around his right shoulder. He took the large items that wouldn't fit inside the knapsack and put them into a large nylon bag. The police were on their way, and his number one priority was to ensure everything he found in Makin's office was smuggled outside to a safer place. He thought of the Turkish House when Nicholas came closer, seemingly anxious to assist. "Can you suggest a way to hide this stuff from the police?" he asked Nicholas.

Nicholas was pressing his jaw with both palms.

"It's important evidence," Jason said. "We could leave it here, but we don't know what may happen to it once we leave the building."

A guard hurried into Makin's office. "The police are parking their cruisers," he said.

Jason wished he had an antacid tablet, but he remembered leaving the whole pack at Villa Oasis.

Helena and Nicholas stood in Makin's office, perplexed. Then Helena said, "The police can't enter the building without a search warrant, and I doubt if they have one at this hour."

"They'll find some other excuse for searching," Nicholas said, and Jason figured he must know from his past experience as a policeman.

Looking outside the window, Jason saw six police cruisers parked alongside the pavement. A dozen officers were patrolling the street. The window offered panoramic views of the harbour and the castle at the far end. "What's that slow-moving thing?" he asked Nicholas.

"The police boat. Four special harbour officers usually man it."

Helena said, "I think we've got three options. We can walk out without the stuff; we can take the things with us and refuse to turn them over to the police; or we can hide them in the basement, by the boiler room, and come back for them later."

Every second seemed like an hour, and Jason had to decide quickly.

"I hate to tell you this," Nicholas said, "but the only way to preserve these things is to smuggle them outside."

"How do you do that?" Jason asked.

Nicholas walked over to Makin's desk and lifted a blank letterhead from a tray that lay by the edge of the desk. "Do you have anything with your father's signature on it?" he asked Jason.

Helena opened her purse and took out the power of attorney. "I have this," she said.

Nicholas examined it. "I must borrow it," Nicholas said. "I'll give it back to you later."

"What do you have in mind?" Jason asked.

"Do you remember the Trojan horse?" Nicholas said nonchalantly.

Not another Greek fable, Jason pleaded inside his mind. "Yes."

"The Greeks left the Trojan horse outside the walls of Troy, and the Trojans took it inside. We'll do the opposite."

"I don't understand," Jason said.

"They," he said pointing to the police outside, "don't know who hired me to guard the building. I'll simply go to them and tell them that you and Helena forced your way in without my guards' permission and that I need their help to get you out."

"What do we do with these things?" Jason asked.

"Leave them with me." Nicholas took the knapsack and the nylon bag. "I'll make sure they're delivered to you tomorrow, or you can pick them up from my restaurant." Before proceeding down the hall to the elevator, Nicholas said, "Stay here. I will need a few extra seconds."

Lack of control unnerved Jason, for he had to rest his blind faith on Nicholas. He sighed and smiled at the same time.

"When the police arrive up here," Nicholas said, "I want you to put up a bit of resistance to make it appear natural."

"Very well," Helena said, her hands holding her waist nervously.

While waiting on the fifth floor, Jason turned to Helena. "If they arrest you, decline to make a statement."

"I was just going to tell you the same thing. Where are you going to sleep tonight?"

"Assuming Naharos doesn't find some excuse to keep me locked up, I hope to be back at Villa Oasis to release Dr. Plato."

"Maybe you should call him now and let him know what's happening," Helena suggested, handing Jason her cellular phone.

After Dr. Plato answered, Jason said to him, "It took us a little longer than we thought. You must be tired."

"Not at all," Dr. Plato responded with a trembling voice.

"We're at the Mustafa building, on the fifth floor to be exact."

"You couldn't wait to assume your duties ..."

Jason sensed that something was wrong. "What's the matter?" he asked.

"I can't stand it anymore. I'm alone talking to my best friend in a monologue that reminds me of some of my psychotic patients."

"But I thought Ismail would be coming over to cleanse and dress my father's body."

"He came, did what he had to do and left."

"Please don't despair," Jason pleaded. "We'll be back soon." He was tempted to brief him about the latest events, but he changed his mind. "Try to rest in the living room."

"I presume what you're doing is crucially important," Dr. Plato murmured.

"Yes, it is."

"You should know that Naharos, the police chief, called here a few minutes ago, asking to know if it's true that your father died."

"That's all he wanted to know?"

"No. He also asked to speak to you, and I told him I was expecting you to be here soon."

"Thank you. I'll arrive as soon as I can." He felt the urge to offer Dr. Plato some words of consolation. "Time is the best doctor for all of us," he said.

"Time is the best doctor, but some people are never cured," Dr. Plato responded.

71

Katerina had to kill time while waiting for Maximus. Anxious to know what happened after they last spoke, she used her cellular phone to call Marianna.

"Did you call Naharos?"

"I'm waiting in his car, outside the Mustafa building."

"What's happening?"

"The building's security manager has asked Naharos's help to throw Jason and Helena out of the building, and he's gone inside with a couple of his men."

Katerina wondered what Jason and Helena were after. "Make sure they don't take anything with them."

"I'll tell that to Naharos."

"Good. Dr. Plato is probably still at Villa Oasis," Katerina said.

"Naharos called the villa a few minutes ago, pretending that he wanted to speak to Jason."

"And?"

"He spoke to Dr. Plato of course. He said that he expected Jason to be back soon."

"How soon?"

"I don't know."

"Call me back when you have more news," Katerina said. As she spoke, she saw a car's headlights and recognized the sound of the car's engine in the quiet of the darkness.

72

The elevator door opened, and Jason saw Naharos, Nicholas and two other policemen step into the corridor.

"So you're refusing to leave the premises, eh?" Naharos chastised Jason.

"Yes, he is!" Nicholas pretended to be upset. "We've told them that they have no business occupying Mr. Mustafa's office." He pulled out a piece of paper, and Jason saw the letterhead of Mustafa Holdings Inc with some writing on it. "Mr. Mustafa hired me with specific instructions not to allow anyone in his office without his permission," Nicholas said pointing at the letterhead.

"We're looking for his personal Qur'an," Jason said. "I need it for tomorrow's prayers." His heart begged for God's forgiveness.

"Is that a crime?" Helena asked Naharos.

"You keep quiet," Naharos said staring at her. "You're coming downstairs. I need to talk to you alone. As for you," he said looking at Jason, "if it weren't for your father's death, I would have arrested you for breach of the peace. Your trial is coming up, remember?"

Nicholas pulled out a pair of handcuffs and stepped in between Jason and Naharos. "With your permission," he said to Naharos, "I'll handcuff him and take him outside."

"Do that," Naharos said, and Jason sensed that Naharos took pleasure in seeing him humiliated once more.

"Let's go," Nicholas said, pushing Jason inside the elevator.

"Take this woman downstairs to the lobby," Naharos ordered his two officers. "She is not to be released until I have a chance to question her."

"Am I being arrested?" Helena protested as the policemen took her by the arms.

"You may be," Naharos shot back, slapping his leg with his baton.

They all got in the elevator and landed on the main floor.

As Nicholas was ushering Jason outside the main entrance, he turned to Naharos and said: "I'll be back in a minute."

"Tell him to go straight to the villa or I'll arrest him," Naharos shouted.

"Did you hear that?" Nicholas yelled at Jason, loud enough for Naharos to take notice of the caution.

Jason nodded, and Nicholas removed the handcuffs. As he was walking away, Jason noticed Marianna cocooned inside Naharos's car. The window was rolled down, and as soon as they collided on each other's glances, she turned her face away.

73

Katerina remained in her car. She watched as Maximus parked his car alongside hers, got out and walked over to her window.

"What on earth happened?" Maximus uttered with a yawn.

"Did you bring the documents?" Katerina asked.

"Yes, they're in the car."

"Give them to me, please."

He strolled to his Land Rover and came back with two thick envelopes.

"Here," he said handing them to Katerina. "Are you happy now?"

Katerina couldn't wait to open the envelopes and inspect the documents. She turned on a flashlight and went over them, one by one. "Thank you," she murmured.

"What's going on? Something is troubling you I think."

"Many things have been troubling me lately, including this." She pointed to the envelopes.

"Well. I have my troubles, too," said Maximus. "I must get going." The moon illuminated the sweat grains on Maximus's forehead.

"Wait," she said. "Don't worry. I won't destroy the papers until the deal is finalized."

He stopped. "I hope so. Modestos won't talk to me."

"Why not?"

"I caught him in bed last night … with a visiting male student. When I reprimanded him, he became belligerent."

"This too shall pass," she said, trying to alleviate his concerns.

"I'm convinced he knows too much about my own affairs."

"Promote him, and then send him to Nicosia to teach."

"He may try to undermine me."

"You worry a lot."

"That's easy for you to say."

Katerina turned her mind to her own plans. "I heard rumours that Faris has only a few hours to live, if not minutes."

"Well, we both knew his days were numbered."

"Yes, but now I learn that Helena, the maid, stands to inherit half his fortune. His will leaves some money for the children, but the bulk of the estate goes to Jason."

"I guess that's it," Maximus said dropping his shoulders.

"We're almost there now. What's the matter?"

Looking at the moon, he said, "Things are happening so fast, so soon. The unknown bothers me."

"Someone will take care of Aziz on Sunday," she said. "You must take care of Jason now before Faris dies."

"Now? It's impossible. I don't even know where to find him."

"He's somewhere in town with Helena. Very soon he'll be back at Villa Oasis."

"It's a very risky proposition. How do I know he's not there already?"

"But that's the idea. You take care of him while he's inside the villa."

"I'm not going inside. If I do anything, it has to be done from a safe distance."

"How?"

"I would have to use my shotgun."

"Then use it."

"It's not that simple."

"You could do it from behind the walls of the villa."

"It will be too dark inside. I won't be able to see him."

"He has to undress, take a shower, read and then sleep." Katerina had no idea about Jason's routine before bedtime, but she had to come up with something persuasive. She hoped Jason would stay up all night, keeping vigil over his dead father.

Katerina thought of reminding him about the money he stood to lose if he didn't kill Jason, but she realized that might not work. "He's been trying to seduce Marianna, you know."

Maximus looked the other way. "Marianna is in love with me."

"Things change."

"I'll see what I can do," he said and walked over to his car.

74

After he left the Mustafa building, Jason pondered whether he should walk to Helena's car and wait. He sensed that he was being followed. Naharos's command was to go straight to Villa Oasis or face arrest. He felt like a kite entangled on hydro cables, spiralling around at the whim of the wind. The prospect of Helena being confined and interrogated shadowed his steps. He feared for her safety. Would she yield under pressure and reveal the whereabouts of Richard's items? Would she tell Naharos everything?

His faith in Helena's prudence provided Jason with some confidence during these otherwise dim developments. Now, with Marianna on the scene, he didn't know what to expect. This air of uncertainty—coupled with the fact that the items he had found in Makin's office were still lying around the Mustafa building—pelted him with feelings of helplessness, with which he was all too familiar.

The Delphi Villa Project lingered in his mind. The villa that Richard had designed was perhaps Richard's last job. Richard's diary notes placed Makin and a client in a meeting with Richard at 5:00 p.m. on April 11, 2001. Apparently, Makin was Faris's right hand man, but Jason was in the dark about Makin's role in the Delphi project. The items that Jason had found in Makin's office pointed to several unanswered questions.

How close was Makin's affiliation with Lagos and Katerina? What was the reason for his acquaintance with Crow the Butcher? Why was he in possession of the three cheque books? Did the cigars that were found in Richard's personal items come from Makin's humidor? And what was Makin's possible knowledge of Richard's relationship with 'Mythic Blue?' Jason couldn't wait for Makin's return to Pafos.

He found a taxi, engine running, outside a nightclub. He decided to hire it and go straight to Villa Oasis, but as he entered the rear seat he realized that he needed to wear a dark suit for the funeral. He asked the driver to make a stop-over at the hotel.

75

Marianna was sitting in the passenger seat of Naharos's car when an officer crossed the street and came toward her. "Follow me, please," the policewoman said.

They walked across the street and entered the Mustafa building. Marianna nodded pleasantly to Naharos and asked, "Can we talk here?"

"Please sit down," Naharos said to her.

Helena was sitting on the opposite side, facing the street, and Marianna noticed how carefully Naharos had adjusted his chair, placing it halfway between her and Helena, at a 30-degree angle.

"Marianna believes that you've stolen certain items from her house," Naharos said staring at Helena. "She also claims that you've used false documents to get a job as a maid in order to spy on her activities for the benefit of her father-in-law, Faris, who I understand died this evening."

"I want this conversation recorded," Helena said.

Look at her, Marianna thought. *I can't believe she has that nerve.*

Naharos asked the female officer to come closer. "Take careful notes of our discussion—"

"No," Helena interrupted. "I want this conversation recorded on video."

"This is not a police interrogation," Naharos sighed. "You're not a suspect yet, as far as the police are concerned."

"Why are you involved, then?"

Marianna waived her hands. "No, no, I can't take this!" She looked at Naharos. "Can you believe this woman's audacity?"

"Just a second," Naharos said waiving his baton. He faced Helena. "Marianna couldn't find you without our assistance. We are interested in finding out the truth."

"You're doing all this to please her!" Helena shot back.

Marianna took a big breath, hesitated and then said, "Did you steal Richard's things from the library and give them to Faris?"

Helena faced Naharos. "Can anything she says be used against her?" she asked.

"No, why would it? You're the suspect. She's the complainant."

Marianna shook her head and stiffened her lips. "Answer my question, damn it!"

"I have a complaint of my own," Helena said.

"I don't believe Marianna has done anything wrong," Naharos said.

"How does she explain," Helena began, "the decorations and pieces of art that adorn the reception hall of Crow's brothel?"

Marianna could not resist the insinuation. "This is ridiculous!" Marianna screamed. She got up and paced the floor, almost ready to leave. She approached Helena. "You have no business prying into my affairs." She looked at Naharos. "You see what I mean?"

Helena said, "But you know as well as I do that an anonymous person telephoned Faris on April 12, the day of Richard's disappearance, to say that a man named Crow the Butcher may know something about Richard's case."

Naharos said, "The police investigated these rumours, and nothing turned out to be credible."

"Ask her how she got to know Crow," Helena pressed on.

Marianna felt the urge to slap Helena, but Naharos's austere expression changed her mind. "It's none of your business, bitch!"

Naharos stood up. "Eh, eh, calm down, please ..." He paused. "Yes," Naharos said. "I don't see what this has to do with the reason we're here."

"Except," Helena said, "Crow refused to share this information with Jason." She paused. "Did he have something to hide?"

"You don't expect her to speak for Crow, do you?" Naharos interjected.

"She might have decorated Crow's brothel," Helena shot back.

"You're jumping too far, too fast, Miss," Naharos said. "Do you have any evidence implicating Marianna?"

"If she didn't do anything wrong, then why is she so concerned that I might be spying on her?"

"You're not really a maid, are you?" Marianna asked.

"I was never your maid. I never said I was working for you."

"But you worked in my household."

"Villa Mustafa belongs to Faris," Helena responded.

"This is besides the point," Naharos said. "Marianna is the mistress."

"Maximus's mistress, yes! She's not my mistress. She's living in that villa courtesy of Faris's generosity."

Marianna kicked the ceramic tiles with her heels. "Shame on you!" her voice boomed out. "I was a fool to trust you!"

"Ha! Trust me?" If you trusted me, you would have told me that it was Maximus you were going to meet when you left me with the children on Sunday after the party."

Marianna sensed that she was not getting anywhere. The more she talked, the more embarrassing the conversation became. "What did you do with Richard's things?" Marianna asked more calmly.

"What things?" Helena responded.

"Some of his clothes, his Rolex watch, a golden chain, his passport, his lighter, cigars, his appointment book, his business cards, his address book, and other personal items."

"Did you have all these things in the library?" Helena responded.

"Yes."

"When did you last see them there?"

"Sunday morning."

"Who put them there?"

"It's none of your business. Did you take them?"

"You were supposed to turn them in to the police to assist them with their investigation." Helena said.

"The police never asked for them," Marianna responded.

"They didn't know you had them," Helena said.

"Look," Naharos interjected. "These arguments are surely making us all dizzy." He faced Helena. "What business did you have sneaking into Faris's office with Jason tonight?"

"Jason already answered that."

Naharos turned to Marianna. "We're getting out of here. I'll drive you home." He waived at Nicholas, who was standing by the entrance. "We're going now," he said. "Thank you for your assistance."

"My pleasure," Nicholas replied with a smile. "And thank you for your help."

Naharos turned to the female officer. He pointed at Helena. "Take her to the station, fingerprint her and charge her with trespassing. Then release her on her own recognizance."

"Yes sir," the female officer answered.

"Only cops understand one another," Naharos muttered as he departed the building.

"I wish I'd stayed home," Marianna complained.

76

As he opened the door of his hotel room, Jason saw a white piece of paper lying on the floor in front of him. He bent down to pick it up. He unfolded it. 'LEAVE TOWN, STRANGER.' Jason shook his head, ground his teeth in fury and tore the paper to pieces.

He grabbed his dark suit, a white shirt and put some underwear and socks into his gym bag. He hurried downstairs to the waiting taxi and asked the driver to take him to Villa Oasis. On their way, the driver looked at Jason through the rear view mirror and said, "You look familiar. I don't know how to say this …"

"Just let the words come out of your mouth," Jason suggested.

"Well, you're supposed to be dead."

Jason realized that the driver mistook him for Richard. "Why do you say that?"

"Are you Richard Mustafa?"

"No. I'm his brother." Jason then stretched the truth just a little. "I've just arrived back from Canada."

"You look so much like him."

"How do you know my brother is dead?"

"It was in the news a few months ago. They found his car by the entrance. The papers speculated this and that, but most people think he's dead."

Jason was quiet.

"Some say it was a contract job."

"Which?"

"His killing."

Jason was taken aback by the driver's bluntness. Gossips abounded. "Have they found the body?" he asked, fully knowing what the answer was going to be.

"Well," the driver answered, "my feeling is that he's buried in concrete."

The thought of his brother's body being mixed with gravel made Jason shudder. "Do you think there are people around capable of doing this kind of thing?"

"There're so many strangers hauling around these days. This place is not as safe as it used to be when I was a boy. I remember sleeping with the door of our house wide open all night."

Jason wondered if the driver knew where Crow lived. "You seem to know the area very well," he said. "Where are you from?"

"I live in the village of Emba," he said. "We've just passed it."

"Do you know someone named Crow the Butcher?"

The driver smiled. "He's not a butcher. He's a pimp."

"Do you know where he lives?"

"As a matter of fact, I do."

Jason gave him forty pounds, the equivalent of $80. "Could you pass by his house?" he asked.

The driver hesitated, but he took the money. "It's around this area," he said. He drove to a brand new subdivision and headed east. He crossed five newly asphalted roads and turned right. He then turned left on the first street, passed by two piles of gravel and cement blocks and slowed down. "There it is," the driver said pointing to the villa.

The house was dark and two cars were parked in the driveway. The electric lamps on the hydro poles offered Jason a good enough view. It was a split-level villa on a sloping lot, with a pool at the front. Jason was curious to see if it resembled the Delphi villa design that he had seen at Makin's office, but its features were very different from those in the Delphi plans. A 'For Sale' sign was stuck in the lawn.

"That's a nice villa," the driver said. "Do you want to buy it?"

"Not unless the price is right," Jason replied.

"I can find out," the driver offered.

Jason knew the normal practice among builders and sellers to pay a finder's fee to intermediaries, who introduced a buyer, if it resulted in a deal. "Where would I find you?" Jason asked.

"I work on my own. This is my taxi," he said proudly. "You can call my mobile any time." He handed him a card, which was also a blank receipt. "My name is Stefano."

Jason took the card, read the phone number, which was easy to remember, and put it in his pocket.

The driver accelerated, found the main road and headed for the hills.

77

"I had to shoot him!" George shouted.

Katerina slammed on the brakes, and the car skidded loudly but harmlessly into a shallow ditch. She stared at her husband, trying to picture him a killer.

George was holding his nose. "My leg ... it's still bleeding," he moaned.

"I told you not to take the gun!" she screamed. "Oh God, I had a feeling something like this was going to happen!"

"As I entered the house from a back window, he attacked me! Do you want to see the bite?"

George lifted the bottoms of his pants, and Katerina saw a gash at least four inches long and one inch deep right above the Achilles tendon of his right leg. Lines of blood, some dried up and some still fresh, disappeared into his sock.

She shook her head in disbelief. "That old quack, Dr. Plato, did that to you?"

"Huh? No." George continued to writhe in pain. "What are you talking about?"

Katerina finally clued in as to what had happened, and began laughing in relief. "It's a dog's bite!"

"I'm glad I took the pistol with me," he responded. "If it wasn't for the silencer, half of the village would have been after me."

She was more concerned with Faris's will than with the dead dog. More seriously, she asked, "Did you find it?"

"It lay open on his bedside table."

Katerina extended her hands. "Give it to me."

"I can't move now," he said uncomfortably. "It's inside my underpants."

Smiling, she manouevered the car back onto the rural side road, and they whisked away.

78

Jason opened the door of Villa Oasis and walked in slowly, anxious to be quiet, just in case Dr. Plato was sleeping. He saw him dozing on the couch of the living room. As he quietly passed by him on his way to the second bedroom, he heard a rustling from the couch. He turned around and saw the old man sitting up on the couch.

"What time is it?" Dr. Plato said rubbing his eyes.

Jason looked at his watch. "It's close to one. I'm sorry I took so long," he said and went over to sit beside him.

"That's fine," Dr. Plato said. "I couldn't keep my eyes open." He looked around. "Where's Helena?"

Jason pondered whether he should tell him what happened at the Mustafa building. He should know, he reasoned. "While we were at the Mustafa building, Naharos and the police came in and ordered us to get out. Naharos then asked Helena to stay behind. On my way out, I saw Marianna in Naharos's car. I don't know what happened to Helena after I left."

"I don't like what I'm hearing," Dr. Plato said.

Jason tried to play down the episode. "Helena is too smart to be manipulated by Naharos or Marianna."

"I hope they don't cause her any harm."

"I hope so, too."

"After you phoned, a stranger called. She said that Richard was alive. She didn't want to leave her name. She said she saw Richard tonight … last night I mean … walking with an unidentified woman in the tourist area of Kato Pafos."

"She probably mistook me for Richard," Jason said.

"I guess so." Dr. Plato got up and headed for the door. "I must get going," he said.

"Why don't you sleep in the extra bedroom," Jason said. "I'll sleep here."

"I have to feed my dog," he said. "He feels lonely without me. I should put it the other way; I'm lonely without him."

"I understand," Jason said. "Would you like me to walk you to the village?"

"It's not necessary," Dr. Plato said. "I enjoy solitary walks, especially at night."

After Dr. Plato left Villa Oasis, Jason took off his clothes, stepped into the bathtub and was about to take a shower when the telephone rang.

"It's me!" Helena said, sounding joyful.

"I'm glad you called."

"Marianna is such a creep!"

"What happened?"

"We had a fight with words. She refused to reveal if she'd done any work for this man, Crow."

"Did Naharos arrest you?"

"They took me to the station, charged me with trespassing and then let me go. I just got out."

"You must be tired," Jason said.

"Ismail is here with me, and we're heading out for a late dinner. There's this nice place; you ought to come out some day. We'll take you there."

"I'd like that," Jason said.

"Tomorrow is going to be a busy day," she said. "I'll let you catch some sleep."

Following their conversation, Jason took a quick shower and went to bed. He couldn't bear the thought of a corpse lying in the next bedroom. It wasn't an ordinary corpse. It was his father's lifeless body. He got up, got dressed and went to the kitchen. He turned on the faucet, let it run and poured himself a glass of water. As he was about to have a sip, the telephone rang. He put the receiver to his ear.

Loud sobs mingled with groans and incomprehensible utterances.

"Who is this?" Jason asked.

All he heard sounded like an old man wailing.

"Dr. Plato, is that you?"

"Yes!" Dr. Plato cried.

"What's wrong?"

"Azor … he's soaked in blood."

"What?"

"Someone broke in and shot him. My place has been turned upside down."

"Were you harmed?"

"No."

"I'll come right over," Jason said.

"No, please don't."

"Have you called the police?"

"They're on their way."

"I'm glad they didn't hurt you."

"They must have come in while I was at your house."

It could have been worse, Jason thought. "Please try to stay strong."

"I lost my two best friends in just a few hours," he sighed.

"You have me," Jason said. "I'll always be here for you."

Dr. Plato said, "I wouldn't have called you if it was not for the fact that I can't find your father's will."

"Where did you last leave it?"

"It was right here on top of my night table."

"Besides Helena and me, who else do you think knew about the will?" Jason asked.

"I don't know."

Jason remembered the nurse. "The nurse was in the other room when my father spoke about his will. Do you think she overheard anything?"

"I wasn't there."

Jason remained silent.

"I'm scared," Dr. Plato said. "I'm thinking of leaving this place. I want to go into hiding."

Jason couldn't blame him. The fear was so intense he felt it travelling the short distance between the doctor's humble home and his heart at Villa Oasis. "Do whatever makes you feel better," Jason said. "Please remember, you can trust me."

"I don't trust anyone anymore," Dr. Plato cried.

"I hope you're not suspecting that I have anything to do with this," Jason stated.

Dr. Plato answered, "I don't know. The police are here", he said, and hung up.

Jason needed fresh air. He opened the balcony doors, walked outside, and stood by the rails. The strong cool wind slapped his face, but he felt no discomfort.

79

As soon as they got home, Katerina went straight to the medicine cabinet and retrieved a bottle of antiseptic, cotton swabs, a pair of blunt-tipped scissors, and an elastic bandage. She began to clean her husband's wound.

George whined.

"It may need some stitches," she said as she examined the gash more carefully.

"You must be joking," he protested. "I was lucky to escape with only one bite. I'm not seeing any doctor!"

His comments made her think again. A visit to the hospital or a private clinic would expose him and raise suspicions, especially if the break-in was leaked to the media. She even regretted alarming George. "You'll heal without stitches." She covered the wound with the elastic bandage and hoped he wouldn't catch rabies. "I'm cold," she complained.

Katerina lit the fireplace, and while he stretched out on the couch she went to the fridge to get the champagne. She felt the bottle. It was cold.

George seemed to be dozing off when the popping sound caused his body to jerk. He moved around and finally sat on the couch.

"Let's celebrate Faris's death," she whispered in his ears. She poured champagne into two crystal glasses and nestled in her husband's arms. "Cheers," Katerina said with both glasses in her hands. "Cheers to you."

She handed him one of the glasses, and George's eyes widened when he saw the bottle. "Since when did you acquire such expensive taste?"

Each imported bottle cost her fifty Cyprus pounds—the rough equivalent of $100—but it was worth it, she thought. "Lately I've been having a lot of second thoughts about us," she said. " I think we should relax the rules from time to time. Don't you think?"

"But you made me swear off anything with alcohol in it," he complained.

"Not when we drink alone in the privacy of our home."

"I'm hurt and I'm tired, though."

"The champagne will relax you before bed."

George took one sip and then another. "It's very smooth," he said. "I don't feel the pain anymore." He gulped down the remaining champagne in his glass, and Katerina filled it up again.

"Let's read the will," she suggested with twinkling eyes. "I'm curious. Aren't you?"

Lagos pulled it out from inside his underpants, all wrinkled up, and handed it to Katerina. He then downed his champagne and wiped his lips.

"I'm glad you like it," she said, filling his glass one more time. She couldn't wait to go over Faris's will. She read it out loud, skipping the technical stuff.

THIS IS THE WILL of FARIS MUSTAFA, made this 11th day of November 2001.

I revoke all Wills and Codicils previously made by me.

I appoint my son JASON MUSTAFA, my daughter HELENA ANDREOU (the child born of my relationship with my former housemaid Angela Andreou) and my friend Dr. PLATO, to be the Executors and Trustees of my Will.

I give all my property to my Estate Trustees upon the following trusts:

1. To pay all my just debts, expenses and taxes....

2. Helena Andreou is appointed to be the guardian and special trustee of my three grandchildren, namely, Andrew, George, and Claira. I direct my trustees to allocate thirty five million dollars for the benefit and use of my said grandchildren. Helena shall administer the children's trust and have their share invested until they attain the age of majority. In the meantime, Helena shall pay or apply such amounts out of the children's trust fund, as Helena in the exercise of her absolute discretion considers advisable for the benefit of my grandchildren....

6. My Estate Trustees shall set aside from the capital of my estate $500,000 and set up an educational foundation for the benefit of the poor, but bright, students of Pafos. I named it the 'Richard Mustafa University Foundation' in honour of my son. They shall pay out to these students $50,000 every year for ten years, and the remaining balance, if any, shall become part of the residue of my estate....

8. All my shares and ownership interests in Mustafa Holdings Inc, Mustafa Bank (Cyprus) International, and all my shares in the Persinaras-Mustafa Group, shall be divided between my son Jason and my daughter Helena, in two equal shares, for their own use and own ownership absolutely....

9. One hundred thousand dollars shall be paid to the village of Peta for the improvement of roads in the area....

10. Villa Mustafa, Villa Oasis and all the adjoining land, including the olive grove shall be transferred to my son Jason for his own use and benefit absolutely. My daughter-in-law, Marianna, shall be given seven days to vacate Villa Mustafa....

11. My Estate Trustee shall divide the residue of my estate equally between my two children, namely, JASON MUSTAFA and HELENA ANDREOU, living at the date of my death, provided that if any of my said two children predecease me leaving issue alive at the date of my death, the issue of any of my children living at the date of my death shall take in equal shares per stirpes the share to which Jason or Helena would have been entitled had he or she survived me....

IN TESTIMONY WHEREOF I have to my Will, which is written upon this paper subscribed my name the day and year first above written.

Katerina felt vindicated for asking George to steal Faris's will. *There's nothing there for Marianna.* She was vaguely aware that her husband had emptied the bottle and was talking to himself, but she wanted it that way.

George began taking off his clothes, and she lost her train of thought. She glanced away from the papers, watched Lagos heading for the bedroom, and she got up to stop him. "I feel very horny," she lied. She took him by the hand and led him onto the thick Flokati wool rug that lay in front of the fireplace. "I'll make love to you," she whispered.

His face was pale, and the colour of his eyes matched the rising flames. He spread out, flat on his back, his legs trembling, and she thought she had never seen him in such a helpless state before. "What were the envelopes in the car," he murmured.

She ignored the question. She looked him in the eyes, and he blushed, conveying a silent message that he wasn't up to it, a message she learned to decipher so well. She sneaked her hand under his underpants and began to stimulate him until she felt his stiffness. She then removed his underpants and went down to suck him. All George did was moan. She continued until he reached his climax, herself frigid and dry.

80

A few seconds passed. Sitting on the couch beside George, Katerina's mind blazed back to the meeting she had with the hotel's security guard, and began seeing images of three men eating and laughing at the seashore tavern. "Do you think I please you enough?" she asked.

"More than I ever imagined," George said to his wife.

His response was not surprising. "I'm scared," she said clinging on to him.

"Why?" he asked, and Katerina sensed the egotistical tone of his voice.

"I suspect you're making deals behind my back."

"You're doing the same thing behind mine."

"You're my best friend," she said. "You can trust me with anything."

"We've been married all these years," he said, "now, for the first time, I hear all your reassurances."

"We all need reassurances from time to time."

"I wonder what goes on inside your mind," he responded. "You're so preoccupied with your family. Sometimes I feel left out."

"Is this why you've been keeping your moves to yourself lately?"

"What have you learned?"

"I don't mind it," she said nonchalantly, hoping to encourage him to open up. "Ever since you arranged the loan with the *Long Nile* people, you've become a different person."

"You should be thankful," he said.

Katerina presumed he meant his words. "Of course. But if they don't have their money by January 31st, all hell will break loose."

"Do you want me to ask for an extension?"

Katerina's eyes widened. "Can you do that?"

"It's possible. You can offer to increase the interest and pay a little bonus on top."

"Where did they find all that money?" she asked.

"They borrowed it from Faris's bank."

He said this with such a straight face it took Katerina a few seconds to regain her thoughts. "But I always thought an offshore bank couldn't lend money to locals."

"They've found a way."

"George …." Katerina fixed him with her eyes. "It's important that you're not implicated in any money laundering scheme." She opened the second bottle.

"It's funny," he said. "I was thinking the same thing about you."

"Why?"

"You've already siphoned a lot of money overseas."

"How do you know?"

"You had to justify them as commissions. How else could you grab the Group's cash?"

"Who told you this?"

He took the bottle. "Ken Stavro, your general manager."

"What else did he tell you?"

George hesitated. "I'm thirsty," he said drinking from the bottle.

"What else did he tell you?" she pressed.

"Niki, your endeared architect, did a good job at designing those bogus villas," he said laughing.

"Stavro had no authority to tell you all this."

"I'm your husband. He *had* to tell me."

Katerina wondered if George had coerced Stavro into revealing the phony transactions. "Have you threatened him?"

He finished the rest of the champagne. "We had a nice time on the boat recently. He bragged about your sharp business acumen."

Katerina saw no point in denying the scheme. "I had no choice," she said. "I had to come up with the money to pay the *Long Nile* people. We're very short of cash these days. Business is slow."

"What about Faris's people?" George asked. "Do you think they're stupid?"

"There's always a way to dress transactions," she said hurriedly, not about to be put down. "There are real people involved."

"You should have come to me. We've set up a nice operation."

Katerina nodded a professed understanding, but she knew that he had little regard for her own concerns. "We'd better be prepared," she responded.

"There's good money to be made for all of us," he said in a tone that was far from re-assuring.

She pretended she did not recognize his opening statement. "Did you know that the Saudis are sending their men to audit Faris's books?"

"I'm not too concerned," he said casually. "Makin's people will take care of that."

"I wonder what his plans are," she wondered aloud. She surprised herself by being able to remain calm.

"Makin and I have been meeting regularly," he said.

"And you're planning something together?"

"Whatever I tell you, keep it between us. I don't want Marianna to know anything."

"Why not?"

"Because she'll get very upset."

"I don't want to upset her," she said reassuringly.

"I'm doing it for us," he said. "For you, for Marianna, for the children, for your parents."

He knows how much I love my family, she mused, *and he's playing with my feelings.* "I love you, and I trust your judgment," she lied.

"When Makin first approached me with the idea, I thought it was too risky. But he showed me the money. Lots of it!"

Katerina remained silent.

"Do you know how Faris made his money?" he asked.

"Not really."

"With Makin's help, he arranged to purchase military equipment destined for the Middle East. The first deal (I think it was completed in the early 1990s) netted Faris's bank ten million dollars. The second deal, a couple of years later, resulted in a $25-million profit."

"I see."

"Then Faris's health worsened and Makin assumed most of the responsibility for these deals. Faris gave him a cut, but Makin thought it wasn't good enough for his efforts."

"I see," Katerina repeated. She didn't need to guess what happened next. "You mean Makin decided to do something on his own?"

"Well … he didn't do it alone. Unbeknown to Faris, Makin negotiated a large purchase of handheld lazers, target-spotting binoculars and ground to surface missiles from Russia."

"No wonder you were so busy," she mused. "Have they paid you well, so far?"

"We've made a million each, but we put it back into the business," George said.

"You bought more?" Katerina asked.

"Our $12-million investment became $16-million, and we loaned it all to your father."

"I would think it difficult to borrow $12-million," she said, anxious to know how they acquired the money.

"It was easy with Richard's help," he bragged.

She tried to conceal her shock, but had an impulse to slap him on the face. "It's quite amazing," she said. "How did it come about?"

"For the love of money, some sons sell their fathers," he laughed uncontrollably.

"Who is the fourth participant?"

"The man you met with this morning."

"I never knew his name," Katerina said.

"No way! I'm not going to tell you his name."

"Why not?"

"Because he'll fucking kill me!" George bellowed.

"Do you really mean it?"

Katerina saw her husband was having trouble breathing. He tried to get up, but he lost his balance and fell on the couch.

"Did he kill Richard?"

"I'm very tired," he grumbled. "Let's go to bed." He got up and dragged himself to the bedroom.

She looked at her watch. It was almost three a.m. She wondered if Jason was dead by now.

Once she heard George snoring, she went to the car to retrieve the envelopes. She hurried back into the house and tossed them into the fire, one by one. As she watched the flames devouring the papers, she whispered, "No more money for Maximus."

She took a big breath. Unable to think, she kept staring at the last flames smoldering the firewood from its very essence, slowly reducing it to ashes.

81

The white-stone wall offered him some shield from the cool, strong wind, but it blocked his view. He climbed an olive tree and leaned against a bough. He was as still as the thousand-year-old trunk under his feet. The moon and the stars were bright, olive branches shook above his head, and he could see his own shadow on the undergrowth.

With a shotgun hidden under his robe, Maximus was thinking about the deal with John Persinaras. He remembered when, in his office, he had signed the private documents, looking forward to a life of financial freedom and carefree subsistence. No more dependence on the tiny stipend from the monastery. The thought annoyed him, for things turned out differently than he had planned, and the olive branches reflecting on the ground gave him the feeling of a pursuing ghost. Maximus had no choice but to put an end to his nightmare.

He was astonished at how pretty the landscape was in the still of night. It was so bright, he could see the branches of hundreds of trees shake aimlessly, and the shadows below them move back and forth, left and right, in a symphony of light and dark, directed by the wind and watched by the solemn moon—the only silent onlooker in that space of creation.

When he'd first seen the monastery under the shine of the full moon, he was only a nine-year-old boy. He had been sad and lonely, recovering from the shock of running away from home, incapable of imagining that the world could ever be kind to him. He had been on a daring journey then, he recalled. Barefooted, he had crossed several miles of the rough terrain of the Pafos interior, with its thinly populated villages, its neglected vine fields, its abandoned houses windswept in dust, and its winding mud roads. He had slept in a cave and under a derelict bridge. Then, three nights later, under the guidance of the same moon, he crossed over the last hill and followed the narrow road that had led him to the monastery.

In the morning, looking at the large dining room, the huge cellar full of food supplies, the airy cloisters, the comfortable rooms, the clean sheets, the lush gardens, and listening to the sounds of Byzantine music drifting in from the chapel, he had thought he was in a mythical king's palace. Later, he had sat with the monks in the huge dining room, drinking mountain tea and eating freshly-baked bread, ripe olives, cheese, roasted hare and fried partridge, and he had thought: I hope this dream lasts a bit longer!

Now Maximus saw a figure moving inside Villa Oasis and then the doors opened and Jason walked out and stood on the balcony. The target was in perfect position. Filled with pain and pleasure, Maximus aimed.

All kinds of thoughts suddenly blitzed his brain, like a tornado twisting about aimlessly. *If I kill him, I will burn in hell for all eternity! No, the concept of hell is an allegory—in fact 'hell' is merely non-existence. I can still be granted admission to heaven if I can show I have good reason to kill him. And I do! Look at him, so at ease standing on that magnificent balcony. He's a wealthy arrogant man who is trying to take away from me the love of my life! Yet, I am a monk, and the pleasures of the flesh are forbidden to me. I agreed to all this when I took my vows. Oh God, give me guidance!*

I must have Marianna, no matter what the cost. He aimed again, but he could not find the energy to pull the trigger. Katerina was the devil in disguise, Maximus concluded. Yes, it was she who was to blame! It was she who had talked him into this. His hands trembled, and his legs wobbled under him. He bent to his knees to avoid falling down. He stayed there, and silently wept behind the tree trunk until Jason went back inside. Maximus thought he would fall into several pieces there and then. It took him a long time to collect himself.

He hurried back to the monastery, unlocked his private storage room, locked the gun in its cabinet, locked the storage room and went to sit on his bedroom terrace.

Watching the sea illuminate under the glow of the full moon, he recalled the first night he had visited the seminary in Nicosia, the capital, at age 13; it had been a difficult time in his life …

In 1963, students were demonstrating in the streets. He could hear the sounds of gunfire between the Greek and Turkish sectors of the capital (the so called Green Line that separated the two communities when hostilities broke out due to a constitutional impasse). The city was engulfed in strife, steaming anger and bitter fanaticism between Christians and Muslims. There was prejudice, mistrust, envy and provocation on both sides. And Maximus had worn a black monk's robe, one hand clinging to a revolver, the other holding a grenade. His schoolmates strode beside him, waving flags, shouting slogans, handing out pamphlets. They all shouted, "Enosis! Enosis!"—Union with Greece.

He heard explosions of mortars and the curses of Turkish fighters across the Green Line.

Further up the street, the roaring engines of the tanks were reverberated more loudly as they approached the Line. Clouds of tense black smoke filled the air, resembling shadows of mythical beasts. The pandemonium pierced consciousness and entered the paranormal. Pain, thirst, hunger and fear disappeared. Crazy centaurs battled and clashed from opposite directions. Thousands of untamed Cerberuses lashed out and devoured the scattered remains. Multi-headed gigantic snakes slithered out of the ground and sniffed the air, while sweet voiced Sirens called the soldiers to their deaths. Up in the sky, giant bats circled the air and plunged to snatch the anguished bodies.

Maximus's father loved and trusted the Turkish Cypriots, because he thought they were honourable, peace-loving, hard-working and loyal to their families and friends. His father had many Turkish Cypriot friends who were ordinary Cypriots: fine farmers, hospitable hosts, jovial and humble. It had always been perfectly obvious to Maximus that special interest groups, and the superior powers, collaborated and plotted to spread the seeds of division and hatred amongst the two communities. He abhorred violence, and so saw no purpose in the strife for segregation.

He suddenly realized the futility of war, hesitated, stopped and turned back. His reluctance to participate in the inter-communal fight led him to throw the revolver and the grenade in a garbage bin and walk back to the seminary, alone and disoriented. It was defiance that moved him and this went against the wishes of the instigators who sought to expel him from the seminary for betraying the cause of patriotism. Maximus had fought off his accusers with determination, which gained the unwavering support of Archbishop Makarios, then president of Cyprus. The president was firmly opposed to the use of violence as a means of achieving political objectives. This defiance had been the start of a long struggle, a struggle that was more powerful and haunting inside him than the outside world around him. This struggle led Maximus to re-evaluate his life.

Now, reflecting on the past, Maximus thought: *Yes, I am greedy and hungry for wealth; yes, I am dishonest and blindly ambitious; yes, I lack the turpitude that causes me to violate the sanctity of marriage that calls for the respect of family and self, but I will never kill anyone simply to achieve any of my objectives.*

He heard a faint noise down below, under the carob trees. He held his breath. The only thing he saw was the shadow of a monk's robe waning into the thickness of the night.

82

Lying in an unfamiliar bed, and knowing that the corpse of a man he used to detest was in the other bedroom, Jason had difficulty getting to sleep. The years he had stayed away from home seemed like split-seconds in comparison to death's eternity. Tonight was an unusual night. The man he had often blamed for being distant, critical and egotistical was no longer alive. It was as if his death drew a veil in the middle of the arches that led to his bedroom, separating the past, pulling a screen at the opposite end that revealed an auditorium full of strange and unfamiliar faces. These faces looked just as formidable as the face of the dead man behind the veil.

The wrath of the wind kept him awake. The hoot-hoot night call of an owl interrupted the lull of the wind. In the crescendo of its cries, he could hear his own anguish thrusting through the essence of his being. Eventually, his ears began to get used to the rhythmic sounds of the outside world, and he fell asleep.

Jason rose at 5:45, his eyes hungry for more sleep. While shaving, he gazed into the bathroom mirror. Black marks covered the skin below his eyes.

He quickly showered, got dressed and walked to the kitchen. He made himself a cup of coffee, sat in the living room and turned on the television set to catch the six o'clock morning news. The satellite dish on the roof offered him a selection of international stations. He used the remote control to click to the right channel.

Stories about the war in Afghanistan poured in from the front. In the north, Northern Alliance rebels advanced steadily against the *Taliban* forces, which held onto the prized city of Mazar-i- Sharif. Rebels serving under the Uzbek warlord Rashid Dostum had pushed the *Taliban* out of Kishindi. To the west, forces loyal to another Alliance commander prepared to seize the village of Aqkupik. *Taliban* soldiers were running away from the battle zones … or defecting. Torched villages. Barricaded homes.

The Pentagon seemed eager to have Mazar-i- Sharif under the control of the Northern Alliance. U.S airplanes blasted *Taliban* lines guarding Majar, aiming to capture the local airport.

The war was shifting south, outside Kabul. U.S. sorties flew daily, and U.S. special operations forces were deployed to the front. The Pentagon began using 15,000-lb 'daisy cutters' which detonated three feet above the ground, rupturing lungs and breaking eardrums.

Terror was everywhere. On the outskirts of Mazar, hundreds of *Taliban* troops took shelter near a power plant and a fertilizer factory. Heavy rains impeded the rebel advance. There were reports that factions of the Northern Alliance were competing with each other for domination of captured areas. The consensus was that the decisive battle would be fought over the control of Kabul. The Alliance forces stationed north of Kabul possessed less than 100 tanks—not enough to capture the city without the support of the U.S. forces.

The telephone rang, and Jason lowered the volume.

"I figured you would be up already," Helena said.

"I might as well tell you now," Jason responded.

"What happened?"

"They broke into Dr. Plato's house, savagely killed his dog, and stole father's will. Dr. Plato is so demoralized, he may go into hiding."

"Bastards!" Helena cried. "I knew she was after me," Helena sighed.

"We don't know for sure."

"Marianna is after Faris's estate. It's obvious. She doesn't want me to get a single penny. Without the will, I won't get anything."

"You could contest the distribution of the estate."

"You know as well as I do that the onus would be on me to prove my claim. I don't think anyone will believe Dr. Plato."

"The witnesses will testify about it."

"Are you dreaming? Most witnesses don't have a clue what's inside a person's will when they sign their names."

"Yes, but they can attest that Faris had signed a will that is now missing."

"Missing. You've said it. A will may be missing for many reasons; that the testator had decided to tear it apart and throw it in the garbage is one of them!"

"I know." Jason said. "I'd rather not inherit anything."

"But you don't have to worry. In the absence of a will, you'll still get your share as one of the heirs. The law provides for that."

"There's supposed to be an older will, the one in the possession of Kamal."

"Yes. I remember Faris spoke about it," she said. "But I haven't seen it. Have you?"

222

"No, I haven't," Jason said. "And I don't even know if it really exists."

"That's another puzzle," Helena declared. "If Kamal does have one, some interesting questions will be raised."

The division of his father's assets was the furthest thing from Jason's mind. "Are you coming over?"

"I should be there in a couple of hours. I'm preparing food for the people who may decide to visit us at the villa after the funeral."

"Do you think it would be more appropriate to ask Marianna if she could allow us to organize the gathering at Villa Mustafa?"

"Did she call you to express her condolences?"

"Not yet."

"I would hate to see her face again. Villa Oasis is just as suitable. I'll make sure the place looks inviting to the guests."

"You've been a tremendous help to me," Jason said. "I'm also grateful to Ismail for cleansing the body."

"I'm sending him with a hearse to transport Faris's body to the Mosque."

"Is there anything I can do to assist?"

"Just be ready. Ismail and the Imam will take care of the funeral service. Make sure you don't send flowers."

"Yes, I know."

"We expect at least two hundred people at the service."

"It just occurred to me," Jason said. "I forgot to notify Manning and his wife."

"I took care of it," she said. "Alex and Cynthia are already in town."

"Are they staying at the same hotel as before?"

"Yes."

Jason said, "Do you have any news from your people in Nicosia?"

"I'm about to find out. I'll call you back if there are any developments."

"I wonder if Makin has returned to Pafos."

"Me, too."

"I'll call his house now," Jason said.

"No. Wait until I speak to my people in Nicosia."

"Alright."

"Talk to you later," Helena said. "Just before I hang up," she said, "I don't want to scare you, but I think you should take measures to protect yourself."

After he hung up the phone, Jason wondered if he should call Nicholas. He didn't want to wake him up, but he was anxious to know if he managed to remove the items from the Mustafa building. He decided to wait a little longer.

83

Jason thought of Dr. Plato. He picked up the telephone, dialed his number and spoke to him. "Good morning. Are you feeling better today?"

"I was about to call you," Dr. Plato said breathlessly. "The police took my statement.

"They want to interview you."

"What for?"

"I told them about the missing will."

"You're aware of the existence of another will?"

"Your father might have mentioned something to me. Frankly, my mind is too much out of focus right now."

Jason sensed the resignation in Dr. Plato's voice. "I want you to rest and be ready for the funeral. We expect over two hundred people at the service. It will give me great relief if you delivered the eulogy."

"I don't think I'll be able to come to your father's funeral," Dr. Plato said.

"Why not? He was your best friend."

"He was. He's dead now."

"Your absence will be felt." Jason added, "If there's anything I can do to help, please let me know."

"I'll be fine," the old man said before hanging up.

Jason sensed that Dr. Plato was more depressed than his words revealed. He sat still, staring at the floor, taking in Dr. Plato's state of mind. He could only hope that Dr. Plato would soon recover from his dejected state.

He searched his pocket and found the little slip of paper that Kamal gave him on Sunday. He thought it would be prudent to inform him about Faris's passing. He dialed the number. A male voice said, "Yes?"

"I'm looking for Mr. Kamal," Jason said. "I must speak to him right away."

"Who are you?"

"My name is Jason Mustafa. I'm calling from Pafos, Cyprus."

"Are you the son of Faris Mustafa?" the man asked.

225

"Yes."

"I'm Mr. Kamal's assistant. My condolences. Is there anything I can do for you?"

"I just wanted to tell Mr. Kamal that my father passed away. That's all."

"Mr. Kamal has gone to Pafos. He will be attending your father's funeral."

"Where's he staying?"

"At the Mustafa Beach Hotel."

"Thank you," Jason said. He hung up the phone.

The telephone rang; it was Helena again. "News from Nicosia," she reported. "Last night Makin showed up at the Mustafa bank and tried to get into the building, only to be stopped by our new security personnel. Four other men were with him. He protested by shouting and fuming. He didn't leave until after he was shown the court order that sealed the building. He drove to the Hilton Hotel where he and his men had dinner. They left the hotel at midnight.

"I'm tempted to call his house," Jason said.

"If you call him, pretend you don't know anything about all this."

"Good suggestion," Jason said.

"Is Kamal on your list of guests?" Jason asked.

"No. I hadn't thought of inviting him."

"I wonder who notified him," Jason said. "He's in town for the funeral."

"He has his contacts, I suppose," Helena assumed.

The door bell rang. "Someone's here," Jason said.

Helena concluded, "I'll see you later."

Jason went to the front door and opened it. A tall, slim man in his early 30s stood on the doorstep. He wore a black leather jacket with shiny silver buckles, black pants, black shirt, and black boots. His black hair danced in the brisk wind; his face was rough and sun-tanned. The man's large black eyes—tired looking and spotted with red dots—emerged under thick arched brows. His nose was long and curvy. With a thick mouth, his unshaven face presented the portrait of a proud buccaneer. Four other men stood behind him holding a wooden casket.

So this is the man who stole Helena's heart, Jason observed. "You must be Ismail," Jason said.

"Correct. Are you Jason?"

"Yes."

"I'm sorry about the death of your father." He turned to face the others. "Let's go, guys."

Jason watched as the men took the body and placed it in the casket. They carried it to the hearse.

"Thank you, Ismail. You've done a lot for me, and I'm grateful to you."

"Don't mention it," Ismail said. "We'll take the body straight to the Mosque and wait. The Imam will be there shortly before three. The funeral service will be very brief. We've arranged to bury the body in the Turkish cemetery, which is on the outskirts of the Mouttallos district."

"I know where it is. Would you be able to join us here for a reception after the burial?" Jason asked him.

"Yes, of course."

When the hearse left, Jason opened all the windows of Villa Oasis, allowing the air to circulate through the villa. He found a sheet of blank paper and sat down to write a short eulogy.

After he finished writing, he picked up the phone and called Makin's number.

"Hello?" a scratchy male voice answered.

"Is that you, Makin?" Jason asked.

"Who is this?"

"Jason."

"I was about to call you," Makin said. "Aisha said you're looking for me."

"I thought maybe you could cleanse my father's body. It's okay now. Someone has done that already."

"I returned late last night," Makin said, sounding sleepy.

"How is business?" Jason asked.

"Which business?"

"Ours."

"Fine."

Jason sensed the moody tone of Makin's voice. "What's the matter? You sound upset."

"You fired my security guards and replaced them with your own men. You've done it both here and in Nicosia. Don't you trust me?"

Jason remembered Helena telling him that the security in Nicosia had changed on Faris's instructions, but he didn't divulge this information. "I didn't think you would object."

"I continue to be the general manager."

"Yes. But I'm the CEO." Jason said.

"Your name is just on paper. I still have the day to day responsibility for this company."

"I have the right to make such decisions."

"You should realize how much I've helped your father."

"What was the purpose of your visit to Nicosia?" Jason inquired.

"Your father sent me there. He didn't tell you that, either?"

"Don't hide behind the instructions of a dead man."

"Look!" Makin asserted. "Your father appointed you the CEO, but you need a lesson or two on how to handle your associates!"

Jason didn't know what to make of Makin's attitude. He wondered if Makin assumed more power than he had. "You're not an associate. You're an employee."

"You know better than to talk to me like this."

Jason could not maintain his composure. "You're a mean son-of-a-bitch."

"The same to you."

"You have some explaining to do."

"*You* have some explaining to do," Makin said.

"I want to see you right away," Jason instructed.

"I'll see you when *I* decide."

"Well, this is what I'm going to do," Jason said. "The moment my father's body is covered with earth, your name will be deleted from the company's books."

"Save yourself the trouble! I resign!" Makin shouted and the phone went silent.

84

Katerina woke up late. The stinking odour of burned paper filled the house and made her headache worse. She sat on the bed and watched her husband snore heavily with his mouth half-open. His dark acne scars and messy hair gave him the appearance of a sleeping dragon. The first thing a dragon does when he opens his eyes is to look for a meal, and she was the prey closest to him. Quite impulsively, her hand covered her mouth.

She crawled out of bed and walked to the kitchen, where she made herself a double-double coffee and sat at the kitchen table. She was mad at herself for underestimating George's abilities. Sure, he'd always been cunning and capable of petty crimes, but she couldn't believe he actually teamed-up with Makin and the *Long Nile* representative (that short, fat man she so loathed). She doubted she could come up with the $22-million she needed by the end of January to retire the *Long Nile* loan. She regretted not monitoring her husband's activities and wondered if he had played a role in Richard's disappearance.

She comforted herself in the knowledge that she no longer had to send money overseas for Maximus's benefit. Anxious to know whether Maximus had killed Jason, she picked up the phone and dialed Villa Oasis.

"Hello," a man answered. She recognized the voice, and her stomach shrank.

"This is Katerina," she said. "I'm sorry." (She found the courage to say "I'm sorry," again but without the genuine feeling of sorrow.)

"His funeral is at three o'clock today, at the Mosque," Jason said. "Will you come?"

"Of course," she said. She sat down abruptly. The calmness of her voice camouflaged her anxiety. She felt betrayed by Maximus; all her efforts had been wasted. "Are you hosting a reception after the funeral?" she asked.

"Yes, here at Villa Oasis."

"Do you need any help?"

"No, thank you. Helena will take care of everything."

"I'll see you later," she said and hung up.

For several minutes she stared at the kitchen wall, trying to find a way to save her family's business from the tentacles of *Long Nile*; but she felt helpless.

She walked to the bedroom and woke up the dragon. She took his arm and saying, "I love you," led him with a measured smile to the kitchen. "I'm glad you opened up last night," she said. "We need each other."

"Yes we do," George said, embracing her, and she felt the firmness of his hold.

85

Jason was on the phone again.

"Hello?"

"Nicholas," he said, " this is Jason."

"Your backpack and the items that I put aside last night," Nicholas said reassuringly, "I have them. Do you want them delivered to you today?"

Jason breathed a sign of relief. "Today is my father's funeral," he said. "I'll pick them up tomorrow. Would you bring them to the restaurant?"

"Tomorrow at noon. We can have lunch."

"I'll see you then."

"I want to see you before that," Nicholas said. "Can I come to your father's funeral?"

Jason hesitated. In light of what transpired at the Mustafa building the night before, I don't want people to see us exchanging pleasantries, he thought. "Yes of course. Be at the Pafos Mosque at three, but stay away from me and Helena ... you do understand, right?"

"I'll be there. I'll pretend I'm present because your father had retained my services."

"You're also invited to the memorial reception which will be held at Villa Oasis, the one next to Villa Mustafa," Jason said.

After he hung up, he went out to the front patio. Why hadn't Marianna called him to express her condolences? Maybe she didn't think he was entitled to accept her pity; maybe she wasn't feeling sad; maybe she was expecting him to call; maybe she was mad at him for teaming up with Helena; maybe.... He assumed the nurse had told her all about Faris's deathbed confessions. He wondered if Marianna gave the order to break into Dr. Platos's house to steal the will.

In a spur of anger, he left Villa Oasis and hurried to the guesthouse. By the time he walked on the lawn, his anger was replaced with calmness and reason.

The nurse opened the door and invited him in. Compared with Villa Mustafa this was a humble place, and Jason regarded it as a very cozy cottage. "I came to talk to you about your future," he said. "Now that my father is dead, I'll need to lay you off. I'll make sure you receive a severance pay until you find another placement."

"Thank you, sir," she said, "but I don't really need your help."

"So be it," Jason responded. "There's something else that concerns me, and I want to discuss it with you now."

The nurse listened attentively.

"First of all, you have nothing to fear from telling me the truth."

She nodded.

"Did you discuss with Marianna anything that had to do with my father's will?"

She suddenly seemed very nervous. "No I haven't," she said, unconvincingly.

He was taken aback by her reluctance to open up, but he understood her predicament. "Very well," he said. "That's all. Thank you."

After he left the guesthouse, Jason pondered whether to confront Marianna directly. After a moment's reflection, he didn't think that was necessary. Besides, he didn't want to give her the opportunity to accuse him of anything. He resolved to wait for the right time.

86

Maximus was awakened at eleven that morning by monk Modestos. He was glad that he hadn't killed Jason. Modestos stood beside his bed with a glass of orange juice in his hand. Maximus sat up and drank the whole glass.

"Today is Faris's funeral," Modestos said.

"How do you know?"

"It's all over the papers. One paper has a half page devoted to his life. In the announcement section, there is a funeral invitation."

Maximus didn't know if he should attend. "Does it say where the funeral service will be held?"

"At the Pafos Mosque."

"I wonder who arranged for that. The Mosque has been closed for many years."

"Could you enter a Mosque?" asked Modestos.

"I don't see why not. But I think I'll convey my condolences in private, after the funeral service. Is there a family gathering?"

"Yes. At Villa Mustafa."

"Call Marianna and tell her I will be attending."

"I'll do that."

Maximus got up, but his movements were slow. All the agonizing and fear he'd felt, while standing on the bough of the olive tree as he lowered his shotgun, came rushing back to him. *How on earth did I reach so low?* His upset stomach irritated his tonsils; a ghost hand grabbed him by the throat. Maximus thought he might vomit. He took a cold shower to help him think more clearly and shake his body from its present sluggishness.

While he was getting dressed, it occurred to him one more time that he had allowed himself to be manipulated by Katerina, and a wave of resentment swept his heart. He realized that his love for Marianna was stronger than ever, but his love for money was beginning to wane once again. Maybe he'd done the right thing by giving the documents to Katerina, he thought. But when he remembered his sister in London, the nausea came back. She could sell her apartment in London's West End, he thought, and perhaps settle in a more affordable unit in a less expensive neighbourhood.

His immediate concern was Marianna and the children. *What will happen to them if they have to vacate Villa Mustafa?* He had some savings to provide for them, if the need arose, but he considered it unlikely that Marianna would ever actually need his financial support.

Maximus left his bedroom and went straight to his office to make some phone calls and look after some paper work. Modestos was there to greet him, appearing peculiarly uptight.

"I have something important to tell you," Modestos hurried.

Maximus grinned and said nothing.

"Someone saw you carrying a gun last night and alerted Bishop Panaretos."

"Is that so?"

"The Bishop called the office a few minutes ago and asked if I knew anything."

Maximus sat at the desk. "Someone around here has a devil mind," Maximus said.

"I could have told him everything," Modestos continued. "But I didn't."

"What do you know?" Maximus asked raising his eyebrows.

"Ever since you threatened to expel me from the monastery, I've found it difficult to remain silent while watching you do all these things."

"Your role is to serve me," Maximus uttered. "That's your place."

"It's unfair that I have to suffer such humiliation for a little indiscretion while you're getting away with conspiracy, embezzlement and attempted murder."

Maximus stood up. He wondered about what Modestos was aware. Certainly, he was shrewder than he'd originally given him credit for. "I've forgiven your sin," Maximus said. "What you've said about me is not true."

"I have the evidence to prove it."

"Show me."

"Contracts, documents, papers, photos, recordings … they're all with my lawyer."

"What do you hope to accomplish by attacking me?" Maximus asked.

"I could destroy you in an instant," Modestos warned.

"Whatever evidence you say you have, it will not stand the scrutiny of my lawyers."

"I knew you would say that," Modestos laughed. "I'm anxious to prove you wrong."

"Forgery, falsification and perjury carry stiff penalties," Maximus cautioned. "Are you ready to spend many years in jail?"

"Are you?"

"Listen," Maximus said calmly. "Why don't we sit down and discuss this?"

"There's nothing to discuss," Modestos said. "I can offer you an escape route … if you care to listen."

"Who sets the rules around here?" Maximus shouted.

"You've no more authority than I do," Modestos said. "We're both plain monks, right now."

"I derive my authority from my appointment."

"Soon, with my help, the Bishop will know all about your conduct, and the Holy Synod will strip your powers and excommunicate you."

"What the hell do want from me?" Maximus said closing the door.

"You can't do anything to me," Modestos said even though he trembled. "It's not that simple anymore."

"I won't harm you," Maximus whispered. He sat down on the couch, next to Modestos. He touched him on the shoulders. "I like you a lot," he said. "Why do you have to be so mean to me?"

"Get your hands off me," Modestos insisted.

"What is this escape route?" Maximus asked.

Modestos hesited. He appeared to struggle with dread, seeking the right words.

Maximus stared at him. Modestos's face was so fresh he could hardly see any creases on his cheeks. He was so young, too young and inexperienced to become an archdeacon, he thought. In his expression, there was a hint of something that Maximus had failed to notice before (perhaps it was jealousy, or innocence, or just plain hatred). He looked lost.

"You scare me," Modestos said, moving away from him.

Maximus heard his own heart pounding, like a thousand drums in the middle of the jungle. Fear and resignation were his only feelings. If Modestos did go to the bishop, with all that incriminating evidence, Maximus's life would be blown out as surely as the candles in the monastery's chapel that reached the bottom of the ashtrays. "I wish to propose an offer," Maximus said.

Modestos's eyes turned the other way; he tried to appear indifferent. "What is it?"

"I'll make you an archdeacon, bestow upon you some privileges—and a handsome salary—and give you a leave of absence to study at Mount Athos."

"No. I hate older monks."

Modestos's stern response made Maximus more unrelenting. He looked out the window at the serene surroundings. He didn't know how to react. Suddenly he was overcome by his own nervous laughter that was so strong, he surprised himself. "Do you enjoy being a monk?" he asked in a sarcastic tone.

"I could do a much better job being an abbot," Modestos said softly.

"I didn't expect this," Maximus said. "That you would like to step into my shoes."

Modestos was silent.

Maximus thought that he was always able to manage all monastery problems with skill and grace, but this time it was a different beast, one that he didn't dare touch. "Well?" he said. "I guess that's what you want."

"I realize I'm too young for the position, but there're so many monks before me who, at my age, were elevated to high places."

"I'm astonished by your audacity," Maximus said, his face twisting into a strange, indignant smile.

"I don't care at all about your sentiments," Modestos said. "I know I can handle things around here."

Maximus moved closer, and Modestos jolted back. "Please," Maximus begged. "Please don't do this to us."

Modestos grinned. "You must pay a price for your sins."

"You are bent on destroying me, aren't you?"

"You destroyed my dignity," Modesto replied. "Tomorrow, you'll announce that you are naming me your first archdeacon to replace you in case of death or other cause. Then, in a few days, you'll disappear. I don't care where you go. Just disappear."

"What are you going to do with all the evidence you've gathered against me?" Maximus asked.

"As soon as I'm appointed – and you leave town – I will make sure that everything is destroyed."

"No. I'd prefer it if you hand over everything to me."

"No."

The monastery bell was ringing, a reminder that it was time for lunch.

Maximus stroked his bushy beard, lost for words. *He wants me to leave town*, he reflected. *I suppose I could always retire rich in London, near my sister. It's Marianna and the twins I hate to leave behind. Maybe they'll join me. She always wanted us to go away anyway. Maybe it is God's wish that I shed the robes, become a normal father. Maybe we could have more children.* "I'll do as you say," he said.

When Modestos left the office, he picked up the phone and called Marianna.

"Hello?"

"I love you dearly," Maximus said to her.

"I love you, too," she whispered. "I hear you're coming to the memorial reception."

"I thought about it afterwards," he said "and I don't think it's a good idea. I must see you tonight. I have something important to tell you."

"You sound troubled," she said. "What is it?"

"Nothing really."

"Maximus? You don't fool me."

"I'll tell you tonight. Meet me in the log cabin at eleven."

"I can't wait."

After he'd hung up, he went downstairs to join the other monks in the monastery's dining room for lunch.

As he was being served, it occurred to him that the other monks would not care less if he left the monastery. They were busy devouring their meals, absorbed in their own worlds, as if, apart from their secluded existence, nothing else mattered. He knew that what he was going to do was disgraceful, but he didn't care.

87

Jason and Helena arrived on time. They got out of the limousine that Helena had hired for the funeral and stood outside the Mosque. Helena, her head covered with a long scarf, was wearing a lengthy dark coat. They walked towards the entrance where a small crowd greeted them with words of condolences. They took their shoes off and entered the courtyard, which featured columns supporting horseshoe-shaped arches displaying geometric designs, birds and foliage. Arabesques proliferated in the form of carving inlay, tile, and painting.

The wall of the courtyard, the *gibla* wall, was facing the direction of Mecca; three other walls were lined with shallow arcades. In the centre of the *gibla* wall stood the *mihrab*, the place for prayers.

Jason watched as Ismail, accompanied by another man, approached him. "This is Imam Rahman," Ismail said as he introduced the other man.

"All women should stay in the back rows, behind the men," the Imam said looking at Helena.

Helena's face turned from pale white to red. "That's fine," Helena said, but Jason could tell she wasn't pleased.

"Viewing the remains is prohibited," the Imam said as he proceeded to the mimbar, a pulpit from which sermons are preached.

The funeral service was simple and respectful. The Imam officiated the funeral rituals with specific recitals from the Koran, while facing the casket.

The Mosque was overflowing with dignitaries, friends and employees. Standing in the front row, Jason took in the solemn and quiet atmosphere. He turned and recognized several people (among them, Kamal, Manning, Nicholas, Persinaras, Naharos, and the Pafos Mayor). Four rows behind him, he was surprised to spot Makin. In the back rows were many scarf-covered women. Jason recognized Cynthia, Katerina, Aisha and Marianna. The children were not with her, and he wondered why Marianna hadn't brought them. His eyes searched for Dr. Plato, but he wasn't in the crowd.

As soon as the Imam finished reading from the Koran, he faced the mourners. "Would anyone like to say a few words?" he asked.

Jason felt all the stares at his back, piercing his neck.

He walked very slowly to the podium. Taking a deep breath, he turned to face the quiet audience. He then raised his eyes to capture the arabesques for inspiration. He wanted the words to come from his heart, but what could he possibly say about a man from whom he ran away several years ago? He was glad that he had written something ahead of time. He pulled the piece of paper from his pocket and placed it on the podium.

"I'll be brief," he said looking at the handwritten eulogy. "'My father was an extraordinary man. Other men regarded him as a trusted friend. Anywhere he went, people greeted him with great admiration. He taught others about his experiences without the harshness of reproof. He was firm in his beliefs. He enjoyed the gift of insight, even when everything around him was gloomy.

"'The trip of life is short,' George Santayana once wrote, 'There is no cure for birth and death save to enjoy the interval.' My father was one of those men who truly enjoyed the interval. He didn't always know where he was going, but he did his work to the best of his abilities.

"I must confess, I often challenged him, without concern for his sentiments. Not understanding what my father's preoccupations were, I would sometimes speak to him in a tone of fierce contempt."

He paused. *Dear father. The time has come to forget the pain we've caused each other. The time has come to forget the love we failed to give to each other.*

"As the Greek poet Constantine Cavafy said in his poem *Ithaca*, 'It is the voyage and the adventures on the way that count, not the arrival itself.' Highways and mud-covered trails may lead us to the same destination. Father, by travelling your own road and reaching your own goals, you taught us that where a person goes is not as important as how he gets there. The journey of life is a difficult one, beset with many dangers and hardships. You enjoyed the voyage. God bless you."

When the service ended, Jason, on instructions from the Imam, walked over to the entrance of the Mosque, ahead of the mourners, and waited to accept words of condolences. As Ismail and his group were busy preparing to transfer the body to the cemetery, the mourners were directed toward the exit door.

Jason, standing quietly under the arched exit, watched the people forming a lineup. It occurred to him that Marianna, Katerina, Lagos, John Persinaras, Alexia Persinaras and Naharos were there as griefless spectators, paying only a token tribute to the passing of a man they cared little about. Watching their dry-eyed faces, he felt more like the Cerberus, the fierce dog guarding the entrance to Hades, than he did a son in mourning.

The sight of Makin, wearing an expression as somber as a mad dog, was even more troubling. The hypocrisy of the moment turned Jason's stomach inside out. He wanted to refuse to shake the man's hand, but the solemnity of the occasion was too severe for such a drastic move.

Nicholas shook his hand in silence.

88

The drive to the Turkish cemetery was brief. Police stopped the busy afternoon traffic to make way for the cortege. Much to Helena's protestation, only men were allowed to attend the site of the burial. Women were asked to wait in the cars.

During the brief graveside service, Jason's eyes filled with tears. He wiped them away fast enough so nobody would notice. He struggled and gained control of his emotions, kissing the casket tenderly for the last time.

When it was over, he felt a hand touching his shoulder, and when he turned he saw Kamal who was wearing a black cashmere suit; a radical change to the traditional attire in which Jason remembered him when they first met.

"I'd like to speak to you privately," Kamal said in his heavy accent.

"Come to the villa," Jason said. "We have plenty of food and juices."

"You must hear me now," Kamal said impatiently.

They walked a few meters away from the grave, far enough that no one might eavesdrop. "I'm listening," Jason said.

"Did someone steal your father's last will and testament?"

Jason wondered who told Kamal this information in such a short time. The police knew about it and … someone else. "Did Helena tell you?"

"Yes."

"It's true."

"Have you seen the will?" Kamal asked.

"No, but I know what it contained."

"From what Dr. Plato told you?"

"From my father's own breath, shortly before he expired."

"I understand that based on that will, you stood to inherit the chunk of the estate."

"Not only me. Helena, my half-sister, also stood to inherit a significant portion. And a trust fund was to be set up for the benefit of the children."

241

Drops of sweat rolled down Kamal's forehead. "I'm very distraught."

Jason was at a loss to understand why Kamal should be so concerned about how the estate was to be distributed. "But why?"

"I'll tell you why, damn it! The will that I have in my briefcase is a completely different document."

"How is this possible?"

"Faris's old will, the one that I have, makes no mention of any inheritance for you or Helena. You'll be sorry to hear that *everything* is left to your sister-in-law, Marianna."

Jason was unmoved. "Why is that the case?" he asked in a casual tone.

"The will that I have is dated November 5, 1999, a few days after your mother's death. It seems that Faris wanted to leave his estate to Richard. The will mentions Richard as the sole beneficiary. A subsidiary clause states that if Richard predeceases him, the whole estate shall go to Richard's wife, Marianna."

Jason wondered why his father, a man conceivably so keen to look after the welfare of the children, neglected to bequest part of his estate for the benefit of the under-age grandchildren. "Is there any bequest in the will for the children's benefit?"

"No. One explanation that I can think of is that perhaps Richard wanted it that way. It seems to me the two of them had discussed the will prior to its drafting and execution."

"Who was the solicitor that drafted it?"

"I don't know. Makin is named as the executor, though."

Jason thought for a moment. "But there's no proof that Richard is dead. Technically, the estate will be transferred to his name, until his death is confirmed."

"That's theoretical. Practically speaking, Marianna becomes the sole beneficiary."

Jason could still not understand why Kamal was so concerned. He saw no point in belabouring the issue. He turned around to face the people who were now going back to their cars, and only a handful remained at the graveside. "The limousine is waiting," he said as he started to walk.

"Wait a minute," Kamal said, blocking his way.

Jason stood there as if someone had put the brakes on him. "Well?"

"I don't want her to inherit your father's estate."

"Why not?"

"For several reasons. She is not a Muslim or an Arab, and we don't want all this wealth to fall into a non-believer's hands. Second, it offends my sense of justice and fairness that she, without a colour of right, stands to become so wealthy. And there are unsettled issues to be sorted out, and I hate to deal with a fragile female beneficiary and an executor whom I no longer trust; I'd prefer to deal with you. Finally, if the old will that I have with me is allowed to stand and the new will is to perish in the hands of some merciless and gutless thief, your father's intentions are going to be shamefully negated."

"Your final point is well taken," Jason exhaled. "However, despite your persuasiveness, my worries do not entirely match yours."

"As the rightful heir of your father's estate, I want you to stand up for your rights."

Jason was skeptical. "My rights derive from my own abilities. I didn't labour for any of these things."

"Come to your senses. In the absence of a will, under the Islamic law of inheritance, you are the first to get the residue in order of succession. Helena is not entitled to anything. According to Islamic law, illegitimate children have no part in inheritance. The grandsons are not entitled to any share either because they're regarded as disbelievers."

Jason could not believe that Kamal wanted him to inherit everything. "This may apply to the law of your land, but not to the laws of Cyprus."

"It's simple. All I have to do is to tear up the will that's in my briefcase. Our thirty five million dollar bank loan to your father is well safeguarded by other agreements; so I don't worry about that."

"I don't want you to destroy the will," Jason said firmly.

"But why? Are you crazy?"

"If I allow you to destroy the will, I will partake in an act of deception and I'll be committing an illegal activity, a crime of the same kind as the one that has already been perpetrated."

Kamal shook his head in obvious bewilderment. "This is not a perfect world," he murmured grinding his teeth. "I think that the West has spoiled you."

"So be it. These are my wishes, and I hope you respect them."

"And I assume you won't be contesting this will?"

"If I can speak for myself only, you're correct."

"Very well then. However, I will continue to have faith that you'll co-operate with our men and assist us in our investigation."

"I have already given you my promise," Jason said, and he rushed back to the waiting limousine wondering why Kamal had expressed his apparent contempt for Makin who was purported to be the named executor of the old will. *What did Makin do to cause Kamal not to trust him? Or is this just a ploy?*

89

Jason's limousine was the last to leave the cemetery. The chauffeur drove through the outskirts of Pafos to the main Pafos-Polis Road, en route for the compound of the Mustafa estate. Jason was sitting in the back with Helena beside him. Ismail, his head resting on the window, was sitting in the front passenger seat, exhausted. Jason glanced at his watch—it was 5:25 p.m. and the road to the Pafos hills was full of traffic.

"Tell me," he said looking at Helena, "did *our* father ever help you, financially?"

"No."

"And you have no resentment toward a man who had taken advantage of your mother's vulnerability?"

"These are choices they made. My mother had her own story; I can't rewrite her life. But I can shape mine. It's easy to blame others. I'm glad that I know who my father is."

He asked the driver to pull over. At an elevation of 1,400 meters, Jason gazed at the orange gash in the afternoon sky, which widened into a bright blue when merged with the vastness of the sea. He turned his head to the right to face the wilderness of the trees and shrubs, with their fading green, yellow and red leaves. He breathed in the coolness of the autumn air. It was, he thought, a good time to remind himself of the reasons for his journey to Pafos. On a day like this, Richard's loss was even more profound.

When the limousine entered the Mustafa compound, Jason saw at least twenty cars already parked in front of Villa Mustafa. Jason, Helena and Ismail got out of the limousine and walked down the garden path to Villa Oasis. The door was locked. Jason tried the spare key, but it still wouldn't open. The two maids who were supposed to meet the guests for Faris' memorial were outside, moving about on the front lawn of Villa Mustafa, re-directing the visitors, ushering them to Villa Mustafa.

"Damn it," Helena shouted, "She's done it again."

"What do we do now?" Ismail asked.

"Let us join them," Jason said and he started off toward the front door of Villa Mustafa. He turned to Helena. "If you see Nicholas, please don't go near him."

"I know," she replied. Seemingly reluctant to follow, she held Ismail's hand and said, "I'm not going in there."

"Please come for the sake of our father's memory," Jason begged.

"Yes." Ismail said. "Come." He pulled her by the hand, and Jason sensed that Helena resented the dragging.

Jason reflected, *I thought that this was going to be a private affair for contemplation*, as he walked into the teeming living room of Villa Mustafa. He felt he was inside a bar, joining a cocktail party. All the Persinaras family members, including Lagos, were present. Most guests held a drink in their hands, and there was a buffet at the edge of the dining room, laden with the same foods and delicacies that Helena had prepared for transport to Villa Oasis earlier that day. Jason saw many faces: the chief of police, Nicholas, the mayor and his wife, Makin and his wife, Alex Manning and his wife, men who appeared to be bodyguards, employees and many others.

Marianna came and extended her hands, touching Jason on the arms. "I'm glad you came," she said smiling.

He could see she was at pains to treat him like an ordinary guest, not as a grieving relative. He felt the stares of the people around her, as if they waited for him to respond with words of appreciation. What a sly front, he thought. Was he supposed to thank her? To smile back? To embrace her? To pretend? She uttered no words of condolence. She showed no signs of sympathy. She offered no explanation for moving the food or changing the lock.

A neutral expression glued on his face, Jason managed to say, "I'm sure you're pleased." He hoped his laconic statement would convey the right message.

Then he walked to the other end of the living room to greet Manning and Cynthia.

"Thank you for coming to the funeral," he said to them.

"Not at all," Manning responded. "It was indeed a sad day for us."

"Let's change the subject," Cynthia said, looking at Manning. "Jason deserves a little break." She turned to Jason. "A rather interesting theatrical group from Greece will be arriving in town on Saturday. They'll use an ancient Greek theater, the Odeion, to stage a fascinating variation of *The Trojan Women*."

Jason welcomed the opportunity to talk about plays. He'd always enjoyed them, but could never find an interested listener. "That would be worth seeing," he said. "I think this particular tragic play turned the focus away from the dilemmas faced by rough male warriors, and onto the women, especially the mothers Hecuba and Andromache, whose lives were ruined by male violence."

"To me," Cynthia said, "the women of Troy have often been made to protest against modern wars or to commemorate their victims. And it seems this particular troupe intends to do just that in protest of the war in Afghanistan."

"Don't be silly," Manning interjected. "They're doing it for the hard cash."

Cynthia turned to Jason. "Will you accompany me to the Odeion on Saturday?" she asked him. Her sweet breath gently reached his nostrils.

Jason didn't know how to respond. If he accepted her offer, he could use the occasion to question Cynthia about Richard's alleged relationship with her, and hopefully get useful information about what led to his brother's disappearance. He was sensitive to Manning's feelings, however, and turned to face him. "If you'll allow me," said Jason, "I would be most honoured—."

"Oh, Alex has some pressing matters to attend to on Saturday," Cynthia interrupted.

"Yes, that's true," Manning agreed. "Enjoy the show," he added.

The tone of Manning's remark was so enigmatic, Jason had difficulty responding. "We can reserve three seats," he said, "in case you finish your duties early."

"Don't worry about him," Cynthia said. "He's happy to see me go out with someone we can both trust."

"That's very nice of you," Jason said, truly thrilled by the compliment. "Shall we meet at the entrance?" he asked.

"No. Please pick me from the hotel at one o'clock," she said. "The play won't start until three, which will give us some time for a leisurely lunch. The weather is going to be fabulous: sunshine and 22 degrees."

"I'll be there," he said, feeling nervous inside. *I'll lease a good car for the occasion,* he mused. "Now, if you'll excuse me," he said, "I must say hello to some other guests."

90

Jason mingled, met and thanked many guests, but he followed his instinct and avoided Marianna, Naharos, Makin, Katerina and Lagos; simply knowing they were there created an eerie feeling within him.

He was happy to see Nicholas in the crowd, but didn't speak to him since they were secretly working together. Nicholas also appeared detached, observing quietly from a distance, as if he were paying his proper respects.

Helena turned to Jason. "She couldn't get her eyes off you," Helena complained in a whispering voice.

"Are you talking to me?" Ismail asked.

"No."

Jason sensed that her comment was directed at him. "What a pleasant couple," he said to Helena, and he smiled at Cynthia Manning.

"You mean what a pleasant woman." Helena responded.

"Are you jealous?" Ismail interjected.

Helena gave Ismail a peck on the cheek. "He's my brother, you fool. I don't want him to get into trouble, that's all."

Jason wondered if he should tell her about the invitation to accompany Cynthia to the play. He thought about it for a split second and decided to keep it to himself. "I'm hungry," he said. "Let's eat something." He picked up a plate and chose a variety of hors d'oeuvres.

While he ate, Jason puzzled over why the children were nowhere in sight. He wanted to talk to them again. He approached Marianna. "I would love to see the children," he said.

"This is not the right time," she snapped back.

Jason retreated. "Fine."

Kamal sat in the middle of the chesterfield and cleared his throat. "Attention, please. I want everybody to get closer."

Jason saw how hastily people gathered around Kamal. "Once again, I want to convey my heart-felt condolences to the relatives and friends of the deceased," Kamal pronounced. "Many years ago, when I was a poor Palestinian kid, without a country and without a home, Faris Mustafa, God bless him, helped me find a job at a bank. He put his trust in me, and I never let him down. I started as a clerk and eventually was promoted to bank manager. Mr. Mustafa's contributions to the Palestinian cause will long be remembered." He opened his briefcase and pulled out a thick document.

"This is the last will and testament of the late Faris Mustafa," Kamal said, holding the papers with both hands. He raised the document up for everyone to see.

Jason remained standing, trying to remain calm, as he sensed the uneasiness in the living room. Marianna, standing beside Katerina, seemed shorter than her normal height, as if a steel bar had fallen on her shoulders. Katerina, on the other hand, stared at Marianna in a bewildering manner, and he sensed she was surprised by Kamal's announcement.

" '...I appoint Nadir Makin to be the executor of my estate.

" '...If my son, Richard Mustafa, is living on the thirtieth day following the date of my death, my executor shall pay and transfer the residue of my estate to my son, Richard Mustafa, for his own use absolutely.

" '...If my son, Richard Mustafa, is not living on the thirtieth day following the date of my death, my executrix shall pay and transfer the residue of my estate to my daughter-in-law, Marianna Mustafa, for her own use absolutely.'"

"I will not tire you with the rest of the provisions in the will," Kamal said, "such as the payment of taxes and debts. It is enough to say that, since Richard is presumed dead, Marianna is the sole beneficiary."

"He left everything to me?" Marianna cried, seemingly uncertain.

"Yes. That's right," Kamal responded.

"Oh, my God. I can't believe this!" she said.

A veil of silence covered the room. Many watched in disbelief, their mouths slightly open as if trying to gasp for more air.

"It can't be true!" Helena shouted out, like a thud from the passing storm. "This is an old will!" she declared, her hands shaking. "The last will was stolen from Dr. Plato's house last night!"

"You're crazy!" Katerina shouted back at her. "Take the maid away," she ordered the bodyguards.

Two tall men with square shoulders and rugged faces stepped in and grabbed Helena by the arms. "Let's go," one of them pressed.

Ismail stepped in to push them away, and he received a punch in the stomach that bent him to his knees. Someone dragged him outside.

Helena was resisting the bodyguards with kicks and pushes, but her neck was clamped, and Jason could see that she was having trouble breathing.

"Wait a minute," Jason protested. "Leave her alone. She's my sister."

The bodyguards hesitated and then relaxed their hold of her.

"You had a brother!" Katerina yelled. "A sister? This is news to all of us."

Makin and Lagos agreed, nodding their heads. Jason heard murmurs and inaudible comments.

"Even if Helena is your sister, what difference does it make, anyway?" Marianna asked in a slow trembling voice.

"The difference is hundreds of millions of dollars that Helena is entitled to inherit," Jason said.

"The will speaks for itself," Katerina said. "Marianna is the sole surviving beneficiary."

"Not according to my father's last will and testament that was stolen from Dr. Plato's house last night," Jason responded.

Makin and Lagos burst into laughter.

"Laugh all you want," Jason said. "Someone has committed a crime. I suspect this someone is here with us today."

"You sound like another Dr. Plato," Katerina said in a sarcastic tone. "We all know what he's capable of manufacturing: hallucinations!"

"Only his enemies would utter such venomous language." Jason snapped back.

"Why isn't he in attendance, so he can tell us what he knows?" Katerina asked.

"He's devastated by the incident," Jason said, "that's why. His house was ransacked and his dog was shot dead."

"Nonsense," Katerina replied. "He's probably caused all this to attract attention to his loneliness." She approached Kamal. She grabbed the will from his hands and handed it to Marianna, who took and held it on her chest. "The will stays with my sister," Katerina asserted in a rather rigid voice. "Now you and Helena get out of here. You've no right to be present in this villa, or this property for that matter." She turned to Marianna. "Tell them to get out. Maybe they should hear it from you!"

"Yes. Get out, now!" Marianna insisted.

Jason could see Nicholas's red face, but he was too proud to have anyone intervene on his behalf. And with so many bodyguards in the room, he didn't want Nicholas to get hurt.

"Fine," Jason said. "We're leaving." He took Helena by the hand, and they both walked out.

Ismail was already seated in the waiting limousine. They got in, and the driver drove slowly toward the gates.

Once outside the gates, Jason felt something in his pocket. He put his hand inside and he touched the keypad that Faris had given him to use for the gates. He was about to throw it away but he changed his mind. "Stop for a second," he asked the driver. He got out, walked about 150 feet at an area where no one could see him, found a rock and hid the keypad under it. *I might need it some day,* he told himself.

91

At eleven-thirty, Marianna looked through the narrow window of the log cabin. She could see the brilliant moon, but her eyes were searching for him. He's usually on time, she reflected. As she was about to put her clothes back on, she saw a shadow and then the dark shape of a man she couldn't quite recognize walked briskly toward the cabin. Fearing that he might be an intruder, she locked the cabin door, grabbed a vase by the neck and retreated in the corner of the room.

"It's me," Maximus whispered. "Open the door."

Marianna heaved a sigh of relief. Wearing nothing but black silk panties, she opened the door to greet him. He looked worried, lost in his thoughts. He wore a black sweater and dark grey pants. "Your robe!" she exclaimed. "Where's your monk's robe? I've never seen you go out without it."

He let go a lungful of air. "I'll explain later," he said.

"You'd better explain to me right now why you didn't come on time! You know how much I hate waiting."

"I'm sorry," he said as he held her by the arms.

"Your hands are cold," she said "Are you nervous?"

"I'm a bit uptight. I'll be okay."

"What happened?"

"I was on the phone arguing with my sister."

The mention of his sister was enough to upset her chemical balance.

Before she had a chance to respond, he kissed her, lifted her off her feet and placed her on the bed. He took off his clothes and made love to her, hastily and wordlessly.

She felt his sperm inside her. So soon; not the usual foreplay; no kissing or sucking; no mesmerizing words; no ecstasy.

They lay together in the darkness, listening to the familiar calls of the frogs. "That was quick," she complained.

"The twins," he said.

"What about them?"

"You remember how anxious I was to know if they were mine?"

"Yes. I remember."

"I don't care, anymore."

"What are you saying?"

"I mean … I don't care if they're mine or not. I promise I won't pressure you again for blood tests."

She was more upset than curious. "You don't care about us anymore. Is that it?"

"I've given a lot of thought about your desire to marry me and move away from this place, to a new land, where you, the children and I can have a normal family life," Maximus stated. "And I'm happy to say that you were right, and I was wrong. I've decided to leave the monastery and move to London—with you and the children. We can get married there and begin a new life together."

Marianna jumped up and stood by the window, her eyes fixed at the splendid exterior of Villa Mustafa, illuminated by the bright spotlights on the lawn. With the hundreds of millions of inheritance she was about to receive, she could choose to live anywhere in the world (the French Riviera would be a good place to start) free to enjoy her life as she saw fit. Why would she want to put up with an aging ex monk and his spinster sister in the smoggy corridors of London? "No!" she said firmly. She stretched out her hands and lowered her torso. "No, no, no!"

He got up and began to put on his clothes. "I can't believe it," he said, shaking his head. "You told me you love me. You insisted I leave the church, marry you and move away with you—and after I've done that, you say no!"

She gathered her clothes and walked to the toilet. She got dressed in a hurry, forgetting to wear her bra. She got out of the toilet and rushed for the door. She opened it and stormed out of the cabin.

She could hear his heavy steps behind her. She stopped and turned around. "Stop chasing me!" she yelled.

He dropped on his knees. "Please don't abandon me!" he cried. "I'm leaving for London on Monday morning … I must. I'll be waiting for you!"

"Leave me alone!" she shouted, pulling off her shoes and running toward Villa Mustafa.

92

Jason left the Turkish House at 11:00. It was a sunny Friday morning and the wind had subsided. He had an hour to look for a rental car before his twelve o'clock meeting with Nicholas. He needed a decent vehicle to pick up Aziz, who was expected to arrive at Larnaca Airport on Sunday. He also looked forward to driving Cynthia to the Saturday's theatrical performance at the ancient Greek theatre. The safe transportation of the items that Nicholas had removed from the Mustafa building on Wednesday night was another reason he thought a private car was necessary.

He walked to the Farmers' Market and asked around for a car rental place. Someone gave him directions, and in just thirty minutes he was able to find a brand new, four-door, Rover with metallic grey paint that glittered under the warm sunrays; its fresh leather seats permeated an irresistible scent. He leased it for seven days. At fifty pounds a day (the equivalent of 100 US dollars) he found it to be the most expensive car he'd ever hired, but it was worth it, he knew.

He drove cautiously around the block for a few minutes to get used to driving on the left side of the road. He then steered toward the Farmers' Market and parked near Nicholas's restaurant. The air was filled with the smell of marinated grilled meat. His hunger was not as intense as his ferocious impatience to pick up the items he had found at the Mustafa building and continue with his investigation.

Nicholas stood up, holding a bottle of wine. Plates on the table in front of him were filled with grilled lamb, cheese, pickled green olives, fried red mullet, marinated octopus and salad. Nicholas smiled broadly, shook Jason's hand and said, "That's a nice car you drive."

"I hired it for a reason."

"Are you hungry?"

The restaurant was crowded. "Yes. I could eat," Jason said gladly, knowing that to turn Nicholas down—after all the effort that had obviously gone into preparing the dishes—would be considered an insult.

They sat down and started eating and drinking.

Jason enjoyed every bite and every sip. "I like the wine," he said. "It washes down well." It was medium-bodied with soft, supple tannins and berry nuances accentuated by hints of vanilla and spice.

"It's a 1995 vintage from the village of Panakas," Nicholas said, "my birthplace."

Jason had heard of the village; some inhabitants were E.O.K.A members and sympathizers, belonging to the first liberation movement that was set up to expel the British from the island in the early 50's. If you were from Panakas, it was presumed that you would have access to at least one pistol. "I haven't been to Panakas," Jason said, "but when my job is done, I'll make a point of visiting your village."

"Apart from vineyards, there's nothing worth seeing," Nicholas said humbly. "Most residents have moved to bigger towns."

Jason found the right moment to mention the items. "Did you bring them?" he asked.

"They're in the back room." Nicholas paused and then he said, "I'm a bit disappointed."

"Why?"

"You don't seem to have a need for our services any longer."

Jason instantly figured out what probably happened. "Did they ask your security personnel to leave the Mustafa building?"

"Shortly before you arrived, I received a phone call from one of our guards, telling me that a man named Makin went there with a bunch of police officers and expelled my people. Apparently he had another security company lined up to take over the job of guarding the building."

Jason couldn't believe that Makin was involved. When they'd spoken yesterday on the telephone, Makin had emphatically resigned, and now this. "I'm sorry about all the trouble," Jason said. "I thought Makin was no longer acting as general manager for my father's company because he resigned yesterday. I'm the CEO of the company."

"After what I saw last night, I'm not surprised," Nicholas responded. "That's why I didn't rush to any conclusions about your involvement in all this."

"I need to find out what's going on," Jason said, "as soon as I leave this place."

"I hope you don't mind me telling you this," Nicholas said hesitantly, "but I think you should thank your lucky stars that you're still alive."

"I know my life is in danger," Jason said.

"I know why you're still alive," Nicholas continued.

"Why?"

"Your enemies underestimate you. They think you're up to no good, but you don't pose a real threat to them—at least not just yet."

Jason appreciated Nicholas's frankness. "Is this how I come across?"

"Well. Really ... I mean, I saw last night how they literally threw you and your sister out of your father's villa, without a hint of resistance on your part. I was astounded. If I were in your shoes ... I don't know. I would have ... done something."

Jason took a big breath and counted to ten. "I came to this town to investigate a crime," he said calmly, "not to commit one."

"I know. Your brother." Nicholas bent his torso foreword. "If you push them any further, they'll cut you into a million tiny pieces and mix your flesh with gravel," Nicholas whispered, conscious of the people around them.

Jason's body shook impulsively. He wondered if that's what happened to Richard. "I can't turn my back and return to Canada," he said.

"You look like you need some help," Nicholas said. "It's time, I think, you take the gloves off ... and ... for Christ's sake, stop being so wimpy."

Jason's pride was insulted by Nicholas's off-the-cuff remarks. "What do I do? Take a gun and go around shooting at every conceivable suspect?"

"You should have guessed who the suspects are by now."

"I have some clues."

Nicholas stood up, forcefully. "Let's go! I've got something to show you."

93

They went through the kitchen, exited the back door, walked on a narrow concrete trail and reached a small house at the back of the property. Nicholas used a key and opened the door.

He turned the lights on and a German shepherd jumped from the chesterfield, ready to leap. "C'mon Achilles!" Nicholas said firmly. "Sit down! Sit. Sit." He turned to Jason. "Achilles won't attack unless I say so," Nicholas said, and Jason's heart went back to its normal pace.

Jason watched as Nicholas went into the tiny kitchen, opened the cupboard under the sink, and removed all the plastic bottles and garbage bags, clearing the area. He then pulled off the vinyl sheet that was covering the top of the wood at the base, and using a hammer, he removed all the nails. Afterwards he plucked out the square piece of plywood. Under the plywood Jason could see a large hollow space. Nicholas inserted his right hand inside the cavity and pulled out a dark, soiled sack.

Jason smelled petroleum.

Nicholas removed the grease with a piece of cloth and placed the item on the kitchen table. "This is a 9-mm Beretta," Nicholas said. "Very popular with the Italian Army during both World Wars."

Jason stared at the thing, as if it was a piece of rock from the red planet.

"This one is a 9-mm German-made Luger. Look at it! Doesn't it look solid? I love the shape." He offered it to Jason. "Feel it."

"It's okay, thank you," Jason said. "I'd rather not touch it."

Nicholas placed it on the table and inserted his hand into the sack. "Oh, here's another beauty," Nicholas said. "American. Colt.45 semi-automatic."

Jason felt nauseated. "I've seen enough," he said touching his forehead.

Nicholas took out a hand grenade. "It won't explode unless I pull this pin."

"You're well-equipped," Jason managed to say.

"I never know when I'm going to need one of these things," Nicholas said. "In your case though, I think you should have one, right now, for your own protection."

"Are you offering me one of your pistols?"

"Yes. Why?"

Jason searched for the right words, mindful that the slightest slip of the tongue could offend Nicholas. "I'm sorry. I'm not trained to handle these things."

"That's not a problem. I'll train you. We'll go up to the mountains, near my village."

Jason looked for another excuse. "But I'm left-handed."

"What a coincidence! Me, too!"

"My ears are sensitive to noise. One of my eardrums is fractured," Jason lied.

"I have earplugs," Nicholas boasted. He pulled out another sack from the bottom of the hole, just as soiled as the first one. "Look," he said. "I have masks, earplugs, and even a camouflaged uniform."

"I'll tell you what," Jason said. "You keep it here. If I need one, I'll come to you for it. How's that?"

Nicholas frowned and began putting the pistols back in the sack. "I know you'll come back a lot sooner than you think. The modern stuff is stored elsewhere. I have machine-guns, shotguns, knives, binoculars and at least a dozen Beretta pistols."

Jason waited for Nicholas to hide everything in the same place, and when Nicholas closed the cupboard, Jason said: "I have a car nearby. I can carry the items now."

"Oh, yes. I almost forgot," Nicholas smiled. He went to another small room and retrieved three large plastic bags. "Everything is in these bags," he said. "Let me help you take them to the car."

They carried the bags to the car.

Jason thanked Nicholas for the fine meal and drove away. While on the road, he called Helena.

"I have the stuff," he said.

"Where are you?"

"I'm driving a rented car. I just left Nicholas's restaurant."

"Where are you planning to take them?"

"I want you to examine everything carefully, especially the bank books." He was also interested to know where Helena lived. "Can I bring them over?"

"I live in an apartment building, and I don't want people to see you carrying things to my unit. I'd prefer you take them straight to the Turkish House. I'll pick them up from there."

"I guess I'll never get to see your place."

"To tell you the truth, I'm a bit ashamed to invite you here. This is a very poor neighbourhood."

Jason wondered if Helena was making excuses for some unknown purpose. "What could be poorer than the Turkish House quarter?"

"Ha! You wouldn't believe it, but my bachelor apartment is so small there isn't enough room for the three of us to sit down."

"How's Ismail?"

"His pride is hurt. He's having a siesta right now."

"Okay. I'm going to unload the stuff at the Turkish House and then drive to the Mustafa building to see what's happening with the business." He didn't tell her about Makin being there, so as not to alarm her.

"Do you think they'll let you manage it?"

"I'll find out in less than an hour."

"I don't know," Helena said, revealing her deep doubts.

94

Behind the wheel, on his way to the Mustafa building, Jason experienced a loss of control. Drivers refused to yield the right of way, and others sped from behind to overtake him, only to make quick turns in front of him. But his frustration with the traffic was no comparison to the irritation he felt whenever he thought about Makin—someone he considered one of the main suspects in Richard's disappearance.

Based on Richard's diary, the Delphi project was the last job that Richard was involved with before he vanished on April 11th. Many questions about the meeting between Richard and Makin remained unanswered. Who was the client that the villa was built for? What did Richard and Makin discuss during their five o'clock meeting? Where did Richard go after the meeting? Whom did he meet and why? Had Makin been present?

If the last forty-eight hours were any indication, Jason didn't think that Makin was going to co-operate willingly. That was a foregone conclusion. Makin's overt hostility towards him could not be explained under normal circumstances, but conditions were nothing but unusual. Thousands of dollars were missing from the vault. There was a Panamanian bank account. Suspicious liaisons existed with Lagos and Katerina. Cigars were found among Richard's personal items; a love letter in Makin's office addressed to Richard from 'Mythic Blue'; a trip to Nicosia on the day of Faris' death; the theft of Faris' will; and above all a photograph showing Makin, Crow and another unidentified man being hugged and kissed by three women at a place that seemed to be Crow's brothel.

Jason considered going to the police with his circumstantial evidence, but his recent encounter with Naharos told him he wouldn't get very far without solid proof.

He wondered why Makin, despite his verbal resignation, had assumed the authority to fire Nicholas's security personnel and replace them with a security firm of his own choosing. He thought about possible reasons. What if Makin and Marianna conspired to remove him as the CEO of Mustafa Holdings? If that was the case, Makin was capable of anything. Still, Jason needed something more to substantiate his suspicions.

He parked behind the Mustafa building. Many cars were scattered through the parking lot, among them a large BMW with tinted windows, which Jason figured belonged to Makin.

The security guards greeted him at the lobby as if he was an expected visitor, a sign that prompted him to be extra cautious. He rode to the fifth floor and walked to Makin's office, only to find it closed. He knocked at the door a couple of times, but there was no answer. Jason heard voices coming from the corner office, the one Faris used to occupy. He walked over to the corner office. Two burly security men stood by the door. One of them asked, "Are you looking for Mr. Makin?"

"Yes."

"He's expecting you."

Makin sat behind Faris's desk, apparently absorbed in paper work.

Jason was about to enter the office when one of the security men stopped him. "We have to search you first," he insisted.

When the search was done, Jason was allowed to enter the office while the two men stood by the open door.

"I'm listening," Makin said.

Jason had to play naïve. "This is the office I'm supposed to occupy," he said humbly.

Makin put on a fake smile. "You don't understand, do you?"

"What?"

"You don't belong here."

"I'm the CEO."

"You were the ... C, E, O," Makin slowly sounded out the letters with a wicked grin.

"You've appointed yourself?" asked Jason incredulously.

"Are you an idiot or pretending to be one?"

"All I want to know is how you got this job."

"Marianna asked me to stay. I agreed on condition that you are out. And so, she hired me as the CEO."

"Are you telling me that Marianna took over Mustafa Holdings?"

"This is not a takeover, smart-ass," Makin snapped. "She's the heir of the estate. She derives her powers from the will! Don't you understand?" he yelled.

"Look, don't raise your voice," Jason said. "I didn't come here for a fight. The will has not yet been probated."

Makin sighed. "Let's not play with technicalities. The fact remains that your father has disinherited you. Everybody knows that."

It was clear to Jason by now that Makin was bent on asserting his power. Jason's purpose for coming to see Makin was to satisfy himself beyond any doubt that Makin was indeed a man to watch. Now he was certain. "Fine. I'll go then."

As he was about to exit the door, the two security men grabbed him by the hair, shut the door and dragged him in the corner of the office. They forced him to sit on a chair and tied his body with copper wire. Then they blind-folded him and covered his mouth with a piece of tablecloth. "You can leave us now," Jason heard Makin say. "Close the door behind you."

"You're mistaken if you think you can fuck with me!" Makin said.

He felt the force of Makin's repeated punches to his head, eyes, nose, mouth, neck, and in his ribs. The pain was excruciating. He felt blood dripping from his nose, and fearing that he was going to die, he began to tremble.

Makin untied his mouth. "Now we can talk," he said.

Jason could barey move his lips. Pieces of broken teeth were mixed with blood, and he spit them out. "Let … me go."

"Where did you hide my things?"

"What things?"

Jason was shaken by another punch on the nose. "You're a liar. Many things are missing from my office. You took them."

"I didn't."

Makin grabbed him by the hair and hit his head on the wall at least three times. "Speak up, or I'll kill you!"

"I don't know."

"Damn it. You're stubborn."

Makin lit a cigar; Jason could smell it though he couldn't see it. He suffered another strong blow to the head that caused him nausea, and at that point he thought he was going to pass out – or die.

95

Jason opened his eyes to see an insane face. "You won't talk, eh?"

Fearing another blow, he shut his eyes on reflex.

"Take him downstairs," Makin ordered the guards. "If he complains to the police tell them he came to attack me, and I had to defend myself."

They dragged him to the elevator, pushed him inside and pressed the button. Once on the ground floor, they carried him to the car and left him, his back against the tire.

It took him at least twenty minutes to regain his strength. He struggled to his feet, searched his pockets and found the key. Trembling, he turned the ignition and slowly drove away, heading for the hospital.

The emergency ward was rumbling with cries, shouts and lots of hurried steps. "Over here sir," a nurse said opening the door to another room. She asked him to lie down, and a doctor came to see him right away.

"What on earth happened to you?" the doctor asked.

"Isn't it obvious?" Jason replied.

"These are very bad bruises," the doctor said as he examined his face and head. "Someone must have beaten you up with a vengeance."

"You're right."

"I'll get the nurse to look after you."

A few seconds later, a slim nurse walked in with a tray of first-aid supplies and started to apply ice cubes on his face. "This will help with the swelling," she said. "Have I met you before?" she asked.

"I don't know" he said, his eyes closed, but her familiar touch caused warm blood to trickle to his heart.

"Jason! Is that *you*?"

He tried to open his eyes. "Do you know me?"

"I'm Penelope, the mother of the child that you saved last Tuesday."

"Oh, yes. I'm sorry, I didn't recognize you."

"It *is* you. I almost didn't recognize you, either."

"How do I look?"

"Don't ask. Who did this to you?"

"A man named Makin."

"Makin?"

"Do you know him?"

"I've heard of him."

Jason took a big breath.

"I think Nicholas should know about this," she said.

Jason didn't want to be the cause of any confrontation between Nicholas and Makin. "I'd prefer keeping Nicholas out of this," he said.

"Anyway, you should rest for at least a couple of hours before you leave the hospital." She handed him several pills and a glass of water. "Here, take these."

Jason swallowed the tablets and drank the water, not so much to take down the medication as to quench his thirst.

"I'll get you a private room." Penelope said.

"I don't think I need to stay any longer. I have things to do."

"No. You shouldn't leave in this condition. The pills will make you drowsy and you may fall. Are you driving?"

"Yes."

"That's even worse. You can easily get into an accident."

Jason did not insist. "You have a point," he said.

Penelope left the room and came back a couple of minutes later with two male nurses who held Jason by the arms as they walked him to a corner room on the second floor. It's clean and quiet, Jason observed, as they undressed him and helped him put on a pair of pajamas. He lay down and closed his eyes. The medication was beginning to have an effect and he started dozing off.

The ringing of his cellular phone interrupted his mending nap.

"Hello," Helena said. "Are you meeting us for dinner?"

"Some other time," Jason said. "I have a few things to take care of tonight."

"How did it go at the office?"

"Not as I expected," Jason said, trying to keep a steady voice.

"What happened?"

He didn't want to spoil her evening by telling her about the beating he suffered. "Makin has taken over as CEO."

"I suspected that something like this was about to happen," Helena said. "Are you alright?"

"Mmm? Yes ... yes, I'm fine."

"I'm looking at the items," Helena said, "one by one. But they raise more questions than answers. The prime suspect is Makin, but he's followed by many others."

"The motive?" Jason asked.

"Maybe money. However, it will be close to impossible to get any particulars of the Panamanian account."

"I think we ought to examine the link between the Mustafa bank in Nicosia and the bank accounts," Jason said.

"That's what I plan to do tomorrow. I'll devote the whole day to scrutinizing the documents I have."

"Can you do all that in one day?"

"If I'm not interrupted."

"I'll make sure I don't call you tomorrow."

"No. You can call any time."

"We know by now who the suspects are," Jason said. "I think we should look for a way to lift their covers."

"Can't you see how organized they are?"

"I'm still hopeful."

"Do you have enough money to get by?" Helena asked.

"Yes, thanks."

"I'm going to use the money Faris left me to pay for the new security in Nicosia and legal costs for the freezing of the Mustafa bank assets."

"Fine," Jason said. "When do you plan to contact me next?"

"As soon as I put the puzzle together."

"I'll be waiting for your call," Jason said.

Penelope walked into the room with a cup in her hands.

"I have to go now," he said to Helena. "Goodbye."

"I brought you some chamomile tea," Penelope said. "Drink it. It will help calm your muscle spasms."

"Thank you," Jason said as he took the cup and began to drink the tea.

"Nicholas is very upset about what Makin has done to you. I had to tell him."

"I'm ready to be discharged. You've been a tremendous help, and I'll never forget it."

"Yes, you can leave now, but go straight to bed. I'll let you get dressed. I'll see you on your way out."

Jason got up, took off the pajamas and got dressed. On his way out, Penelope waived goodbye with a broad smile, and he returned the favour.

Once back in the car, he pondered whether he should go to the hotel to check for messages (and change his clothes) or drive straight to the Turkish House. He didn't want the hotel staff to see his bruised face, so he opted for the latter.

Parking the car a safe distance from the house to avoid detection, he walked through the narrow streets of the Mouttallos neighbourhood and eventually reached the gates. As he was about to open the door, his cellular phone rang. It was Helena, again.

"You won't believe this," she said.

"Go ahead," Jason said anxiously.

"Among the items in the envelopes, I found your passport, driver's license, birth certificate, health card and several business cards."

"I lost those things two years ago!" Jason exclaimed.

"What should I do with them?"

"Um, put them in an envelope, and I'll pick them up when I see you."

96

On Saturday, Jason left the Turkish House, drove to the Mustafa Beach Hotel and arrived there at half past noon. He parked, went to his room, shaved and showered. He put on his grey corduroy pants, casual leather shoes, white cotton shirt, light blue cotton vest, and dark blue blazer. He picked up a tie and was about to wear it but changed his mind. He left the room and went to the lobby of the hotel on time, waiting for Cynthia.

His main reason for accompanying Cynthia to the Odeion was to seek information about the circumstances that had led to Richard's disappearance, but trepidations filled his mind. What if Cynthia had a hidden agenda? What if Manning was after something? What if someone planned to kill him? He tended to think that Cynthia would not attend a 'public event' with him if she intended something sinister. Perhaps she wanted to 'be seen' in his company, a motive Jason could not discern. Despite these misgivings, he looked forward to a social outing with Cynthia alone, a woman whom he found highly spirited.

At exactly one o'clock, he saw her exiting one of the elevators, and their eyes met. She walked towards him with a worried look, and when she came closer he could see black bags under her green eyes. As they shook hands, he felt her uneasiness. She was wearing a smart-looking grey faux suede pantsuit. Her hair was wet, and (as usual) her face had no make-up. She was holding a black bag, small enough to be a wallet but big enough to hold large items, such as a PDA or a cell phone.

"Oh my God!" she exclaimed, holding his chin with her slender fingers. "They beat you up!"

Jason looked the other way. "I'm fine," he said.

"No, you're not! Those bruises on your face, and the dark blue marks around your eyes ... you look awful. What happened? Who did this?"

"Makin and I had a skirmish yesterday."

"Damn it!" she exclaimed. She snapped her fingers and narrowed her eyes. She sat down, holding her head.

"It's okay," he said. "Don't worry. Let's go."

Cynthia got up, and Jason sensed that they were being watched. A man with Hispanic features walked by and stood in front of him for a second with his hands in his pockets. He then pulled out a camera and took a picture.

"What are you doing?" Jason asked the man. "Give that to me!"

But the man turned around briskly, walked away, opened a door and disappeared into the vast corridor.

"Did you see that?" Jason said to Cynthia.

She shrugged her shoulders. "Where is your car?"

"In the parking lot."

They exited the hotel through the main entrance and walked to the parking lot. Behind a van, Jason saw two men with cameras. "We're being photographed," he said.

"Evidently," Cynthia affirmed.

They got into the car. Jason followed the main road, driving towards the harbour. They reached the crowded tourist zone, and Jason had to slow down.

"Are you ready for lunch?" Cynthia asked.

"I know a nice little place by the Farmers' Market," Jason said. "A friend of mine—"

"Let's go to *The Pelican*," she interrupted.

"You'll have to give me directions."

"It's on this street, by the harbour."

He drove another four hundred meters and he saw a police officer redirecting the traffic, preventing the cars from driving towards the harbour. "They do that during lunch and dinner," Cynthia said, "to allow the patrons to enjoy their meals without noise and exhaust fumes."

"Are you sure you don't want to go to my friend's place?"

"Wait a second," Cynthia said. She got out, approached the police officer, and Jason saw her pulling a card from her purse and showing it to him. She said something, and the officer nodded with a smile.

Cynthia came back and got into the car. "He'll let us through," she said.

Jason thanked the officer and drove slowly.

Cynthia pointed. "That's the place. There's parking at the rear."

He parked, and they walked to the front where stone arches and columns adorned the restaurant's arcade. There were no empty tables. Jason glanced across the street and spotted more tables, covered with the same blue and white-checkered tablecloth. They crossed the street, passed through the sitting patrons and stopped at an empty table.

"Is this spot all right?" he asked Cynthia.

"Well," she paused, "I'd rather sit over there." She pointed at a table that was isolated from the rest. "It's more private."

They walked over to that table, and Cynthia sat down. "I wouldn't mind a cold glass of Carlsberg," she said.

"That's my favourite beer," Jason grinned.

"Let's see how many other things we have in common," Cynthia smiled.

Jason sat opposite Cynthia, with the marina behind him. A male waiter came to their table to deliver the menu, and Jason ordered the beer and a bottle of mineral water.

"The salty breeze tangled with the smell of fried fish makes me hungry," Cynthia said as she flipped the glossy menu pages.

Jason could smell her perfume, a mix of almond blossoms, fresh roses and pine oil. "Have you been here before?" he asked.

"Many times," she said as she got up. "I've got to wash my hands. Please order me the shrimp scampi al fresco and a small village salad." And away she went.

Jason surveyed the area around the little harbour. A strip of restaurants extended from one end to the other and hundreds of patrons were eating on the patios. Small kiosks lined the quay, selling snacks and drinks to unhurried locals (mothers, fathers and young children), who swarmed all over the street eating sandwiches, corn on the cob or cone ice-cream. Some tourists snapped pictures of the harbour. Porters pushed wheeled carts loaded with boxes. He turned his head to see motorboats and sailboats; the people on them seemed busy cleaning, while others sat idly chatting.

97

The waiter returned, and Jason ordered Cynthia's choice and artichoke bottoms with scallops and a garden salad for himself.

He turned his head around again, feeling the soft touches of the breeze caress his face and soothe his bruises, as if an invisible sea goddess applied curative herbs to his wounds.

Cynthia returned to the table, carrying a cellular phone. "I just spoke to Alex," she said. "I've told him we're both doing fine."

Jason nodded.

"You see that yacht over there?" she pointed, and Jason turned his head. "It belongs to George Lagos. I've been on it. It's very comfortable and roomy, but it reminds me of a fishing boat, which is what it was, really, before it was converted into a passenger boat."

Jason saw porters loading boxes on it. He couldn't care less about Lagos's boat. He wondered, though, if Cynthia was trying to tell him something. Encouraging her to open up some more, he said, "It looks big enough to accommodate at least eight people."

"Actually it has sleeping quarters for four," Cynthia said. "The rest of the space is used for storage ... you know, wine, beer, food ... other things."

"Do you like boats?"

"I prefer small sailing boats," she said. "I hate large motorboats. I find them a nuisance. What about you?"

"I like sitting on the shore, watching the ships cross the sea, but when they disappear past the horizon, I turn away. They remind me of everyone I've ever loved who is no longer with me."

He was surprised to see tears in Cynthia's eyes.

"Are you feeling all right?" he asked.

"I'm touched by what you said. Your voice, hair, eyes, hands, posture and even your lips ... all remind me of Richard."

The waiter emerged with two plates of steaming seafood and two salads.

Jason waited for the waiter to leave the table again. "Now that you mention his name, may I ask you a few personal questions?"

"I know what you're after," she responded. "Yes, we were lovers."

What a bold revelation! Jason thought as he was about to eat a slice of artichoke crowned with a scallop. "Obviously, you miss him."

"A lot!" More tears ran down her cheeks. "Your brother ... is ... dead."

"Is he ... really dead?" Jason asked.

"But it happened very recently. He hanged himself the morning of your father's funeral."

Jason held his head. "Oh, God. Why?"

"Apparently he was very depressed; your father's death triggered the suicide."

"Where was he all this time?"

"His captors found him in his cell, dangling from the ceiling with a pair of sheets wrapped around his neck."

"You know his captors?"

"I was involved in the negotiations for his release.

"Where is his body now?"

"They won't tell me."

"Who are they? "

"Men working for the *Taliban*."

"Why did you agree to get involved?"

"Because I didn't want him killed."

"And you didn't notify the authorities?"

"Your father begged me not to. They threatened to kill Richard if anyone went to the police."

"Are you telling me that my father was aware of reasons behind Richard's abduction?"

"Yes. He was hopeful that they would release him to Aziz."

"Aziz? The same man who's arriving on Sunday from Riyadh?"

"Yes. Your father delivered the money to him."

Jason was angry now. "What the hell is going on? Tell me everything, damn it!"

"Okay, okay. Behind your father's back, Richard and Makin skimmed the Mustafa Bank in Nicosia to the tune of millions of dollars. They used the bank as a go-between to purchase large shipments of small arms on credit. They resold the arms to two opposing groups. They got money from Kamal, the *Taliban* and a warlord. They channelled the proceeds to an offshore bank, sunk the Mustafa bank in the red and left the participants in a mess."

Cynthia paused.

271

"Tell me more! Give me names!"

"Kamal loaned the Mustafa bank $110-million for the purchase of the arms. Richard and Makin ordered the arms through Manning's company. Alex was supposed to receive $110-million dollars for the shipment, but he wasn't paid a cent. The arms were delivered to Kamal at a specific destination. He won't deliver the shipment unless he's paid $115 million. Alex and Kamal thought the arms were destined for a warlord, whose forces are fighting the *Taliban*.

"Richard and Makin sold the arms to the *Taliban* and to the warlord at the same time. They got their money but didn't ship the arms. When Richard and Makin began quarrelling among themselves about the money and where to ship the arms, Richard sent the money – at least $370-million – to an offshore account. Upset, Makin notified the *Taliban* about the scheme, and they abducted Richard."

"What were the abductors' demands?"

"Originally they asked for three hundred and seventy million dollars. Subsequently, they modified their demands and insisted for either the weapons or the return of their money."

"How much money did the *Taliban* pay for the arms?"

"One hundred and thirty million."

"And the warlord paid the same sum?

"Yes."

"Did they get their money back?"

"No. There were complications. The money was nowhere to be found. Richard had refused to divulge where the money was, not even to Faris. To secure Richard's release, your father had agreed to deliver $355-million of his own offshore money to Aziz, a man whom all parties agreed upon to handle the mess. The plan was to deliver Richard to Aziz. And Aziz would then return the $130-million to the *Taliban*, pay Kamal $115-million, pay Manning $110-million, and deliver Richard to Faris. Next, Kamal would deliver the arms to the warlord.

"Alex, however, did not want Aziz to return the money to the *Taliban* because of pressure from the CIA, who didn't want the *Taliban* to use the money to finance their war against the USA and its allies."

"Is there any good reason why you kept me in the dark?"

"Your father feared you wouldn't have handled it properly."

"What was Richard's motive?"

"Three reasons: ideological indoctrination; power; and money—lots of it!"

Jason shook his head. "Are you sure? Maybe his abductors wanted to portray him that way."

"I'm certain. Your brother was a sensitive man, but he was also depressed and overly susceptible to influence."

"Did he tell you everything?"

"I don't know. He disclosed a great deal of information to me the day before his abduction. He sensed something bad was going to happen to him, and he handed me his travel documents for safekeeping."

"Did my father deliver the $355-million to Aziz?"

"Yes."

"So what is going to happen to all that money?"

"Aziz was a close friend of your father. He won't deliver the money unless Richard is delivered to him."

"But Richard is dead."

"Aziz doesn't know that. He's coming on Sunday expecting to have Richard delivered to him at midnight. Once he finds out Richard is dead, he'll refuse to give the money to Makin, the *Taliban* and Alex. All hell will break loose."

Jason said, "If Richard had the money, why didn't he give it to the parties owed?"

"He couldn't get hold of the offshore money because he'd switched accounts and transferred it into a new bank account in Panama bearing a different name."

"Well, under whose name is the new account?"

"Jason Mustafa." She pulled out her small black notebook. "Canadian Passport #VE68543BX29B."

His shock rolled into anger. He let out a loud groan that shook the tranquility of the little harbour and scared the seagulls away. The patrons turned their faces disapprovingly, and two dogs began to bark nervously. The waiter rushed to the table, his eyebrows dropped and eyes narrowed.

Cynthia stood up before he had a chance to get closer. "It's okay, waiter," she said calmly. "I'll take care of him."

The waiter shook his head, turned around and walked back inside the restaurant.

98

"If the abductors wanted 370-million dollars ransom for Richard's release and all that money was sitting in a Panamanian bank account in my name, why haven't they come after me?" Jason asked.

"If they knew you had it, you wouldn't be sitting here," Cynthia countered.

"Did Makin know about the money being transferred to my name?"

"Of course not! I'm the only one who knows this."

"Why didn't you tell me? I would have paid the money to them."

"That's the problem." She started to cry again. "I knew that ... Richard was going to be killed ... even if the money was paid back."

"What do we do now?" Jason asked, anxious to gauge Cynthia's motives.

"You see that boat ... over there?" She pointed with her head at Lagos's boat.

"Yes."

"I leased it from Lagos. He doesn't know ... what I intend to do with it once I'm on the open waters. Alex will soon come after me. I want you and I to escape. The boat will be ready for us by seven. It has enough fuel to take us to Haifa. Once we arrive in Haifa, we can hire a taxi to take us to the Ben Gurion Airport, and from there we can fly to Madrid. Once in Madrid we can purchase tickets for Panama City. With the money you have, we can live very comfortable lives with new identities somewhere in the Caribbean."

Jason was stunned. "How on earth will I forgive myself for running away?"

"Your brother is dead. Your father is dead. Your mother is dead. You have no reason to stay on this island. Besides, it's only a matter of hours before they find out that you have the money. And they'll come after you, too!"

"You think I'll simply take off with you?" Jason replied trying to stay calm.

"You have no choice ... if you wish to remain among the living."

274

Jason wasn't convinced that Cynthia was telling him the whole truth. "Tell me more about my brother."

She said, "He was so depressed. He looked for something to give him a sense of purpose, I suppose." She paused. "He doubted that Marianna's children were his, and he wanted to avenge his wife's infidelity."

"And you? Where do you fit into all of this?"

Cynthia hesitated. "I … cared for him. I wanted him to be happy."

Jason gave a stern stare. "You and Richard planned to disappear with the money!"

Cynthia was shaken. "No!"

"Why did Richard transfer the money to my name?"

Cynthia stroked the edges of her mouth. "You and Richard are so alike; it's difficult to tell you apart. He had your passport, your driver's license and other personal items. He planned to start a new life under an assumed identity, and you were the only logical person he could impersonate."

"Once you learned that his life was in danger, why didn't you do anything to protect him?"

She started sobbing again. "I didn't take him seriously. If I knew they were going to abduct him, I would have done something to stop them."

"Are you sure they don't know the money is now in an account bearing my name?"

"Yes."

"Did you love Richard?"

"Yes," and then she whispered, "I would have given my life for him."

"But he betrayed his own father. He let many people down."

"Maybe he was coerced. Maybe he had no choice. Maybe he was too depressed to think straight."

"Maybe … you led him into this mess."

"No! I did not!"

Jason wondered why an American would be so sympathetic to an alleged criminal who—according to her version of events—had dealt with the *Taliban*, an enemy of her nation. "Is Alex aware of your plan to escape by boat?"

"No, I hate him! He's responsible for Richard's death! The negotiations were delayed because he wanted the money—and Richard dead. If he knew I was telling you this, he'd kill me. Please don't mention his name. It makes me shiver with fear."

"I'm not sure I want to follow your plan."

"We don't have much time left."

Jason rubbed his forehead uncontrollably. He wondered how the Saudis would react if he failed to protect their loans. "I don't know what to do," he said. "I need some time to think."

"That's a huge amount of money to turn over to them."

"Fuck the money! I don't want to be an accomplice to a crime."

"You haven't done anything to worry about."

"But the money's not mine!"

"You have it now. Let's enjoy it together."

It was an offering Jason found utterly unacceptable. But he feared that if he refused it outright his life would be in greater danger. He decided to play along, to pretend that he was a willing – albeit hesitant – accomplice. "Your plan does seem workable," he said carefully.

"Good," Cynthia said. "Very good!"

He couldn't wait for the opportunity to alert Helena and Nicholas. "What do we do now?"

"It's two thirty," Cynthia said, looking at her watch. "We can't get in the boat before sunset. How long will it take you to get your passport, other I.D. and some clothes?"

"About half an hour."

"We have plenty of time. We don't want to arouse any suspicions. The play is about to begin in half an hour. Let's go."

"Oh, yes, 'The Trojan Women,' he said apathetically.

99

There was a long line-up outside the open air Odeion Theatre but Cynthia and Jason didn't have to wait. A man, seemingly in charge, recognized Cynthia and rushed to welcome her. She introduced Jason to Andreas Petrides, the director of the Pafos Theatre Club. Petrides handed them two programs and asked them to follow him. They walked through a narrow passageway, *the parodos*, passed under an arch, and reached the front row, next to the round orchestra.

"These are the best seats in the house," Petrides declared.

Cynthia smiled. "Can we sit higher up, at the back?" she asked.

"Certainly," the man replied.

They climbed up the radial stairs of the ancient theater, and reached another walkway, *the diazoma*. Finally Cynthia found two empty seats that were to her liking on the upper story of *the theatron*.

Jason started reading the program but couldn't focus his concentration on it. He folded it and let his eyes drift about the theatre, when suddenly he saw Marianna and Katerina, both fitted in long beige gowns, entering the theatre, accompanied by Makin and Lagos. Aisha was not among them, Jason noticed. An usher helped them to their seats at the left edge of the second row.

"I just saw Marianna and Katerina," Cynthia said.

Jason jerked to attention but couldn't find anything to say in response. "Oh." He wondered how Marianna would react if she knew for a fact that Richard was dead.

"You're awfully quiet," Cynthia said.

"I'm trying to capture the spirit of the ancient times," Jason responded, but he was frantically looking for a chance to notify Helena and Nicholas. He stared at *the skene*, on stage, the power source of the place: several military tents were scattered around. Jason imagined the captive Trojan women being quartered there. Columns ranging from eight to thirteen feet in height were placed next to *the skene*.

"Ladies and gentlemen," Petrides said. "The play is about to begin. I would ask that you shut off your mobiles and remain silent during the duration of the performance."

The action was set in front of the tents of the Greek warriors.

"The City of Troy lies in ruin," Poseidon said. Hecuba, the Queen of Troy was lying on the ground in obvious misery, crying.

Each part had a corresponding meaning, a message that amplified Jason's anxiety. Goddess Athena reversed her prior enmity against the Trojans and was now retorting to manipulation designed to convince Poseidon to "make the Aegean Sea roar with huge waves and whirlpools and fill the hollow bay of Euboea with the corpses of the Greek warriors."

Hecuba said, "Why should I be silent? Why should I be not silent? Why should I lament?"

The chorus began to sing. Messengers appeared, bringing even more bleak news.

Jason realized instantly that he had to act fast to verify Cynthia's story. He thought about the money. Three hundred and seventy million dollars was a huge sum by any standards. Cynthia may have held back a great deal of information, which he needed in order to make real sense of the situation. *Did she truly love Richard? Is she genuinely concerned about saving my life? Or is she after the money?* Hating Manning, wanting to distance herself from him, was fair motive for wanting to take off with him, he guessed, but Jason had no way of knowing for sure. He experienced an eerie feeling sitting beside her, a noose pulling tighter and tighter around his neck. He waited. As soon as the first part concluded, he turned to Cynthia. "I don't think I can stay until the end of the play."

"Do you think Athena is being a bit unforgiving?" Cynthia responded nonchalantly.

"She's hurt."

"Poseidon is right, though. She swings between excessive love and hate, as the situation permits."

"Now is the best time to leave."

"What's the matter? You don't like the play?"

"I don't feel well."

"As you wish," Cynthia said.

They walked down the same steps, stepped upon *the diazoma*, turned left and landed on *the parodos*, hurried under the arch and ended up outside the theatre.

"I hope you understand," Jason said apologetically. "I just couldn't—"

"It's okay. Lets go."

They walked another fifty meters and reached Jason's car. Anxious to test Cynthia's reaction, he reached for his cellular phone and began to call Helena's number.

He put the phone to his ear, but Cynthia grabbed it, severed the connection and slipped it in her black bag.

"What are you doing?" Jason protested.

"I don't want you to speak to anyone until we leave the island."

Jason faked surprise. "You can't do that!"

"I have to. One wrong move and we'll both be killed."

"How do I know you're telling the truth?" Jason asked.

"Would I meet you in public if I had anything to hide?"

"You are hiding a lot of things from me."

"Stop being overly suspicious," Cynthia interrupted.

"Suspicious, eh? I want all the facts, damn it!"

"Look, I'm risking my life for you."

"I want some proof that Richard is dead."

"You have a choice. Either you do as I say, or we go our separate ways ... and you handle the mess."

"We can stay and fight," Jason proposed.

"No. We're all living on the edge. Someone is going to fall. And it's not going to be me, for sure!"

"We need each other," Jason said.

"How can I be sure I won't be blamed for whatever may follow? The last thing I want is to be branded a traitor, back home, and find myself rotting away in an American prison."

"If you're clean, you have nothing to fear."

"I feel like a bee, which has entered a sun room from an open window, hitting the glass walls, the ceiling, unable to get outside."

"You must have entered, sensing there's pollen to collect."

"We must go back to the hotel," she demanded. "We have to get ready."

They got inside the car, and Cynthia placed her hands on his shoulders. "You have nothing to fear from me."

Jason started the engine and began to drive. He looked through the rear view mirror and saw two cars following closely. His biggest challenge now was to find the right moment to escape Cynthia's net.

100

It took Jason less than ten minutes to arrive at the Mustafa Beach Hotel and park in the parking lot. They exited the car and began to walk toward the entrance of the hotel.

"Are you afraid?" Cynthia asked as they reached the main entrance.

"Not really," he lied.

The lobby was crowded. The bells of a huge clock on the wall began to ring.

"I need to go to my room to get my things," he said.

"Not now," she insisted. "It's quarter to five. We won't leave until seven. We should stick together all the time."

The last thing that Jason wanted to do was to stage a scene. "Fine," he said.

"Will you buy me a drink?"

"Of course," Jason answered. They walked over to the bar and sat on the stools. "I'll have a *Bloody Mary*," Cynthia said.

Jason ordered a scotch on the rocks.

The female pianist in the corner was playing *Amaryllis*. As he was about to have a sip, Jason felt a heavy hand touch his right shoulder. He turned his head to see the serious bearded face of a short fat man in his mid-forties. The man had the other hand in his pocket, and Jason felt a firm pipe-like object press against his ribs. Frightened, Jason looked at Cynthia, who looked mystified.

"I carry a pistol," the man said to both of them. "I want you to exit the hotel quietly."

Jason walked out of the bar first, followed by Cynthia. Once outside, the man waived and a black Mercedes pulled up to the entrance of the hotel. Another man got out and opened the back door. "Get in," he ordered.

Cynthia hesitated but obeyed the man's command. Jason felt a hand grabbing him by the arm and lowering his head into the back seat. The man with the pistol settled himself in the front passenger seat, and the other man who was holding the door hurried in, sat beside Jason and shut the door.

101

Seven minutes later the Mercedes left Pafos proper and drove north.

"Close your eyes, both of you!" the man at the back ordered, and Jason obeyed. He felt a piece of cloth being wrapped around his eyes and a tight knot made behind his head. His hands were forced to his back, while he felt cold handcuffs on his wrists and heard the snapping sound of the lock. A few seconds later, he heard a similar sound, guessing that Cynthia had also been handcuffed.

The sudden acceleration of the car jerked Jason's body backwards and increased his heartbeat. After the car travelled for about thirty minutes, it slowed down and finally stopped. A strong hand pulled Jason out, held him by the handcuffs and pushed him forward. "Keep walking," a rough voice mumbled.

A moment later there was a knock on a door, and Jason heard voices inside. A hand grabbed his left arm and pulled him inside.

"Why did you bring us here?" Jason protested.

"What did Cynthia tell you," a man asked.

"Please don't tell them," Cynthia's voice pleaded.

"Who are you anyway?" Jason asked.

"None of your business."

"They work for the warlord!" Cynthia shouted.

"Take this bitch out of here!" the man bellowed.

From the grunting and scuffling sounds which followed, Cynthia was apparently taken elsewhere.

"What do you want from me?" Jason asked.

"You will assume your brother's identity."

"You want me to pretend I'm Richard?"

"Not to *pretend*. You're going to *be* Richard."

"But why? How—"

102

After watching *The Trojan Women*, Marianna's bewilderment about men's inclination towards aggressiveness and war exasperated her, and she needed to clear her mind. She concluded that women must rely on powerful men for their protection, and this did not entirely please her.

Accompanied by Katerina, Lagos and Makin, she left the Odeion Theatre and they climbed aboard her BMW SUV.

She drove north until she reached the main Pafos-Limassol route and headed east for the *Petra Tou Romiou* (The Rock of Aphrodite), the legendary place where the goddess Aphrodite was reputed to have emerged from the surf of the sea. Along the way, she turned on the radio and found Channel Three of the Cyprus Broadcasting Corporation, which was playing Greek romantic songs.

"Lower the volume so we can talk," Katerina pleaded, but Marianna did not respond. Instead she lowered her window to allow the cool air to blow her hair and make her feel liberated. She kept tapping her fingers on the steering wheel and glancing at the Mediterranean landscape, dotted with panama fields, bare hills, shrubs and farmers' huts.

Twenty-five minutes later, she stopped her car in a parking lot, and they walked to a café overlooking the shore and the Rock of Aphrodite.

Once inside, they chose a private corner, far from the rest of the crowd. Marianna sat on a chair facing the wide bay window. The last sunrays shone on her face and warmed her forehead. She saw the waves rolling in and hitting the shore, and seagulls circling in the air. Marianna enjoyed observing the birds flying towards and away from the setting sun. It was her way of escaping the thoughts of the day, thoughts that lingered in a ball of wound-up hopes, feelings, curiosity, helplessness, nostalgia and sadness.

Relentlessly, surf hit the rock and she pictured the naked body of the goddess Aphrodite coming out of the sea, her hands extended high up in the air, her bare breasts, followed by her belly, hips and legs, only to disappear and then re-emerge in a different, yet similarly seductive, shape.

She thought about Maximus. Marianna refused to believe he was leaving the church because of her. If he truly loved her, surely he would have proposed to take her away a long time ago, when she had longed for his commitment and a life together abroad as a normal family. Something else quite apart from their affair, she suspected, had propelled him to leave on such short notice.

Marianna's mind jumped back to the moment and she glanced at her sister. *She's so strong*, she mused. *Why can't I be like her? I wouldn't have to worry about anything.* She then thought of Jason and Cynthia. "I must say I'm a bit surprised to see Cynthia and Jason together," she said looking at Katerina.

"You shouldn't be that surprised?" Katerina responded. "Cynthia is everyone's friend."

"Even Jason's?"

"Why not? Maybe she feels sorry for him."

"You know what?" Marianna hesitated. "I ... feel sorry for him, too."

"I'm going out for a smoke," Lagos said. "They don't allow smoking in here, anymore ... bloody tourists!"

"I'll come with you," Makin seconded. "We'll be back shortly."

Marianna waited for the two men to exit the lounge. "He wants me to go with him."

"Who? Where?" Katerina asked.

"Maximus. He's flying to London on Monday. He's asked me to join him, but I told him I'm not interested."

"How unusual."

A waiter came to their table. "What can I get you ladies?"

Katerina said, "I'll have three scoops of vanilla ice cream on a cone."

"Maybe we shouldn't order until they come back," Marianna said.

"Too late," her sister smiled.

Marianna turned to the waiter. "I'll have one scoop of the same."

Once the waiter left, Marianna curled some strands of hair around her index finger. "I think Maximus is after my money."

"Could be," Katerina said.

"That's all you can say?"

"I'm hungry," Katerina said.

"Never mind! You're so indifferent."

"Listen," Katerina said angrily. "All you can think about is you, you, and you! You and Maximus, you and the money, you and the villa, you and the galleries, you and your children, you and your happiness. What about me?"

"You have a husband," Marianna responded. "I'm all alone now."

Katerina shook her head. "You're impossible, you know that? I refuse to waste the rest of my life giving you re-assurances and being there for you. It's about time that I look after myself."

"Why are you being so mean to me today?"

"Don't you understand? You've inherited hundreds of millions of dollars which you've done nothing to earn, and I must continue to struggle to keep the family's business afloat."

"You want some of my money. Is that it?"

"Your money? Be careful how you talk to me. Show some consideration for people's feelings."

Marianna bit her lower lip. "You never asked for anything."

"Those who really love me should have the sense to ask me what my needs and desires are. I'm so bitter! Do you honestly think George and I are happy together?"

"I know you. If you weren't happy, you would have divorced him a long time ago."

"That's easy for you to say."

"What's really bothering you?"

Katerina didn't respond.

"Are you thinking about your child again?"

"Why do you have to remind me, damn it?"

"Because I care."

"You don't care! No one in my family does! Mother and father made me keep that information from as many people as possible. No one helped me through my grief. I wasn't allowed to express my feelings at the dinner table. I had to hide my feelings after the birth, just as I had hid them during my pregnancy."

Marianna left her seat and sat beside Katerina. Their shoulders rubbed. "I hate to see you so upset."

"The truth is," Katerina said, "I never loved George. I married him for convenience, and I needed someone to boss around."

"George likes being used, anyway," Marianna tried to reassure her.

"That's what I thought. The truth is he's been using me. He's a manipulator—an egomaniac."

Marianna found Katerina's confessions difficult to believe. She stared. "What makes you say such things?"

"He's made some deals without my knowledge or approval. He teamed up with Richard, Makin and others. They traded in weapons. His 'associates' are pressuring me to come up with all the money our family owes to them by January 31st, or else—oh, I'm afraid! If I don't come up with the money, they'll kill me or at least take over our family's business."

"That's terrible! Does father know?"

"Of course not. You want him to have another heart attack?"

The waiter brought them the ice cream and left again.

Marianna's thoughts ran amok. "Do you think George and Makin might be involved in Richard's disappearance?"

"Who knows? I dare not ask them."

"How did you learn about their activities?"

Katerina licked the top of the ice cream four times. "I got George drunk on Wednesday night, after he stole Faris's will from Dr. Plato's house."

Marianna felt her heart palpitating rapidly, and she could hardly speak. "So, it's true … what Helena and Jason were saying. It's true!"

"Yes, it's true," Katerina whispered slowly. She crunched the bottom of the cone, her eyes staring at the floor away from Marianna's face.

"You planned all that?"

"Marianna, I have to pay off the loan and get them off my back once and for all."

"How much do you need?"

"Twenty-five million dollars."

"I wish I could help you, but the money Faris left me belongs to the kids."

"You know how much I love them. I don't think you understand my situation."

Marianna had never seen her sister so desperate. "Katerina, I know you'll overcome, somehow."

"Let me manage the Mustafa estate, please. We can share the profits."

"Based on the terms of the will, Makin is the executor of the estate. He's the one who's administering it."

"I wouldn't trust Makin if I were you. He has at least four faces."

"What choice do I have?"

"The money should stay in the family. We can go to court and ask to change the executor. You're the sole beneficiary. The judge will most likely grant your request."

"I'm sorry. I can't afford to let Makin down."

"Do you realize that Makin and George may be planning their future without us?"

Marianna took in a big gasp of air. "Stop controlling everyone around you! Let them do what they want."

"I hate to see them taking off with our money."

"We have ownership. They have nothing. They're bound to work for us."

"Are you being sincere? Somehow I think you prefer to work with Makin because he 'appears' to be more powerful than me."

"I need a ruthless man to protect my assets, you understand?"

"I'm in deep trouble," Katerina said. "If I go down, you'll fall with me."

"What do you mean?"

"A Pafos lawyer called me this morning. I won't reveal the name because I promised to keep it secret. The lawyer has been consulted by monk Modestos who provided incriminating evidence against Maximus and me. The lawyer wants out of the case because I'm involved. I didn't hear about specific demands for money, but I think I can pay this lawyer one hundred thousand dollars to bury the case."

Marianna noticed Katerina had chosen her words carefully, and she hadn't indicated whether the lawyer was male or female. "What did you and Maximus do?"

"I can't tell you."

Marianna turned her head. She saw Makin and Lagos approaching. "You mean, you won't tell me?"

"No," Katerina said firmly. "And don't press me."

"We must leave now," Makin said solemnly. "I have to be somewhere."

"Listen," Marianna said to the others. "I think we're all a bit gloomy today. I wish we hadn't watched *The Trojan Women*. Let me organize something to cheer us all up."

"What do you have in mind?" Lagos asked.

"A memorable dinner party. Be at Villa... Marianna, at 7:00 tomorrow night. I'll invite all my other friends."

"You mean Villa Mustafa," Katerina said.

"Do you mind?" Marianna reacted. "I'm changing the name."

"What's the occasion," Makin asked.

"My freedom." She looked at them, waiting for an answer. "Well? Shall I expect you or not?"

"I wouldn't miss it for a million dollars," Makin said.

"We'll come, too," Katerina said without waiting for Lagos to respond.

"There might be one or two surprises," Marianna said.

"That's typical you," Lagos said. "I enjoyed the group of dancers you brought in last Sunday."

Marianna grinned. "George, flattery will get you nowhere." She frowned. "Whatever you do, don't get my twins drunk."

103

"We ask the questions around here," someone cut him off. They tied Jason to a cast iron chair, hands and feet bound by a rough, thick rope. The pain from the tight knots on his knees and ankles was excruciating, but he tried not to show it. He felt the sharp prick of a needle piercing his arm.

At exactly every single second interval, he would feel the force of a hard, hot, ball hitting the back of his neck, precisely at the same spot, causing an involuntary spasm below his chin. He couldn't see who was administering the torture, but he sensed that the tactic was designed to break down his defenses and render him prone to influence and submission.

Any time the ball beat the nerve, a man's deep, slow voice would utter, "Richard, Richard, Richard …" thousands of times.

After sixty minutes, the ball still drumming his neck, the man close beside him kept whispering, "You *are* Richard, you *are* Richard, you *are* Richard…."

The bad breath and stale perspiration of the torturer's face reached Jason's nostrils as if the air around him had drifted past an open drain.

"Now," the man was saying, "you must repeat after me: "I'm Richard, I'm Richard, I'm Richard …." The ball never stopped pounding Jason's nerve. "Say it after me."

Jason hesitated. "I'm not Richard, I'm not Richard. I'm Jason, I'm Jason, I'm Jason!" he shouted.

The ball continued beating his neck; the noise inside his head intensified. Jason swam inside his own body, gasped for air, drowned in blood.

He felt the spike of a sharp needle in his right arm, causing him to shake. The ball hammered at the same spot. "I'm Richard, I'm Richard, I'm Richard," the tormentor uttered relentlessly. "Repeat after me."

Jason resisted. "Fuck you, asshole!" But his body weakened. His legs went numb. He began to hear voices, sirens and deafening screams. To prevent his head from exploding, he tried falling asleep. He began to lose his sense of smell; then he couldn't feel anything. A few minutes later the only noises he heard were the beats of his heart.

104

When he woke up, the words he remembered were: 'Wake up, Richard.'

Now he could see. A fair-skin woman with blonde hair and blue eyes, in her early thirties, sat beside him, holding a glass of orange juice. She smiled two perfect rows of bright teeth. Through her thin silk blouse, he saw the shape of her nipples, erect, begging to be devoured.

"This is for you," she smiled, as she handed him the glass.

His thirst was so intense, he grabbed the glass and drank the juice in one big gulp. "Who are you?" he asked.

"You don't know me," she answered, "but I want to be your friend. Come to bed with me."

She must be Russian or Romanian, Jason guessed. He knew that beautiful girls from Russia and Romania left their countries and went overseas in search of a better future. Many of these girls ended up in Pafos. They managed to find half-decent jobs, some had married Cypriots, yet a number of girls—perhaps the most vulnerable and desperate—ended up in the nets of pimps. He had seen some of these girls at Crow's brothel.

As she removed her blouse and skirt, he surveyed the suite. It looked more like a substandard hotel room than an ordinary apartment. The white walls were decorated with paintings of the same variety as those he'd seen at the brothel and at Villa Mustafa. The floor was covered with a thick Afghan rug. His eyes searched for a window, but there was none. His chest felt itchy and when he scratched it, he noticed he was naked.

"Come to bed," she urged him again.

"Is there a washroom around here?" he asked.

She pointed at a side door, by the entrance. "There."

He went to the washroom, closed its door and looked for a window hoping to get a glimpse of the outside surroundings. Disappointed he remained there for several seconds, flushed the toilet and got out. As he turned, he put his hand behind him, got hold of the main-door handle and tried to turn it, but it was locked.

He glanced at her. Her naked body was as trim as the frame of a lurking leopard.

She lifted the white bedspread and crawled her body under it. "C'mon Richard," she pleaded. "Please come to me."

His erection was stiff. She's too much to resist, he thought. Overwhelmed with lust, he lifted the cover and huddled into her arms. He kissed her mouth, sucked her nipples, tantalized her clitoris and tasted the moisture that flooded the hair between her thighs. She fitted him with a condom, and as he entered her, he gave and took pleasure.

"I need some fresh air," he said after they finished their lovemaking.

"We can't go out."

He got up. "I'm hungry," Jason lied. "Let's get something to eat." He looked for his clothing. "Where are my clothes?"

She removed the cover and jumped up. "You can't leave this room," she said with a sharp tone and a vicious stare.

"Well, can we order something to be delivered?"

"Let me see what I can do." She searched her purse, retrieved a mobile phone and dialed a number. "He's hungry," she said. "Send us some food."

When she severed the connection, Jason asked: "What time is it?"

"I don't know," she said. "I don't keep track of time."

Jason had to act. Nonchalantly, he approached her from behind before she had the opportunity to suspect anything, firmed his hands against her mouth, held her head tight against his chest and whispered in her ear, "I won't hurt you." She resisted for a few seconds, but she gave in. With her blouse he muzzled her mouth. Then he placed her on the thick carpet, face down, removed a sheet and used it to tie up her hands and legs. Then he carried her to the washroom. "You'll be alright," he said. "Can you breathe?"

She nodded.

A few minutes later, he heard knocks at the door, the sound of keys, and he saw the door handle turning.

As the door opened, Jason faced a rough-faced bearded man of medium built. He was wearing a military uniform and a hat similar to those worn by Afghani warlords who were directing the war against the *Taliban* in Northern Afghanistan. The belt around his waist had a holster, and a pistol was protruding from it.

Jason smiled widely.

"Where is she?" he asked with a frown.

"Come in mister," Jason said. "She's shy." He pointed at the washroom door that was closed. "She's freshening up."

"Mmm."

"Honey, the food is here," Jason said. "She likes tea. Did you bring some tea?"

The man firmed his lips. "No." He put the tray on the table and stared at Jason with envy.

Jason smiled again and used his hands to cover his genitals. "Pardon me."

As the man turned around heading for the door, Jason grabbed the pistol with the left hand and punched him in the face with the right. The blow was strong enough to cause the guard to lose his balance, and as he was falling, Jason hit him again and kicked him between the legs. Before the guard had a chance to regain his strength, Jason grabbed him by the hair and shoved the pistol in his mouth. The guard lifted his arms in the air. "Take your boots and clothes off," Jason demanded. "Do it, fast!"

The guard obeyed.

"Now lie down and face the floor."

Jason tied the guard's hands with the belt. He then took another sheet and bound his legs with it. The sheet was long enough to cover his mouth and tie up a knot behind his head. Then he got dressed in the guard's clothes and boots and put on the hat.

He took the tray, went to the door, opened it and locked it behind him with the guard's key. With the tray in his hands he walked through the narrow corridor, past two more guards, found the exit door, opened it and began running in the darkness of the night. He stumbled and fell, got up, heard dogs barking and commotion behind him. "Stop him!" someone shouted.

He saw a shadow ahead pointing a gun at him. "Don't shoot," Jason screamed. "He's over there." He began to run at the direction he had pointed and abruptly he moved to the opposite direction, found a wall, climbed over it and landed in a vineyard. He crossed the vineyard, jumped over a low fence, ran down a steep slope and followed a pathway that led him to a road.

Jason stopped briefly to catch his breath. He looked back, dimly discerning the outline of the building that had been his prison only a few minutes ago. It was nestled among the vineyards high up on a hill. Its arches and style reminded him of the Delphi architectural plans, but he'd have to view it during daylight in order to convince himself that this was indeed the Delphi project. Trying to determine his location, he saw

292

flashing lights on the horizon emanating from three slow moving objects, presumably ships crossing the sea. Then he looked for the shoreline but couldn't see the usual lights that illuminated the seaside hotels. He couldn't see any cluster of streetlights that would indicate the existence of any villages or villas. And where was the lighthouse that marked the western boundaries of the Pafos harbour? The town of Pafos was nowhere to be seen.

For a moment he feared that he had been transported by boat to another land outside Cyprus. On second thought, that seemed unlikely, but the only remote area in Pafos he knew about was the Akamas peninsula on the western edge of the Pafos district. Local authorities had declared the Akamas region a natural conservation and wild management zone.

The distance between where Jason stood and the shoreline was about six kilometers. He heard car engines roaring. His safest bet, he reasoned, was to abandon the road, cross the fields and aim for the shore.

When he reached the sea, he panted happily with relief. Thorns had pierced the clothes he wore, reducing them to rags. Scratches and bruises on his body caused him some pain but he was happy to be alive – and free! He was pleased that in the span of an hour, he managed to cross the rough terrain, from the hills to the lower plateau, and overcame at least six unknown creeping creatures along the way. Jason was aware that his determination had allowed his escape from a forced personality transformation. *But who had masterminded the scheme and why?*

He heard no cars travelling. It was nearing dawn, for he could see faint strokes of natural light reflecting on the scattered clouds in the eastern horizon.

Jason stumbled upon a rural road and decided to follow it. But when he saw lights moving down from the hills, he left the road and walked beside it, stepping over underbrush, rocks and wild vegetation. A shadow suddenly moved, and he feared someone was lurking behind the trees, ready to cut him down. He ran as fast as he could, east, the direction in which he thought the town of Pafos was situated.

Out of breath, he slowed down. He walked another kilometer when suddenly his body could no longer move. He began to shiver, and he thought he was going to faint from over-exhaustion, apprehension, hunger and lack of sleep.

He searched the pockets of the pants he wore and found a matchbook, a pen, a lighter and money. He counted it nervously. There was thirty-two pounds in paper money and some coins—enough to hire a taxi. And the gun? Holding it nervously, he wondered what to do with it. *Maybe I should keep it for my own protection.* Jason dragged himself another fifty meters, found a tall olive tree and collapsed under it.

105

The trilling of the sparrows woke him up. Early morning rays of sunshine warmed his body and he felt re-energized. The first images that came to his mind were those of Claira, Andrew and George. They're so innocent, he reflected. *I miss them and I don't know what I would do if anyone harmed them.* He thought of Marianna and ruminated over whether he should tell her about his ordeal—not to seek her sympathy but to alert her to the possibility that Richard was dead. While that thought lingered in his mind, he wondered whether it was safe now to step onto the rural road and walk its length until he found the main road. What would they think if they see me wearing a torn military uniform, he thought. What if someone calls the police? Shall I throw the pistol away now? Shall I hide it? He hesitated.

Jason walked another two kilometers until he came to a banana field. Hungry, he peeled off several raw bananas and ate them gluttonously, like a boar devours its food. Studying the area, he saw a farmer mounted on a tractor cultivating a nearby field.

After removing the boots, the shirt and tearing the pants, reducing them to shorts, he buried the gun, the boots and the discarded clothes and hurried toward the tractor. To make himself visible, he walked in the middle of the field and waved at the burly farmer.

The man stopped the tractor, jumped off and approached Jason. "Get off of my land!" the farmer yelled in Greek.

"I'm a fisherman," Jason pleaded in English. "I need your help."

The farmer scratched his head in obvious puzzlement.

He probably didn't understand English. "Look," Jason pleaded in Greek. "My little fishing boat capsized. I'm lost. I need to call a taxi."

"Sure, sure," the farmer said. He reached for his pocket and pulled out a mobile telephone. "I know no taxi number," he said with sadness on his face.

"Let me call someone I know," Jason pleaded. The farmer handed him the phone, and Jason called Stefano's number.

Stefano answered with "Stefano's taxi."

"Hello Stefano," Jason said. "I need your services again."

"Who are you?"

"You drove me to the Mustafa Villa past midnight on Thursday. Do you remember?"

"Are you the man I mistook for Richard Mustafa?"

"Yes."

"Where are you now?"

"I don't really know. Let me hand the phone to a gentleman here who can explain my location." Jason gave the phone to the farmer. "Would you please explain to him how to get here?"

The farmer nodded and—in Greek—he gave Stefano directions. "He'll be here in forty-five minutes," the farmer said. "He said he knows the area. There's a rural road over there," he pointed. "Wait for him there."

"May I ask one more favour?" Jason said.

The farmer nodded. "Are you hungry?"

"No, I'm okay. I need to borrow your phone again for a few seconds."

"Sure," the farmer said and passed him his mobile phone.

Jason dialed Nicholas's home number, and he walked a few feet away from the farmer.

"Yes?" Nicholas answered.

"Nicholas, this is Jason. I'm sorry to wake you up."

"I'm glad you called. I've been looking for you."

"I need to see you."

"Where are you?"

"I'm out of town."

"Are you okay?"

"I can't discuss anything right now. Can we meet privately somewhere in a couple of hours?"

"Come to the restaurant. It isn't open for business today – the Farmers' Market is closed on Sundays – but I'm going there in any case to do some bookkeeping and prepare the food for tomorrow."

"What time is it, please?"

"Six-fifteen."

"I should be at your restaurant before nine-thirty."

Jason then dialed Helena's number.

Helena answered, and Jason got straight to the point. "Any progress on your review of the bank books and records?"

"I have some startling revelations," she said. "I've been trying to reach you since four-thirty yesterday, but you didn't answer my calls. What's the matter?"

"Meet me at Nicholas's restaurant at nine-thirty," he said.

He cut off the connection, thanked the farmer, crossed the field and sat on a rock at the edge of the country road, waiting for the taxi to arrive.

106

"I almost didn't recognize you," Stefanos said.

"I look awful, I know."

"Are you sure you're not Richard Mustafa?"

"Why do you ask me that again?"

"Uh, no reason. What happened, anyway?"

Jason ignored the question and said quietly, "How long will it take to drive back to town?"

"Forty-five minutes."

He needed to shower and put on some decent clothes before he met with Nicholas and Helena. Jason had an hour and a half to spare, which he could put into good use. "Before you take me back to Pafos," Jason said, "I'd like to drive around the area for a few minutes."

"Which direction?" Stefanos asked.

"Drive west for a couple of kilometers."

"I don't like the roads around here. They're full of gravel and rocks."

"Please, it's important."

"All right."

As Stefanos drove, Jason made mental notes of the area.

When Stefanos covered the two-kilometer distance, Jason said, "Can you go up those hills?"

"I have to find a decent road first," Stefanos groaned.

"Try."

Stefanos maneuvered through rough terrain, followed rural routes until the taxi reached an altitude of about six hundred meters. Jason could distinguish the building clearly. He estimated the distance between the taxi and the building to be less than two kilometers. "Stop here for a second." Jason said.

"Yes sir."

"Can you tell me a bit about the area?"

"Yes, of course. The land around us belongs to some foreigners who come and go as they wish. Rumour has it they couldn't buy this much land because of local laws banning ownership of large parcels by outsiders, so they teamed up with two locals who purchased it in trust for them."

"And who is the owner of that large villa up there?" he pointed at the building in which he had been detained and interrogated.

"Oh, I've never been up there, but I think it belongs to an Arab."

Jason could see two trailer trucks parked outside. "Do you know how many people live there?"

"No. Are you interested in purchasing the villa?"

"Maybe, if the price is right."

"We can try to reach the place if you want," Stefanos offered. "I think there's a good road leading to it from the interior. To get to it, we must go back to Pafos and head north."

"Not just yet, thanks." It occurred to Jason that the Delphi project was more than just a villa. "Can you tell me the shortest route to Villa Mustafa?"

"Drive east about twenty kilometers, and then head north another seven."

"That would take us another twenty minutes, I suppose."

"Just about."

"Let's go to Villa Mustafa now," Jason said.

"Yes, sir," Stefanos responded.

As the taxi was cruising toward Villa Mustafa, Jason wondered how Marianna might react to his impromptu visit. After she'd thrown him out of the compound on Thursday, he had no reason to believe she would welcome him warmly. He also worried about being recaptured, even killed, by the torturers from whom he escaped the night before. I came to look for my brother, and I ended up being the one on the run, he mused. *The more I discover about him, the deeper the crater gets.* Jason had looked for challenges all his life, but this one was far more complicated and dangerous than it had originally seemed. He recalled eating those raw bananas by the edge of the field and he smiled.

"Why are you smiling," Stefanos asked.

"It's better than crying," Jason sighed stoically.

"Mmm."

He tried to check his emotions before the big encounter with Marianna began. Deep down, he liked her. Jason saw in her a vulnerable woman struggling to establish stability in her life. He wondered what she'd do if she knew that Cynthia and Richard had been lovers.

He was convinced that Marianna cared deeply about her children. She wouldn't do anything to jeopardize their welfare. It was the children who stood to lose a great deal if the Mustafa estate was nothing but an empty nest. As the taxi made a sharp turn, he saw the villa. Will she be willing to listen to me? he wondered. *She was an intelligent woman, after all.*

"What time is it?" Jason asked Stefanos when the taxi stopped outside the gates.

"Seven thirty-five."

"We've got enough time." He got out, crossed the street, walked a few feet on the rough terrain, found a rock and lifted it. Under it he found the transmitter for the gate that he'd hidden on Thursday night.

He walked back to the waiting taxi, used the keypad and opened the gates. "Wait for me here," he said to Stefanos. "I'll be back in twenty minutes."

107

George's loud snoring woke her up, but Katerina was thankful. She had to speak to Makin alone. She glanced at her watch. It was six o'clock. She tiptoed out of the bedroom, showered hastily, got dressed, exited the villa and got into her car. Before she turned on the ignition, she dialed Makin's number.

"Hello," Makin answered.

"We must speak. Meet me in my office in thirty minutes," she said.

"Today's Sunday," Makin protested. "I planned to spend some time with Aisha."

"It's vital."

"Very well. I'll be there as soon as I can."

She then started the car and drove straight to the hotel.

Katerina opened her office and sat behind her desk, thinking about how she could sway Makin. She was determined to purchase Mustafa Holdings at a fraction of its assets' market value and take firm control of the Persinaras-Mustafa Group. Once she controlled the consortium, she thought, she would be able to retire the loan to *Long Nile* and get rid of George.

Wearily, Katerina pondered afresh the dilemma that had troubled her for the last few days. *Should I tell Makin that I know about the arms dealings? Shall I pretend I know nothing about it? Who can I go to if he refuses to co-operate?*

Her door was ajar, and since it was almost time for Makin to arrive, her heartbeat accelerated. She was convinced that Makin and George had close ties to *Long Nile*. What she didn't know was the extent of their involvement and who was pulling the strings. Her whole life seemed to lead up to the control of the Persinaras-Mustafa consortium. There were obstacles to overcome, but she resolved not to be discouraged—even though Marianna had been unwilling to help her, and George was scheming behind her back.

Makin stood at the door, apparently hesitant to enter.

Katerina walked over to greet him. "Welcome," she smiled as she extended her hand. He stepped forward, they shook hands, and she closed the door.

"Please sit down," she said.

Makin sat at the edge of one of the leather chairs facing her desk.

"I must tell you," she said, "I have every faith in your abilities."

"Thank you."

She looked him in the eye. "Let's work together."

"What do you have in mind?"

"On behalf of Persinaras Estates, I want to purchase Mustafa Holdings. I think it's time the consortium dissolved and a new, more dynamic company emerges to replace it."

"You'll need a lot of money to acquire Mustafa Holdings," Makin said.

"We can work out the figures later. All I need from you at this stage is your commitment to help bring my plan into fruition."

"What's the reason behind your plan?"

"I want to use the cash flow of Mustafa Holdings to retire the *Long Nile* loan that's due on January 31st."

"I'm simply the executor. Marianna would have to agree to this."

"You know how much she listens to you. You can do a good job convincing her that my proposal is sound."

Makin said, "What's in it for me?"

"Once the acquisition is finalized, I'll appoint you the CEO of the new entity, double your salary and offer you a bonus based on your performance."

"No. Thanks."

Obviously, Katerina thought, he thinks he's better off now. *He must already be making big money, I suppose.* "Why not?"

"I don't need the extra headaches."

The carrot did not do the job, Katerina concluded. She wondered whether if it was wise to use the stick and decided to go for it. "I know about your arms dealings," she said with a dour expression. "I hope you're not so naïve as to believe you can continue trading without being caught."

"What the fuck are you saying?"

"I can't believe that you have close ties to *Long Nile*, which is nothing but an instrument to channel funds and arms to terrorists."

"I don't know what you're talking about."

"You and George had lunch with their representative at the St. George restaurant on Wednesday afternoon."

"George is lying."

"I have an independent eye witness who saw you there."

"Let's say I've met with him. Does it prove anything?"

"Leave proof for the lawyers," she said. "If someone adds up all your actions, one can draw a very clear conclusion."

Angrily, Makin stood up. "If you think you can blackmail me, you're mistaken!"

"Sit down," she said firmly. "You can leave this office, but you can't escape."

"Oh, listen to this! Are you threatening me?"

"I haven't reached that stage yet," Katerina said calmly. "Now, do we have a solid understanding that you'll work with me?"

Makin scratched his head. "Sure," he said. "You know I'm easy to go along."

Katerina wasn't convinced he meant his words. She always saw him as having at least four faces. "I'm going to draw up the purchase agreement," she said. "And I want us to take it to Marianna to sign today. You sign as the executor. She signs as the beneficiary. I sign on behalf of Persinaras Estates."

"What's the hurry?"

"Marianna is too emotional," she said. "As soon as you transfer the estate assets to her, she may sell them to the highest bidder, take the money and squander it in London with Maximus by her side."

"Does she plan to go to London?"

"Yes," she lied.

"Let me know when the documents are ready for signing," he said.

"I will." They embraced and she handed him the phone.

"What?"

"Call her now."

"To tell her what?"

108

"My God!" Marianna exclaimed. She saw dried blood inside his nostrils. Scratches and bruises covered his rough face and upper torso. His eyes were begging for sleep. "What happened to you? "

"I must speak to you."

She saw a tattoo on his back. "Are you trying to trick me?"

"Why?"

"That thing," she said pointing at his back. "Richard had the same ... on exactly the same spot."

He turned his neck. "What is it?"

"It's a tattoo."

"Those sons of the bitches! They must have burned it into me!"

She felt sorry for him. "Where have you been?"

"When I was with Cynthia ... they forced us into a car. We were blindfolded and taken someplace. They tortured me. I escaped, but I don't know what happened to Cynthia."

"You need medical help. Leave! Go to the hospital."

"I came to tell you that there's someone out there who wants me to assume Richard's identity."

"What?"

"Cynthia claims that Richard really is dead, but that he died recently ... while in captivity."

"She never told *me* anything!"

"According to her, she and Richard were lovers."

Marianna laughed. "Richard couldn't satisfy *me*."

"Unless she's lying."

He's gone mad, Marianna thought. "Who were his captors?"

"The *Taliban*. They wanted millions of dollars."

Marianna's doubts increased. "Are you here to get money from me?"

"No. I'm here to warn you to take care of the children and yourself. If Richard's abductors don't get what they want, God knows what they will do next."

"I'm surrounded by friends and relatives who take good care of my children and me."

"Are the children okay?"

"They're sleeping."

"I want to see them soon."

"Last time you saw them, they got upset because you reminded them of their father."

"They're more resilient than you think."

"Don't counsel me about my children."

"What bothers me," Jason said, "is that you continue to maintain close associations with Makin, Crow and Lagos."

"You see what I mean? You sound like Faris."

"They may have had a hand in Richard's disappearance."

Even if what he's saying is true, Marianna thought, I'm too helpless to do anything about it. "I don't believe a word you're saying," she said.

"I found out where Villa Delphi is located," Jason said. "It's a chamber of torture and brainwashing."

"You are surely losing your mind."

"I know it's hard to believe, but it's true. I was tortured there."

"You've made some enemies, I'm afraid. You shouldn't have come to Pafos."

"Richard may still be alive."

The thought of Richard alive caused her to flinch. "I've heard that before. I won't believe it until I see him."

"The question is: Do you want him to be alive?"

She realized she was better off without him but answered, "Of course I do."

"Can you go on living like this if you suspect, that some of those who surround you are involved in deception, abduction and even murder?"

"Put yourself in my shoes. Where can I turn?"

"You're afraid."

"I don't think talking to you will take us anywhere. You'd better leave."

"Yes. I'm going to leave right now." He searched his pockets. He pulled out the pen and the matchbook. He cut off the cardboard folder and scribbled down a number and a name. "Here," he said as he handed it to her. "If you need anything, call me at this restaurant. I'll be there from nine-thirty to noon."

"It's not necessary," she said. She took the paper, tore it in half and threw it in the wastebasket. "I don't think I'll ever need your help. Thank God for that."

109

"**Y**ou can take us back to town now," Jason said to Stefanos.

"Yes sir."

Jason was pleased; Stefanos found the right shortcuts, drove swiftly, and by nine o'clock his taxi pierced the heart of the Pafos town centre. He asked Stefanos to drop him off at a quiet street near the Farmers' Market. He gave him all the paper money he had in his pocket for the fare. The coins jangled. But for his concern for Stefanos' pride, he would have got rid of the coins, too.

"The fare is only fifteen pounds," Stefanos said. "Here, keep the rest."

"No. It's okay," Jason said waiving his hand. He thanked Stefanos and began a fast walk toward the Mouttallos neighbourhood. He hoped to arrive at the door of the Turkish House in less than five minutes. To save time, he took all the shortcuts he knew around the Farmers' Market. The closed shops and the absence of any vehicles or other pedestrians presented a ghost town setting.

When he arrived at the Turkish House, Jason realized he didn't have the key. His wallet, driver's licence, the door key and about five hundred Cyprus pounds were in his dark blue blazer. He wondered who had possession of these items now. The only other person who had a spare key was Helena.

He left the Turkish House and hurried over to the telephone booth at the intersection of Mechment Pasa and Aphrodite Avenue. He needed twenty-five cents for the local call, and he was pleased that he had not given the coins to Stefanos. He emptied his pocket and counted them: twenty-four cents in all. "Shit" he murmured.

Jason jumped out of the telephone booth and stood at the corner, scouting the area, hoping to spot someone who could give him a penny. He saw an old man with a soiled blanket wrapped around his shoulders dragging himself down an alleyway. He's homeless, Jason noted, as he approached him.

"Hello sir," Jason said.

"Hi brother," the old man responded.

"I need a penny to make an urgent phone call," Jason said.

"What did you say, brother?"

"I need a penny."

The old man stood, shrugged, shoved his hands in his pockets and emptied them.

A coin fell, rolled on the ground and landed near Jason's feet. Jason bent down and picked it up. "Can I have it?" he begged.

"I have no need for only one penny," the old man responded in muted surprise.

"Thank you." A penny from a homeless person can open doors, Jason mused.

He had been careless to give all the paper money to Stefanos. He remembered Faris's $14,000 gift to him, which he'd refused. He thought of the $370-million plus that Cynthia wanted him to share with her. At that moment, one penny was just as useful as all that money. If one penny is so important, he reflected, $370-million could be 370 billion times more valuable. On the other hand, $370-million dollars can be a lot less important than a penny, he reasoned. *It all depends what one does with one's money, I suppose.*

He rushed back to the telephone booth, inserted the coins in the receptacle and dialed Helena's number.

"Hello," Helena answered.

"Would you please come to the Turkish House now?" Jason asked. "I need your spare key to open the door."

"I'll be over in a few minutes."

Even with the sun shining on his bare back, Jason felt cold because the cool wind was blowing from the southwest and he could see dark clouds swelling on the horizon. He hurried back to the Turkish House, sat in the backyard and waited.

Ten minutes later, he heard the banging of a car door and footsteps on the pavement at the front of the house. He got up and looked. It was Helena. He walked to the front yard to greet her.

She frowned. "You look like a homeless man. Your face ... what happened?"

As Jason went closer, Helena took a step back. He saw alarm in her eyes. "Don't worry," Jason said to calm her fear.

"There's a tattoo below your right shoulder," she said. "It's a letter R, in Old English typeface. When did you have that done?"

He tried to maintain his composure. "I'll explain later," he said. Right now, I need to shave, take a bath and put on some decent clothes. Nicholas will be waiting for us."

Helena unlocked the door and stood back, seemingly reluctant to go inside. "I'll wait for you in the car," she said.

As he was shaving, intermittent spasms pounded the nerves of his neck, and as his pain intensified so too did his anger. He turned his back to the mirror and twisted his neck to see the tattoo. It looked exactly the same type and size as that which had fashioned Richard's back. He was determined to seek revenge on his Delphi torturers. In defiance, he uttered into the mirror: "I'm Jason, I'm Jason, I'm Jason," as if he was struggling to exorcise Richard from his subconscious.

He wondered if Helena thought he'd gone mad. *Should I give her the true version of events or sell her the capsized boat story? I could keep all my cards pretty close to my chest and, depending on what she has unravelled, reveal to her only so much as I deem fit. But I trust her, and it would be unfair to keep her in the dark. Besides, I'm interested in her input on things.*

Jason then thought of Nicholas and the assistance he could provide. His aim was to connect his observations with Helena's findings and arrive at a possible explanation for everything. Only then, he thought, would it be wise to come up with a plan of action. Yet, a troubling topic lingered in his mind and made him feel uncomfortable.

110

The phone rang and Marianna answered it.

"Marianna," Makin said. "Listen carefully. Katerina wants to buy all the Mustafa assets from you."

"Why?"

"You don't need the headaches, and the price is right."

"How much?"

"Twenty million dollars."

Marianna had always believed the estate was worth over $300-million. "That's all?"

"Yes, but she'll assume all the liabilities, don't forget."

"How much are the liabilities?"

"Enormous."

"You're the CEO, and you don't know the exact number?"

"Relax. It's not easy to figure out. Faris made secret deals. Things are not as they are recorded in the books."

"I'll think about it," she said. "I'll let you know soon."

"No. We can't afford to wait. The papers must be signed today."

"I'll tell you what," she said. "Bring them with you when you come to dinner. We'll review them then."

"You won't have the time then. I think we should do this before dinner."

"I can't. I'm up to my neck in tasks. See you at eight." She hung up and called the Mustafa Beach Hotel.

"Mustafa Beach," the female voice said. "Where may I direct your call?"

"Alex Manning, please."

"One moment, Madam."

"Hello," Manning answered.

"Hi Alex."

"Marianna?"

"May I speak to Cynthia, please?"

"She's not in right now. She's out visiting some friends."

"Would you have her cellular phone number handy?"

"She didn't take her cell with her, I'm afraid."

309

Marianna suspected something wasn't right. "I called to invite you and Cynthia for dinner."

"When?"

"Tonight at eight."

"Thanks. What's the occasion?"

"To cheer us all up a bit."

"Sounds good. We would be delighted to attend."

"Bye," she said and hung up. *Let's see if Cynthia shows up,* she said to herself. She thought of the remaining guests she'd planned to invite. She picked up the phone and began calling the first number when a gloved hand came out of nowhere and grabbed the phone.

Marianna felt the cold edge of a knife on her neck. Her upper body shook by reflex, but when she felt the sharp point of the knife against her skin she gave up any resistance and froze. "What do you want from me?"

"Where is he?" he asked.

A black veil concealed his face. His voice was tense, almost trembling. The English was accented.

"Who?" Marianna feared she might be killed on the spot.

"Jason."

"I don't know."

"He was here an hour ago," the voice insisted.

"Yes, but he left," and she pointed nervously towards the doorway as if that might make him believe her.

"What did he tell you?"

"Nothing unusual," she lied.

"What did he tell you?" he repeated.

"He said he wanted to see the children." The children, she thought. *I hope he doesn't harm them.* The maid was watching over them upstairs, and she heard them laughing.

"What else?"

"Nothing."

"Did he promise you any money?"

"No."

"The bastard! He thinks he can get away!"

"What do you mean?"

He suddenly jumped out the window, ran, climbed up the wall and disappeared behind the olive trees.

111

Marianna was on the phone again. "I'm very upset," she said to Makin. She was reluctant to tell him about Jason and the intruder who was looking for him. "I worry for my safety and the safety of my children."

"Are you hiding anything from me?"

"You are the one who's hiding things, damn it!" she exploded.

"Relax."

"All you can say is 'relax.' I want you to come over right away."

"I should be there in thirty minutes," he said.

She hung up, walked to her private patio and sat down, trying to regain her composure. She felt the coolness of the brisk wind blowing from the southwest and saw dark clouds moving inland. She went inside, closed the window and sat on the bed.

How can I trust Makin? she wondered. *He's been less than sincere the whole time, she realized. A few days ago he'd begged me to appoint him the CEO, after promising me he'd do a good job as administrator of Faris's estate. Now he's pressuring me to sell everything to Katerina at a ridiculously low price. I don't like it when people try to manipulate me!* The words "huge liabilities" and "secret deals" reverberated in her mind and gave her a headache. She couldn't wait to confront him.

She debated whether or not she should call Naharos and tell him about the intruder. He'd probably send half a dozen officers to turn the place upside down looking for fingerprints, but since the intruder was wearing gloves, their work would be pointless. Also, her celebrity status in the community would attract the attention of the media. And she hated answering reporters' questions about the incident, which some locals would probably twist into colossal gossip.

She hurried to the bathroom, took off her clothes, jumped into the bathtub and took a warm shower. The water pressure invigorated her body. She dried her body, changed clothes, combed her hair and walked to the living room, waiting for Makin to arrive.

The gate entry system rang. "Let me answer it," Marianna said to the elderly maid. "Who is it?"

"Open the gates," Makin said and Marianna pushed the numeric access code.

When she glared at him, he couldn't look her straight in the eye. "Who do you work for?" she demanded.

"Calm down."

"Something's wrong. You've given me a lot of referrals, and I've made a fair amount of money decorating Crow's brothel. I thought you did it to help me after Richard's disappearance. Now I sense you've benefitted more from it than I have."

"Why do you say that?"

"You admitted you were an insider on secret deals. Don't tell me you were a silent onlooker."

"When you work for others you're always a silent onlooker."

"Bullshit! You have a luxury villa, drive a Mercedes and live better than any of the other employees."

"Faris has rewarded me handsomely. You've also given me a cut from all these referrals."

"If you're such a good manager, why are there 'huge liabilities,' to use your own words?" she said raising and moving her index fingers for emphasis.

"There's only so much a manager can do," he said.

"I'm not happy with the answers I'm getting from you."

"I'm afraid we all have to live with reality."

"Are you saying that Mustafa Holdings is bankrupt?"

Makin scratched his head. "I know there aren't enough assets to meet the liabilities."

"If that's the case, why do you want me to sell them to my sister for twenty million dollars?"

"Maybe she can turn the company around."

"No, no, no! I know my sister. She wouldn't buy an insolvent company."

"I'm sure she'll accept that risk."

"You want me to benefit at my sister's expense?"

"Katerina wants this. I can't go against her wishes; you know she can be vicious."

"You're trying to turn me against my sister, damn it!"

"Look! The truth is I care more about you than her. You have children to consider."

"There you go again. Stop manipulating me!"

"You can't handle problems. She can."

"Why do you assume I'll just continue to let others manage my affairs?"

"So far you haven't done anything on your own."

"You're wrong. The galleries are doing just fine, thanks to my efforts."

"Thanks to the jobs I've sent your way."

"Words are cheap. What can you do for me now?"

"I'm just as helpless as you are!" Makin yelled.

Marianna was taken aback by the humble words of a man who, up until now, she had thought strong and powerful. "What's going on, anyway?"

"I don't want to cause you any more worry."

"Tell me, for Christ's sake!"

"Okay. All the money is now in Jason's hands. He's sitting right now with $386-million in an offshore account in his name."

"Who gave him the money?"

"Who else?"

"Richard?"

"Yes."

"I'm going to call Naharos."

"No! Don't do that."

"Why not?"

"It's too complicated to get into."

"Is my sister implicated?"

"All of us are."

"I haven't done anything wrong."

"The authorities won't believe you."

"Are you *trying* to implicate me?"

"You are part of this whole fucking mess!"

Marianna began to see where Makin was leading her. If I dig deeper, she thought, he might harm me. "What do you suggest?"

"I told you. Let us sort things out."

"Very well." She paused to change topic. "Are you coming to dinner or have you changed your mind?"

"We're still friends, aren't we?"

"Yes, we are," Marianna said, struggling to maintain her composure. "I'll see you tonight."

By the time Makin left the compound, she knew what she had to do.

112

When Jason and Helena walked in, the restaurant was empty. But, a few seconds later, Nicholas emerged from the kitchen. He welcomed them cordially and shook their hands. Achilles, the German Shepherd, approached Jason, sniffed his shoes and wagged his tail. "Sit, sit," Nicholas ordered and Achilles obeyed. Nicholas turned to Jason. "I heard that someone smashed your face on Friday, and I don't like it. I can see the bruises."

Helena gave Jason a bewildered stare.

Jason stood in the middle of the restaurant and took a moment to gather his thoughts. The same unsettling topic lingered in his mind. *Should I tell them Cynthia's story about Richard depositing at least $370-million in a Panamanian account under my name?* Maybe later, he decided. "We need to discuss some important developments."

"Please sit down," Nicholas replied. "Would you like some coffee?"

"That would be nice," Helena said as she sat down. "A strong Greek coffee with a teaspoon of sugar sounds great."

"Make it two," Jason said. He pulled out a chair and sat on it facing Helena.

"I'll be back in a few minutes," Nicholas said and left the sitting area.

Jason was anxious to begin, but first he wanted to understand something. "When you hear the word *'Delphi'* what comes to mind?" he asked Helena.

"The ancient site in Greece," Helena answered. "A shrine on the slope of Mount Parnassus about, oh, nine kilometers inland from the Gulf of Corinth, a sacred spring, the Sacred Way, pilgrimages to priestess Pythia, rich offerings, cryptic answers, the god Apollo and the god Dionysus. But you know all this, don't you?" she grinned.

"I thought the shrine was dedicated only to the god Apollo."

"Well, the ancient Greeks thought it was the centre of the earth, Delphi was once the site of an oracle of the earth, um, goddess Gaea. According to mythology, the god Apollo defeated the monstrous serpent

314

Python, who guarded Gaea, and expelled her from the sanctuary, which he then shared with the god Dionysus."

"God against goddess."

Helena smiled. "All in the name of gold."

"Who do you think among our suspects could use Delphic symbolism?"

"It takes a touch of sophistication. I can think of your late mother ... and perhaps ... Marianna."

Jason nodded. Helena's opinion has merit, he thought. His mother was an admirer of ancient Greek monuments. And Marianna had a sizeable collection of paintings and other works of art depicting Ancient Greek life. Her decorative style was also predominantly Greek. "What about Lagos?" he asked.

"He's from mainland Greece. I imagine he's well acquainted with Delphi."

Jason remembered *The House of Adonis and Aphrodite*, Crow's brothel on Parthenon Avenue. He thought of the huge painting behind the desk of the hall of the brothel depicting ten hetaerae dressed in fawn skins, surrounding, touching and feeding Dionysus, the god of wine. Female slaves were carrying trays of fruit, food and drinks. Dionysus was holding a drinking horn and wearing a crown made of grape vine branches. Jason further remembered the classical Greek art adorning the walls of the brothel's atrium. "Crow also seems to be an ardent admirer of ancient Greek themes," he said.

"That's right," Helena said.

"What if Makin hired Marianna to do the job at Crow's brothel?" Jason asked.

"It may show that Makin is running the show."

"Do you remember the photograph?"

"Which one?"

"The one revealing Makin, Crow and a third man being hugged and kissed by three women."

"I was looking at it yesterday."

"The backdrop in that photo shows the same artwork I saw hanging on the walls of the brothel."

"If so, that places Makin in the brothel premises," Helena said.

"And increases the possibility of Makin and Crow working together."

Nicholas returned, holding a tray with two cups of Greek coffee and two glasses of water. He placed the tray on the table and headed for the kitchen.

"Where are you going?" Jason asked him.

"I thought you were discussing private matters," Nicholas said.

"Well, we could use your input."

"Yes," Helena said. "Please stay."

"Very well," Nicholas said, sitting firmly on a chair as if he was obeying an order from a military superior. "I'll keep quiet," he said, "unless I'm asked to speak."

113

Jason said, "First of all, I've located the Delphi project. It's a building high up on the hills overlooking the Akamas peninsula. It looks like a luxury villa but it's just a fortress. Yesterday, I was held there for many hours before I managed to escape. They tortured me, and attempted to brainwash me into thinking that I was Richard. They also tattooed my back with the letter R. What do you make of this?"

"How did you end up at that place?" Helena asked.

"They abducted Cynthia and me from the Mustafa Beach Hotel."

"I'm sorry for my attitude this morning," Helena responded. "You looked strange. You must have been through hell."

"It's okay."

"What happened to Cynthia? Did they torture her, too?"

"I don't know. They took her away, roughly."

"How did they try to brainwash you?"

"They wanted to change my identity by convincing me that I was Richard. They kept hitting me on the neck with a ball after they injected me with something."

"Why would someone want you to take on Richard's identity?"

"Maybe they planned to mislead somebody."

"Can you identify them?"

"No. They blindfolded us before they took us there. But I think I can identify the man who came inside the hotel to abduct me. There was one other guy who sat beside me in the back seat of the black Mercedes. I was too nervous to notice his features. And the guard …. I could identify one guard if I saw him."

"They must be looking for you. Do you think they're the same people who beat you up on Friday?"

"How do you know I was beaten up on Friday?"

"Nicholas just mentioned it a few minutes ago."

"I'm sorry. I didn't tell you about it because I didn't want to ruin your evening. It was Makin who assaulted me on Friday when I went to the Mustafa building."

"The son of a bitch," Helena muttered.

317

"If he wanted me dead," Jason said, "he would've found some other, more discreet, way to finish me off. Obviously he wants me alive for some reason."

"Mmm," Helena thought. "Perhaps. Does the tattoo on your back remind you of anything?"

"It's the same tattoo Richard had, on exactly the same spot of his body."

"So they're very anxious to pass you off as Richard," Helena said. "Obviously they know some details about Richard's life."

"Yep."

Helena sighed. "It seems Makin has the connection with Crow, but I feel Marianna wants to avoid implicating Makin."

"Could be. What can she gain by hiding his involvement?"

"Maybe Makin *wants* it that way."

"You mean, she's afraid of him. What's also important," Jason continued, "is to find out if Marianna did that job at the brothel and if its before, or after, Richard's disappearance. And how much money, if any, she got for the job … and who paid her. But I don't think Marianna is going to share any information with us."

"That's obvious, isn't it?"

"Well, I visited Villa Mustafa this morning, before I called you the second time—"

"You dared to go back?" Helena interjected.

"I was concerned. I also had to inform her of Cynthia's claim that Richard is dead. At the same time I gauged her reaction by stating that Richard may be alive."

"How did she react when she saw you?"

"She was uncomfortable. She doesn't believe that Makin, Lagos and Crow may be involved in Richard's disappearance. But it's clear to me she's afraid of them."

"You're giving Marianna the benefit of the doubt."

"To her, I think, keeping quiet is a matter of survival."

"In fact, Jason, she might well be a collaborator."

"I doubt it, although someone is definitely planning something. I've seen porters moving boxes on carts and loading them onto Lagos's boat."

"They may be planning a trip," Helena said.

"Or an escape," Jason said. "I wonder—"

The telephone rang, and Nicholas picked it up. "Nicholas' Restaurant."

There was a short pause.

"Yes, he's here," Nicholas said. He turned to Jason. "It's for you."

"Hello?" Jason answered.

"I'm sorry for what happened this morning," Marianna said. "We need to talk."

Jason was startled. "Now?"

"Yes."

"Where?"

"Anywhere safe."

"Well … I'll call you back in a couple of minutes."

"Yes, please do."

He hung up, took a big breath and said, "That was Marianna. She wants to meet with me."

"Obviously, she knew where to find you," Helena noted.

"That surprises me, actually," Jason said, "because she ripped up the piece of paper I gave her with Nicholas's phone number on it."

"Something's wrong. I don't like this."

"I should listen to what she has to say," Jason said.

Helena shook her head. "She's up to no good."

Jason turned to Nicholas. "What do you think?"

"I would tell her to meet me on my turf," he answered.

"Do you mind if she comes to the restaurant?" Jason asked Nicholas.

"She must agree to come alone and not to tell anyone that she's here. To be on the safe side, I'll place ten guards inside and outside the restaurant."

"I'll call her back now," Jason said and dialed her number.

"Hello," Marianna answered.

"Okay," Jason said. "We'll meet at Nicholas's restaurant."

"All right."

"No one is to know we're meeting, and you must agree to discuss things in front of Helena and Nicholas, as well as me."

"That's fine," Marianna said. "Where is his restaurant?"

"It's near the Farmer's Market."

"I'll find it. I should be there in forty-five minutes."

Jason hung up, and Nicholas picked up the phone and dialed a number. "Send ten men over to the restaurant. I want five at the door and five inside."

After he hung up, he said, "They'll be here in half an hour."

114

While waiting for Marianna to make her appearance, Jason turned to Helena. "So, what did you uncover in your audit of the books and the Mustafa bank records?"

She opened her briefcase, took out a large notebook and flipped the pages. "The Mustafa Bank in Nicosia shows three directors: Faris, Makin and Richard. Any one of the directors can approve loans of up to $100,000 from the bank to a customer. For any lending over $100,000 at least two of the three directors must approve. My audit finds that in October 1995 Richard and Makin approved a $12-million loan to a company called *Long Nile Development Corporation*."

Helena cleared her throat and continued. "In January 1997, Makin and Richard approved four additional loans to *Long Nile*, totalling $386 million. They are sectioned into four separate payments to *Long Nile*: $16-million, $110-million, and two payments of $130-million each. Except for the $12-million loan, from the bank's cash fund, it seems clear the bank received the other funds from third parties and then rechannelled them to *Long Nile*."

"What's the significance of these loans?" Jason asked.

"Based on local regulations, an offshore bank can lend money only to an entity that does not trade or carry on business inside Cyprus. I searched for *Long Nile* in the registry of companies and I couldn't find any such name. It appears that *Long Nile* is registered in another country. While the loans were made to *Long Nile*, the Mustafa bank borrowed $110-million from a Saudi bank – and Kamal Kamal signed on behalf of it. At the same time, the Mustafa Bank in Nicosia received two simultaneous deposits of $130-million each from two different sources. The first was an offshore bank that operates in the Cayman Islands. The second deposit was from a Bahraini offshore entity."

"So the bank had deposits totalling $260-million during that period," Jason stated.

"Actually deposits at the time totalled $386-million. That includes the $110-million from the Saudi bank and a $16-million deposit from the same Bahraini source earlier."

"When Kamal spoke to my father last Sunday, he mentioned only the $35-million loan."

Helena replied, "I found that one. It was made to your father from the same bank in September 1990. That was the sole loan secured by a mortgage and a general security agreement."

"What was the purpose of the loan?"

"The agreement I reviewed refers to 'for the financing of the operations of Mustafa Bank (Cyprus) International.'"

"But why did Kamal not mention the $110-million loan?" Jason asked.

"Maybe he didn't want your father to know about it."

"Why do you say that?"

"First of all, as I said, that loan was approved by Makin and Richard. Secondly, the $386-million was transferred to *Long Nile* as 'loans for the purchase of construction equipment and the undertaking of major infrastructure projects.' Makin and Richard also approved these loans. It appears Faris knew nothing about them."

"That's a lot of money to be transferred to a construction company," Jason said. "Who signed the papers on behalf of *Long Nile*?"

"The agreement refers to three participants. The first is the Mustafa Bank. The second is *Long Nile*. And the third is a company named *Sudan Star Construction Inc*. Makin and Richard signed on behalf of the Mustafa Bank. Abbas Azim and Badi Latif signed on for *Long Nile*. Finally, George Lagos and Dimitrios Fermouras were the *Sudan Star* signatories."

"These are three new names we don't know anything about," Jason remarked.

"I think I know who Dimitrios Fermouras is."

"Oh?"

"He's Crow the Butcher."

A stunned Jason muttered, "Are you sure?"

"I went through the town's names in the telephone directories and the rolls of taxpayers, and I found out he owns the brothel on Parthenon Avenue. He also has a house in the hills. I drove to the area. He has a 'for sale' sign on the lawn."

"Yes." Jason remembered his own excursion and discovery. "Do you think he plans to leave the country?"

"Maybe."

Jason saw Nicholas shaking his head in complete bewilderment.

"Do you think Lagos and Crow are front men for other, silent, partners?" Jason asked.

"It looks like it," Helena said. "Abbas and Badi may also be front men."

"I wonder who the real partners are."

"Me, too." Helena rattled on, "But listen to this: I've come across another agreement between the Mustafa Bank and a number company. It was signed by Faris and Makin on behalf of the bank back in September 1990. It refers to a loan to the number company for the purpose of 'engaging in international trade of surplus military equipment and supplies from and to approved and accredited governmental sources in compliance with United Nations regulations and embargo directives'."

"I can't believe my father financed the trade of arms," Jason said. "That's shocking!"

"Not if it was legitimate," Helena said. "What's really interesting is that Alex Manning and Cynthia Manning signed the loan contract on behalf of the number company."

"This is becoming more revolting by the second! How much was that loan for?"

"Fifty million dollars."

"Was it repaid?"

"Yes. Two years later, the bank received from the same company $75-million dollars."

"So the bank made a $25-million dollar profit?"

"Apparently."

"Did you discover any other dealings between Manning's company and the Mustafa Bank?"

"No. But that doesn't mean Manning hasn't entered into similar agreements with others."

"Good point. Let's go back to the loans from the Mustafa Bank to *Long Nile* and *Sudan Star*. When were these loans due?"

"January 31, 2001."

"Two months and eleven days before Richard's abduction," Jason said after a pause. "Did you find any offshore bank accounts that belonged to Richard or the Mustafa Bank?"

"I looked for any reference to a Panamanian bank account in the books in connection with the cheque book we found in Makin's office on Wednesday, but nothing popped up. It will be very hard to get any information from the Panamanians about that account. My guess is it belongs to either Richard or Makin."

Jason smirked and whistled in the dark, "Any more earth-shattering revelations?"

"That's all I've managed to put together so far," Helena said. "A more thorough audit will take months to complete and at least four more auditors."

"Just as well," Jason exhaled. "I don't think my heart can take much more at the moment. Thanks, Helena, you've done a great job!"

"Let's eat something," Nicholas said. "We have a busy day ahead of us." He went to the kitchen and came back with a tray full of *mezedes*. "This is my version of fast food," he said smiling broadly.

They were in the middle of their meals when three vans arrived. The guards got out and Nicholas interrupted his meal to greet them and give them instructions. He took something from them and asked Jason to follow him to the back of the restaurant. They walked over to the small house at the back of the property and Nicholas outfitted Jason with a tiny camera. "When you are ready, click the top of the pen and the camera will begin to transmit color video via the wireless transmitter to the wireless receiver. We'll tape everything Marianna says."

"What else do you have?" a surprised Jason inquired.

"The receiver will be connected to a VCR 150 feet away."

"Fantastic!"

By the time they walked back to the restaurant, Marianna was already at the front door, posturing like a stray cat.

115

She didn't expect to see so many people inside the restaurant. Marianna recognized Helena, who was sitting alone at a round corner table. God, I don't know if I can withstand that contemptuous stare, she thought as their stares clashed.

Seeing Jason emerge from the kitchen made her feel better. A mustached man, whom she swore she had seen before, accompanied him. *Isn't he the man who was in charge of security at the Mustafa building?* She also saw him at Villa Mustafa on Thursday, after Faris's funeral. Strange.

"I feel so bad," she said, going closer to Jason. "I've been pretty mean to you."

"I understand," Jason said. "This is Nicholas."

"Pleased to meet you again," Nicholas said as he shook her hand.

"Now I recognize you," she said to Nicholas. "I didn't know you owned a restaurant."

"I like to eat well," Nicholas responded with a smile, and Marianna was thankful for his jovial mood.

She turned to Jason. "Jason, the truth is I'm afraid ... of everybody. I've been living in fear ever since Richard disappeared. I feel lonely and helpless. When I saw you last Sunday, I vowed never to allow you to get too close to me because I was afraid you'd take away from me the things I enjoy. I worried you may control and dominate me. You proved me wrong. You are unselfish and decent." She threw herself into his arms. "I'm sorry. I'm sorry."

"It's okay," he said, holding her tight.

"We must do something about it," she said.

"First, let's sit down," Jason said and he pointed to the corner table where Helena was sitting.

Marianna hesitated, but she realized that the only way to reconcile with Helena was to let her vent her feelings. She walked over to the table and extended her hand. Helena didn't react. "I'm sorry," Marianna said.

Lips stiff, Helena nodded in silence.

"Please sit over here," Jason indicated a chair next to Helena.

Marianna sat down, resigning herself to the fact that Helena (even through her piercing silence) was calling the tune. The last time she'd been in a similar situation, was when father had chastised her for fooling around with Maximus.

Jason sat on a chair across from her facing the door, while two of Nicholas's security men stood behind him.

"Would you like some coffee?" Nicholas asked, eager to break the ice.

"Yes, please," Marianna responded, "with three spoonfuls of sugar."

Nicholas turned to one of his men. "You know how to make coffee, don't you?"

"Ah, yes sir, I do."

Nicholas sat next to Jason and stroked his mustache. The German shepherd walked from the kitchen and sat behind Nicholas. "It's going to rain," Nicholas said.

"Yes," Marianna replied fidgety.

"Well," Jason said looking at Marianna, "we're ready to start. By the way, you should understand that we're video-recording whatever you say."

"I have nothing to hide."

"Please tell us all you know about Richard's disappearance and any wrongdoing on the part of Makin, Lagos, Katerina, Maximus, Manning, Cynthia and others."

"Before I say anything, I want your pledge that whatever happens to me, my children will be protected – financially and otherwise."

Jason nodded. "If it's up to me, I'll make sure of it. I love those kids."

"I don't know what happened to Richard," Marianna said. "He just … didn't come home one day. I don't give any credence to rumours."

"Makin, Lagos and Crow are close friends," Marianna continued. "Crow owns a brothel. Makin introduced me to him after Richard's disappearance and Crow hired me to decorate his brothel. He paid me thirty-five thousand pounds for the job. I also sold him a number of art works, including all the paintings he has hanging on the walls of his brothel.

"Katerina claims her husband made some deals with Richard, Makin and others—without her knowledge. They bought weapons, she says, but I don't know if that's true. Lagos's associates are pressuring Katerina to pay off a loan by January 31st. My sister fears if she doesn't

326

come up with the money, they may kill her or take over the family business.

"Katerina used Lagos to steal Faris's will from Dr. Platos' house. Yesterday she asked me to give her twenty-five million dollars, but I refused. She asked me to let her manage the Mustafa estate. When I refused, she teamed up with Makin—whom she describes as having at least four faces. He pressured me to sell the assets of the Mustafa Estate to Katerina for twenty million dollars, but so far I've held back.

"Makin claims the liabilities of Mustafa Holdings are huge and that Faris made secret deals. He also said Richard transferred $386-million into an offshore account in your name. Is that true?" Marianna noticed her question caused Jason some discomfort.

He smiled and then frowned.

She sensed that Nicholas and Helena were just as eager to hear what he had to say.

"Frankly I don't know," Jason said. "Wouldn't Makin have given you all the details?"

"Makin didn't explain how this happened, and Richard seldom confided in me about his financial dealings."

"What else do you have to say?" Jason asked.

"Katerina thinks Makin and others are planning a major scheme. She's afraid Makin and Lagos will take off with our family's money. She told me that a Pafos lawyer called her on Saturday morning and told her that this monk, Modestos, supplied incriminating evidence against Maximus and Katerina. Apparently, Katerina says, the lawyer wants out of the case because she's involved. She thinks she can bury the case by giving this lawyer a hundred thousand dollars. I don't know if this lawyer is male or female, for Katerina was careful not to disclose this information to me.

"Maximus plans to leave the church for good. He told me he's purchased a one-way ticket to London. He flies out on Monday morning. Maximus and I had an affair before I married Richard. Three months after I married Richard, Maximus made love to me only once. We stopped seeing each other for a long time. We resumed our affair after Richard's disappearance.

"This morning a masked man broke into my house, put a knife to my neck and demanded I tell him what you said to me. He also wanted to know if you had promised me any money. I answered that you just wanted to see the children."

A guard returned with the coffee and two glasses of water. Marianna took a sip of coffee and used her handkerchief to wipe some sweat from her forehead. "I'm still in the dark," she sighed, "as to what is going on."

"You're not alone," Jason said, as he held her hand. "Do you have anything else to say?"

"One other thing," Marianna said. "I'm planning a dinner party at seven o'clock. I've already invited many friends and relatives, including Manning, Katerina and Lagos. Do you think I should cancel it?"

"You should go ahead with your plans. Have you invited Maximus?"

"No."

"You should invite him, too."

"Okay."

"What about Crow? Have you invited him?"

"No."

"Invite him also," Jason suggested.

"Yes. I have his number."

"We know who the main suspects are," Nicholas said. "I've heard of Makin, Crow, Kamal, Lagos, Cynthia and Manning. Anyone else?"

"Maximus and Katerina," Jason said.

"Do you know where they all live?" Nicholas asked Marianna.

"Well, Manning is supposed to be at the hotel. I don't know where Cynthia is. Kamal may have gone back to Saudi Arabia, but I'm not sure. Maximus should be at the monastery. As for the others, I know where their houses are."

"We could always storm their homes, then abduct and interrogate them one by one," Nicholas offered.

"That's a bit like overkill," Jason smiled. "I'm thinking of something different ... but I'll need Marianna's cooperation."

"Such us?" Nicholas asked.

"They seemed anxious to condition me into thinking I was Richard," Jason said. "I should impersonate Richard. Only then can we get to the heart of the matter."

"Both options are extremely dangerous," Helena said. "We have enough information to call the police and have them arrested."

"I don't think so," Nicholas said. "By the time the police get involved, these guys will either escape or do something crazy."

"Let's plan how to handle Marianna's dinner party," Jason said.

"I rather like your idea," Nicholas said to Jason. "However, before we discuss how to carry out this mission, I must warn you that you have entered point zero."

"What's that?" Jason asked.

"Simply put, if anything goes wrong, they'll kill us all."

"I'm scared," Marianna said, "but I'm prepared to follow Jason's plan."

"I don't want any violence on our part," Jason said.

Nicholas shook his head. "That's close to impossible. You'd need my guards to assist you. These guys are trained to defend themselves, if necessary. What happens if they start shooting at us?"

"We must try to do it in such a way that the enemy won't have an opportunity to use their guns," Jason said.

"You're talking to an ex-police officer and the head of a security company."

"Our problem is we don't really know who's against whom," Jason stated.

Helena stood up. "What about your sister and Maximus," she said looking at Marianna. "Are you prepared to turn them in?"

My sister betrayed me by teaming up with Makin, Marianna thought. *Maximus has his own plan, it seems.* "Katerina admitted she's done something illegal; she should be punished for that. As for Maximus, if he's guilty, he should also bear the consequences."

As Helena was about to say something, her cellular phone rang. "Hello?" she answered.

She listened for several seconds and Jason saw fear on her pale face. "Ask them to please wait until I come home. I'll be there in a few minutes."

After pressing the end call button, Helena took a big breath. "That was Ismail," she said. "The police are at my apartment with a warrant to search the premises."

116

"I need to speak to Jason in private for a minute," Helena said to Nicholas and Marianna.

Jason got up and walked with her to the kitchen. "All those records and Richard's items are at the apartment," Helena said. "What are we going to do?"

"Let me look after something first while Marianna is here. Let's go back in. I don't want them to think we're planning something behind their backs."

They returned from the kitchen and Jason approached Nicholas. "Do you have enough aprons for ten guards?"

Nicholas look befuddled. "Yes. Why?"

"We'll dress them as waiters and send them to serve Marianna's guests." He looked at Marianna. "Mmm?"

Marianna nodded.

"Before they go there," Nicholas said, "I'll want to take my technician to the villa to help me set up the surveillance equipment and to bug the place."

"Concentrate on the library and dining room," Jason said. "How long will it take to get that under way?" he asked.

"At least an hour."

"I think Marianna should go home now," Jason said. He faced his sister-in-law. "Invite all your friends and relatives to the party as usual. Get everything prepared. Remember to invite Maximus, too. Nicholas and his technician should be there well before dinner begins."

"Expect my technician and me before four," Nicholas added.

When Marianna left, Jason turned to Helena. "We don't want to antagonize the police, especially since they have a warrant. Let them take what they want, but insist on having all documents sealed for examination by a judge."

"At least the records will be in the hands of the authorities," Nicholas agreed. "We can find a way to explain how you came into their possession later on."

330

"I suppose I don't have to make a statement. I have the right to remain silent," Helena said. "Okay. I'll call you later to let you know what happens, if I'm not in custody."

She took her briefcase, opened it, placed the notebook inside, and headed for the door. She stopped, turned back and said, "I'll leave my briefcase here."

With Helena gone, Jason's anxiety intensified. "Who do you think tipped the police about the location of the records?" Jason asked Nicholas.

"The police have their own informants," Nicholas said.

"I don't know what Naharos might do with those documents. I don't trust him"

"I have a friend in Nicosia. He's from my village. He's the head of all the police chiefs. I can ask him to ensure that the documents are not touched by anyone until a judge has had the opportunity to review them."

Jason said, "Your friend will want to know your knowledge of our findings, and I don't want the police mucking things up at this crucial stage. Eventually we'll go to them, but not now. Helena, Marianna and I may be killed or abducted." He glanced at his watch. "It's almost eleven. We have only thirteen hours left."

"I can simply mention to him that Helena has some important documents, and he should ensure they are sealed. I won't tell him what I know."

"Excellent!"

Nicholas used his mobile phone and dialed a number. "Ariste?" he said. "My wife and I have prepared some wine-marinated sausages, the ones you enjoy, remember?"

A few seconds ticked on.

"Yes, anytime. Just give me a call before you get here."

....

"Listen," Nicholas said. "By the way a lady friend of mine has some documents that the Pafos police are after. They have a warrant to search her place. Can you see to it that the documents are sealed and kept intact until a judge has the chance to go over them?"

....

Nicholas turned to Jason. "What's her last name?"

"Oh!" Jason cried. "I don't...know! Let me call her," he offered.

Nicholas waived his hand. "Her first name is Helena," Nicholas said on the phone.

....

Nicholas turned to Jason for the second time. "What's her address?"

Jason raised his arms and shook his head.

"I'm sorry, I don't have her address. "I'll find out and call you back in a couple of minutes."

Nicholas severed the connection. "Give me Helena's number," he asked Jason.

Jason gave him the eight-digit number and Nicholas called.

"Hi Helena. This is Nicholas. I just spoke to a friend of mine in Nicosia. He's the chief of all police forces. I've asked him to ensure that the records are sealed and remain as such until they're taken to court. He needs your last name and address."

....

"Give me a pen," Nicholas asked Jason.

Jason struggled to find a pen. He opened the briefcase and found one, which he handed to Nicholas.

"Come again?" He wrote down a name and an address. "Thank you. Don't worry. Let them take the stuff."

Then he clicked off that connection and called another number. "Ariste?" he said.

"Her last name is Andreou. Her address is 156A Chlorakis Avenue, Apartment 9."

....

"Thank you. See you soon."

As soon as he finished his telephone conversation with Ariste, Nicholas turned to Jason. "I find it incredible that you don't know Helena's last name and where she lives."

"She's my half sister."

"Isn't that something?" Nicholas exclaimed. "How do you know that she's on your side?"

"I trust her the same way you trust me, because she earned my trust the same way I earned yours."

"There's so much you can trust people with. The talent is to know what to hold back."

"I'll remember that."

"Anyway," Nicholas said, "If what I've heard is true, the Mustafa bank is doomed. Someone out there has all that money and others are after it. The person with the money may be you. What I don't understand is why they want you to be Richard?"

The answer to Nicholas's question finally dawned on Jason. "Do you think my brother is not alive?"

"Hmm," Nicholas pondered. "That is very interesting."

Let's go over the plan," Jason said. "Oh, yes, one more thing. We should also make sure Aziz is protected when he arrives at Larnaca Airport."

"Let's have some Zivania first," Nicholas said. "It'll warm our blood."

He went to the kitchen and came back a few seconds later with a bottle of Zivania and two shot glasses. "It's nice and chilly," Nicholas said as he poured the colourless dry aperitif.

"Isn't it too early for that deadly stuff?"

117

Maximus woke up miserable. The night before he'd summoned the monks to the chapel, and, during a brief ritual, he'd ordained Modestos an archimandrite. After the ceremony, he invited the monks to the *synodic* room and announced Modestos's appointment as his assistant and second in command to replace him in case of illness, death or other emergency. He remembered the monks' surprised expressions when they learned that Maximus had chosen a young and inexperienced monk to take on so much responsibility and play a vital role in the affairs of the monastery. *Lord*, he prayed, *please forgive me.*

He missed the Sunday liturgy, but he didn't care. On Thursday night, he had hoped to persuade Marianna to follow him with the children to London, but he now realized that the likelihood of marrying her (and living a normal family life with her in London) was nothing but a distant dream.

Maximus had less than twenty-four hours to prepare for his Monday-morning flight to London. The plane was due to take off at nine o'clock, and he had to be at Larnaca Airport at least an hour and a half before departure time. The Pafos-Larnaca route was a two-hour drive during normal traffic hours, which meant he had to get up at five the next morning.

His mind travelled back in time again to when he was nine and entered the monastery walls for the first time. It was night then, as he walked under the arches, but the moon welcomed him inside.

Now looking outside the window, he saw heavy clouds hung low on the southwestern horizon, and he heard the wind whistling through the rafters. He could tell there was going to be a long rainstorm extending well into the night. Maximus was thankful to be leaving the monastery forever during rainfall and in the thickness of night, this time without the moon illuminating his path. It would be unbearable, he thought, to face the moon from the monastery grounds, as if it was a beloved dog he couldn't bear to leave behind.

He took a shower and was about to shave off his beard, but decided not to discard it just yet. *I can shave it off when I arrive in London.* It was nearing lunchtime, but Maximus would skip lunch, for he didn't want to face the monks' curious stares one more time. He rushed instead to his private office, anxious to collect his personal items and remove the cash from the safe.

As he was going through some documents, the telephone rang. "Hello?"

"I called your office at least seven times," Marianna said.

"I got up late."

"You don't sound well."

"I'm sure you know why."

"Are you leaving tomorrow, for sure?"

"Yes."

"I don't know what to say," Marianna said. "I'll pray for you."

"And I'll pray for you. I hope you'll reconsider."

Marianna said, "I've invited some friends over for dinner tonight, and I think it would be a good idea if you'd join us."

Maximus became concerned. "I hope you didn't tell anyone that I'm leaving tomorrow."

"No, I haven't."

"I don't have much time left. I still have to pack."

"Travel light. You'll find good clothes to buy in London."

Maximus was flabbergasted by Marianna's casual attitude, as if she was talking to a friend who was bound for a brief vacation. "I may never see you again," he said, his voice trembling. "The thought alone makes me shake. I don't think I'll be able to stand sitting in your dining room."

"Dinner starts at seven," she said. "But I want to see you at 6:45."

She knows I can't find the strength to say no. He was pleased that she wanted to see him early. That would give them sufficient time to make love right in her own house, and he could persuade her to change her mind, he hoped. "I'll see you then," he said joyfully.

118

Maximus arrived at Villa Mustafa at 6:45 sharp, but Marianna was not at the door to welcome him. The elderly maid invited him to follow her. "Come. The mistress will be down in a few minutes," she said as she escorted him to the library. She opened the door and left.

While waiting for her, Maximus looked outside the bay window on the north-end of the library. The rain was relentless and floods of water were running into the drains. *I might as well survey the room, since I've never been in here before.*

A rectangular area rug of Greek design, ivory and black, with gold tones covered the centre of the hardwood floor. The larger exterior border was lined with diamond-shapes, presenting a flower in each corner. Inside its borders a small wreath in wheat-like style encircled its flower-like design. A black satin and moiré-stripe sofa was placed by the western exterior border of the rug. Two needlepoint cushions rested on the corners of the sofa. In front of the sofa stood an occasional table with Chinese motif and lotus engravings. Its brass fret was engraved with Chinese cultural symbols. An antique Latique vase filled with cyclamens rested on it.

Hand-carved child figurines in Carrara white marble adorned the Italian crafted fireplace mantel. Three pumpkins of varying sizes sat in the centre of the mantle. They were balanced on either side with a grouping of candles and basket of fall leaves. On top of the mantel stood a three-foot arched mirror with a beveled edge. The cherry-finished frame had column-like sides with flower accents in the two lower corners and in the centre of the top arch.

A large basket next to the hearth was filled with pine cones.

Two leather chairs faced the desk.

An inviting chair with antique brown leather back and cushion sat behind the desk. The leafy designs covering its apron and cabriole legs gave it an elegant touch. Maximus walked over and sat behind the desk. This place is much better than ... what used to be mine, he mused.

He looked behind him. A console with subtle hand-painted detailing, gentle curves and antique brass finished hardware pleased his eyes.

An ottoman with smooth and lizard grain leather and hand-carved claw feet in walnut finish rested beside the desk. Fitted in its own stand with intricate hand carvings and adorned with a marble fossil stone top, an illuminated globe stood on the other side of the desk.

Maximus placed his hand on the globe. As he was about to turn it, Marianna walked in.

He got up, rushed toward her and embraced her. He tried to kiss her, but she turned away her pale face. "I don't want anyone to see us kissing," she said.

"I haven't given up hope that we'll get together soon … in London," Maximus whispered in her ear. "Every hour apart seems like a year."

"I'm too confused right now."

"The twins. Are they mine?"

"I was so wicked to cheat on Richard," she said sadly. "Yes, they are yours … yours and mine."

"I feel better now."

"I don't think it makes a difference to them. You aren't going to be in their lives, anyway."

"Oh, don't say that. I've saved enough money all these years, so we can all live comfortably."

"I don't know if I can trust you anymore. Katerina told me something that I didn't like."

"I hope she didn't spread malicious lies."

Her expression was anxious. "Did you kill Richard?"

"No! Of course not."

"Modestos and Katerina know more about your secrets than I," Marianna complained. "I would have thought that I was more important to you—"

And I feared I would lose you to him. She wanted me to kill Jason. I came so close. I'm glad I didn't shoot him."

"How could you, a man of God, reach so low?"

"Your sister is an evil woman—when she spoke to me, she froze my conscience. I am so sorry. I have begged for God's forgiveness."

Her sharp stare unsettled him.

"That's an easy way out," she said. "You should confess to the authorities and accept whatever punishment is fit for your crime."

"But I spared his life. I've committed no crime!"

"Stop it!"

"Give me credit for changing my mind. Good prevailed over evil."

"I'm not the one to pass judgment."

He grabbed her from the waist and pulled her toward him. "Will you please forgive me?"

She jerked her body away from him. "You should be asking this of Jason."

"You don't care about us, or what may happen to your sister! What on earth has happened?"

Marianna looked at her watch. "It's almost seven," she said. "The guests are due anytime. "We must go into the living room."

"But we haven't discussed anything ... about us."

"There's no need to."

A frustrated Maximus followed Marianna out of the library.

119

Shortly before seven, Katerina drove, with George in the passenger seat, to Villa Mustafa and parked her car. She got out, opened the back door and took out her brief case.

"What are you taking that for?" George asked.

"I'm buying the Mustafa estate. I presume your good friend has already briefed you on this," Katerina said. She wanted to sound as sarcastic as possible. That was the only way she knew to silence her husband.

He shook his head disapprovingly.

Katerina's main concern was to convince Marianna to sign the contract before dinner. When she entered the villa, she was puzzled to see so many waiters. In the living room, hoping to find her sister there alone, Katerina was taken aback when she saw her sitting next to Maximus, chatting cozily with him. It nearly triggered a headache in her. *Has Marianna changed her mind?* Katerina was afraid. *Is this the surprise she spoke about? Are they getting married?*

"Hello," Katerina said.

Maximus stood up and extended his hand. It felt cold and sweaty.

"Hello," he replied icily. Then he turned and greeted George.

Katerina looked at Marianna. "I have something to show you."

"What's the big rush?" Marianna asked.

Katerina took Marianna's hand. "It's important," she said.

"Let's go to the library," Marianna said. "Would you excuse us, please?"

Maximus nodded, and George didn't respond in any way.

Once in the library, Katerina hurried to the desk, opened her briefcase, removed a document, and placed it on the desk. "This is the agreement that Makin spoke to you about," Katerina said. He handed her a pen. "Sign it here." She pointed to the dotted line.

"Don't you think I should have a lawyer look it over before I sign?"

"I'm your lawyer," Katerina responded. "I've been your lawyer all my life. Have I ever let you down?"

339

"Tell me what it is."

"You're selling the Mustafa estate to our company."

"What's the price?"

"Twenty million dollars."

"Does the sale include the two villas and the land?" asked Marianna.

"Well, yes."

"Where am I going to live?"

"With twenty million, you can live anywhere you want. I'll build you a nice villa by the sea. You shouldn't stay here. This place will only haunt you with bad memories."

"What are you going to do with the villas and the olive grove?" Marianna asked.

"I'll lease them to some rich Arab, and use the rent to pay down the debt we have."

"Makin said the liabilities are huge. Is this true?"

"I'm just as anxious as you to find out."

"Before I sign it," Marianna said, "I want to know a few things."

"I don't know much myself."

"What was it that you and Maximus did to prompt the telephone call from Modestos's lawyer?"

Katerina hesitated. She wondered fearfully, *What shall I tell her?* Finally, she said, "It's better if you don't know."

"What I want to know is whether or not Maximus has told me the truth."

"What did he say?"

"Why don't we hear it from his own mouth?" Marianna turned around and headed for the door.

"Please don't," Katerina begged. "Don't bring him here. Come back. I'll tell you."

Marianna turned around and walked back to Katerina. "I'm listening."

"Let's sit down," Katerina said. She took Marianna by the hand. "Your hand is very warm" Katerina said in a friendly way.

"Take your freezing hand off me!" Marianna protested as she pulled her hand away.

They sat on the sofa, a few feet apart.

"Did you ask Maximus to kill Jason?" Marianna asked.

"Yes," Katerina said.

"Obviously you didn't think about the consequences."

"Honey, no one cares about us. Don't you understand? No one cares!"

"Honey?" Marianna repeated. "Maybe you should get professional help."

Katerina began to cry. "Please don't say that," she said wiping her tears.

"You don't want any man around me! You think that either Maximus or Jason is going to marry me, and you don't want either one to have me."

"That's not true," Katerina said weeping softly.

"You want my children and me close to you so that you can control us!"

"You wouldn't talk like that if you knew how much I suffer in silence."

"I know you've been through a lot of pain. You're so afraid of pain, you won't hesitate to destroy anything that threatens your sense of control."

Katerina gasped.

"Now you want me to sign this paper. What will you do if I refuse to sign?"

"I don't know. I wish we could reverse roles. I hate myself for being who I am, but I feel helpless to do anything about it. I would give anything to be you."

Marianna said, "I often thought the same thing about you."

"But my life is empty!" Katerina replied. "It's been like that for years! You don't know what it's like not knowing where your own child is!"

"This is the first time I've heard you talk like that."

"I blame myself for everything. If something turns out well, I still feel guilty for feeling pleasure. When things go wrong, I blame myself again. I can never find happiness."

Marianna walked over to the desk and took hold of the document. "Why don't we tear it up? It won't make a difference to us whether I sign it or not."

"No," Katerina begged extending her hands. "Give it to me. I'm afraid if you destroy it, I'll lose you and the children forever."

"So, I'm right!"

Katerina did not respond.

"Okay. Here." Marianna signed it and gave it to her. "Are you happy now?"

"Thank you," Katerina said. "I feel bad for putting you through all this." She took the document, opened her briefcase and shoved it inside. "Will you please forgive me?"

"My guests are arriving," Marianna said. "Let's go greet them."

120

Lightning jagged the dark clouds and thunder brought rain. At 8:55, a black van pulled outside the Turkish House. Jason, dressed in a black trench coat and a Greek fisherman's hat, slipped outside and settled himself in the back seat.

He felt positive. In only a few hours, he and his group had accomplished a great deal: Marianna was briefed and agreed to co-operate. They had sketched out in detail the process of the operation, and so far it was working without a glitch. Nicholas kept him informed via cell phone. By five o'clock, Nicholas and his guards had bugged Villa Mustafa as planned.

Nicholas's guards were now dressed as waiters and serving Marianna's guests. At Nicholas's request, the police in Nicosia had notified Cyprus Airways about a possible assassination attempt on Aziz's life. Ariste sent two secret police agents to the Larnaca Airport who whisked Aziz off to a waiting car, escorted him through private customs, and drove him to Villa Mustafa.

The Pafos police searched Helena's apartment, took all the documents they found, sealed them, and moved them to the station. But they didn't charge her.

To ensure the children's safety, Marianna delivered them to Helena at a location near the Peta village. Then she drove back to the villa in time for her meeting with Maximus. Fitted in chef's clothes, his mustache newly shaved, Nicholas was now directing the operation from the kitchen of Villa Mustafa.

Thirty minutes later, the van sped through the gates of the Mustafa compound and stopped inside the garage of Villa Mustafa. The garage doors closed. Jason exited the vehicle and two waiting guards greeted him. He walked with them through the service hall, galleria, and rotunda. Once they reached the library, one of the guards opened the door, and Jason stepped inside.

A chandelier hung from the library's cove ceiling. Its rich polished finish and hand-rubbed patina highlighted the solid cast brass arms that reminded Jason of ancient Greece.

"Everything's in place," Marianna said waiting for him.

They embraced.

Jason took off the hat and trench coat. He wore a black gabardine suit, black silk shirt and a black silk tie.

"Your hands are shaking," Jason noticed.

"I'm afraid Makin may recognize you."

"That's why I'll see him last. How did it go with Maximus and Katerina?"

"Well, I think," she said. "I've made sure you have enough water to last you the whole evening."

"Thanks."

"Are you ready?"

"I need a few minutes."

After Marianna left the library, Jason walked over to the shelves and examined the family pictures. He looked at a photograph of Marianna's three children together, outside by the pool, wrapped in towels. Another picture showed his father and mother, sitting together on a sofa. Next to it, there was one of Marianna. She sat on the swing that hung from one of the trees in the grove. The fourth photograph was of Richard ... and himself. They weren't even teenagers at the time.

The two boys, their smiles wide, were covered in sand and playing in the shallow water by the shore. *We used to go swimming together. He was always so much stronger than I, always there to keep me afloat. I used to cough and choke on the water, and he would be underneath me in a flash, helping me to the shore. He was too good to me.*

121

By nine-thirty, Marianna's struggle to maintain a lively atmosphere had paid off due to several factors: her hospitality, the good food and wine, excellent waiter service, and Aziz's presence at the dinner table.

Aziz was an overweight man in his mid-thirties with large prying black eyes. He had a pointed nose, and sported a trimmed mustache with a goatee. Wearing a permanent scowl on his face, he also wore a brown woolen Thobe, (a loose, long-sleeved ankle-length garment), a Tagiyah (a white knitted skull cap) a Ghutra (a square scarf folded across his head over the Tagiyah), and an Agal (a thick, double, black cord on top of the Ghutra to hold it in place).

He was the centre of attention, for he spoke constantly in a loud voice that reverberated in the dining room and kept everyone alert. Much to Marianna's quiet displeasure, Aziz often cut others off in mid-sentence to make his point.

Dinner began with baked pita wedges filled with hallumi cheese, eggplant dip, crab salad on toast, grilled shrimp pieces with scampi sauce, cocktail meat balls in Cyprus sauce, and smoked salmon. The main course consisted of classic Greek salad and Mousaka, green vegetables, baked potatoes and roast goat. Wine poured freely, and a waiter was assigned to get Lagos drunk. Since Aziz was a devout Muslim, he naturally abstained from alcohol, unlike everyone else present.

While the waiters served baklava, coffee and port, Marianna walked over to the kitchen and thanked Nicholas for his wonderful assembly of so many dishes in such a short time. Wearing a chef's hat and white aprons, Nicholas smiled broadly. A German shepherd was sitting quietly at the corner. "It's nine-thirty," Nicholas said."

"Right." She smiled and went back to the dining room.

Marianna counted her guests: eighteen in all, including her parents. Cynthia and Kamal were noticeably absent.

Taking her glass of clear, fiery Zivania (a drink something like the Mexican Tequila), Marianna walked slowly, around the dinner table, toasting each individual guest starting with Aziz. Then Marianna stood near him and said: "We have a very special guest tonight." She touched Aziz on the shoulder. "Are you having a good time?"

"Oh, yes!" Aziz said. "It's a great dinner given by a beautiful hostess!"

"I have a surprise for everyone," she said.

"Surprise is your middle name!" Lagos shouted across the table and everyone laughed.

I hope he's not too drunk to talk, Marianna mused, thinking of Lagos. "Please, everyone, remain seated until I come for you," Marianna said. She turned to Aziz. "Let me start with you. I have something to show you," she said.

She took him by the left hand and they walked toward the library.

122

"Richard is back," Marianna said as she opened the door.

Jason remained seated behind his desk. "Come forward," he waived.

Holding hands, Marianna and Aziz walked over to the desk. "Richard, this is Mr. Aziz," Marianna said smiling broadly.

"Pleased to meet you sir," Jason said extending his hand.

Aziz hesitated at first. Then, puzzled, he extended his right hand. Aziz was confused; his face was red.

"Isn't it wonderful!" Marianna said still holding Aziz's left hand.

"It's a miracle," Aziz murmured.

"Please be seated," Jason said.

Aziz sat on one of the leather chairs facing the desk.

Some waiters entered with a pull-cart of coffee and fruit. They left the cart by the fireplace and walked out.

"Now if you'll excuse me," Marianna said, "I must get back to the dining room." She exited the library and closed the door.

Jason knew that the two waiters, ex-commandos who Nicholas had handpicked for duty, were standing behind the door, ready to act if needed.

"I expected them to deliver you to *me* at the airport," Aziz said.

"I thought you were supposed to meet with my brother Jason, not me."

"That was going to happen afterwards. Nobody told you?"

Jason didn't know what Aziz meant. "I had an idea."

"I wonder why they changed the plans."

"I escaped."

"How did you manage that?"

"It's a long story."

"What am I going to do?"

"Aren't you happy to see me alive?"

"Hmm." He scratched his forehead. "Do you know your father is dead?"

"Marianna told me."

"We have a problem."

"Such as …?"

Aziz pointed at the door. "Do they know you've escaped?"

"Why?"

"Your father gave me 355-million dollars in order to secure your release. Now that you are free, I … don't know what to do."

"I don't want you to give them the money," Jason said.

"They will still want to get paid."

"If my father was alive, he wouldn't approve the release of funds to them."

"Why not?"

"Because I escaped, damn it!"

"So, what do I do with the money?"

"Turn it over to me. After all, it belongs to my family."

Aziz placed his hand on his head and removed his Agal, Ghutra and Tagiyah. "They … may kill me, if I refuse."

Jason saw a small folded vanilla envelope inside the Tagiyah.

Aziz tore off an edge of the envelope and removed three bank drafts.

Jason reached out his hand.

"No. I'm not giving them to you. Not yet," Aziz said.

"I know," Jason said. "You're concerned about your safety."

"If I go back empty handed, Kamal will kill me, provided I stay alive after I leave this place."

"Who do you think saved your life today?"

"Was it you who'd arranged for my escort at the airport?"

"Of course."

"May peace be upon you."

"And upon you may there be peace," Jason responded.

"You must understand my difficulty. Kamal wants the return of all the money he loaned to your bank to finance the purchase of arms. He will not release the arms to The Lion of Mazâr-e Sharîf unless I pay up."

"I know," Jason said nonchalantly.

"The Americans are not very happy with these developments. They want the war to end soon."

"You're under a lot of pressure."

"I'm mad at myself for agreeing to act as intermediary."

"Let me get the figures right. How much is Kamal asking?"

"One hundred and fifteen million dollars. I have the draft right here."

"I thought it was a bit less."

348

"What about commissions?" Aziz complained. "Kamal claims you agreed to pay him five million in commissions."

"If I let you give this cheque to Kamal, would you turn the rest of the money over to me?"

"Manning wants to get paid, too. That's part of the deal."

"Manning has some explaining to do."

"He knows how to get his way."

"How much is the cheque you have for him?"

"One hundred and ten million."

"I think he wants to get the *Taliban* money, too," Jason added.

"That's preposterous!"

"Can you say that to Manning's face?"

"Sure. Bring the bastard in here. I can't stand him, anyway."

"I'll invite him to join us in a couple of minutes." Jason fixed his stare between Aziz's eyes. "How did you meet Manning?"

"I introduced him to your father many years ago."

"Why don't you like him?"

"He has his own agenda."

"I get it. Your concerns are different than his."

"Well, yes. Can you imagine the uproar back home if they find out that two warring groups are fighting to get hold of the arms Kamal financed through your bank?"

"Whom do you favour?"

"Personally, I don't give a shit whether it's the Lion or the *Taliban*."

"It was Kamal's idea to supply The Lion of Mazâr-e Sharîf with arms in the first place."

"Call it the American plan."

"Anytime something goes wrong, you people in the Middle East blame the Americans. Kamal put up the money, remember?"

"He financed the deal. But it was Manning's idea. I'm sure you know by now that Manning didn't come here to bask in the sun."

"You're telling me the Americans supplied the arms to Manning?"

"How do you think Manning managed to go on doing business without any interference?"

"You mean, the *Taliban* and The Lion of Mazâr-e Sharîf were competing for the same shipment?"

Aziz furrowed his eyebrows in a suspicious way. "Come on, Richard. Don't pretend you don't know."

"You don't know what I've been through. I have difficulty remembering."

"Something is wrong," Aziz said. He got up. "Let me call Kamal."

"Wait a minute," Jason said. "Sit down. If you start calling people, I can no longer guarantee your safety."

Aziz sat at the edge of the chair. "Have the *Taliban* brainwashed you?"

"Why do you say that?"

"I find it hard to believe you escaped from them. You are sitting here like a warlord, as if nothing happened."

"How do you know the *Taliban* kept me captive?"

"Makin told us, unless he's lying."

"I'm very upset. My father didn't act fast enough to secure my release."

"Don't let this get out of the room. Your father and I had engaged in secret negotiations for your release to us. We didn't know whether you were dead or alive."

"Obviously you failed."

"Yes, because the *Taliban* members were afraid they were going to lose the war. So they insisted the arms be shipped to them, or they get their money back. The Americans weren't happy with either proposal."

"What should we do to make everyone happy?"

"Let me pay Manning and Kamal. I don't have to turn over the draft to the *Taliban* because you're a free man."

"But the Americans may want the $130-million turned over to them."

"That's your problem, not mine."

"What do you know about the Delphi Project?"

"Kamal financed the bloody place, but he wasn't responsible for its operations!"

"Who runs it now?"

"It must be the Lion's men. All I know is that it's supposed to be a recruitment centre."

"For what?"

"Look, every war has many twists and turns. I suppose The Lion of Mazâr-e Sharîf worries that someday he may either have to flee for his life, or be captured. He doesn't trust the other warlords. So, elite guards are being trained outside Afghanistan for his protection."

"I see." Jason picked up the phone and dialed a number. "I'm ready to receive Manning." He gave Aziz a sharp stare. "Come." He got up, walked over to the door of the conference room and opened it. "You stay here and listen."

Aziz entered the room and stood there fidgety. Then Jason closed the door, walked behind the desk and sat down. He knew that Manning would recognize him instantly. And that's exactly what he wanted.

123

"Surprise!" Marianna said as she walked into the library holding Manning's hand. "Richard is home." She pointed at Jason. She left Manning in the middle of the room, turned back and exited the library. Someone closed the door behind her.

"I don't ... understand," Manning mumbled as he approached the desk.

"It's been a long time Alex," Jason said. "How's Cynthia?"

"She ... she's ... fine." As he came closer, he looked at Jason and his eyes widened. "You're not Richard!"

"Sit down," Jason ordered him.

Manning did so.

Jason got up and removed his coat and his shirt. "I'm not Richard eh! What are you talking about? Take a look." He turned his back. "Whose tattoo is this?"

"Richard is dead."

"You didn't tell Aziz that."

"I wasn't at liberty to disclose the information to him."

Manning held his ground, Jason noticed. "I guess you don't want your money."

"I didn't do anything. In fact I didn't learn that the *Taliban*'s men had kept Richard captive until I spoke to Makin."

"Where's Cynthia?"

"She was with you yesterday. I don't know what happened to her."

"Did you kill her?"

"You're so ignorant. What did you do with the money?"

"What money?"

"The money that Richard transferred to you."

"Who told you that?"

"Richard received $370-million, and we didn't know what he'd done with it until we found out that he'd transferred it to another offshore bank under your name."

"Answer the question."

Manning kept quiet.

"Aziz told me that Kamal would not release the arms to the Lion of Mazâr-e Sharîf unless he receives one hundred and fifteen million dollars. Is this true?"

"Fuck you! You and Richard let us all down."

"Watch your language."

"I agreed to let the Mustafa bank act for me on condition that Richard would sell the arms to the Lion of Mazâr-e Sharîf. Instead he negotiated deals and received money from two rivals at the same time. Then he transferred the money to your offshore account. He put Kamal and me in a very tight spot."

"What do you want?"

"I will cut off Aziz's head if he doesn't give me the money."

"Why should he have to give you the money? The deal was to have the *Taliban* deliver me to him. And that's not going to happen now."

"Richard caused a rift between my friends and me."

Jason slapped Manning across the face. "You had that coming."

Manning staggered, shook off the blow, then pulled out a cellular phone from his waist.

"Don't," Jason demanded. "Give me that!" He grabbed it from his hands. "No phone calls until I finish talking with my guests."

"What do want from me?"

"It's up to you. We can stay here all night. You can choose to co-operate or you can face the consequences."

"I'm leaving!"

"You can't. We have to get to the bottom of things."

Manning turned around and rushed toward the door. Before he reached the door, the two commandos opened it and walked in. "Go back to Richard," one of them uttered. "Do it quietly."

Manning obeyed, like a child caught doing something naughty.

Jason said, "Let's see if we can find a compromise."

"I need guarantees," Manning said.

"Tell me what you propose, and I'll consider it."

"Give me my money, and I'll leave the island tonight."

"It all depends, I suppose, how much information you're willing to share with me."

"First I want to see the money."

Jason walked over to the door of the conference room and opened it. He waved at Aziz. "Come here, please."

Aziz exited the door and faced Manning.

"Give him the draft," Jason said to Aziz.

Aziz hesitated.

353

"Give it to him," Jason said grinding his teeth.

Aziz gave Manning one of the cheques.

Manning grabbed the draft, looked at it for a few seconds, then shoved it in his pocket. "What information do you want?"

"How do you know I've transferred the money to my brother?"

"Stop pretending you're Richard!" Manning yelled. "You don't make a very good impressionist, you know!"

"I don't want to repeat myself."

"Cynthia was questioned by the Lion's men. Under pressure, she told them all about the money, and they alerted Makin who notified me."

"Was she tortured?"

"Yes."

"Where is she now?"

"She's in the boat, waiting for me."

"What else did Cynthia say to the Lion's men?"

"She told them everything. She said that she and Richard were lovers, and they planned to escape. She tried to convince you to leave the island with her when she learned that Richard was dead. She made a grave mistake and apologized for it. I forgave her."

"I presume Makin told you all this."

"Yes. He was present during her interrogation."

"Why was she abducted?"

"Makin and I suspected that she was planning something with you."

"So you and Makin hired the Lion's men to abduct her?"

"Yes."

"How do I know you're telling me the truth?"

"I'm willing to confess this in front of Makin."

"He may deny everything."

"He may."

"Where is my brother?"

"He's dead."

"My brother Jason is dead?"

"Your brother Richard is dead!"

"Since you insist that I'm Jason, can you explain to me why you didn't come after me for the money?"

"We didn't know that Richard had transferred it to your name until yesterday."

"Where was I yesterday?"

"After Makin learned that Richard was dead, he formed an idea. He arranged for the Lion's men to capture you, brainwash you and pass you off as Richard to Aziz. His plan failed when you escaped."

Jason was convinced that Manning was telling the truth. He dialed an extension. "Send the waiters in."

The waiters entered.

Jason turned to Manning and Aziz. "Let's have some refreshments in the adjacent room," Jason said. "Follow me, please." He led the way and the three of them entered the conference room and sat down.

124

Marianna took drunken Lagos by the hand, held it firmly and helped him keep his balance as they began to walk to the library. At one point he staggered and almost fell.

When they entered the library, the waiters closed the door behind them.

They sat on the sofa. "Why did you steal Faris's will?"

"Who told you?"

"Katerina."

"The bitch! To be honest with you … I'm sorry. I'm ashamed."

"What happened to the will?"

"I do what I'm told. I'm a good husband."

Marianna shook her head, impatiently. "Never mind that. Who has the will?"

"Katerina burned it."

"Do you know what happened to Richard?"

"Crow. I mean, a brick layer is a brick layer … I don't know if you get exactly what I mean."

"Who's a brick layer?"

"Crow is."

"Did Crow kill Richard?"

"He buried him."

"Where?"

"On top of the arches, in his house."

Marianna gasped. "How do you know?"

"I watched. But I didn't help … just watched. I feel … ashamed."

Marianna began to shake. "Why didn't you do anything to prevent it?"

"He was dead already."

"Please, help me to find out why Richard was killed."

"They'll kill *me*."

"Who?"

"Makin and Crow."

"No, I won't let them."

Lagos started to cry. His moan was deafening. Then he began to tremble. "They're here."

Marianna heard a commotion outside and seconds later the door burst open. She saw Makin and Crow struggling with the waiters.

"Let go of me," Crow shouted.

Marianna saw Makin pull out a shotgun and point it at the 'waiter' who was holding Crow. "Get your hands off him, damn you!" Makin said. His face was red. "Hands up!"

The two waiters raised their hands and put them behind their necks.

Marianna began screaming. "He has a gun!" she shouted. "Help!"

125

Jason heard Marianna's pleas for help. He felt an urge to open the door and rush to her side, but he hesitated when he considered that someone out there had a gun.

Manning and Aziz appeared restless. Manning jumped up quickly. Jason tried to stop him; however, Manning escaped his clasp and bust into the library.

"We've been trapped!" Manning shouted.

Jason walked out to face Manning, who now stood between Crow and Makin.

Manning pointed his finger at Marianna and then at Jason. "They tried to fool us!"

Marianna, still sitting on the sofa, covered her face with her hands.

Lagos looked mystified.

"This idiot," Manning pointed at Lagos, "is a traitor."

Jason tried to walk slowly to one side, thinking their attention was mostly on George Lagos for the moment. *Maybe I could pivot around and kick the gun from Makin's hand.*

Makin pointed the gun at him. "Don't move!" he yelled.

Jason stopped.

Crow rushed over, punched him in the face—and Jason fell. Crow then grabbed Jason by the hair and dragged him to the door. "I'll take him with me," he said.

Jason heard screams and commotion inside the villa.

As Crow pulled Jason, Lagos ran for the door. Makin shot him in the leg and Lagos fell on top of Jason, in front of the door. He began shaking and moaning, holding his leg. Blood trickled from Lagos's wound, soaking Jason's clothes.

Katerina came inside. "No!" she screamed. She ran toward Lagos, bent to her knees and held his head. "Please don't kill him!" she begged Makin. "You've destroyed us as it is!"

"Everybody on the floor!" Makin yelled.

Jason's eyes went blurry. He heard a male voice shout, "Now!" and he recognized it as Nicholas's voice. Five men with guns drawn appeared at the door. A gun discharged and Jason watched as Nicholas bent, and then collapsed on the floor.

Achilles jumped Makin, bit his hand and his jaws didn't let go. The gun dropped from Makin's hand.

Marianna fainted and was carried outside.

Katerina looked lost in shock.

Nicholas's men handcuffed Makin, Manning, Crow and Lagos.

Jason struggled to his feet and approached Nicholas. He knelt down and held his hand. Panic swept through him as he saw Nicholas, lying on the floor with a big wound in his chest, gasping for air. "Somebody call an ambulance!" he ordered.

"Let me in, let me in," a man shouted.

"It's Naharos," a guard said.

"Let him come in," Jason said.

Naharos was trembling. "What—what happened? he asked. He pulled out his cellular phone and dialed a number. "Send in the emergency squad and three ambulances to Villa Mustafa," he ordered.

Jason cradled Nicholas's head in his lap. He touched his hand and tried to feel his pulse. There was nothing. "My good friend. Please! What am I going to say to your wife?" Jason cried.

Someone tapped him on the shoulder and helped him get up. Then Jason walked over to the window. The rain had stopped; the sky was clear. Stars burned bright in the black sky, but the moon was missing.

He felt numb. "It was all futile," he whispered. "We all lost."

Turning around, Jason nodded at Nicholas's men and approached Naharos. "We've gone as far as we can," he said. "We're ready to turn in the evidence."

"What evidence?" Naharos asked.

"The police in Nicosia will take it from here."

EPILOGUE

At Ariste's insistence, the evidence gathered at Villa Mustafa the night of Nicholas's murder, and the Mustafa Bank records that were sealed and kept at the Pafos police station were turned over to the Nicosia police that same night. The Nicosia police, in consultation with the Assistant Attorney General, intervened and took charge of the investigations. Makin, Crow, Manning and Lagos were transported to Nicosia, facing several charges.

On Monday morning, the police raided the Delphi Villa but found it empty. The villa's owner, Abbas Azim, was nowhere to be found, and a warrant was issued for his arrest. The police also searched Makin's house and recovered documents and lots of cash. The numbers on the bills seized matched the numbers on the bills that had disappeared from the vault of the Mustafa building. Maximus was arrested the same morning at Larnaca Airport, while he was boarding a Cyprus Airways plane. In his luggage, police found $200,000.

The police also questioned Modestos. He gave them tapes, photographs and documents. Then he shaved his beard and left the monastery.

On Tuesday, police went through Crow's villa. They found Richard's body encased in a reinforced concrete cask right above the middle arch of the villa's patio. A warrant was issued for Cynthia's arrest.

On Wednesday, Aziz was arrested by the Cypriot authorities, questioned and released. Instead of returning to Saudi Arabia, he sought asylum in Cyprus.

A week later, Kamal was arrested in Saudi Arabia and charged for violating the kingdom's banking and trade laws.

The same week, Lagos consulted with his lawyer and agreed to testify against Manning, Makin and Crow.

Two weeks later, John Persinaras was arrested and charged with tax evasion and fraud. He suffered a massive heart attack when he was denied bail and collapsed in court. He was pronounced dead on arrival at the Nicosia hospital.

In February 2002, the Haifa police notified the Cyprus authorities that a boat believed to be registered in Cyprus was abandoned in the

1

Haifa harbour. The same month, authorities in the United States requested Manning's extradition to the U.S. to face money laundering charges and trading in arms without government approval. While the local authorities were debating the legality of the U.S. extradition issue, Manning was assassinated when he was about to be transported from the detention centre to the courthouse to face additional charges. His unknown assassin escaped.

In March 2002, Naharos, under pressure from Nicosia, resigned his post as Pafos police chief and was forced into early retirement.

By May 2002, the authorities gathered sufficient evidence for them to conclude that Abbas Azim and Badi Latif were ex-lieutenants of the The Lion of Mazâr-e Sharîf, one of the warlords at large in northern Afghanistan.

Other than what she'd told Jason, it wasn't clear what role Cynthia played in Richard's abduction and subsequent death.

Meanwhile, authorities could find no evidence to implicate the late Faris Mustafa of any criminal activity.

The three money orders totalling $355-million dollars, representing the ransom Faris had given to Aziz for Richard's release were confiscated and returned to the Faris Mustafa estate in July 2002.

Jason cooperated fully with authorities. After inquiries with the Panamanian authorities and banks, he confirmed that $386-million had indeed been transferred to a Panamanian account in his name shortly before Richard's abduction. Jason turned the money over to the authorities.

In August 2002, Dr. Plato resurfaced. He had been hiding on the island of Rhodes since the day of Faris's funeral. He went to the authorities and gave them a copy of Faris's will which he'd been keeping in his bank's safety deposit box.

Marianna agreed to have Faris's old will declared null and void and recognized the new will as authentic and representing truly Faris's intentions.

Jason and Helena were appointed executors and trustees of the Mustafa estate. Under Helena's trusteeship, they transferred $35-million to a special account for the benefit of Andrew, George and Claira.

In January 2003, on the initiative of Jason and Helena, the Persinaras-Mustafa Group was dissolved. Immediately thereafter, the company's creditors petitioned Persinaras Estates into bankruptcy.

Villa Mustafa, Villa Oasis and the olive grove were transferred to Jason. Marianna vacated Villa Mustafa and went to live with the children at a Pafos apartment, near the Pafos Harbour. Helena and Jason split

Faris's remaining assets. Jason kept the villas and the land for a few months, but he never visited the compound. It reminded him too much of the loss of his brother and Nicholas. He sold these properties to a local businessman for four million dollars and gave half of those proceeds to Marianna and the other half to Penelope, Nicholas's widow.

In February 2003, Katerina, Lagos and Maximus pleaded guilty to several charges and sentenced to lengthy jail terms.

In the spring of 2003, Jason and Penelope fell in love and moved with Penelope's son to a villa Jason had purchased on the hills of Pafos.

As it turned out, the Turkish House belonged to Ismail's parents. Ismail was the little Turkish boy who gave Helena the scoop of ice cream the day his parents were shot.

Proximity talks for the unification of Cyprus began in 2000, and Ismail managed to cross the so-called Green Line in the spring of 2001. In the spring of 2003, the people of the divided island were allowed 'free' movement between the north and the south, albeit their property and civil rights remained unsettled.

On May 1, 2004 Cyprus became an official member of the European Union, but the island remained divided.

One Sunday in the summer of 2004, Jason, Penelope, Helena and Ismail travelled north and the two couples got married in the Saint Andreas Monastery, located on the eastern tip of the island. They exchanged their vows before God and friends. They swapped presents. Among the presents to Jason and Penelope was an envelope from Helena.

Jason opened it outside the church, under the hot sun. It contained a note and some money. He read the note: "Dear son, this envelope contains fourteen thousand dollars. I want you to have it. This is the money I saved for your fourteen birthdays when you were away from home. Your father, Faris."

Jason smiled and put the envelope with the money and the note in his pocket. He knew he deserved every single dollar. He turned to his wife. "We have a nice present from my father," he said. "Oh, great!" Penelope exclaimed. "We can use it for our honeymoon."

In September 2004, Makin and Crow were found guilty of numerous offences and sentenced appropriately.

Marianna found a new lover.

Helena and Penelope are now pregnant.

The strife in Afghanistan continues.

ISBN 1-41205094-4